A Modern GENIE

A Modern GENIE

Brandy Sizemore

Rev. date: 10/26/2019

To order additional copies of this book, contact:
Xlibris
1-888-795-4274
www.Xlibris.com
Orders@Xlibris.com
795440

Contents

1

God's Allowance

Thousands of years ago, the devil made a decision within his heart. He felt that with his combined wisdom and beauty, he was the rightful ruler of the throne of Heaven. The Lord stripped him of his cherub status and cast him from the mountain of God. Satan, knowing the power of his beauty, vowed vengeance against the Lord and purposed to claim as many souls as he could.

The corruption of the world that followed after, led God to make the decision to flood the earth. Only his chosen ones would survive.

Now there was a certain great sorceress named Dalia. With the evil decisions she continued to make, she would not be among the chosen. Her power was unrivaled by any else on Earth and her spirit was on the verge of death. If only Satan could contain and use her power, he'd be able to corrupt the entire world in a day's time. His greed and wrath wouldn't let that opportunity die.

He approached her in a human form, clothed in royal purple robes fit for a king.

"You and the power you possess will soon be destroyed! Pledge your loyalty and service to me and I will let you live!"

Dalia scoffed. "The power I possess is greater than any other, what could you possibly have to offer?"

Satan smirked. "Your power *is* great, but I can offer you *greater* power if you serve me."

She turned away from him, "I serve only myself!"

Angered, Satan left her.

Days passed, and the rains continued to fall.

Satan returned to her again.

He faked concern. "You are about to die! Let us make a bargain."

She refused yet again, "I rely only on myself. Leave me!"

He left her alone once more to prove that she wouldn't be able to save herself from the flood.

A week later, he approached her a third time.

"Pledge your soul to me, and I will let you live to see many generations to come!"

She remained hesitant despite the continued rain. "I still know not who you are."

He stood tall and proud, "I am the devil, Lucifer himself. I will save you and your power from this flood if you'll only pledge your soul to me."

Dalia treasured her power above all else, including her soul.

"We have a deal."

His perfect lips formed a sinister grin.

When the deeds he required of her were complete, he eagerly lay claim to her soul.

Her eyes glazed over instantly.

Dalia seemed . . . hollow now.

Satan trapped her inside an ornate glass vessel and brought her back to the very edge of Hell.

More than a year had passed, and Dalia had grown bitter waiting for him to fulfill his promise to her.

The devil waited until God had divided up the generations of Noah across the earth before returning her, just as he promised. When she came out of the vessel, her waist down was churning black and red smoke; her upper body was still solid and normal sized. He gave her an attractive jeweled outfit that was pleasing to the eye.

"This is not what we agreed upon!" she complained.

The devil laughed, "You and your power are still alive! Do not be ungrateful to your master."

"Yes, master." She gasped, not knowing why she had said that.

Satan grinned.

"Why am I dressed the way I am?" she asked.

He answered happily, "Lust is a powerful tool."

"Why do I have to be attached to a vessel?"

Satan didn't answer; he was quite content with himself. He commanded her to go back inside, he skillfully plopped the lid in, and then he waited until the right moment to test out his new weapon.

*   *   *

In a nearby village, a young man by the name of Nuqi had just awaken to attend to his sickly mother. His skin a sandy brown, his eyes the color of dessert mud, and his hair as black as an Arabian night.

His mother coughed. "Son, I do not know how much longer I have, but I have one last wish for you."

Hope still dwelled in his heart.

"Mother do not talk like that, the Lord will provide."

Her cloudy yellow-ochre eyes met his. "Son, just promise me that you will live an upright life, and I will not have lived in vain."

"Yes, Mother, of course." He took her hand and kissed her forehead.

She smiled, satisfied.

Nuqi caressed her face gently. "I will get you some more water."

Her eyes closed peacefully.

He took the empty drinking pot by the bedside and walked the short distance to the village oasis when the sun suddenly caught his eye in the sand.

"What is this?" he asked himself out loud.

He had discovered the stained-glass vessel and bent down to brush the hot sand away.

"Hmmm, I can use this to get more water," he thought. He proceeded to rub the grit off. "I will give it to Mother as a gift. This will be the most beautiful thing she owns."

Nuqi removed the cork to examine the inside; it felt like something was in it.

Inside, Dalia was too enraged to realize that someone had picked her up.

When Nuqi popped the cork out, Dalia couldn't help but fade into smoke and wisp out of the vessel. Satan watched secretly nearby.

"Ahh!" he yelled out.

The hot sand caught him and the vessel as he watched blackish-red smoke twist and turn to reveal a beautiful strange woman.

Dalia, blinded by the sudden brightness, shielded her eyes. She slowly glanced around to discover a man on the ground staring back at her in terror.

"Who are you?" she asked, still angry.

"I-I . . . I am, uh . . ." His expression was horrific.

Dalia looked at herself attached to the vessel; she wanted to escape. "Here, hold this!"

She thrust it into his hands. He did what she said out of fear.

"Do not let go!"

She darted away as fast as she could but was slung back into the vessel. Nuqi stared at it, petrified. After a moment, he snapped out of it and quickly fumbled with the fancy cork to seal the vessel before she'd be able to escape again. A sigh of relief left his lips and he then proceeded to bury it frantically. Satan appeared and rushed to him.

"What are you doing, boy? Why are you burying a perfectly good water vessel? Do not be wasteful!"

"There is an evil spirit in here! It must be hidden forever!" He continued to dig as though his life depended on it.

Satan stole the bottle and opened it quickly.

"No!" Nuqi shouted.

His hands chased his voice.

"There is a woman inside, boy," he stated while Dalia appeared again. "She has the power to give you anything you want!"

Nuqi slowly stood and brushed sand off his legs. "Anything?" he asked.

Satan grinned. His voice echoed around Nuqi, "How about some servants so you no longer have to fetch your own water? Or, how about a chest full of gold so you do not have to work? Or, I know . . . How about your sick mother? She can be well again! There are no limits to what you can wish for! All you have to do is *ask*!"

Nuqi took an innocent step forward and squinted at him suspiciously. "How do you know all this? Who are *you*?"

Dalia saw the boy as an opportunity to be set free.

"He is the devil," she crossed her arms, "and he tricked me into trading my life for this!"

"Ah, ah, ah, Dalia. If someone sets you free, you will lose *all* your powers."

"What?" She turned to him. "How did you read my mind?"

"I am Satan, the greatest angel to ever exist!" he revered in himself.

In that moment, Nuqi made a decision and swiped the vessel from him. "You *both* are what my mother warned me about. I wish that this would be hidden forev—"

"NO!" Satan shouted, horror-struck. He couldn't act fast enough in his human form and only managed to knock Nuqi back to the ground.

POOF!

In an instant, the vessel vanished and was hidden away.

2

September 27

Jenny Ann Delemonte began each morning with a cup of cocoa, not coffee like normal people. Coffee probably should've been her drink of choice though because she was typically very unrested in the morning. She had no idea why and she usually woke up without a voice as well. The hot cocoa fixed her voice. Jenny's long hair consisted of several shades of natural blonde. Her skin was the color of cream, and she was built like a woman who could hold her own. Her eyes were grayish-blue, like a rainy day, and they were always full of thankfulness. Today, however, they were full of annoyance. She'd been looking for the perfect piece of land for almost four years now.

"Ugh, that's not right either . . ."

Her fingers cycled through property listings on her "smart" phone.

"Oh c'mon, work please."

The phone apparently wasn't having a very good morning either; it didn't want to cooperate.

Despite her young age, she was one of the best interior designers for a major renovation company in her hometown and was looking to buy her own plot of God's masterpiece to build her dream home on.

Sigh. It needs to be close to a water access. Her eyes glanced at the stove. Seven o'clock. "Uh-oh! Is that the time?" she asked herself out loud. "I'm going to be late!"

Jenny zoomed out the kitchen door to the garage and headed off to work, nearly backing into her neighbor's garbage can . . . again.

UGH! I asked Mr. Mitts to move that thing. It's always in my driveway! I really need to get out of this apartment.

Just then, Jenny noticed a bouquet of flowers on her front doorstep.

"More flowers? C'mon. I don't have time for this today! AGH."

She hopped out of her truck and grabbed the flowers anyways.

"Yup. Another carnation in the center. Who keeps leaving these for me?"

Flowers in hand, she sprinted back to her truck and sat them in the seat next to her. There wasn't time to put them in a vase. Little did Jenny know, beady little eyes watched her from next door as she drove away that morning, and . . . *every* morning really. She headed off to work, hopeful as always for the things that life might have in store for her that day.

*I feel good about this morning. Today is going to be a . . . a very **important** day! I can **feel** it!*

She was right; this day *would* mark the day when her life would change forever. For better or for worse, her life would never be the same.

* * *

Jenny arrived at work and fast-walked as normally as she could manage until she reached the automatic entry door.

Her feet carried her over the threshold right on time.

"Good morning, JD," Cali called from the front desk.

That was Jenny's nickname around the office. Jenny smiled.

"Oh, boss man wants to see you."

Cali had been Jenny's best friend ever since Jenny had started working at Conroy Renovations and Design. Her short black hair poofed up a little in the back and curved along with her face. Large, bright, oval-shaped, brown eyes complimented a big smile for each person who walked in. She was thin and nearly six feet tall with almost snow-white skin.

"Oh, what about?"

"I don't know, he didn't say, but I have a feeling something is up. Nothing bad! Just . . . something different." She squinted and propped her elbows up on the shiny black counter.

"You and your feelings, Cali." Jenny grinned. "Oh well . . . You've never been wrong before. I'll go see him." She headed straight over to the elevator. "See you later!" *Hmmm, and it sounds like **my** important feeling is going to be right too.*

"See ya! Good luck!" Cali called.

"Hey!" Jenny called back to Cali while she walked backward into the elevator. "Let me know when your new boyfriend gets here. I want to meet this one!"

"No promises, but I'll try to remember to call for you." Cali's eyes flashed with uneasiness.

Jenny was too far away to notice; she stared back at Cali as the elevator doors closed. "See that you do," Jenny said in a serious tone. She pointed her right index finger at Cali, "Or else . . ." she winked and then laughed.

"Ha! Oh, Jenny . . ." Cali didn't finish. She just shook her head and smiled. *I'm glad she works here too, or this job would be seriously boring.*

Jenny arrived at the top floor where her boss, Mr. Conroy, worked in his private office. She bounded over to him.

"Good morning, Kurtis. What can I do for you?"

Jenny always called him Kurtis when it was just the two of them, but she tried to call him Mr. Conroy in front of everyone else. She'd known him all her life. She spun the guest chair around, hopped up on his desk to sit, and snatched up a piece of candy from the bowl. His six-foot three, firm figure loomed over you. He was fifty-three years old but looked easily ten years younger. His medium-toned brown hair had a touch of blond and he didn't have a bald spot . . . yet. His eyes were bright-blue like the sky, and they were always full of business. He had an old-school style about him with a high-class taste, which Jenny really appreciated. He was a gentleman, and Jenny viewed him as a second father. He was a dedicated worker and always seemed to make the right decision whether it be about work or his personal life.

"Jenny Ann Delemonte, get off my desk this instance, young lady."

His fingers stopped shuffling through papers. He stared up at her. "You really know how to push my buttons, missy."

"Oh c'mon, what gives? You know those chairs are too soft. They make it hard to reach the peppermints when I sit—"

He held up his hand and cut her off. "Jenny," he said forcefully.

Jenny stopped and met his serious eyes. "Oh . . . I'm sorry, sir." She slid off his desk. "I'm just excited. I have a feeling this day is going to be *different*!" She beamed brightly before him.

"Never mind." He let out a breath of air. "Never mind. I apologize for the sternness, but once again, your intuition is correct. We have an important partnership opportunity today that could mean more job opportunities *and* great savings." He stood up and continued. "We're looking into partnering with the biggest construction company in the state, Dayton Developments, and the owner of the company will be here any second. I can't have my chosen company ambassador goofing off when he walks in. Now can I?" He raised an eyebrow at her.

She stood still; her eyes full of surprise. "You've chosen *me* to be your rep?"

He sat up a little taller and gave her a gentleman's smile. "Of course, I did."

Jenny turned to face the elevator door with him. She smoothed out her flowy knee-length black skirt and straightened her light-blue blouse.

"Good girl. I have decided that *you* will be the one to work with him today. See what his vision is, help him in any way possible, and then report back to me ASAP." He crossed his arms. "I need to know what *you* think of him before we even start talking about making a deal."

Jenny turned to him wide-eyed. "Wait . . . You want *me* to do *all* that? That sounds kind of, *really* important! Are you sure *I'm* the one you want for this assignment? There's lots of people who've been here way longer than I have."

"Yes, Jenny. I've given it a lot of thought." He smiled at her reassuringly. "You are newer, but the results of your past judgements have only grown my company. I want *you* to judge if he's partnering-worthy or not. You're a better fit than anyone else here. I'm confident in that."

"Oh." She was flattered. Her cheeks blossomed into a dark shade of pink. "Well, I just let my conscience guide me." She looked back up at him and smiled brightly. "Like you do!"

He gave her an amused smile. "Yes. You're an *excellent* judge of character, especially for your age."

Jenny gave him a humble smile.

Mr. Conroy furrowed his brow sincerely. His voice was mellow. "You're . . . you're like a *daughter* to me, Jen-Jen. Carrie and I don't have anyone to leave this business to when we retire, and we've discussed it and decided that you will be the one to inherit it. If you want it. You know we don't have any . . . *kids* of our own, and we both see you as a daughter." He turned and smiled proudly at her. "This mission I'm sending you on today is something *I* would normally do, but I want to start giving you more responsibility for two reasons: One, is to see how you handle it so I can give you advice and train you accordingly, and two, is so that you can see if this business is even something you would *want* to run someday. If you don't like it, we'll figure something else out."

"Oh." Jenny swallowed. She couldn't believe her ears. "Kurtis . . . you don't have to do that!"

"I know," he took in a deep breath and gave her a positive look, "but that's what Carrie and I have both agreed on. Why, if you weren't practically already an adult when . . . well, you know, we would've adopted you ourselves officially, and then as my adopted daughter, you would have no choice." He smiled playfully. "I'm teasing. Of *course*, you'd still have a choice."

Jenny studied him, surprised, thankful, and almost teary-eyed. There were at least five different emotions churning and mixing inside. She felt bad about the way she had paraded in earlier.

"I . . . didn't know you guys felt that way. That means a lot to me . . . Thank you, Kurtis. Tell Carrie thanks too." She straightened up along with him and put on a focused smile. "I won't let you down today! I promise. I'll be professional, and I'll let you know what I think of him at the end of the day."

She was so excited she had to mentally tell herself to calm down three times. This was all such an honor and so unexpected, she didn't want to let Kurtis *or* Carrie down. Ever since her mom and dad died, she'd thought of them as parents as well. The last memories she had of her real parents tried to find their way in, but she quickly brushed them away.

Focus Jenny! Think of something positive, she thought to herself.

Kurtis smiled at her.

It warmed her heart to know that the Conroy's thought of her as their own. She let out a breath of relief, thankful for his distracting smile.

"Mr. Conroy," Cali's voice echoed over his personal intercom, "your seven-thirty is here."

"Thank you, Cali. Send him up, please." He turned to Jenny and added, "Ahem, yes. Well, now he will be here any moment, so we will talk about it more later. Remember, Jenny, focus on the mission above all else. That is my secret to success." He winked.

"Yes, sir, dad, sir!" She gave him a semi-joking salute and stood at attention for half a second. *Wow, I can't believe he told me his secret to success!* she thought.

He leaned his head back in surprise and then gave her a loving look. "I . . . like being called dad, Jen-Jen."

She smiled, "I like the thought of having a dad again."

He briefly returned her smile and then quickly turned back into business mode. "Well, he's off to a good start because he is five minutes early."

"To be early is to be on time," Jenny recited.

Mr. Conroy nodded in agreeance to one of his mottos.

Diiiinnnnggg! the elevator announced.

"Ah," Mr. Conroy whispered to Jenny. "There he is. Smile! We need to make a good first impression."

Jenny nodded and looked toward the elevator expectantly.

The elevator door opened, and a cool breeze blew in along with the most handsome man Jenny had ever seen. He seemed to enter the room in slow motion as his slightly curled darkish-blonde hair bounced. The soft morning light coming in through the wall of windows caught the tips of his hair, and his face seemed to glow. He was as tall as Mr. Conroy with broad shoulders and had white, sandy-colored skin. He wore a long-sleeved light-purple button-up shirt and dark bootcut jeans. His face was clean-shaven but his whole manly appearance reminded Jenny of a lumberjack. His summer-field eyes were different colors of greens and yellows, and they drew you in and held you down to earth when you looked into them. Well, that's what Jenny thought about them anyways.

She froze, and her mouth parted slightly.

Even though he wasn't looking at her, she let his warm eyes hold her to the ground.

"Hello, Mr. Conroy, I'm Demetri Dayton." He shook Mr. Conroy's hand. His voice sounded like a smooth baritone.

He stepped back from Mr. Conroy to look at Jenny for the first time. He couldn't help but form an entranced smile as he looked her straight in the eyes.

Wow, are her eyes gray or blue?

Demetri continued to stare into them; he might've inched closer to try to find out had this not been a business meeting.

Jenny's heart began thumping louder; she was too enticed to smile back.

Her brain worked overtime. *Wow, he's who I'm working with? I love the name Demetri.*

11

"Uh." Mr. Conroy leaned over a little to get Demetri's attention off Jenny. "Nice to meet you, Mr. Dayton. I'm Kurtis Conroy, Conroy Renovations and Design."

He turned to Jenny and waited a moment for her to introduce herself but quickly realized that she was too awestruck to speak.

Oh great. Looks like she needs more training than I thought. "And uh, this is JD, my top designer."

Demetri raised his eyebrows. "Oh, *you're* JD? It's certainly *nice* to meet you."

He took a couple more steps toward her and shook her hand; he had to practically grab it from her side as she only had enough strength to lift it halfway. He was very close now.

*Hmmm, I guess they're blue **and** gray,* he noticed.

Mr. Conroy tried but failed to divert Demetri's attention away from Jenny. "Yes. She really has eagle eyes for design. I'm sure you'll come to find that out for yourself soon enough."

Yeah . . . eyes, Demetri thought, still entranced.

Mr. Conroy's proudness quickly faded when he realized Demetri and Jenny were still staring at each other.

He sighed quietly. "I hope the two of you can come to a *business* agreement . . ." He eyed them both. *I guess I forgot that Jenny is a young girl who is subject to normal feelings toward men.* He sighed and continued, ". . . that will benefit both of our companies. *Ahem!*" He still couldn't get either one's attention. *Ugh great, he's dumbstruck too.* Mr. Conroy rubbed his eyes with his right hand. *Am I doing the right thing? Maybe she isn't ready. . . No, I can't bring her down just after I brought her up. She can do this, despite Mr. Romance over here.* Kurtis shot daggers at Demetri.

Jenny sensed Mr. Conroy's irritation and tried to snap out of it. "Uh, nice to meet you . . . Demetri," she finally said. She smiled at him shyly.

Wow, she has a cute smile, Demetri thought.

Their handshake must have been longer than it was supposed to have been because Mr. Conroy interjected again, *"Ahem!* Yes."

Demetri finally gradually let go and turned back to a now stern-looking Mr. Conroy. "Uh, when you said that I would be working with JD, I kind of thought I would be working with a man. This is a . . . pleasant surprise." He returned his eyes to Jenny who still blushing brightly.

I'm sure it is, Mr. Conroy thought. "I trust you'll take good care of my . . . um . . . *our* JD here. She is the only one we've got." He stared at him with an "Or else!" glare.

Demetri realized instantly that Mr. Conroy was super protective of Jenny. He felt like he was back in high school reassuring a father that he would have his daughter back by eight. Um, make that seven. He nearly began to sweat under Mr. Conroy's stare, but managed to keep his demeanor.

"Yes, sir, she's in good hands, I assure you."

Mr. Conroy crossed his arms and thought again to himself, *does he have to say it like that . . . **good** hands?* "All right!" He turned to Jenny slowly. "Please report to me in an hour, and then at the end of the day, please, oh, and make sure you tell me *everything.*"

His eyes glanced sideways to give Demetri a once over one more time.

"Yes, sir, Mr. Conroy." Jenny said quickly. She could tell Demetri was uncomfortable now, and she finally figured out Mr. Conroy was giving him the third degree with his stares. *Well, I guess for **both** of our companies' sakes, I had better get us both out of here as soon as possible.* "Don't worry about a thing, Kur . . . uh, Mr. Conroy, I've got this." She put her hand on his arm and smiled.

*Oh brother, you've certainly got **something**, all right, something **he** wants.* He exhaled and whispered to her quietly, "Jenny, I think I should just take care of this instead."

Jenny's eyes went sad. Her shoulders began to deflate.

That look tugged on Mr. Conroy's heartstrings.

He sighed and thought to himself, *Ugh, not the puppy eyes, Jen-Jen! Agh!* "Fine!" He whispered to her again but not too quietly this time. "Remember your pepper spray that I gave you."

"OK!" Her eyes went even wider as she walked up to a patient and unsettled Demetri. She looked up into his coppery emerald eyes. "Shall we get started?"

"Yes . . . please!" Demetri escorted her out by her arm under Mr. Conroy's watch. *Whew! I am glad to get out of here.*

"Be careful, Jenny," Mr. Conroy called as the elevator door started to shut.

Jenny nodded at him and smiled reassuringly, "Don't worry, Mr. Conroy!"

Mr. Conroy went around behind his desk and kicked his roller chair. *Why didn't I do a background check on him first? I should have at least figured out how old he was, or if he has a love interest. You're losing your touch, Kurtis,* he scolded himself. He took a deep breath and retrieved his chair to sit down. He rested his head on his hands and sighed. *What have I done? I just sent Jenny away with some strange guy for half a day. Some **father** I'm turning out to be.* He set a timer for one hour and stared at it. *I have a bad feeling about today.*

3

Old Wounds

In the elevator, Demetri let out a breath of relief.

"Is he always like this?" he asked Jenny.

He stood in the middle. He couldn't help himself; he felt drawn to her. Maybe it was the skirt? Girls hardly wore modest skirts these days, if at all. It was very feminine and was a breath of fresh air for him.

She smiled up at him nervously, only briefly meeting his eyes. "Uh, only with me. I'm like a daughter to him. Mr. and Mrs. Conroy um . . . have never been able to have kids of their own."

"Ah, I understand. Did they ever think about adoption?"

"I don't know actually."

The weight of the responsibility that was just engraved into his mind by Mr. Conroy's stare stayed there.

He let out a sigh. "Sorry, I'm not typically quite like this either. This day just isn't going as expected."

She quickly glanced up at him from the side and then back to the floor. She didn't want to risk getting caught up in his eyes again.

Focus, Jenny, focus . . . Focus!

He beheld her and continued, "Did he call you *Jenny* back there?"

She tilted her head to the right out of habit when she tried to think of a way to sequence her words. Doing this exposed her neck, and he gazed at it openly. He found himself to have no choice in the matter.

"Oh, yeah, that's my real name, but everyone here calls me JD. I'm not sure how that got started actually."

"Hmm. Cool," he answered. He smiled to himself. *I like the name Jenny. Where have I heard it before?*

He forgot about trying to figure out the answer to his own question. He studied her hair instead. Jenny's golden hair was braided and wrapped up like a rose on the top of her head, near the back.

It's so beautiful, he thought. He couldn't hold the intended compliment in, "You have . . . um . . . a lot of hair."

Demetri changed what he was going to say mid-sentence. He lifted his right hand up to rub the back of his neck.

Her eyes widened and focused themselves into her wedge shoes. Her cheeks turned rosy pink.

"Oh, right. You weren't expecting a woman." She tried to laugh off what she hoped was a compliment.

"Yeah," he smiled at her, even though she still wouldn't look him in the eye. He wondered why she wouldn't and decided to step away a little in case she felt uncomfortable.

She continued with the first thing that popped into her mind, "Well, I guarantee you that I'll be more interesting to be around than a man would be."

She stopped, and her eyes opened wider.

"Umm . . . that came out wrong, I think." She looked up, disconcerted, into his amused eyes for the second time now. Red replaced the pink in her cheeks. *Great first impression, Jenny,* she scolded herself.

He laughed and noticed her cheeks this time. "I agree, girls are more interesting to work with. I think that's why my, uh"—he looked down and furrowed his brow, troubled now— "girlfriend wanted to know who I was working with today. Anyways, because of your nickname, I told her that I was working with a man."

He rubbed the back of his neck again and waited for her reaction.

Jenny's heart felt afflicted, and her chest echoed painfully with disappointment.

She looked down again. *Ugh . . . he's taken.* She tried to act normal and looked back up at him. "Oh . . . yeah, she probably won't like how this turned out. Not that she needs to worry or anything," she added quickly, trying to seem as normal as possible. She couldn't bear to look into his eyes after his statement; it was too painful now. She continued, "I don't think Mr. Conroy was expecting someone like you either."

"Someone like me?" He tilted *his* head now and wished that she would look him in the eyes again. Demetri continued, "He knew I was a guy, we've talked over the phone."

"Oh." She kept her eyes glued to the golden buckles on her wedges. "Well, then I'm not sure what his deal was."

"Hmm." Demetri examined her hair again. "He sure is protective of you. I think it was just sinking in with him that you would have to be alone with me all day." He tried to move his head to meet her eyes. "Uh, I apologize. . . that *did* come out wrong."

Jenny promptly flashed him an amused smile. "It's OK." She concentrated on the thick cork-colored bands that held the tops of her feet to her shoes.

The elevator stopped on floor 3, but no one was there to get on.

Demetri thought about her smile again and changed the subject. "So, you're the best interior designer around here? Tell me about your work."

"Oh, um . . ." She took a deep breath. "I don't know if I'm the *best* . . . I just seem to get a lot of thankful feedback. I love helping people fall back in love with their homes. I started here when I was eighteen. Kurt . . . Mr. Conroy took me in here and gave me a chance. I guess I actually intimidated another one of our designers so much that she quit—"

"Wait," Demetri interrupted her. "Oh wow . . . OK." He remembered now where he had heard the name *Jenny*. "I didn't realize you were *that* Jenny." He looked at her with truly tormented eyes now.

She gave him a bothered look. "What?"

"Was the other designer named Mel O'Brien?"

Jenny nearly shuddered at hearing her name. "Yes . . . why?" she asked, even though she was afraid that she already knew the answer.

He considered her expression. "She's, my girlfriend."

The word that Jenny had dreaded him saying tainted her perfect delineation of him. He tilted his head again and studied her; he shoved his hands in his pockets.

Jenny's heart regressed a little, and she turned her head away just a touch.

He continued, his voice a little more robotic than smooth this time, "That's probably why she made a point to ask who I was working with today. I just assumed you were a guy. How long have you been called JD around here?"

"It *is* pretty recent. She wouldn't know that it's me. If she would've known that, she would *not* have been OK with it." Jenny crossed her arms and stared at the elevator wall now.

"Why?" Now Demetri was confused. *I wish she would stop turning away from me.*

Jenny squinted and tried to think of a vague way to answer. "Well, her and I" —she turned away a little more, holding the memories back— "never really got along. I don't know how she is now, but no one liked her around here. She was very conniving and jealous. She'd do anything to get what she wanted, even if it meant hurting someone."

"What?"

Demetri came closer, and she straightened up a little when she realized how close he was. He noticed her reaction and abruptly turned away and scratched his head. "This is the first I've heard of this."

Jenny let out a silent breath of relief when he turned around. It wasn't that she felt uncomfortable around him —well, she did, but in a good way— it was just that she wanted him close and knew that was wrong because he was already taken.

"We were all glad to see her go. Ask anyone." She turned to face the elevator door now.

Demetri thought for a moment and took that in. He believed Jenny even though they'd just met. There was just something about her, and she didn't seem like the lying type.

He turned around again, only to face her back. "Well, she isn't like that anymore."

Sure, Jenny thought. She kept her head forward, and her voice came out a little harder than she had meant it to. "People like her don't just change on their own."

He went up on the defensive at hearing the stubborn change in her tone. "She *has* changed. I think I know her pretty well."

"Maybe," she said.

After the words left his mouth, he reconsidered them.

*Or do I? How well **do** I know Mel? We haven't been dating **that** long.*

His eyes returned to Jenny, who stood with her back completely to him. He couldn't help but notice her figure since he was standing on the other side of the elevator now.

What am I doing?

He turned away again and tried to clear his head. He was disappointed with himself for not being able to combat his attraction to her.

Ding.

Finally! Jenny thought.

She was beginning to feel claustrophobic and her stomach was tied up in knots. She couldn't believe that the man of her dreams was dating someone so self-aggrandizing.

The doors took their time in opening to reveal a man kissing Cali over the front desk. Cali heard the doors open and broke the kiss.

"Oh! Jenny, you're back!" She pulled away quickly. "This is Stefan."

Jenny walked briskly out of the elevator; she desperately wanted to get her mind off of Demetri.

Thank goodness, Cali's new boyfriend is here right now. I need a distraction!

Demetri gave it his best to control his eyes so as to not notice her feminine walk over to the front desk.

"Hi, Stefan. I'm Jenny. It's nice to meet you." Jenny held out her hand with a smile.

He turned around and stood all the way up, and she could see that he was even taller than Cali and had midnight-colored skin and matching dark eyes. Except, the left one was light-blue.

"Oh." Jenny couldn't stop herself from saying it, and her expression quickly changed from all smiles to seriousness.

Stefan's voice was deep and booming. He laughed. "Don't worry. I get that a lot. It's OK."

Jenny grabbed her right arm. "I'm so sorry. I just wasn't expecting . . ."

He gave her an understanding smile. "It's OK, and I got, uh, clawed in the eye saving my little sister from a bear."

She hadn't even noticed the two awesome-looking claw scars going straight down the left side of his face. Her brain needed to seriously get out of the clouds; Demetri had fogged everything up and the Mel announcement just added more dry ice.

Demetri arrived at the front desk as well and tried to keep a safe distance from Jenny. It hadn't been something that he was able to help though. It was as if he was magnetized to her. He'd already discovered that being too close *and* being too far away were both on the edge of dangerous.

The marks on Stefan's face weren't very deep, but Jenny couldn't believe that she'd nearly missed them. She snuck a quick look at Cali, who had just changed her facial expression from happiness to worry. Actually, it was almost fright. Jenny furrowed her brows, thinking that Cali's fright made no sense.

I must just be misreading this one. My mind isn't where it should be right now. Jenny smiled at Stefan, "That was really brave *and* sweet of you." She felt that she would be able to focus for Mr. Conroy now. "I think your scars look awesome!" Jenny said. "I've never seen anything like them in real life before. I love different . . . and so does *Cali*!" she winked at Cali, teasing her.

Cali looked horrified.

Demetri nodded to Stefan, "Nice to meet you. I'm Demetri."

Stefan returned the greeting.

Cali changed her expression before anyone else noticed and leaned back over the counter again but in Demetri's direction. "So, Demetri, what do you have in store for our JD today?" Cali could sense something about them; she winked at Jenny to get her back.

Jenny raised an eyebrow, "How do you know that we are supposed to . . . go out on business today?"

Cali ignored her playfully and waited for Demetri's response.

Demetri leaned against the countertop on one elbow and tried to catch a glimpse of Jenny's eyes again. "Does *everyone* in this place care about you this much?"

Jenny's cheeks developed another pink tinge. "I don't think *everyone* cares. Cali is just my best friend." She pressed her teeth together under her smile, upset that her cheeks had lost focus.

Demetri was disappointed that she still wouldn't look him in the eye.

"Oh, OK. That makes sense." Demetri turned back to Cali, "Cali, I felt like Mr. Conroy gave me the 'You'd better have my daughter home before *seven* speech' up there."

"No worries, Demetri!" She smiled one of her huge smiles at him and noticed Jenny's now-completely-pink cheeks and continued, self-satisfied, "But yes, I would *definitely* have her home by seven if you care about what Mr. Conroy thinks. He is *very* protective of Jenny."

"So I've noticed. But it shouldn't be an issue because we're just going to be looking at dirt for a couple hours."

Cali yawned automatically. "Sounds boring."

Demetri laughed and rubbed the back of his neck again when he looked at Jenny. "Yeah, it probably will be, but I'll see what I can do to make it a little more interesting."

Jenny's face blossomed, betraying her wishes again; she grabbed her right arm with her left on cue.

Why am I blushing? He's dating my old, iconoclastic rival.

Everyone silently stared at him, and he realized that what he said could be taken two ways.

"*Professionally*, of course." Demetri turned to Cali abruptly. "Please don't tell Mr. Conroy I said that." Demetri never had this much trouble speaking before.

Cali beamed at Jenny this time and raised both eyebrows twice. "Of course."

Demetri noticed. "Um, we really need to get started before it gets too hot outside."

"All right, lead the way." Jenny started following him out, glad to finally be getting out of there as well. She was doing an awful lot of escaping today.

"Have *fun*, you two!" Cali waved. She was trying to have as much of a good time as possible.

Jenny's eyes went wide. *Oh, Cali, I am so going to get you back for this!*

She decided Demetri wasn't walking fast enough, so she nudged him out of the modern style building before Cali could think of any other embarrassing things to do. Jenny already felt so awkward—she didn't want Demetri feeling that way too, or else it would be a very, *very* long day.

"Whoa, easy there, JD." Demetri smiled with one eyebrow raised. He was surprised at her capability to push him so easily.

"Sorry. I just really wanted to get out of there." She hoped he wouldn't ask why; luckily, he didn't.

They walked side by side in the parking lot; Jenny made sure to stay at least three feet away, for professionalism. It turned out to be more difficult than she thought it'd be, as she found herself gravitating toward him.

He looked down at her; she kept her eyes fixed ahead.

"May I just call you Jenny? I like it better than JD."

He hoped she wouldn't ask why; luckily, she didn't.

She sighed, happy to be out of Cali's teasing range. "You may call me what you like."

He smiled to himself. *Good.*

They walked through the parking lot until they came to an old dark-blue Chevy 2500 Duramax Diesel in pristine condition. Demetri stopped next to it and turned around to face her.

"wow! Is this yours?" Jenny let a wall down and turned into a kid on Christmas morning.

He was taken aback for a moment and let a laugh escape. "Um . . . yeah, it's *one* of my vehicles."

She kept inspecting it. "This is *awesome!*"

He tilted his head and watched her. "Normally, girls aren't interested in my truck."

"I'm not normal. And yes, I meant for it to come out that way." She smiled at him briefly, and he raised an eyebrow again at her comment.

Jenny pointed. "*My* truck is over there!"

The direction of her finger revealed another Chevy Diesel from the same year a few parking spaces down. It was almost completely identical, except hers was black and definitely not as pristine.

It was his turn to be surprised. "Whoa! You have excellent taste in vehicles." Demetri smiled, impressed; he let down his guard from earlier without realizing it.

Jenny walked back up to him and actually looked him in the eyes. "Yours is beautiful!" She looked back at hers. "Mine is dependable, but needs work, if that makes any sense."

"Ah." He shrugged and uttered a small laugh. "That makes perfect sense actually. From over here it looks like you just need a new paint job."

She moved her lips to the right side of her face and studied the faded pavement. "Yeah, I've been putting it off. I just . . . can't bring myself to do it."

He turned back around to her. "Oh, why is that?"

She furrowed her brows and found herself suddenly needing to keep more memories from escaping. "That's how it's been for as long as I can remember."

The memories of her parents escaped anyhow. She stood there, staring off into space. Her eyes were beginning to glaze over.

Demetri studied her and realized after a moment that something was off. "Um . . . Jenny?" He walked up to her.

No reaction. He waited a moment longer.

"Jenny?" He dared to reach out and gently touch her arm. It seemed like such a natural thing to do.

"Huh?" She shook her head and looked back up at him but didn't let herself notice his eyes. "Sorry, um . . . let's get started." She turned around and headed for the passenger side.

Demetri followed quickly, beat her to the door, and opened it for her.

"Oh." She looked up into his eyes, intending to do so only for a brief moment. He had enough time to step closer and hold her eyes for a moment.

His heart beat faster the longer he held her eyes.

Jenny swallowed and felt her face warm up. She snapped out of it. "Thank you, Demetri." She hadn't expected him to do that for her.

He was glad that she finally looked him in the eyes for more than a split second since they met.

He noticed her surprise. "Please tell me that I'm not the *only* guy to have ever opened a door for you."

Demetri grabbed her hand and helped her up. He knew she didn't need help, she had a truck just like his after all, but he helped her anyway.

Jenny's heart reminded her that it was still beating alive and well at the touch of his hand. "Um . . . It's been a while—well, besides Mr. Conroy, but that doesn't really count." Her face warmed considerably from his consideration. *Geez. My face might as well just* stay *pink! Why can't I control my emotions better?*

He looked down and shook his head. "What's the world coming to?" He peeked back up at her. "I . . . take it that you don't have another man in your life then?"

"Nope," Jenny said with a simple smile; stealing one last glance at him.

He shut the door for her; a smile appeared on his face. His long legs carried him around to his side and helped him hop in.

"*That* explains why Mr. Conroy was so protective earlier. You're single. He also doesn't know if *I'm* single or not, so he views this as a, well, date pretty much. A date with a guy that he hasn't had the chance to get to know yet." He noticed her wide eyes as he pulled away. He laughed. "Don't worry, Jenny. I'm not going to let anything happen to you, and I'm not going to *do* anything that you don't want me to."

Jenny noticed that he didn't mention anything about Mel in his last comment. She also thought his wording was weird again.

*He won't do anything that I don't **want** him to. OK, that's good. I understand that part, but does that mean . . . oh, never mind. This is business, **not** a date! He's taken anyways. I need to focus!*

Mr. Conroy's office overlooked the parking lot. He had seen it all.

Jenny pushing Demetri out of the building.

Them walking what he thought, was too close to each other.

Demetri touching Jenny's arm.

The staring they'd done into each other's eyes.

His hand on hers while he helped her up.

None of it had been even remotely ok with him.

"What have I done?" he asked himself out loud. He let out a long, aggravated sigh as he watched them leave.

4

Good Ideas

hey'd only been driving for a minute or so when Jenny broke the silence, "I wish the inside of my truck was still as nice as this." She ran her hand along the perfect, non-peeling dash.

"Well, with a reupholstering, yours can be."

"Yeah."

She thought she should probably start talking about business stuff now.

"So how did you manage to create something as successful as Dayton Developments?"

He kept his eyes on the road and didn't try to look into hers, for which Jenny was thankful. She didn't want to get trapped in them again.

"It was my parents' company," he answered. "They built it themselves. They're retired now."

Jenny felt a little more at ease being away from everyone and opened up a little. "Mr. Conroy just told me that I am to inherit his business when he and his wife retire."

"Wow, that's awesome. Congratulations!" Demetri smiled at her briefly before turning his eyes back to the road.

"Thanks. That's why he assigned *me* to come with you. He wants to see what I think of you before you guys go any farther."

Jenny's conscience had told her to be honest with him. She wasn't sure why, but she felt that she could trust him with anything.

"Wow, so I guess I better make a good impression, then." He laughed.

She let out a breath of laughter and smiled back at him. She decided to put Mel out of her mind. *I am not going to let her ruin my day with Demetri. She isn't even here.*

Demetri continued, "My parents are happily traveling all the time now, so it's completely up to me on every decision. They bought one of those tiny houses—"

Jenny perked up and felt brave enough to turn half her upper body toward him, "Oh! I've designed a few of those!" She smiled brightly, then realized she'd interrupted him, "Uh, I'm sorry. I guess interrupting when I'm excited is a bad habit of mine. Please continue."

Demetri smiled. "Don't even worry about it. I can tell you love what you do. That's great!"

She wasn't as upset this time when her cheeks exposed her embarrassment, but that might've just been because she knew he wouldn't see on account of him driving.

He continued, "They pull it around and visit all the places on their bucket list."

A small sigh escaped her lips. "That sounds like a dream. Someday, I hope to be that free." She stared at her faint reflection in the window. "Sometimes, I just feel trapped, living the same day over and over again." She looked up at him, "Sorry, we're supposed to discuss business, not my personal life."

"No, it's OK. It's important to get to know people that you plan on doing business with." He smiled and pulled over along a neighborhood curb. "Here we are, let's get out, and I'll go over my plans with you and see what you think."

"Sounds fun," she replied.

Demetri hopped out and swiftly walked over to the other side and opened the door just as Jenny finished unbuckling her seat belt.

"Thank you, Demetri." She grinned at him while he helped her down.

"You're welcome, Jenny." He looked into her eyes again.

Her heart pounded at the sound of him saying her name.

He moved his right arm to gesture to the lot. "This lot is half an acre." He opened the back door to retrieve his clipboard. "These are my blueprints for it." He removed a print from the clipboard folder and rested a pencil on his ear in case she had any suggestions.

She examined it. "This is a great design. But I would put the driveway on the *right* side of the property, not the middle, so that it allows for one large front yard. It will be harder to play catch if you have to throw the ball over vehicles in the driveway."

He laughed. "Hmm, that *is* a good idea. I meant for you to look at the house part, though. I didn't know you were an exterior designer too."

Jenny laughed. "Oh, sorry . . . I'm not officially, but we have one at the office, and I've learned a lot from him."

"No, it's OK. It's *great* actually. This is why I need someone like you— someone who knows more than just one thing and can help me see the creative side of things. My mom had the creative eye for my dad, and I'm starting to run out of new ideas alone."

Jenny blushed. Maybe it was just her, but she thought that the way he worded things were, not flirty, but close. Maybe that was just the hope in her. Demetri didn't seem like the flirty type, especially with already having a girlfriend. She found herself disappointed and tried to send the ridiculous thought to be forgotten somewhere in her hippocampus.

"Just callin' 'em as I see 'em," she was thankful that Demetri hadn't seen her bright-pink cheeks again. They didn't seem to want to fade back to normal anytime soon.

He took the pencil from his ear and made a few notes. "I'll get that changed on here. All right. Anything else you think this place needs?"

She pointed. "Maybe add a tire swing to that tree over there to the left."

It was the only tree on the lot; she hoped it wouldn't come down when the house was actually being built.

Jenny gave him a smile, "This is a kid-friendly neighborhood, and no one else has one. It's a perfect tire swing tree."

That wasn't exactly what he was expecting either, but he did, nonetheless agree. He found Jenny very amusing. "OK. Tire swing it is. I'll have to make sure they don't cut the tree down for that."

Good. I just saved a tree, she thought.

Jenny wasn't an environmentalist or anything, but she didn't think trees needed to be cut down just to make building a *tad* bit easier. Especially if it wasn't even going to be in the way.

"OK, then, next property! I'll let you look at the blueprints some more in the truck where it's not as bright."

Jenny's phone rang. She rolled her eyes at Demetri. "It's Mr. Conroy. Was he really serious about me checking back with him in just *one* hour? Has it even *been* an hour?"

Demetri laughed. "Wow . . ."

Jenny answered, "Yes, Mr. Conroy?"

"ARE YOU OK?" Mr. Conroy asked loudly into the phone.

She yanked the phone away from her ear a little. *Ow! My ear!* "Yes, Kurtis. I'm fine."

He didn't sound convinced. "You are? Are you sure?"

She raised an eyebrow in disbelief at him even though he wasn't there. "I'm *sure*, Kurtis. We've just looked at the first property. Everything is going very well."

Mr. Conroy hesitated. "All right, well . . . good, then. I will let you get back to it."

"Kurtis, I will call you later today, all right?"

He thought about it and calmed a little. "OK, I'm sorry. Look, Jenny, I just have a funny feeling that I can't shake off. I don't know if it's Demetri or something else, but it just won't go away."

She furrowed her brows. "I'll be *fine*. Thank you for worrying about me, though. I haven't had anyone worry about me in a long time."

"Jenny, Carrie and I are always concerned for you."

"Aw. You're making me *blush*, which is unprofessional, so I'd better get off here." Her eyes widened in sarcasm. *How ironic*, she thought.

"OK . . . just promise me you'll be *extra* careful today? And don't forget about your pepper spray."

Jenny turned away from Demetri. She tried to keep her voice level and professional. "Yes, sir. Thank you, Kurtis. I'll talk to you later."

"Bye, Jenny. I'll be waiting."

Mr. Conroy sighed after he hung up and then scolded himself. He felt so off today, professionally anyways. The last thing he wanted to do was bother Jenny, but her safety was all he could think about.

Jenny hung up and turned towards Demetri. "Yup, he was serious about the one-hour call. But I got him to agree to only one more check-in call that *I'll* make later."

Demetri studied her face. "Wow. That seems like quite the accomplishment."

They both laughed.

Demetri cleared his throat, "You should've told him that I have a girlfriend. That might've made him feel better."

His attempt to get another look at her eyes was in vain because even before he said the word *girlfriend*, they were glued to her black phone screen.

"Yeah, you're right. I didn't even think about that. Oh well!"

Jenny tried to brush it away like it was nothing. She didn't want Demetri thinking she was interested in him, even though she was hopelessly interested now. She peered back toward the truck and started walking.

He helped her into the truck again.

She found the will to meet his eyes. "Thanks." Or maybe she just wanted to see his unique green-and-yellow eyes again.

He gave a satisfied grin and went and climbed into the truck himself. He handed her the blueprints to look at, then headed to the next property.

She held them and stared at them blankly, and a thought came to her. "So, uh, doesn't Mel help you figure out designs? She *did* use to be a designer too."

"No, she just likes to . . .," Demetri thought for a moment, "well, I guess, spend money. Her parents are both wealthy lawyers, and they are giving her a huge allowance until she gets married."

"Oh, good for her, I guess." Jenny already knew that. She tried a final time to clear her mind of Mel.

"All right, back to business. Why do you want to team up with our design company?"

"I've heard great things about Mr. Conroy. People love their homes after he remodels. He is also into advertising design, which can potentially help my name get out there a little more. His company is probably the best in the business around here. I think we can help each other. You design 'em, and I'll build 'em."

He glanced at Jenny and noticed her reddened cheeks this time, "Uh, I mean your company, of course." He mentally admonished himself, *I have got to be careful with what I say.*

She smiled at him politely. "Mr. C. is always up for good changes."

"This was *actually* Mel's idea," Demetri started.

Great, Jenny thought. *Just when I was able to rid her from my mind.*

"She thought that if I partnered with someone, it would free up some time for other things. I don't . . . really have extra time to spend with her. All my focus is on my business. We hardly even see each other."

Guilt weighted Demetri down. He couldn't help his feelings towards Jenny. He'd always been *completely* faithful in the past to each of his girlfriends. He didn't understand why he was having such a hard time today.

Great! Jenny thought. *I need to just give up. I'm not going to come between anyone. He obviously truly cares about her, or he wouldn't even* **be** *here right now.* Jenny tried to clear her head, and she commanded her stubborn heart to move on. *Let's focus on the mission, Jenny. Don't let Mr. Conroy down.*

"Here's property number 2." He pulled over against the curb and then helped Jenny down again.

"Thank you, *again*." She looked him straight in the eyes for a long, controlled moment and gave him a grateful half smile with her lips together.

In the broad daylight, Jenny's eyes illuminated and appeared only gray. He froze and stared back as she looked up at him.

Jenny broke off her gaze and strode casually over to the lot. She felt disappointed for the thoughts and feelings she had for him having been all for nothing.

I never even had a **chance** *with him. He's taken. I've been sidetracked by him all day. Maybe I'm not ready for this. I've let Mr. Conroy down.*

Demetri hadn't moved yet. He wasn't sure what to think about her eyes, other than they were the most beautiful and the hardest to read that he had ever seen. He shook his head and tried to get back into work mode.

"Um . . ." It took him a minute to focus, and he cleared his throat.

He pointed to the plot sheet. "I call this property the Bean."

With the help of the curved sidewalk, the rest of the lot was a connect-the-dots that formed the middle indentation of the bean.

Jenny tried to suppress her emotional disappointment and let out a small laugh. "I can see it . . . cool."

She wanted to keep the talking to a minimum; turned out, getting to know someone like Demetri only made her want him more. She made a desperate attempt to dissolve her attraction.

Demetri smiled; everyone else he had shown it to couldn't see the bean. He talked some more about the property, but Jenny hardly heard him.

She didn't understand why it was so hard to just put her feelings aside.

5

"Africa"

Jenny gave what little input she could muster, and they soon moved on to the third property. This time, the truck ride was much quieter.

Demetri took out his phone to play some music and turned on "Africa" over his Bluetooth. He didn't prefer riding in quietness, and he could tell that, for whatever reason, Jenny didn't feel like talking.

She refrained from rolling her eyes. *Great, he even likes the same music as me. Maybe if I sing, I'll feel better, or at least be able to get my mind* off *him. I have* **got** *to focus for Mr. Conroy.*

Music always made her feel better. She quietly sang along, matching Toto's low and high notes.

Wow, she's good. I've never heard a woman hit those low notes, Demetri thought.

He was so charmed that he almost ran a stop sign and had to slam on the brakes. He protectively placed his hand on her thigh and held her down so she wouldn't come out of the seat. The tires screeched for a few feet in protest.

"Oh man! I'm so sorry! Are you OK?" Demetri kept his hand on her thigh out of concern and waited wide-eyed for an answer.

"Um." She stole a look at his hand but didn't attempt move it. "Yes, it's OK. I didn't even move an inch. Your grip is *very* strong." She smiled in his direction; her mind was racing with her heart, but it wasn't because of the skid.

"Oh, sorry." He slowly removed his hand. "I guess I didn't see the stop sign in time. I had my eyes on the road, I don't know how I could've missed it." He furrowed his brow and turned his head toward her, "I . . . didn't hurt your leg, did I?"

Her face was downcast. "No. No harm done."

There was silence for a moment. She noticed he still looked worried.

"Don't worry about it, Demetri. It happens to all of us. That stop sign *is* hard to see. They need to cut the shrubbery down. You are still stopped behind it, so it's all good," she assured him.

He considered her soft expression. "Right. I apologize again." He tried a small, sincere smile, "Um, the next property is down this quiet road a little way." He turned right. "Although, I'm not sure it's necessary that we go. I already like what I've seen . . . I mean, I already like what I've heard!" he added quickly. "Your ideas are great!" He turned his head to his window briefly.

That was the truth. But the other half of the truth was that he didn't want to be around Jenny for any longer than he needed to be. He felt as though he was cheating on Mel because he was constantly fighting off innervation; he'd *never* had this problem before.

"Thanks." She tried to ignore his words and smiled a little. Something was bothering her, and almost against her own will, she finally addressed it. "So does Mel live with you?" she asked bluntly.

Demetri's eyes shot open. "Huh?"

"It's just . . . um, it's been awhile since I've seen her. I just want to know how she's doing. If you say she's changed, maybe she and I can patch things up." Jenny let out a silent breath, glad her brain was able to conjure that excuse. It sounded plausible.

"No, she doesn't live with me. She lives at the Dickson. It's mainly a short-long distance relationship, meaning she lives about forty minutes away, but I don't get to see her much because of work," he explained.

Good, Jenny thought. "What has she . . . told you about me?" She didn't look at him when she asked.

"Um," he scratched his head, "hardly anything really, except that there was this girl at work she didn't like . . . at all. I think she only mentioned you once when we started seeing each other."

Jenny frowned, unbeknownst to Demetri.

Demetri turned his head to meet the back of hers. He sighed quietly to himself, wondering why she was being so evasive. It was killing him inside.

He continued, "She never mentioned the reason being because she was intimidated or anything. Not that, *that* isn't the real reason or anything, that's just all she said."

"Hmm. Interesting."

Demetri was about to ask her what she meant by that, but they had arrived. "We're here," he said instead.

He turned down a private driveway with lots of trees blocking the view of the plot. They passed a pond that was a part of the acreage for sale and a small field. They arrived at a rare flat spot covered in tall grass. There were woods on the opposite side of the flat area from where they parked. He helped her down once again, but this time she didn't even look at him.

Jenny instantly forgot about everything, "Wow, this is a beautiful piece of land." Her brain took in all the images that it could. *This is exactly what I've been looking for! I love it!*

He took a good look at it too. "Yes . . . it *is* actually. This one gives *my* land a run for its money. Well, I guess the best one's for last."

Jenny tried to mask the disappointment in her voice. "Oh, you only wanted to show me three?"

He looked out his window. "I did have more plots to take you to, but I should get off work early for once and take Mel out. I already know that I'd like to look into making some sort of agreement with Mr. Conroy, but if we need to come back and look at more land tomorrow for you to make *your* decision, then I can do that."

Demetri really needed to see Mel; he was sure that when he saw her, he would be able to forget all about Jenny. He was pretty sure that in the course of the last three hours, he had asked God to forgive his desire about fifty times too many. It *had* been a while since he last saw her, and he figured seeing her would fix his appetency for Jenny.

Jenny gave him a smile that wasn't strong enough to show her teeth and turned away again. "I understand. Family and relationships are very important and *should* come before your job. I'll tell Mr. Conroy that you'll be an inestimable partner. There's no need to meet again tomorrow." She commended herself. *Good job, Jenny. That was very professional.*

She felt very cheerless inside but kept a civil composure.

He retrieved his prints and showed her his house design ideas for this acreage.

———

Jenny tried again to clear her head and glanced over them. *No. Uh-uh. Not gonna happen. I need more of those.*

She wanted this land, and she'd already had the perfect house design down on paper back at her house.

"Is this land even on the market yet? I didn't see a sign." She knew she hadn't seen it listed anywhere either.

"Um, no, not yet. I happen to know the guy who owns it, and he hasn't talked to a real estate comp—"

"How much is it?" Jenny interrupted.

He looked up at her and raised an eyebrow in confusion. "Seventy. Why?"

"Awesome! Tell him no need to waste his money with a real estate agent. *I'm* going to buy it, and I already have a house design for it." She put her hands on her waist and looked around at the land.

Demetri wasn't sure how to respond. "Oh, that's . . . unexpected."

Jenny began walking as quickly as the untamed grass would let her. "The walkway will start over there. There will be a big wooden double door at the front, right about, here."

She continued on with her vision excitedly. Suddenly, her wedge knocked against something and caused her to lose her balance.

"Woah!"

She'd been so caught up in her design that she hadn't noticed Demetri had been walking right behind her trying to imagine everything as she'd said it. He quickly moved forward to help her but tripped over the same thing. He managed to catch her anyhow, and quickly spun so that he would be the one to break their fall.

Thud!

The hard-rocky ground showed Demetri no mercy and the tall grass had offered no help in padding the fall.

Ow, my head, he thought, disoriented. "Are you OK, Jenny?"

He opened his eyes, only to see her uneasy, now bright-blue ones, just inches above his. His heart began racing. She was fully on top of him, and his right arm was still tight around her waist.

"Um, yeah. I'm . . . good," Jenny replied, her cheeks beet red.

He gave a small laugh and a half smile as he closed his eyes in pain.

"Are . . . *you* OK?" she asked. *His lips are so close. Mmm, his breath smells like chocolate.*

Her conscience fought with her brain and her heart.

Brain: *Kiss him.*

Her conscience fought back, *No. He's taken.*
PLEASE? I love him!
If it's meant to be, it will work out.
I want to kiss him now!
That's immoral. Have some patience.
But I want him right now!
Absolutely not. We are better than that.
Ugh.

His arm was still around her, so she didn't rush to get up. She stared into his eyes for a long and rare moment. His heart beat even faster; he was sure she'd be able to feel its thumping against her own chest.

He unwillingly let his arm fall away from her, knowing he had kept it there too long. He tried to reason that it was just because he was still trying to figure out what hurt and what didn't, but there was really no use in making excuses.

Jenny placed her hands on the ground on either side of him and started with her chest to get up. Her blouse shifted with the movement, and her breasts teased to reveal themselves, just inches away from his face. They moved with even the slightest of her movements, while she decided on the most professional way to proceed.

Oh man . . . wow! I shouldn't be thinking that, he rebuked himself, *and I shouldn't be looking! I don't have anywhere else to look.* "Uh . . . I . . . uh . . ." he clenched his eyes shut.

Jenny paused and tilted her head down to see what was wrong. "What is it?"

Oh great, she stopped moving, he thought. "Nothing, nothing, take your time," He said awkwardly with his eyes still shut. *Oh boy, I hope she gets up quickly, or something will beat her to it in a moment.*

She noticed his clenched eyes. "Are you in pain?"

You have no idea, Demetri thought. "Uh, no . . . I'm great actually."

He opened his eyes and smiled to reassure her. He was careful to look only at her concerned eyes, which he noticed were bluish-gray again.

They were a welcoming distraction for him.

She studied him a moment longer and finally carefully rolled off. She sat on her calves and straightened her blouse, not realizing what she had put him through.

Demetri still lay there trying to decide if he was conscious or not.

Please be knocked out right now. Please be a dream.

He wanted to be dreaming because he had enjoyed the fall despite his aching head. He offered what seemed like his hundredth prayer in the last three hours.

Dear Father, please forgive me.

Jenny stood up. "Here, let me help you." She extended her hand and leaned over.

Demetri opened his eyes to accept her hand.

*Oh boy, **they** are not going to stay put, are they?* "No, that's OK." Demetri closed his eyes again.

She backed away. "Oh . . . OK. If you're sure."

This is embarrassing, Demetri thought. *I hope she didn't notice me looking at her.* "Thanks, Jen, but I don't want to hurt you. I'm three times your size." He half smiled up at her painfully and sat upright.

She smiled on the inside. *Jen?*

"I hit my head on this rock," he said, tossing the heavy nuisance into the woods effortlessly.

"Oh, my goodness, are you sure you're OK? I didn't realize you hit your head. Let me see!" She bent down on her knees right next to him and moved his hand to take a closer look. "You're bleeding!" Jenny gasped. *This is all my fault!* she thought.

Demetri was petrified; he didn't know what to do. Three hours ago, he was worried about working with a woman for Mel's sake; three minutes ago, he found himself uncontrollably glad that he was. He still wasn't sure if he was awake.

He shook his head and tried to clear his mind. "I'm OK, really, Jen . . . uh . . . *Jenny.*"

Jenny was relieved; she brought her hand and her eyes down to his chest.

"Thank you."

She let her eyes fall to the ground, embarrassed that she'd caused them to fall. Her left arm held on to her right.

"For what?"

Demetri looked up at her, only to notice that the position of her arms pushed her breasts together. They were really close to his face again.

OK, yup, they are definitely bigger than Mel's. Wait, what am I thinking? No, that's the problem—I am thinking! Ow. Please help me, Father.

"You landed where I didn't get dirty or hurt. That was . . . sweet." She smiled; eyes still shied away.

"Huh, oh, you're welcome." He studied her face briefly to try to figure out if she had noticed his intrusion, then tried to change the subject. "Um . . . what did we trip on?"

They pushed some weeds back to reveal a dirty blue knob sticking out of the ground.

"Here, I'll get this out of the ground before someone else trips." *Or heaven forbid we trip again*, he thought. He pulled and twisted, but it wouldn't come out. "What in the world is this thing?"

"Here let me try."

Jenny bent down again, still not noticing what her breasts did when she leaned over.

Instead of arguing, he just quickly jumped up and looked anywhere else.

"OK, yeah, my head *is* starting to hurt actually, so have at it." *Ugh, I am **not** that guy. I do **not** like her for her body. Well, I mean I do, but not **only** because of that. I like her for other reasons too! Her eyes are like diamonds in the sunlight, she has a cute smile, she's really smart, she can sing really well . . . wait! What am I **doing**? I **have** a girlfriend . . . I—*

Thoomp!

Dust burst into the air, and Jenny fell backward off her knees.

She smoothed her skirt quickly and flashed him a triumphant smile. "There! I got it!"

"What? How did you—" He stopped mid-sentence when he noticed what it was. It was a light-blue bottle about a foot or so tall.

Jenny examined it. "Wow, this is beautiful! This looks very old."

The bottle had a long straight tube which led down to the main part of the container. At the bottom of the tube, the glass bowed out and then curved back in to create a chamber to hold liquid.

"It has to be an artifact," she continued excitedly. "I wonder how old it is? Look at these markings and engravings!"

The light-blue gradually faded to a rich, dark-blue as it got closer to the bottom. Strange silver and black swirls wrapped themselves around the bottle.

"I wonder if there is anything inside!" She grabbed the rounded-off glass knob that kept whatever was inside from getting out. She pulled and twisted. It didn't budge. She tried again.

"Here, let me help you," Demetri offered as he reached for it.

"No, it's OK. I . . . GOT IT!"

The cork came out, and she peered down the tube and saw blackness.

* * *

Down in the bottle, Dalia's heart raced with hope for the first time in a long time. She, along with her vengeful heart, evaporated into soulless-black smoke.

Jenny's eyes shown with excitement at Demetri. Both completely unaware of how much their lives were about to change.

6

Jenny In A Bottle

POOF!

The evil genie appeared; her red-and-black smoke engulfed Jenny.

"JEN!" Demetri yelled and reached for her.

He would've been able to save her had her body not faded away. In her place was a short woman with hair as black as coal and skin as tanned as the Sahara Desert. Her eyes were deep brown and seemed to heat your soul the longer you locked eyes with her. She had thin red lips and a cunning look on her face.

Demetri's arms were instead wrapped around the strange woman's hips.

"WHOA!"

He let go quickly and fell backward.

"AHHH! Hitna'er!" the mysterious woman shouted. Free!

She took in a horror-struck Demetri on the ground and thought he was attractive.

Demetri could only wrap his head around one thing.

"Jenny? Where are you?" he asked firmly.

"Bah'ura?" The girl? The strange woman pointed to the sealed bottle in her hands.

A pale Demetri ran his shaking fingers through his hair. "What? That's impossible!"

Also impossible was what he just saw; he had to be dreaming. They were in the middle of a field in the middle of nowhere. He had decided last minute to take Jenny to this plot of land instead of an old fixer-upper. It couldn't have been a prank, a mirage maybe, but more likely just a dream.

For some reason, he felt as though his heart had been wrenched from his chest.

It was painful.

Dalia rubbed the bottle with one sharp-nailed finger.

An empty grin plastered her face.

* * *

Jenny found herself on the glass floor. She no more than had time to warily take in her surroundings before turning invisible again. She appeared a second later in a silvery-blue wisp of smoke, human-sized and visible, except for her bottom half. Below her hips were turning gusts of silver-and-blue smoke; the smoke led to the bottle.

"Jen!"

Demetri's heart began beating again.

He rushed to her and hugged her protectively.

A frightened and confused Jenny clung to his neck and buried her face into his chest.

They stayed there in that moment until their hearts slowed to the same beat again.

Dalia took in her new surroundings.

When Demetri realized what he was doing, he reluctantly backed away.

Jenny unwillingly let her hands fall from his neck.

His face showed red. "Um, I apologize . . . I'm just really, *really* confused. What's going on?" He took in the new Jenny before him. "Where are your legs?" He furrowed his brows and then gave her a look of unbelief. "I knew it! I'm dreaming! Thank you, God!"

It was the only explanation that his brain could accept.

The woman, bottle in hand, wished to speak and understand their language so she knew what they were saying.

POOF!

"Ahhh, so *this* is your language? What is it called?"

Both were too shocked to answer. Demetri instinctively moved between Jenny and the potential threat.

Dalia squinted harshly. "Hmm, fine then. I will find my answers elsewhere. Thank you for freeing me from that prison. It's been a long, *long* time. Bahahaha!"

She gave the bottle a disgusted toss over her shoulder, finally glad to be free from it.

Jenny was yanked along with it.

"WHOA!"

Demetri lunged for it and caught it just before it hit a bald spot with more rocks. His chest landed on another football-sized rock.

"Ow!" he mumbled. He just played off the pain so Jenny wouldn't notice.

He scrambled to his feet as quickly as he could manage and stood guard again to make sure the strange girl didn't intend on trying anything else.

Dalia turned back to Demetri. "When you get tired of the little blonde, just call for me, darling." She winked at him, blew him a kiss, then mumbled to herself, "This sure is a *strange*-sounding language."

Jenny attempted to float around Demetri after Dalia, but he stayed in front of her. "Wait! What did you do to me?" she pleaded.

"Dear," Dalia turned around, "think of it as a gift. You now have *unmatched* powers, and you have done a great thing in freeing me." An evil smile formed across her lips. She placed her right hand on her hip, snapped her free fingers, and vanished in a sparkle of lingering black-and-red dust.

Demetri waited a few moments to make sure that Dalia was gone and then turned back to Jenny when he felt it was safe to do so.

She had no body below her hips, only smoke. The clothing she did have was essentially a dark-blue bra dusted with silver sparkles and adorned with an intricate silver design that embroidered the top of the cups. The most noticeable thing about it was that it pushed her breasts up where they were held together attractively.

Jenny was too busy trying to figure out the smoke pillar out of which she spouted and didn't notice Demetri's ogling. She waved her hand in and out of it in bafflement.

Demetri's mouth opened slightly. *Again with the breasts? Oh, Father, please help me. And I thought I was having trouble* **earlier.**

But he couldn't look away; he was too confounded and enraptured.

Besides, he was *one hundred* percent sure he was dreaming, so he didn't even try to stop himself.

Jenny too finally took a good look at her upper body for the first time. *I'm dressed like a harem girl,* she thought in unease. *I look so stupid. I'm nothing more than half of a floating body now.*

She moved her left arm to her right again.

Not the arm thing again! Demetri tried to look away but failed miserably.

"Demetri, what happened to me?" Jenny looked to him, desperate for an answer.

He gazed into her eyes and thought, *I don't know what's happened to* **you,** *but I know what's happening to* **me.** "I don't know, Jen," he told her instead. He lowered his eyes to stare again. It was a sexy dream come true standing right in front of him. He pinched the side of his leg, unbeknownst to her.

It doesn't matter what I do or say, right? This is **totally** *a dream.*

Jenny's eyes fell and her cheeks blushed. "You're staring at me," she finally realized. She braved meeting his eyes which matched the color of the bright, summery tall grass around them.

"Oh," he apologized to her sunlit, sky blue eyes. "Um . . . sorry, I'm just trying to wrap my head around this."

His face was red; he tried to think straight but quickly gave up.

Wow. She. Is. Hot. I need to fix myself in case I'm conscious. He turned away for a moment. "Um, give me a second. My head hurts."

That *was* true; his head felt cloudy with pain.

Poor Demetri. This is all my fault! Some **day** *this has been. OK, I need to try to get out of this costume—it is so* **not** *professional.*

Jenny started with the thin silver cuffs that had appeared on her wrists, but they wouldn't budge even a little bit. The captive bangles were about three and a half inches long.

OK . . ., she thought, a little more freaked out now.

Next, she tried the silver veil around her new updo; it came off, no problem.

Whew! Thank goodness! At least something *will come off. But taking things off shouldn't be the problem here. I need my cloth—*

A breeze blew. It finally sank in that she was hardly wearing a thing. Jenny had never exposed so much skin in front of someone before, even including times at a public pool. Her cheeks were instantly fiery red and toasty warm. She turned a little from Demetri, *extremely* uncomfortable now.

"Um, Demetri?" she asked meekly. "Do you see my clothes?"

He turned back around, and his eyes gravitated to her chest again. "Jen . . . you're not really . . . *wearing* any clothes."

If it was possible, she felt her face burn a few degrees hotter. "Um, I know." She turned away from him completely. "That's why I'm asking you if you've *seen* my clothes . . . from earlier."

She reached back down to retrieve her veil, not that it would cover much, it was see-through.

Demetri felt dumb. "Oh! Right! I'm sorry!" He shook his head to focus and began searching around. "I don't see them anywhere." He awkwardly turned back to her. "Um . . . what's wrong with what you're wearing?"

If he was going to have a dream like this, it might as well be a good one where she doesn't find them. He forgot everything and admired her again. The whole day —meeting Mr. Conroy, going around with his dream girl who got transformed into a genie and was not wearing enough to be called decent in public view— was all just an amazing dream.

She bent her head down shamefully. "Um . . . there *isn't* anything wrong with what I'm wearing. It's really comfortable actually. I kind of like it."

Me too, he thought.

She continued, "It's just . . . I shouldn't wear it in *front* of you. Especially not for a *business* outing." *He's probably ready to call off the whole thing.*

His conscience was finally able to wake him up and convince him that even in his dreams, he should be a gentleman. Especially with his dream girl.

His eyes were finally able to focus on her uneasy ones rather than her body. "Hey, I have a jacket that might fit you in my truck." He turned and headed for his truck. "C'mon, I'll get it for you."

Jenny started to follow but was quickly stopped by her bottle. "Uh . . . Demetri?"

He turned and noticed. "Oh, um . . . please, let me help you." He walked back to her, trying desperately to just look at her eyes.

"Thanks," Jenny mumbled. She kept her embarrassed eyes away from his.

Demetri picked the bottle up and walked up to her. "Is it all right if I carry you?" he asked softly.

She drifted back toward her bottle, then shrank down to about five inches and held on to the rim. That was a lot more bearable for Demetri; it clouded over all the weirdness of the situation.

"Yes, it's all right," Jenny said dolefully. She wasn't even phased by her new tiny size.

Demetri held her bottle with both hands in front of his stomach and headed for the truck. He felt a breeze and heard some whip-poor-wills in the treetops nearby.

His conscience tugged at him, telling him that this *wasn't* a dream. His brain was holding up a wall, however.

Now he was unsure of everything. He peered down at her. She'd shrunk down and was holding on to the rim with her back to him. With her being so small, he could think a little clearer. Demetri started to head around to her side of the truck first; then he remembered she was inside a bottle in his hands.

"Right. This isn't weird at all. Totally normal! I'm *not* having a bizarre dream from hitting my head."

Jenny sighed.

Demetri walked in a bit of a daze around to his side and hopped in. He sat her bottle down next to him, in the middle seat, and buckled it in so it wouldn't tip over.

Jenny drifted out of the bottle a bit more and "sat" as normally as she could, given her situation, and put her seat belt on. She wanted to feel as normal as possible.

Don't *look, Demetri. Just turn away. You are **not** that guy. Why am I having so much trouble with this? You're with someone right now, so this **isn't** ok!* He quickly reached in the back and retrieved his jacket. "All right! Here's my jacket. Please use it!"

"Thanks." Jenny accepted it and slid it on as quickly as she could and then turned toward her window again. She was seated as far away from him as possible.

Jenny sighed. *He must be disgusted. This outfit is **entirely** too inappropriate.* "Thanks for your jacket."

"Yeah, no problem," he said quickly.

Her fingers began buttoning; they began with the bottom button first. When she buttoned the last one, she noticed how perfectly it fit her.

"Wow, this *does* fit me." She turned to him, "Why do you have such a small jacket?"

He stared into her eyes, a little heavily from all the excitement, but it was not enough that Jenny would notice. "My mom did some cleaning and sold most of their things so they could travel, and she found my favorite childhood jacket. She thought I'd like to give it to my son someday," he looked back through the windshield, "if I ever have one."

It was an old worn black leather jacket with silver buttons.

She closed her eyes for a moment and smiled. *Mmm, it smells like the woods.* "It's still in great condition for being so old."

A bit of comfort was able to set in and she faced the dash this time instead of the door.

He felt more in control of himself now. "Yeah, I took really good care of it, it was my favorite. My dad picked it out for me. I wore it outside all the time when I was about thirteen. It was my photography jacket." He laughed slightly. "I remember one time, a button fell off. I was so upset. I spent all evening looking for it and happened to actually find it. I brought it to my mom, and she fixed it."

"Aww." Jenny smiled. She felt a little better and more normal inside. "Your parents sound great."

"Thanks. They are. I'm really lucky to have great parents. Not everyone has that blessing." Demetri felt a little better as well with the recollection.

Jenny smiled a small smile and nodded solemnly.

It was silent for a moment.

Demetri let out a breath and raised an eyebrow, wondering if he had woken up yet; he felt so much like himself again. "OK, so what's going on? Am I knocked out right now from hitting my head? I mean, if I didn't know any better, I'd say that you have been turned into a . . . genie."

Jenny had heard enough fairy tales to already know what she was: she was just confused as to how this power existed. Maybe *she* was the one dreaming; it would make more sense.

Demetri began to recall all the events out loud.

"The last *normal* thing that happened was you explaining your house plans and then you tripped. After that, I pulled you on top of me—wait, that's not normal. What am I saying? Gosh, I can't even *think* right now."

Demetri was rambling; yet another thing he never did. He sighed and rest his head on his steering wheel.

Jenny hung her head humbly. She felt as though she had failed everyone today, including Demetri. "I'm sorry," she said.

Demetri's head shot up in befuddlement. *Why are **you** apologizing?* he thought to himself. *If anyone should be sorry, it should be me with how much I've violated you with my eyes in the last few minutes. But I'm **not** telling you* *that. That would probably make things worse. Not that things are bad. I mean, this has been, like . . . Wow.* "Um, why are you apologizing?" he asked.

"This was supposed to be an important day," Jenny started, "Kurtis . . . *Mr. Conroy* was counting on me! I've let him down, and I feel . . . like I've let you down too. Your head is bleeding, all because I can't watch where I'm going."

Demetri took a long breath in and out. "So . . . this *is* real?"

Guilt weighted his conscience.

She slowly looked up at him. "Well, we aren't *both* dreaming the same dream. I guess I'm a . . . *genie* now."

Demetri hoped she was wrong, for his conscience's sake. He didn't know how much longer it could hold up the three tons of guilt that'd just been dumped on it.

"That's impossible, Jenny. There's no such thing."

He also didn't want his feelings to be real; he had a girlfriend, and his feelings for Jenny had disrupted his moral way of thinking.

"Well, what do *you* think happened? All the stories I've heard growing up about genies pretty much explain my situation." She looked specifically at the churning blue-and-silver smoke that attached her to the bottle.

"I agree, but *I'm* not an astronaut."

Jenny held in a snicker and rolled her eyes at his reference. She was having a hard time trying to convince herself, let alone Demetri too. "This isn't a joke, Demetri."

He looked her over again, but just to try to understand this time.

I guess that would actually explain everything. "OK, so . . . let's say you *are* one. Why did it happen to you? *How* did it happen?"

"I think that woman was trapped in here," she looked at her bottle, "so when I opened it, she . . . trapped *me*, I guess."

It began to sink into Jenny's gut that she may be stuck like this forever.

Her heartbeat picked up speed at the thought of actually being trapped.

*How can I explain this to Kurtis? How can I even move around by myself? How can I even go to Bible Study now? Or to town, or **anywhere** for that matter?*

So many questions twisted in her head.

Demetri thought to himself, *OK, so my genie dream wasn't far off . . . nice! You've got to stop thinking, Demetri. You have a girlfriend. You love your girlfriend. But . . . do I **love** Mel? Do these feelings count if I **don't** love Mel? . . .*

46

Of course I love her! I wouldn't be with her if I didn't . . . right? I don't even know anymore.

He wanted someone to answer his questions for him and tell him what to do.

Yet another silent, small prayer helped clear his mind a little.

Jenny's eyes glazed as she stared off into the distant woods. "Demetri?"

"Huh? Oh, yes?" He sensed her sadness, so he drew close automatically, half trying to comfort her, half trying to prove to himself if this *was* real.

She kept her eyes straight ahead. "Will you . . . take me home with you?"

His eyes burst open. *Oh, great! Just great! The nearly naked genie wants to go home with me! This couldn't get any better—I mean worse, or do I mean better?* He cleared his throat. "Uh . . . why?"

Jenny seemed to grow a little smaller, but it had nothing to do with being a genie.

"I'm . . . scared . . . I don't understand any of this, and I don't have anyone else to figure this out with." She gazed into his summery eyes. "I feel like I can trust you."

He leaned back a little with how sad her stormy gray eyes were. Demetri sighed and tried to run the requested scenario through his head. *A sexy genie, in a bottle, at my house? I can't explain this to Mel. Something tells me she isn't going to be OK with that, especially since the genie is Jenny.* "Um, OK . . . uh, how about we get your best friend . . . what was her name again . . . Cali!"

Her eyes went wide with fear, and she straightened up completely. "NO! Cali couldn't handle something like this! This is bizarre enough as it is without more people getting involved. If word gets out, they might take me away and do some kind of test or experiment on me! No one needs to know about this, not even Cali." She looked down, saddened that she may never see Cali again. Or anyone else for that matter. *And I thought I was trapped before,* she thought sadly.

He understood and scratched his head. "Well, what about your parents? They love you no matter what. They'd keep it a secret."

Jenny kept her head down and closed her eyes tightly in pain. "They . . . aren't alive anymore." She turned to face the passenger door since she didn't have knees to bury her face in. *He doesn't want to help me. I don't blame him—I don't know if I'd help me either if I was him. He only just met me.*

Demetri stared at her solemnly and sighed. "I'm *so* sorry. I wouldn't have said that if I had known. What . . . happened to them? If you don't mind my asking."

She kept her concealed position. "I'd . . . really rather not talk about it right now." Silent tears slid down her hidden face.

"Oh, OK, I understand."

After a moment, he heard her sniff.

Aw, man, he thought. He softened his voice. "Hey, I'm sorry I asked about your parents." He moved the bottle carefully and scooted over right next to her.

"It's not that . . ."

She tried her best to hold back as many of her tears as she could. If she thought she was unprofessional before, the tears were the light to ignite the candle on top of it all.

"It's just, I'm *barely* here. I can't go to work like this. I can't go to town or see anyone. I can't even move *around* on my own. I won't . . . be able to live a normal life anymore."

Saying it out loud only made it worse, and more tears raced each other down her cheeks.

Demetri let those words sink in. He hadn't even thought about that and felt so badly for her.

His hand found its way to the middle of her back.

"Hey, it's going to be all right. I'll help you." *I owe you that much for all the things I've imagined*, he thought to himself.

She lifted her head; her face was lined with tear streaks, "No, Demetri. I'm sorry I asked to go home with you. I don't want to be a burden to you. You don't even know me. I don't want to drag you into this mess." She turned back to the window.

He tilted his head a little to try to see her face. "Jenny . . . I *want* to help you."

She slowly turned to face him. "Why?"

He gave her a soft smile and reached his thumbs to her face to dry her tears. "Because you need help, and I'm not the type of person to leave someone in need."

Jenny's heart beat uncontrollably.

She felt so comforted by his touch that she couldn't help but lean into his chest.

Demetri let her; he knew she needed someone. He wrapped his arms around her and held her tightly.

Poor girl. This isn't about Mel right now. This is about helping someone out, even if they are a half-naked, female stranger, who I'm pretty sure is the girl I've been waiting for my whole life.

It felt so right with her in his arms; he held her even closer.

Jenny instantly felt a lot better.

"You're the only one who knows, other than that woman. It needs to stay that way. You won't tell anyone, will you?" Her heart-wrenching gray eyes pleaded with his.

As he stared back, his heart speed up with every second that passed. Vanilla suddenly overwhelmed all his senses.

Wow . . . she smells so good! He breathed in deeply, then answered her, "Hey, I promised Mr. Conroy I'd take care of you, didn't I? I won't tell anyone." He gave her a warm smile.

Jenny felt relieved that her intuition and feelings had thus far been correct about him; she closed her eyes, and they stayed there for another moment.

"Thank you, Demetri."

He didn't want to let go. He felt so . . . he wasn't sure how he felt actually. He tried to hold his feelings back, but he'd never felt this way about anyone before. He didn't know how to describe it other than *right.*

"All right, all right, let's just forget about it for now. I'll take you back to my place. It's still early. We'll figure this out there."

Demetri reluctantly let his arms fall, and she slowly sunk into her seat and buckled herself in. He slid back over to his own seat and buckled himself and the bottle in again. His hand found the key but hesitated to turn it. He wasn't sure if he would be able to safely drive or not.

I need to be able to concentrate, he thought to himself.

An idea came to him.

"Uh, what song would you like to listen to?"

He tried to act as if everything was normal, for Jenny's sake. Maybe it was also for his.

For once, she didn't feel like listening to music. She noticed Demetri looked kind of pale, almost as though he had just seen a ghost.

What did I just ask of him? she asked her brain. *He has a life, a business, a girl he loves—I'm sure he has tons of friends, and who knows what else. Even if he's willing, I'm **not** going to screw it up for him.* "Um, hey."

Demetri's uneasy eyes easily found hers.

"This really isn't your problem." She continued, "You just met me. It isn't your job to watch after me. I'm an adult, and this is *my* problem. If you really want to help me, please just take me to my house. I've been through tougher, I think, believe it or not."

Jenny didn't want to go through this alone, but she didn't want to interrupt Demetri's sanity any more than she already had.

Demetri wasn't sure how to respond. He wanted to help, but if he was being honest with himself, he didn't know if he *could* help her—he wasn't sure how.

"OK, um, if that's what you want, then that's what we'll do."

He thought that Jenny might've changed her mind on account of him being a stranger, so he didn't try to convince her otherwise. He sighed quietly, a little disappointed that she didn't seem to trust him all of the sudden. He glanced down at her bottle and then picked it up a moment later.

Jenny was pulled a little. "Whoa!"

"Oh, sorry." He glanced at her confused face and then went back to studying the bottle. "I just wanted to get a closer look at it. Maybe I can figure out a way to get you out."

She raised an eyebrow. "I doubt it's that simple. That lady seemed to be from a completely different era, I'm sure she's tried everything already."

"Possibly, but she didn't have help."

Demetri wanted to prove that she could trust him.

"Wow, I can't believe you're *really* a genie." He turned it upside down.

Jenny was pulled a little again.

"Demetri!" Jenny crossed her arms.

"Jen . . . look! It has your name on the bottom."

Her arms dropped. "What?"

He showed her. Her name was written in black cursive on the bottom.

"Great!" She rolled her eyes.

"Wow! It just did that on its own. This thing is seriously cool."

Jenny cast it an annoyed stare. "Yeah, well, you can have it since you like it so much."

POOF!

A silver band appeared on Demetri's right ring finger in a flash of blue dust.

Jenny continued, "I'll just hold on to it for you until I get out."

Demetri froze. "What in the world?"

She looked over at him, puzzled. "What?"

"Look!" He held up his hand to show her, palm side facing himself. He noticed something written on the bottom of the ring.

"What about it? Hey . . . it's the same silver as my bracelets—or imprisoning *cuffs* is probably more accurate." She sighed.

He looked at her with all seriousness. "Jenny, this ring *just appeared* on my finger. And check this out!"

Demetri showed her his palm; she saw her own name staring back at her.

Her eyes went wide. "It's just like the bottom of my bottle."

He picked it back up and examined it again to compare them then nearly dropped it.

"Woah! Demetri! Please put it down before something happens to it." She crossed her arms again.

A flabbergasted expression overtook his face. "Look, Jen!"

Gasp! "It has *your* name on it now! But . . . but . . . it just had *my* name on it seven seconds ago!"

Jenny's eyes searched along with her mind for answers, and Demetri set the bottle down gently.

She couldn't come up with any plausible reasoning for all this. After a moment, she noticed him studying his ring.

"Take the ring off, Demetri."

"What, why?" He glanced up at her briefly and then went back to admiring it. "I . . . kinda like it."

She turned away again and lowered her voice. "*Mel* won't like it. It has *my* name, of all people, on it."

"Oh, I guess you're right." He'd forgotten about Mel for a minute. "This is like something that couples do when they've promised themselves to each other isn't it?" He threw her a quick look and then tried to take it off.

It wouldn't budge.

"Don't tell me." She didn't even have to look at him. "It won't come off, will it?"

He looked over at her sheepishly even though she was turned away. "No . . . it's stuck."

She sighed and met his hopeless hazel eyes. "I'm sorry, Demetri, but you *cannot* show that to Mel."

"I know—she'd kill me!" Demetri rested his head on the steering wheel again.

Jenny watched the wind sway the tall grass. "I'm sorry that I'm ruining your life. Maybe if you take me home now, it will disappear or something after you drop me off." The thought of him leaving made her heart lurch.

He sighed; he really didn't want to be apart from Jenny. "All right," he said, despite every atom in his body screaming, *No!* He looked over at her one more time and felt saddened himself.

7

Into Motion

"**B**wahahaha! FINALLY! So, *this* is where the bottle has been hidden for the last few thousand years."

Satan had seen everything.

"Dalia was resourceful for figuring out how to trap another and escape. She *will* soon lose all her power and be useless to me, but no matter. I know Jenny Delemonte well. This will *not* be easy, but I can corrupt *any* soul. I will simply use her *purity* and *innocence*"—he said the words with revulsion—"to corrupt her!"

A mighty but soft voice from above echoed in his head, "You won't prevail."

"Oh, *I* don't *have* to!" Satan yelled up to the sky. He composed himself again, upset that he had lost his cool. "I can make that *boy* do it all for me!" He grinned viciously. "Demetri Dayton is already so enthralled, and lust driven toward her—this should be a piece of cake. Even with both of their *near* perfect records."

Satan sent his best devil to go sit on Demetri's head, and disappeared.

ACROSS THE SEAS

Dalia appeared on a sidewalk back at her hometown. It was almost dark, so hardly anyone was out. She took in her surroundings; there were tall foreign structures everywhere she turned, but for the most part, the people looked and dressed the same.

A man saw her and wasted no time in rushing over. He had slightly tanned skin and sandstorm-colored eyes. He was about a foot taller than Dalia and wore a long, thin white robe with a black band like a crown on his head.

He pushed Dalia back into a narrow alley. "What are you wearing?" He didn't wait for a response as she started to go up on the defense. "If the Mutaween see you, you will be in trouble! Are you trying to get yourself arrested?" He looked at her as though she had lost her mind.

She forgot about her amplifying fury for a moment and glanced down at her outfit. It was fiery red with matching gems and hardly covered her body. Her top barely covered her breasts; her red veiled pants covered her legs, but with see-through fabric. She did have on shorts underneath the pants, but they didn't even fully cover her there either.

He gave her a good once-over . . . or maybe it was a thrice-over. He'd never seen a woman showing this much skin.

Dalia gave the man a once-over herself and rolled her eyes. "Are women *still* forced to cover themselves from head-to-toe?"

She'd been trapped so long she'd forgotten about the customs of her own country.

He took too long to answer.

"Fine. If I *must*."

She peeked out of the alley to see *exactly* what the other women were wearing these days.

How repulsive. Women's attire has not hardly evolved at all! We are still wearing blankets with peepholes! she thought when she saw another lady walking by with a man escorting her.

Dalia snapped her fingers, and a replica of that lady's outfit appeared on her own body. She grabbed a clump of slack fabric. "Why do we still have to wear this?"

He stared back at her in horror and flattened himself against the alley wall. "You . . . you are a genie!" He remembered her costume. Genie legends were a common marketing idea in this area.

She flashed him an outraged look. "Tell me what a genie is! If it's an insult, you can say bye to your puny life!"

He tried to compose himself. "A genie is . . . an attractive woman, or man, who is normally trapped in a lamp and has the ability to grant wishes."

Dalia narrowed her eyes, "Yeah . . . that sounds about right."

She snuck another look out at the few people walking by. She thought back to what she saw Jenny wearing when she had been examining her prison of a home. Jenny had been wearing a knee-length skirt that showed her calves and a short-sleeved shirt that showed her arms; she even had her hair exposed.

"I just came from a place where women wear what they want. Why is this still an issue *here*?"

The man answered, afraid for *his* life now, "The laws are firm. A woman cannot be in public wearing what you were wearing. I do not know why they will not change them."

Harsh memories from thousands of years ago of women getting stoned, raped, and beaten reappeared in her mind.

Dalia studied him. "Why did you not turn me in or rape me?"

He gave her a grave look. "I promised myself a long time ago I would not be that man."

She gave a slight nod. "What language are we speaking?"

"It is called English," he replied, a little more at ease now.

"Why do we still not speak Hebrew here?" She put her hands on her hips.

"I do not know. People here speak Arabic or English. English is the third most spoken language in the world, so many here learn it, including me. It is good for business."

"What do you mean, 'good for business?'"

He looked away for a moment. "I own a small market. When English-speaking tourists come, they are more willing to buy if you can speak their own language to them. So, I learned it."

Hmm . . . he is resourceful, and adaptive. He could be useful.

She tossed around the idea of casting a locust plague upon him, even though he hadn't done anything besides help her, but ultimately decided against it. "How about you come with me."

It was not a question, and Mimir could tell, "I was going to anyways."

Dalia hadn't expected that reply. He must've noticed her surprised expression.

"You need a male escort. You cannot walk the streets alone."

"You have *got* to be kidding me." She crossed her arms and bit her bottom red lip out of anger.

He walked up to her. "I apologize. Again, *I* do not make the rules."

She squinted, clearly aggravated, and then stared directly into his dark eyes. "What is your name, man? I need something to call you."

"Mimir, madame." He slightly bowed his head. That was *not* customary, but he felt that she deserved some respect. "What is *your* name?"

She seriously considered not telling him, as he was absolutely *nothing* to her, but it just kind of came out on its own.

"Dalia. *Now*, Mimir, where is the closest oasis?"

She wanted to get down to business.

He pointed to the north. "There is one not far from my shop, and I can take you there in the morning." He came out of the alleyway and started walking north. "It is getting dark, and neither of us should be out here at dusk. You can come stay at my place for the night. You will be safe there." *I hope*, he thought to himself.

Mimir would be breaking the law for a stranger, but he could tell that she needed help.

She agreed only because almost everything about her hometown had changed, and she'd be completely lost in the dark. She began to follow him.

He soon realized that his stride was too fast for her, and so he slowed until she walked almost directly beside him. After a bit of walking, she was able to see how much her old world had changed with what little light was left.

"Mimir, what is that yellow thing over there?" She did not point; it was probably *still* rude to point too. She hated being obedient to anyone or anything, including the firm, unfair laws of her land.

"That is called a car. You put fuel in it, and it will take you wherever you want to go until it runs out. It cannot go into water, though."

"Hmm," she muttered, unimpressed. "How much farther?"

"Just a bit. It is not far." He continued walking.

"Are men *still* allowed to have as many wives as he wants?"

"Only four." He looked back at her briefly.

"*Four*? A man should have *one* wife! And he should let her speak when she wants, as he does."

Dalia didn't like competition; she thought of the way Demetri had looked at Jenny, and it fueled her angry fire.

He gave her a slight smile, which she ignored.

"How many wives do *you* have?"

She couldn't believe she even cared enough to ask. A strange, unknown feeling began to develop inside of her while she waited for an answer. She tried to ignore it.

"None," he answered. "I hope to have *one* someday, though."

The feeling went away.

Good riddance, she thought.

She didn't like whatever that feeling did to her. It made her feel vulnerable. She did not answer him.

"Ah, here we are."

It was a small simple place with an empty fruit stand in the front.

Dalia stared at the glass door that he held open for her. "I am *not* going in there! It is a trap! Do you *know* how long I have been *trapped*? Try about four thousand years, give or take a few . . . I lost count!"

He raised his eyebrows and then offered her caring eyes. "Dalia, this is my store and my home. Look around, everyone lives in one of these."

She studied him coldly. "Fine, but *you* first, and you have to shut the door behind you and then open it, from the *inside*."

Mimir did just that for her without a word and then waited patiently for her judgement. She eyed him cautiously as she timidly stepped through the threshold. As soon as he let the door shut them inside, she opened it quickly.

It opened right back up again.

"OK, I will stay here tonight," she announced cautiously.

"Um, I *do* have to *lock* the door so no one can break in."

Her eyes went wide. "I knew it! It is a trap! You want me for my *beanie* powers!" She began to head back outside.

He wanted to roll his eyes but refrained. "*Genie* powers, not *beanie* powers. And no, I do not. Here. This is the key, it locks *and* unlocks the door." He held the set of keys out to her. "You lock it and keep them until morning, if you want."

She had the door open, but it was completely dark outside. Even with her powers, she knew it was not safe out on the streets, especially at night.

The memories haunted her again. Fear washed over her. Dalia turned to look at the key. She crossed her arms and gave him a warning look. "Fine, but if you *do* try to trap me, I will *destroy* your little market as soon as I wake up!"

Mimir suppressed a laugh. "Fair enough."

He was glad she was staying; he wanted her to be safe. This wasn't her world anymore and she needed help even if she didn't want it. He showed her how to lock the door and then escorted her to a secluded room in the back of the market that she could sleep in for the night. It was a small rectangular room with a simple bed and a plain nightstand. It had a rack against the left wall, and some regular white robes hung from it.

"Well, it *is* bigger than what I just came from." Dalia walked over to the bed and slid out of the burka. "Ahh, that is better. It is way too hot in there." She started to lie down.

"Um," he turned away, "may I shut the door?"

She sprung back up quickly. "No! I will *not* be trapped *inside* of a trap!"

Dalia was back over by him with one foot in the doorway in less than a second. Mimir didn't even bother trying to convince her that he wasn't going to trap her this time. Dalia was standing really close to him, wearing almost nothing. He glanced at the bed and then back at her. Sweat began to form beads on his forehead.

"OK, I will let you get some rest, then, it sounds like you have had a big day! I will be in the other room if you need me." He pointed to a room to the right of where they were.

She crossed her arms. "OK. Be gone with you."

His eyes widened at her crossed arms, and he quickly turned away.

Dalia waited for him to leave and shut himself into the other room before she decided to shut her own door partway. She dragged her feet to the bed, and as soon as her head hit the pillow, she fell asleep.

8

"867-5309 / Jenny"

Jenny felt like she could have a good cry, but instead, she let it build up inside. She just wanted to go home and pretend that this day had never happened. Even though she had no idea *how* she was going to do that.

She rested her head on the window and closed her eyes, trying to trap the tears.

A strange sensation came over Demetri.

"Whoa!" he whispered. His eyes started welling up with tears. "What in the world?"

He dried them before Jenny saw. Not that she would've noticed anyways; she hadn't stopped looking out the window for the past fifteen minutes, which was pretty much how it had been all day with her. He still didn't understand why she had barely looked him in the eyes all day. *He'd* been trying to *only* look at her eyes since he met her.

Jenny sighed. "What is it?"

She wanted to get her mind off her situation. She actually looked over at him now.

He was surprised. "I have . . . no idea. I can't explain it, but I just got an immense feeling of—"

Jenny averted her eyes again but not before he saw. She didn't feel like making conversation.

He glanced at her again. "Jenny?"

She didn't answer.

He thought for a moment and then tried again. *"Jen?"*

She straightened up a little. Butterflies fluttered in her stomach.

He smiled.

Jenny kept her face positioned toward her window. "What?" It came out as more of a whisper.

"Is anything wrong?"

"I'm f—"

She tried to tell him that she was fine, but something wouldn't let her.

"Yes. I mean, n—"

She gave up and tried a different response.

"Just don't worry about me, all right?" She gave him a big fake smile and then continued staring at the passing landscape.

Her eyes trapped a sad story inside.

Demetri thought a moment, and an idea came to him. He went to his "favorites" playlist and clicked on a song, all without taking his attention off the road.

The song he chose began to play.

Jenny's heart started dancing, and it recognized the song all too well. A tear escaped.

"Why are you playing *this* song?"

She couldn't hold it in anymore, and she started crying again.

He glanced over at her.

"I'm sorry, please ignore me. We're almost there."

Jenny was no more than able to wipe away one tear before three more spilled out.

Demetri pulled over.

"No, *please*, I'll be fine! I just need a minute. Keep going." She covered her face.

Demetri felt the feeling increase. It was beyond arduous. He tried to fight it off and began singing to her. Singing had always cheered him up, and maybe it'd also cheer her up.

"Jenny, Jenny, who can I turn to? / You give me something, I can hold on to."

Her heart felt caged inside her chest and began to bang on the door to get out.

He turned his body toward hers as much as he could and continued, *"I know you think I'm like the others before."* His eyes focused on her broken composure. *"Who saw your name and number on the wall."* He smiled at her, painfully trying to fight off sadness and something *else* . . .

She'd managed to stop sobbing and just stared at him as though he'd lost his mind. He was serenading a girl he just met, like he was back in grade school or something.

"C'mon, Jenny, I *know* you know this song."

Demetri sensed a different feeling; he didn't know what it was, but it wasn't as sad.

"Jenny, I got your number. I need to make you mine. Jenny, don't change your number. 867530-9, 867530-9, 867530-9, 867530-9." He kept his confident gaze fixed on her and met her eyes anytime she peeked over at him.

Jenny shook her head and closed her eyes. *This is so corny.* She wanted him to *mean* those words so badly.

Demetri felt another feeling, and he was pretty sure he recognized this one. He smiled. "Don't you wanna sing with me? I know you love to sing."

She gave a small laugh and looked over at him with red-tinted eyes. *How?* she wondered.

He kept singing. *"Jenny, Jenny, you're the girl for me / You don't know me, but you make me so happy."*

Demetri felt the emotion overwhelm him, and he knew what it was now.

Jenny quietly started singing. *"I tried to call you before, but I lost my nerve."*

They both sang. *"I tried my imagination, but I was disturbed."*

Tell me about it, Tommy, Demetri thought to himself.

Jenny let a laugh escape and was able to successfully dry her eyes. She sighed and reached for the volume dial and turned it all the way down.

Her heart wouldn't be able to take him singing the chorus to her again.

She was glad he went all weird to cheer her up, but she didn't want to get her hopes up again. The song hurt her too much when *he* sang it.

"Hey, what are you doing?" He reached for the volume dial too to turn it back up, but she grabbed his hand.

She looked at him with pinkish cheeks and then let it go. "Thanks. I feel better, but . . . I don't want to listen to it anymore." She gave him a small grateful smile and returned her eyes to the window once again. "Let's keep going, please."

Demetri didn't move, he wanted to figure her out. "Do you feel . . . how can I put it into words . . . *torn*?" He tilted his head a little.

"What? N—yes." Her eyes went wide as she swung her face back around to look at him. "AGH! Why can't I say what I *want* to say to you?"

"Jen, calm down." He reached over and took her hand for a moment. "I know you feel torn. I can *feel* it." He looked into her eyes, concerned.

Her face turned pinker. "What? What do you mean?"

"I don't know. It sounds crazy, but I think I can *feel* what you feel."

She looked at him as though he'd lost his gourd. "How? That's ridiculous!"

"Well, it's probably because . . . well, I don't know, but I'm sure it has something to do with you being a genie."

"Well . . ." She looked at the floorboard.

Jenny didn't want Demetri feeling like there was a connection between them; not when he was taken.

"That's *all* it is, then. It's just because of this genie thing, that's *it*. So, you might as well just ignore whatever you're feeling and take me home now because it isn't even going to matter tomorrow."

She turned away, hoping that would be enough to satisfy him so they could get going again.

He furrowed his brows. "Jen, I—"

"*Don't* call me Jen . . . please."

It killed her to tell him that; she loved her new nickname.

"Oh . . . do you not like it?" Demetri's eyes fell for a brief moment before returning to her.

She still had her body turned slightly away from him. "N—yes, I do . . . agh! Stop asking me questions!" She buried her face in her hands.

"You feel hurt and torn again," he said quietly.

He felt just as bad as she did.

"No, I d—" She crossed her arms. "Stop trying to read my feelings and please just take me home now!"

He peered at her sadly. "Jen . . . *Jenny* . . . I'm not trying to read you. They just come—"

"*Please*, Demetri!" She clenched her eyes shut and rested her head back on the window.

He turned back to the steering wheel. "Fine!" It came out almost too angrily; he tried to overcome the sensation. *She must really be upset with me.* He sighed. "I'm sorry Jenny, I just thought . . ."

His eyes scanned her over one last time.

She was trying desperately to just ignore him.

Demetri fixed his jaw to the side and shook his head. "Never mind." He started the truck and pulled back onto the highway.

A mix of emotions come flowing through him; he felt completely awful.

9

Interrogation No. 1

They passed by her work along the way.

"I can't even bring my truck home!" Jenny complained, still frustrated, as she looked down at her nonexistent legs. "And Mr. Conroy wanted me to report back to him."

Aw, man, she feels so . . . I'm not sure there are words for it, but it makes me deeply depressed. "Um, you can call him!" He tried saying it in a positive tone. "I'm not sure what we're going to do about your truck yet, though."

We? Jenny thought. "Demetri, *I* can take care of it. *I'll* think of something."

Demetri didn't say anything. He didn't want to argue with her; he knew she felt bad enough.

Jenny spoke only to give him directions; soon they arrived at her little apartment. It was white with dark-blue trim accented with a little landscaping. Two stories tall and not much more than twenty feet wide. It looked kind of like a giant birdhouse.

"Thanks for bringing me home," Jenny said to the floorboard.

"No problem, really. This is on *my* way home actually." He gently grabbed her bottle. "Um . . . maybe you should go all the way in, so no one sees?"

"Right . . . here goes nothing."

She thought about going back into the bottle, and down she squeezed. Her upper body just grew smaller and slid right down all the way.

My whole life is literally in his hands.

She stood in the middle of her empty prison and noticed that she was actually standing.

"Cool! I have legs when I'm inside!" She perked up a little.

"What?" Demetri didn't quite hear what she said.

Jenny floated back up just past the spout; her tiny eyes filled with hope. "When I'm inside, I have legs!" She wafted back down and sat so she wouldn't fall over when he carried her.

Demetri suddenly felt a lot better. *Thank God*, he thought. He peeked down into the hole. The glass let some light in; she was sitting at the bottom. He slid out of the truck and walked up the path until he reached her door.

"Um . . . what's your pass code?" He felt very intrusive having to ask that question.

"Ten-thirteen." Her voice echoed up from the bottle.

"No way!" Demetri gasped.

She quickly got up, thinking something bad had happened. "What? What is it?" she called up. The curved glass made her voice come back at her. "Ow," she mumbled.

"It's just, that's my pass code too." He grinned down at her as the door clicked opened.

He sensed a new feeling coming from her. Was it surprise? Maybe a mixture of surprised and—

"HEY, YOU!" a strange weaselly voice called over to Demetri.

Jenny recognized that voice all too well. She whispered frantically up to Demetri, "Oh no! That's Mr. Mitts, my nosy neighbor!"

Demetri hid the bottle behind his back, with one hand still on the opened door. "Uh . . . hello!"

"What do you think you're doing? Are you trying to break into Jenny's house! I'm gonna call the cops, so don't move!"

The short, scrawny man was in his late thirties but looked five years older with his unkempt hair and bald spot. He was not overly threatening to Demetri; at all. His stubbly face and short brown mustache just added to his creepiness. His breath always overpoweringly smelled like sour pickles, and Jenny had to keep her blinds shut all the time because he kept a pair of binoculars on his window seal. He hated that Jenny called him Mr. Mitts, as he wanted her to call him by his first name. He looked like a real weasel with the rodent hunch and everything. He'd always reminded Jenny of a warlock who accidentally turned himself into vermin; and honestly, that didn't sound so crazy anymore given her current situation.

"No, wait, I'm a friend of hers. She gave me her pass code so I could drop this off." He gestured to the bottle.

Mitts squinted his eyes and turned his head to the left a little. "Who are you? I know *all* of Jenny's friends—"

"No, he doesn't!" Jenny called up quietly.

"—and I've *never* seen *you* before."

Only one thing came to mind.

"I'm her . . . boyfriend."

Jenny gasped quietly to herself, but it resounded all around her.

"Bahahaha! Likely story! Jenny never mentioned having one before. *I* would definitely know about any . . . *boyfriend*." He said the word with disgust.

Demetri stood a little taller. "Well . . . that's what I am." He tried to sound as convincing as he could; he wasn't used to lying.

Mitts waited a moment and considered the possibility; then looked at Demetri suspiciously. "If you're her *boyfriend*, then what's her favorite color?"

Great, Demetri thought. He sighed and tried to get out of answering. "Um . . . we just started dating."

"Hmm, *that's* what I *thought*." He opened his seriously out-of-date flip phone and began to dial 9-1-1.

Demetri's eyes tensed. "NO, WAIT! Her favorite color is . . ."

"Blue," Jenny whispered up at him.

Mitts peered up at Demetri with one large doubtful eye. "Let's *have* it."

"It's blue." He waited warily.

Mr. Mitts sneered a little. "What about her favorite thing to drink in the morning?"

Demetri accepted that he would have to be interrogated in order to help Jenny. He sighed.

"Hot cocoa," Jenny muttered.

Demetri answered, "Hot cocoa."

Mr. Mitts rolled his eyes. "Her favorite song?"

"I don't have just one favorite." She sighed too. She knew how persistent Mr. Mitts was.

"She doesn't have just one favorite."

"The color of her eyes?"

"Grayish-blue," Demetri answered immediately.

Jenny inhaled a sharp breath out of surprise.

Demetri felt her astonishment and smiled to himself.

Mitts growled a little. He wanted to know how much Demetri had paid attention to her.

"What kind of blonde is she?" he asked.

His eyes narrowed and proceeded to stare Demetri down. He wanted the *exact*, right answer.

"She's a . . . she has lots of different colors of blonde."

Mitts shook a little with bitterness. It was time to ask harder questions. "What does she smell like?" He knew Demetri would not be able to know that one unless she had let him get really close to her neck. Mitts only knew it because he'd recently ambushed Jenny with a hug while she was headed for one of her occasional jogs to the park.

Demetri stiffened. *Seriously? What a perv!* "She smells like vanilla."

Jenny's cheeks warmed. She turned her head to the right and sniffed her shoulder. There was a faint wisp of vanilla.

*I **do** smell like vanilla.*

She, herself, hadn't even been aware of that.

I can't believe Mr. Mitts knows that! How did he find out?

She stood in her bottle, slightly confused, and very creeped out.

I can't believe Demetri knows that either!

Demetri could've sworn that he heard Mr. Mitts hiss. He proceeded with the questions.

"What does she do when she's embarrassed?"

Demetri sensed Mitts's increased displeasure. He really didn't want to answer this one, but he guessed he had to if he wanted to keep the police out of this for Jenny. He tried not to mumble. "She blushes and grabs her right arm."

I do? Jenny thought. *I didn't realize that.*

Mitts sneered a little more.

Demetri mentally rolled his eyes. *Great, if that's the answer he's looking for, then this perv has probably seen Jen's cleavage.*

This news awakened Demetri's anger despite the sense of surprise and . . . something *else* that he was receiving from Jenny.

Mr. Mitts wanted to know how far Jenny had let Demetri go if he was her supposed "boyfriend."

"What kind of underwear does she wear?"

"All right, dude, seriously? Do you really know the answer to that?" His anger shook his body; he took four large steps toward Mitts.

Mr. Mitts hunched down; he could clearly see how irritated he'd made Demetri.

"Oops. Ah, no, I *don't* know that one."

He focused into Mitts's beady little eyes. "Good! It had better *stay* that way."

Demetri backed up to Jenny's door again, not realizing that he'd even moved towards Mitts at all.

Mr. Mitts perked back up a little. "Well . . . do *you*?"

Demetri's blood boiled. "NO! I am not a *creep* like *you*! I'm Jenny's boyfriend, and I'm dropping something off for her! If you call the cops, they aren't going to be happy to find out it's a false alarm because some jealous old pervert is prying into his neighbor's business!"

Demetri had taken a few stomps toward him again.

"Ah, don't worry. I won't call anyone. I'm sorry, Mr. uh . . ."

"Dayton," Demetri answered, still staring him down. *Am I sweating?*

"Mr. Dayton." *Gulp.* Mr. Mitts dropped his phone into his red-and-white-striped flannel PJs and backed away from his fence with his hands up by his shoulders. "Just tell Jenny I said hi?"

He seemed to shrink in fear.

What a wimp! "Yeah, sure, whatever."

"All right, I'll leave you to it." He quickly scurried back inside his own house.

He was really glad that Demetri didn't know the answer to his last question.

Demetri stood there for a moment, trying to cool off; soon, two little beady eyes revealed themselves from in between Mr. Mitts's blinds.

10

Interrogation No. 2

What a stalker!

Demetri let out a sigh of relief and went inside.

He had passed the interrogation.

"Nice place."

"Thanks!" Jenny called up.

He noticed there weren't any pictures on the walls, or *anything* for that matter. He looked around the kitchen. There were no decorations whatsoever.

She wisped out of her bottle, still invisible from the hips down.

Demetri set her bottle on the small kitchen island to their right and stood in front of her. "That guy is a total pervert!"

He tried to not sound provoked; he could tell she was feeling a lot better. He was actually thankful for the distraction that Mr. Mitts had been to Jenny. The upset feelings that had previously radiated from her had ceased since running into Mitts. Demetri hoped that he, himself, hadn't been the cause of her torment.

Jenny "sat" on the counter; she was almost his height now.

"Yeah, I know. It's hard to live with him next door sometimes." She smiled at him. "Thank you for putting up with him. I'm glad you didn't just give up and leave me there or anything."

"Hey," he gazed into her eyes, "I would *never* do anything like that to you."

Jenny blushed and held her right arm. "Oh." She gave him a coy look briefly and then looked down. "I guess I *do* hold my arm when I'm embarrassed."

Demetri laughed; it was a *lot* easier to look her in the eyes now that she had his jacket on. He leaned against the counter, closer to her. "Why are you embarrassed?"

She bit the side of her bottom lip gently as he adhered her gaze. He wouldn't let her look anywhere else.

Jenny didn't fight the hold and tried to keep her emotions under control. She sighed and answered him. "Let me count the reasons." She checked things off with her fingers as she spoke. "Maybe because you're a guy who I'm supposed to be making a *business* decision with. I *barely* know you and you've seen me in this outfit, which hardly covers"—his commanding eyes wouldn't let her look away, so she just let out a quick uncomfortable laugh instead—"um, *never mind*."

Demetri refrained from glancing at her chest and rubbed his neck instead.

She continued, "And to top it all off, I've been on top of . . . you." Jenny said the last part quietly.

He finally let her gaze go.

Jenny looked anywhere except his face. She couldn't bear to know how disgusted he'd been to see her dressed like a slut when it was supposed to be a professional outing. He was the most old-fashioned, courteous man she'd ever met; he surely thought it was unprofessional and awkward.

Demetri looked down at the same time she did. He thought to himself, *Yep. And that's going to be very, very, VERY hard to forget.*

He'd tried to get the images of her body out of his head, but they seemed to be engraved there. When he closed his eyes, the appealing images were what he saw.

This day has been something else, he decided secretly. *I'm not any better than that creep next door.*

Demetri felt embarrassed now, and ashamed.

He sighed and then noticed all her blinds were drawn. "You better *keep* your blinds drawn because Mitts is definitely into you."

Great, he didn't even acknowledge what I said. He's probably ready to just forget about the partnership. "Mitts doesn't like me like that," Jenny said confidently.

Demetri raised an eyebrow at her. "Uh, *yes*, he does, a lot, too much actually!" His voice got louder. He mentally calmed himself back down. "Did you *seriously* not know that? It's obvious!"

The rise in his voice didn't affect her. "He's always been like that, from the second I walked up the sidewalk for the first time. I've never known him to act any differently. He acts strange around *everyone*. He's just a . . . strange guy."

Demetri kept his serious expression. "OK . . . well, he's hooked."

And so am I, his heart announced.

Jenny considered what he said and thought for a moment. "Maybe Mitts is the one who leaves me flowers every month."

Demetri moved his head back a little. "Someone leaves you flowers every month?"

She nodded and looked down thoughtfully. "They are different every time, but they always have a carnation in the middle. I know I've never told him that carnations are my favorite, though, so maybe it's *not* him."

Demetri made a mental note of that and sighed. "I would just, stay away from him as much as possible. There's no telling what he'll try to do, especially now that he thinks he has competition."

Jenny nodded. "Why *did* you tell him that you were my boyfriend?"

She regretted asking it as soon as the words left her lips.

The question caught Demetri off guard. "Uh," he rubbed his neck again, "I just figured it would be a way to shut him up quickly. But boy, was I wrong. I think that's the worst thing I could've said to him. Now he might actually try to get your attention *more* often. Agh, I'm really sorry."

"Great. Thanks," she rolled her eyes at the idea, "that's all I need. As if I don't already have enough problems. If he were to find out that I am a . . ." She couldn't say it.

Demetri froze. "If he figured out you're a . . . genie . . . and got ahold of your bottle, it would be like Christmas every day for him! Who knows what he'd make you do!"

The thoughts that came to mind were appalling. His blood began heating up again.

"Demetri—" She tried. "This is my life now. I don't want to be a burden to you. You've already done enough for me. You have a life. It sounds like a wonderful one with lots of promise. Go live it, all right?

Please, just . . . *forget* about me. I can take care of myself. I've been doing it for over three years now. It's what's best for everyone."

Her heart felt seven pounds heavier after finishing that statement.

Demetri could've saved himself a lot of trouble, and pain, if he would've taken the easy way out and walked out the door. He didn't care though.

"NO! I'm probably the *only* one who won't take advantage of you. I'm going to make sure that you don't get hurt. I won't let you go through this alone, Jenny."

He grabbed her hands and didn't let go. He was really close now . . . too close. Every word out of his mouth was exactly what she wanted to hear, but it wasn't realistic.

"Look, be real. You can't have me in a bottle and resume a normal life. For starters, what would *Mel* think?"

Demetri let go of her hands and stepped back.

He hadn't realized how close he was standing, or that he'd grabbed her hands. It was just a natural reaction. He turned away briefly and rubbed his neck again.

She continued, "You can't keep me a secret from her, she'll find out. She's a woman, and we *always* find out."

"Because women have a sixth-sense?" He faced her again.

"Uh . . . that's not exactly what I was referring to." She glued her eyes to the white countertop for the time being and played with her thumbs.

Demetri examined her. "Oh . . . you mean she would think I'm cheating on her . . . with you, right?"

Her answer came out instantly against her will. "Yes." She peeked up at him quickly with balmy cheeks. "I mean, if situations were reversed, *I* would be furious that you were hiding a barely dressed woman inside a bottle that would come at your every beckon call."

The little devil on Demetri's head finally began playing its part. It wasn't about to let them go their separate ways. That situation suddenly sounded awesome to Demetri, though he tried to shake the thought away. That wasn't why he wanted to help Jenny.

"Look, she *won't* find out, and I can't just leave you here. Can you even move more than, like, fifteen feet from that bottle?" He'd gravitated towards her again.

Jenny glanced over at the stairs and moved forward. Her smokestack only stretched so far.

No! She closed her eyes, with her back to him. *OK, think . . . I've got to get him to leave.* "Ah!" She floated back to the bottle, picked it up, and tried moving around.

It worked!

"There! See? I can take care of myself. It'll just take some getting used to. Like carrying my phone around all the time. I'll be able to get used to the other things too, whatever they might end up being."

Demetri wasn't convinced; there still wasn't any way to be sure that she'd be safe, especially with that creep next door. If she fell into the wrong hands, literally anything could happen.

If anything happens to her, it'll be my fault for not protecting her. I'd never forgive myself. "Jen," he breathed out and looked down. Both of his hands rest on the counter. "You're coming with me," he said firmly. "That's final."

POOF!

Jenny suddenly appeared right in front of him.

She went wide-eyed. "Um . . . *what* just happened?"

Her heart raced, but that might've also had something to do with Demetri standing in her kitchen demanding that she come with him.

"I did *not* move over here on my own!"

Even though she'd startled him with her teleporting stunt, he hadn't moved away, not even a millimeter.

"Um . . . I don't know for sure."

She looked down again; her cheeks were hot. Her heart was beating too loud for her to think clearly. He was too close for comfort, but she didn't want to back away.

"Jen," he said with focused eyes. He knew she was nervous, and he wanted to test something out.

She slowly looked up at him, her cheeks sizzled. He was only a few inches away and gazing attentively into her eyes.

Oh, dear God.

Her stomach flipped; a thousand butterflies tried to escape.

Her hasty heartbeat throbbed in her head.

She held her breath.

"Get me a drink," he commanded.

The moment ended as quickly as it had begun.

"Huh?" Jenny asked, confused.

POOF!

There was a fresh glass of water in her hand.

"Wow. I don't believe this!" While he had expected that to happen, he was excited to see it in action. "OK, you are *definitely* not going anywhere without me. Do you know what someone with the wrong ideas could do with your power? They could probably turn everyone into mindless slaves!"

That's the idea, the little villainous devil thought.

She handed him the water and found herself disappointed that a drink was all he had wanted.

"Thanks." He set it back down beside her.

Jenny knew he was right; no one needed to get ahold of her powers, unless they were going to be responsible with them. Demetri had helped her and thus far proven himself to be at *least* trustworthy, and she didn't want to get anyone else involved. There was no choice but to trust him. She sighed and turned her head to the right a little and looked down yet again.

"How old are you?" She asked.

"What?" He wasn't expecting a question to be her response to all the important things he had just said.

She kept her head down. "I just . . . need to know more about you before I . . . move *in* with you, I guess." She met his eyes now, and her heart started its engine accordingly.

Demetri raised an eyebrow but understood. "Oh, right."

He didn't get any uncomfortable vibes from her, so at least that was good. He offered a gentle smile, glad that she was agreeing to go with him where he could ensure her safety, *and* the world's.

"Of course," he continued. "If a few questions are all it takes to get you to agree, then fire away."

POOF!

He sprung back, "whoa!"

A yellow fireball appeared in her hands, and she reared back to fire at him.

He shielded his face and bent down. "no! I take it back!"

Jenny halted and shook her hand to put out the flame. Her terrified expression matched his.

"oh my goodness! I'm so sorry! I didn't do it on purpose!" She wisped over to him and placed both hands on his shoulders out of concern.

He slowly stood; a wary look consumed his face. "All righty then! So I *obviously* have to be careful with what I say to you." He hesitated and then slowly walked back to the counter. "I wonder if *anyone* can order you around with what they say."

She followed him back. "Oh, that would be awful! I would literally be a slave." She "sat" on the counter again; her head fell.

I won't let you be anyone's slave, Demetri thought. "Are your hands OK?" he asked. He took them in his and examined them.

The feeling in her chest slithered back in, and she kept her head bowed. "Yes . . . not a scratch."

She gently retrieved her hands; they were warmer than they should have been, but no harm done.

Her stomach was doing gymnastics inside.

Demetri looked down too.

He was glad that her hands hadn't gotten burned. Jenny's overpowering emotions swept over him. He wasn't exactly sure what any of them were, though. He felt warmth on the right side of his head.

Demetri laughed and ran his fingers through his hair in that area. "I think you singed my hair a little."

Jenny gasped; both hands covered her mouth. "I am so, so sorry!" Her fingers touched his hair to feel the damage. She gave him a guilty half smile and tilted her head a little. "It's *barely* noticeable, really."

A side smile appeared on his face, "Don't worry about it. It will grow back."

Jenny returned the smile and noticed his dried blood from earlier. "Let me clean your wound."

She floated to the sink and grabbed a clean, dry rag and wet it with warm water.

"Oh. I completely forgot about it," he said as he touched that spot too. "Hold still."

Jenny hovered at his side as she gently cleaned the blood off and washed the dirt out. She made sure to avoid meeting his eyes at all costs. Her touch was gentle; Demetri smiled inside. When finished, she rinsed the rag out, washed her hands, and floated back to him. It had taken longer than she thought it would've; he had a thick head of hair.

"All clean."

He noticed her expression and smiled back. "I guess I've got to be careful with what I say, or we could *both* get hurt."

She nodded.

"Now . . . let's try this again. Um . . . ask away . . . if you please." He came a little closer again and noticed the strange feelings increase; he felt fluttering in his stomach. The feelings radiating from her would be hard to get used to.

"All right, how old are you?" she started again, bravely.

Easy enough, he thought. "I'm twenty-seven. How old are you?"

Jenny's stomach flipped; she couldn't believe he was *that* much older than her.

Awesome, she thought. "I'll be twenty-one in February."

Wow, she's seven years younger than me! "You're twenty years old?" He raised both eyebrows in surprise. *That's hot*, he thought to himself. *Ugh . . . is that wrong?*

He didn't have time to answer.

That's right, the little devil thought. *Now just admit to yourself that you want her.* **Tell her your feelings, and she will want you too!** It rubbed its little hands together wickedly.

"Yes." She looked back down again. "Is that too weird for you?"

"Weird? No . . . no, not at all." He looked down too. "Um . . . why would it be weird?" He tried to meet her evasive eyes.

"Because it's quite the age gap if we were to date," she blurted out with no choice. She gasped.

It hadn't seemed to affect Demetri.

"Forget I said that!" Jenny felt exceedingly shy all of a sudden and went on to the next question. "Um, where are you from?" Again, she kept her eyes away.

"Here." He kept his eyes on her face. He studied her expressions and compared them to what he felt from her.

Jenny sensed his eyes perusing her. Her cheeks burned.

She continued her questioning. "What is your favorite kind of food?"

"Um, anything really if it's Italian or Mexican."

"Mine too!"

Jenny moved her hand in excitement and knocked over the half-filled glass of water on the counter.

"Oops," she groaned.

Demetri laughed. "Wait, stay there. I'll get it."

Jenny stayed; she couldn't move.

He retrieved the dry hand towel draped over the oven handle and cleaned the water up. He wrung the towel out, draped it over the middle ledge in the sink, rinsed the cup out, flipped it upside down to drip-dry on her drying mat, and came back over to Jenny. With Jenny hovering directly in front of him and full sized, he noticed for the first time how his jacket fit her. Or maybe he gave into his human nature like the little devil wanted him to.

"Hey, my jacket looks really good on you." He looked her over.

Jenny stiffened.

"You should keep it," he finished with an overly satisfied grin.

Demetri knew that had made her feel . . . not uncomfortable, but maybe . . . He couldn't put his finger on it, but he was sure she had actually liked that he'd just checked her out.

"I . . . I can have it?" She looked down at the jacket and then back at him. "But what about your future son?"

"I want you to have it, Jen." He studied her face again. He wanted to be able to understand all her emotions.

Her eyes shone with excitement and appreciation.

"Wow, thanks! I really love it! It's so soft inside."

Ugh! Stop with all the mushy stuff! Just kiss her already so she will want you! The devil was growing more impatient by the second; he didn't think it would be this hard to try to get a twenty-seven-year-old man and a half-naked young woman to have sex.

Demetri smiled at her and tried to keep his eyes on hers, but he just had to look again.

Jenny didn't notice; she was still appreciating her new jacket.

Man, it fits her perfectly everywhere! It even shows some of her stomach. That's attractive! Not to mention what it does to her chest.

He didn't stop his thoughts this time.

"You really think it looks good on me? I might just start wearing it everywhere, then." She looked into his eyes a little longer this time and waited patiently for an answer.

"Yeah!" Demetri's eyes lit up. "You look ho . . . uh . . . a *whole* lot better in it than I ever did," he saved himself. His face turned slightly pink to match hers. "But you probably shouldn't wear it *everywhere*."

He didn't want any other guys seeing her in it.

She cocked her head to one side. "Why not?"

"Uh, just . . . because . . . um . . . something might *happen* to it. It's pretty old." *Nice save,* he commended himself. He rubbed his neck again.

"OK, if it'll make you feel better." She smiled at him, thankful. "I really, *really* love it actually! It smells like the woods. I grew up playing in the woods too, so it brings back good memories."

He could feel how much she loved it, and he felt better knowing she wouldn't wear it everywhere. "That's cool."

Now he was certain what love felt like coming from her. Well, at least, one type of it.

He smiled.

"Why *did* you do that again?" Jenny asked, changing the subject.

"Do what?" His heart started racing. *Oh no, did she notice me checking her out?*

"Rub your neck. I've never seen anyone do that."

"Oh. That." He was relieved. "Um . . . I'm not sure. I guess I don't realize when I do it. What was going on when I did it earlier?"

"Well, you've done it several times today, like when we were with Cali and Stefan. You said you would try to make things more"—she forced herself to keep eye contact—"*interesting.*"

"Oh, I guess I do it when I'm . . . uncomfortable, maybe?"

"Why are you uncomfortable right now, then?" She felt a little more confident and asked the question directly to his savanna eyes.

"Uh. I'm not sure . . ."

He didn't want to tell her why. He started to lift his right arm up to do it again but caught himself.

Jenny laughed, and that made him smile again.

She continued with the questions. "Um . . . what's *your* favorite color?"

Demetri fell deep into her eyes; he hadn't been able to see them this close yet. He completely gave up trying to fight his feelings. He had been fighting them from the first moment he saw her for Mel's sake. He felt a connection with Jenny for whatever reason, and he needed to see if it meant anything.

Oh! Good boy, Demetri, give up and make her want you! the devil thought.

It, and Demetri's personal devils, continued feeding and stoking the fire of passion that were his own thoughts.

He folded his arms on the counter and leaned closer to her. "Blue . . . and *gray.*"

Jenny tried to move back, but she couldn't budge.

He was inches away again.

Her heartbeat could have powered a locomotive. *Great, I guess I can't move until he says I can. That's cool . . . I think.*

Demetri confidently moved a little closer still.

Her eyes grew wide.

The butterflies flew around like their lives depended on it, still trapped. Her breathing increased, and she hoped he wouldn't notice.

But he did.

Demetri was fueled by her strong feelings, and the devil's. He was beginning to figure out what the feelings she was having earlier meant.

She wanted to ask another question to distract him; there was only one that had been on her mind all day. She blurted it out before he could move any closer.

"Have you done it with anyone?"

Jenny couldn't believe she *actually* asked it. She regretted it instantly. If he had, her perfect picture of him would be blemished. Jenny turned her head to the side and looked down. The probability of the gorgeous, courteous man standing in front of her still being a virgin at the age of twenty-seven was like one in a million—maybe even one in a billion. She braced herself for the impact of the answer that she was pretty sure that she really didn't want to know.

Demetri stopped moving forward but didn't lean back any. He was surprised by the question. But she *should* probably know how many girls he'd had in that way before she was going to be staying under the same roof. He saw how the answer to the question could potentially make her feel safer. He continued with his experiment and with analyzing her face.

"I've never had sex, Jen."

Jenny couldn't believe it.

Her heart smiled inside her chest, and she found herself relieved.

She tried to maintain a calm composure and continued with the questions. She dared to turn her head back to face his.

He was still so close.

"Do you like caramel?" she asked weakly. *What a dumb question*, she thought.

He grinned; his eyes were half-shut. "No." He looked at her lips.

Even though she didn't have knees at the moment, she felt them go weak.

"I prefer vanilla." He breathed in through his nose; vanilla overwhelmed his senses again. He leaned in the rest of what little space there was, tilted his head, and closed his eyes. His lips were millimeters away.

Yes. Do it! DO IT! The devil was dancing around on his head now.

"You can move if you want," he whispered.

His breath was hot and smooth against her coffee cream-colored skin.

He had wanted to find out if she felt the same way; he needed to find out if this was indeed what her feelings were calling for him to do.

His chocolate breath filled her mind.

Mmm! she thought.

He'd made it clear what *he* wanted, and he let Jenny decide if she wanted the same thing. He didn't want to force her into anything, especially since he *actually* could.

YES! *Just lean forward another inch! Do it!* The little devil's eyes were wide with nefarious excitement.

Jenny turned her head to the side and looked down. "We . . . *shouldn't . . .*"

It exposed her neck, and even more vanilla teased him.

No! the little devil thought. *You dumb girl! You know you want him. Just kiss!* AGH! It turned around. *If I don't get them to fall for each other completely, Satan will end me!*

It started formulating another plan.

Demetri stayed there for a moment longer and quietly inhaled a couple times. He knew she felt something for him—he could *feel* it.

Ugh. If only I wasn't dating Mel. Would she want to kiss me then? "I'm sorry, Jenny. Please forgive me."

His words lingered around her neck; It ticked. He turned the opposite way and tried to clear his head.

"I forgive you!" WHOA, *where did that come from? Wait, I know where. He* **told** *me to.* She sighed. "Don't even worry about it, and please . . . *don't* feel bad. Just forget it."

Her hand rested on his for a second. She cleared her throat. "Right." She lifted her hand away.

He sensed disappointment, but he wasn't one hundred percent sure why. Was it because they didn't get to kiss? Or because he'd tried to?

"Let's go get you some more comfortable . . . um, covering clothes, and anything else you need."

She furrowed her brows. "You're still going to take me home with you?"

He picked up her bottle, and she shrunk down just above the lid again.

"Yes Jenny. I'm not going to let anything happen to you. I'm *not* leaving you here alone with that creep next door."

Jenny gave him a soft smile.

"Where's your room?"

"First room you come to upstairs."

He took her upstairs and into her room.

Great, it's on the side of the house where that pervert can look in.

Demetri's temperature rose again; he tried to calm down. He was again thankful for the distraction that Mr. Mitts was. This time, it was for his own attraction to Jenny.

*At least he's good for **something**.*

It was very clean with white walls: no pictures in here either, or on the stairwell walls coming up. Her queen-sized bed had a gray comforter. She had one white chest of drawers with a mirror on top to the right of her bed. He stood in the middle of the room. The closet was to the right when you walked in.

"Do you need any help?"

"I don't think so. Thank you though." She hovered there for a moment and stared at her bed.

"What's wrong, Jenny?" He wanted to be as formal as possible.

"It's just . . ." Her eyes still fixed on her bed, almost in a trance. "I'm trying to wrap my head around it all. This morning, my biggest problem was trying to find the right piece of land to buy. Now, I'm a genie somehow, and the world could be destroyed if someone bad gets ahold of me. It's just too surreal. Not to mention, now I have to move in with a total stranger who happens to be a *guy*. Ordinarily, I would *never*, under *any* circumstances, move in with a guy before marriage. That isn't how I was raised." She studied her soft rug that she wouldn't be able to stand on anymore.

Demetri lifted her chin up with his right hand and stared gently into her gray eyes. They spooked him because they had changed colors since earlier. "Jenny, I don't want to make you do anything that you don't want to do. I just want you to be safe. Do you trust me?"

Her cheek pulled up a slight grin; someone else had told her the same thing once. Her mind melted at Demetri's touch; the only thing that kept her from sinking to the floor was the sincere hold he had on her eyes. She didn't know if she should or not, but she trusted him. She felt that she could trust him with her whole heart if she gave it to him.

"I trust you, Demetri."

"Good. I'm glad."

He loved how he'd just made her feel; it made him feel comforted and sure. He reluctantly let his hand drop.

"Take as much time as you need. I know this will be a hard adjustment."

She turned away and scoffed, *"Big* surprise there. Seems I've been doing nothing *but* for the past few years . . ."

Jenny vanished into her bottle before Demetri could ask what she meant. A few moments later, she came back out.

"There isn't any furniture in there." She looked her bed over. *I wonder if this will work.*

She imagined it being smaller and inside her bottle.

POOF!

Her bed vanished and reappeared inside.

"Whoa!"

Jenny's whole body was jolted.

"Sorry! I've gotcha. Did you just bring your bed inside there?"

She tilted her head and gave him a sassy look. "Yes, I did, and you are not helping yourself with the trust thing here by almost dropping me . . . again."

He locked eyes with her and gave her a reassuring smile. "Jen, I would *never* let you fall."

Again, he was satisfied by the feeling that radiated from her.

He peeked down through the silvery fog. "Well, how about that? That's awesome!"

She shied away a little. "Now let me actually put a . . . shirt on.

Jenny picked one out from her closet. It was gray with mid-length sleeves and a few small white buttons on the front. She began unbuttoning his jacket but stopped and cleared her throat.

"Oh, sorry!" Demetri closed his eyes and turned around. *Just a few more moments. Don't turn around,* he thought to himself.

No, you stupid boy, turn back around! the devil complained. *AGH! You're one of the hardest ones we've ever been able to get through to! Agh!* **Fine, boy, have it your way! From now on, it will be eleven times as painful for you to resist!**

The little devil couldn't physically harm Demetri, or anyone else for that matter; but a person's human nature is an easy thing to give in to, especially during a time like this.

Jenny thought about their almost-kiss. *Should I have let it happen? Ugh. What am I thinking? He's with Mel right now. It's not right to want him, no matter how much she's done to me.* "You can turn back around now."

Demetri turned back around and snuck a look at the shirt before she was able to slip the jacket on again. It hugged her skin and showed the top of her cleavage just a bit, even with the buttons buttoned. But the jacket hid all that again. She skimmed through her closet, deciding which clothes to take, or if she should take them all.

Control yourself, Demetri, he thought.

He tried to look at a different part of her body. Her stomach was covered by the shirt; he noticed she wasn't celebrity skinny, but she didn't quite have love handles either. Maybe she enjoyed a cheeseburger or a pizza every now and then. That was very attractive to him. He thought he was like most men and didn't want to see a near starving girl underneath. His eyes tried to look at something other than her body in general, but they couldn't.

*What's my problem today? This has **never** been an issue for me! Please, Father, give me strength.*

He was finally able to will himself to look around her room again. "I thought your room would be more . . . decorated, I guess, since you're a designer."

"Well, to be honest, I try to live simply."

"No TV down in the living room or up here in your room?" He furrowed his brow.

"Oh . . . no, I spend my free time reading the Bible or other stuff . . . *Crazy*, right?"

Demetri liked that too.

*Gosh, is there anything I **don't** like about her?* "No, that's awesome! So did your parents use to live here?"

"No. I've sold everything my parents had, including their house, but I did keep a couple reminders of them, like pictures and my truck.

Where's the pictures, then? he thought, but he still didn't get a chance to ask.

She continued, "That's . . . why I haven't painted it yet. It just reminds me of a time when they were still here." She looked at him with a smile to say, *It's hard.*

Demetri could feel the love she felt and the aching sadness that she was trying to move past. "Wow, I understand. Thanks for telling me." A genuine smile took over his face.

Now he understood what love for her parents felt like; it was different from what the love towards his jacket felt like.

She returned his smile and then looked away thoughtfully. "It feels better telling someone. Maybe it *is* time I paint it."

"Oh, what changed your mind?"

"Well, I don't know if I'll ever get to drive it again . . . but my dad would want me to take care of it. It really needs one." Her eyes were full of sincerity, "Thank you, Demetri."

He looked puzzled. "What did I do?"

"I'm not sure exactly. Just thank you." She gave him a small smile, with her head tilted slightly.

Jenny couldn't explain how natural it felt to tell Demetri things, but it made her happy. She poofed a few other things down to size; she would figure it all out later.

"OK, I'm ready to go now."

"All right, if you're sure, then I'm ready when you are. We have a lot to figure out." *A whole lot*, he thought. "Not to mention even trying to see what all you can do."

Jenny hadn't even thought about what she might be able to do. She'd only been caught up in the things she knew she couldn't do anymore. A smile appeared on her lips, she was thankful for Demetri's optimism once again.

He brought her back downstairs.

"Um, you should probably hide again."

Jenny nodded and hid inside.

He grabbed the cap from the counter and put in on the bottle so he wouldn't lose it.

11

Guardian Angel

Demetri heard something.

What's that noise? It's coming from . . . OH, YOU HAVE GOT TO BE KIDDING ME!

He opened the door to the outside to find red and blue lights. A police siren just stopped its wailing. Mr. Mitts was hiding behind a female officer.

"Mitts! This had better not be another one of your false alarms," a woman warned in a stern sassy voice. She had dark-chocolate skin and straightened black hair in a low ponytail.

Demetri smiled and thought to himself, *So, he makes a habit of this?*

He locked the door back.

"No! No, Officer Kelly, I promise there's—THERE! There he is!"

He pointed to Demetri walking toward his truck, then hid behind the officer again. He peeked out from around her.

"You took *too* long to be *'dropping'* something off."

He hid again.

Officer Kelly sighed, as though she had done this several times before. She began in a monotone voice full of boredom and annoyance. "Good afternoon, sir. I'm Officer Shannon Kelly. I'm sorry to bother you, but Mr. Mitts here seems to think that you're breaking in and stealing things."

Officer Kelly had noticed that Demetri had punched in a code to lock the door back and knew he wasn't the issue here.

"A-HA!" Mr. Mitts proclaimed. I knew it! You're not dropping anything off. You're still carrying that vase thingy!"

Officer Kelly rolled her eyes. "Mr. Mitts, if he knew her pass code and walked out of her house with the same thing he walked in with, how is there a crime here other than your *third* false alarm this *month*?" She turned around and challenged him with her crossed arms.

"Uh . . . I don't know. But he's *guilty*, though!"

She turned back to Demetri. "I apologize, sir. Mr. Mitts says your Jenny's *boyfriend*?" She mimicked his rackety rodent tone as she said the word.

Demetri suppressed a laugh. "Yes, Officer." He gave her a reassuring look. "I tried to explain that to Mr. Mitts over there earlier so that he wouldn't have to bother you. False alarms waste valuable police time. Do you need any of my information or anything?" he asked respectfully.

She let out a sigh. "No, sir. Mr. Dayton, I presume?"

"Yes, that's me."

"I got the name and number from your truck decals if I need anything, which I can pretty much assure you that I *shouldn't* have to bother you with any of this. You may go."

"Thank you, Officer." He nodded at her—"Have a nice day"—and got into the truck.

"Thanks, you too." She gave him a small nod. "As for you"—she turned back around to Mitts—"ONE more false alarm, and you are in *trouble*. There is *no* evidence here. You said yourself that he was carrying the *same* vase."

She turned to leave and mumbled angrily to herself, *Next time, it's Officer Rankin's turn to come out here and deal with this psycho. Now I have to go file away **another** report in the Mr. Mitts False Alarms folder! Ugh! I wonder if there's any more room!*

Mitts sneered after her. "Bah! You'll see someday, Officer!"

He shooed her away with both arms and scampered back inside.

Demetri noticed beady little eyes peek out from between Mitts's blinds again.

What a creep!

He pulled away out of Mr. Mitts's view.

"OK, Jenny"—he took the lid off—"you can come out now."

He continued down the main road to his house; It was about ten more minutes away.

She slid her way out and sat as best she could in the passenger seat again and buckled what was left of herself in.

"What was all that noise I heard?"

"Your creep of a neighbor ended up calling the cops because we took too long."

"Wow." She stared straight ahead. "You've *got* to be kidding me."

"Nope." He rolled his eyes and shook his head.

She sighed and then perked up a little. "So where's your house?"

"It's up here, just a bit farther."

They drove for a few more minutes and then pulled into a private drive. Beautiful tall trees lined both sides of the road; they were preparing to change into their fall colors. A large, modern-style house was soon revealed. It was mostly windows with a mix of black steel and medium-toned wood. Soft slate-colored pebbles made up the circular driveway.

"Wow! This place is beautiful!" Jenny stated in awe.

Demetri smiled. "I'm glad you like it because you're staying here for as long as I am.

Again, his words rushed out with no filter. He reprimanded himself silently.

Jenny turned to him. "How long are you planning on keeping me?"

That question didn't come out like she intended either. They were both getting used to it.

"I guess . . . as long as you need me." He rubbed his neck and hoped for longer.

Jenny nodded a little. "Thanks."

She smiled on the inside. She'd just have to try to keep hidden from Mel; she had no idea how she was going to do that, or even how Demetri planned on it either, but she trusted him.

12

Letting Go

Demetri pulled into his garage and slid out. The garage door automatically closed. He brought her inside.

The garage entrance led to a modest foyer, which spilled into a spacious living, dining, and kitchen. All modernized, clean, and simple. The living room had a two-story ceiling with an open staircase that separated the dining and living area. All the other walls were about ten feet tall. In the living room, there was a slate-gray leather sectional and two comfy-looking burnt-orange accent recliners across from it. A large glass-topped coffee table stood in the middle of it all. A floor-to-ceiling stone wall with a fireplace sat behind the two burnt-orange recliners. Across the room from where they were standing, was a huge windowed wall with an extraordinary view of a field and some woods in the distance.

Jenny loved the design. "This is a *lot* nicer than my place."

Demetri smiled.

The sunsets must be beautiful here, she thought.

He brought her to a large room off the living room. "This is my room."

Demetri's room was very spacious. His bed was the first thing you came to when you walked in. On either side of his bed was a dark metal nightstand. He had his own sunken mini living room to one side with a dark-blue curved sofa big enough for about five people. A massive television hung off a rock wall, so you could easily see from part of the couch and the bed. On the opposite side of the entry was another glass wall. The view was of a small modest patio outside and then the green wooded forest. To the left of the TV was an opening leading directly to the bathroom. An office desk sat patiently to the left of the bedroom door.

"It's yours too now," he offered.

Her heart lurched. "You want me to stay in *your* room?"

"Uh . . . only if you're ok with that." Demetri gently sat her down on his work desk. "I mean, you've got your own room inside there." He pointed to her bottle. "I figure there's no better place for me to protect you."

Jenny saw his point. It didn't seem so weird when he put it like that. "Yes, that's fine with me."

Her eyes admired his room again.

"OK, well, how about we eat lunch now?" he suggested. "It's three. Are you hungry?"

Jenny hadn't realized how much her tummy hurt until now. "Wow, yes, I am. Well, at least we know I still need to eat food."

Demetri laughed. "What would you like?"

"I would like . . . some clam chowder and biscuits." Jenny crossed her arms and gave him a teasing smile.

He laughed and crossed his arms too. "Clam chowder?"

"Yeah! I know . . . I know . . . you're going to tell me, 'Ew, gross. How can you eat that stuff?' Right?"

"Yes. That's *exactly* what I was going to say, believe it or not." Demetri laughed again. He sat down on his king-sized bed; a dark-blue comforter that matched Jenny's newest outfit covered it protectively.

"Well, I wish I had some for you."

She blushed brightly.

POOF!

A hot bowl of chowder and a plate full of biscuits appeared in both of his hands.

"Whoa!" he said, balancing the meal that appeared out of nowhere. Demetri smelled the chowder. "And apparently, I *do*. Yup. Definitely clam chowder." He gave it a disgusted look.

"Ha! Wow. Be careful what you wish for, Demetri." She said it as a joke, but her eyes were serious. "You have a lot of power now, you know. Use it for good, because it seems that I will have to give you anything no matter what."

Demetri considered what she said and thought about all the possibilities it would bring. He also thought her wording was suggestive, but maybe that was just his darker side being wishful.

He had let the little devil in, convincing himself that everything he and Jenny were doing was all ok.

It was a dangerous game.

"I really intend to not use it as much as possible," he decided. He set down her food on his desk and pulled out the chair for her. "Here."

She mumbled shyly, "Thank you," and then "sat" in the chair. "Mmm. Wow! This is *really* good! You're a good wisher."

He laughed. "Thanks. I'd really like something to eat too. My stomach aches."

POOF!

A plate of chimichangas appeared in his hands.

"Whoa!" he said. "Hot. Hot. Hot." He set it down next to Jenny's food. "But I don't understand. I didn't wish for it."

"You didn't have to say 'wish' earlier today either when that fireball appeared."

He furrowed his brows. "I really hope it's just me who you have to obey. It wouldn't be a very fun life doing what you're told all the time, especially if someone was making you do something you didn't want to." He pulled out the other chair and sat down beside her.

She managed a weak smile and hoped the same thing.

"Mmm, this *is* good," he said, taking a bite of a perfect-looking chimichanga.

"What do you have to drink?" Jenny asked.

"Um, I'd have to go look. It's been such a weird day. I can't remember." He started to get up. "What would you like?"

Jenny ran through several different drinks in her head. "Hmm, I'd really like some water actually."

POOF!

A fresh glass of water appeared in front of Jenny on the table.

"Well, I guess that answers my question." He sat back down next to her.

Gasp! "How did that happen?"

"I don't know, but if you're a genie, you can probably make anything you want happen too. You downsized your whole room essentially, remember?"

She nodded.

"Here, we're at my computer, let's just research about genies."

"Good idea."

Demetri typed in "genie powers" on the Internet. He clicked on an article that looked promising and began reading.

"All right, so genies are slave to a vessel, which would be your bottle. The person to possess the vessel controls them. So that's me, I guess." He stole a quick glance to see what her reaction would be.

Jenny leaned back, remembering the movies she had seen with genies. "I guess . . . you're my . . . *master* now." Her eyes darted away, embarrassed. *Jeez. That's so kinky*, she told herself.

*Did you hear that, boy? You're her **master**. Command her!* the little devil chanted Satan's bidding.

Demetri turned to her and placed his fingers on hers. "I promise I'll be a good . . . *master*." He tried a small smile.

Her heart burned inside her chest.

"Thank you. I know you will, Demetri," she whispered. She leered into his eyes.

She wants you! She's so close to you, boy. Look at her lips! That's right, you want to taste her lips. The devil grinned and rubbed his hands together. *Go on . . . TASTE!*

Demetri felt a new emotion overcome him.

His heart pounded in his head, or maybe that was the devil knocking.

He glanced down at her lips. *I can smell her orange-flavored lips from here. This would be really easy. All I would have to do is tell her to hold still, or to kiss me. I know she . . . wants it. I . . . I can **feel** it.*

Demetri's heart beat faster.

Just one taste! As soon as I see Mel, I'll break it off with her. I've got to taste! He leaned forward a little with his eyes locked on hers.

Good, good, the little devil thought. *Breaking it off with that girl will make Jenny want him more. Now we're **getting** somewhere!*

Jenny's heart raced against itself.

Oh, no, he's going to kiss me this time!

Demetri sighed and let his head fall. The extra flow of blood caused his head to ache from the rock incident. He grimaced and held his right hand against his temple for a moment.

"Are you all right?"

Jenny found herself disappointed that it had been *another* almost-kiss. She clenched her teeth, upset with herself for wanting a taken man.

Forgive me, Father, she prayed quickly.

"Yeah . . . just give me a second please."

He kept his eyes shut and tried to think of something that would slow his heartbeat down. Jenny's feelings didn't help with the pain any.

"It's been a second."

It came out automatically.

She half-grinned an apologetic smile at him.

He laughed. "Wow . . . I really have got to think about things before I say them, huh?"

She nodded and smiled shyly. "I'm just glad that it's only been small things so far."

He lifted his hand from his head and focused into her beautiful blue eyes. "Jenny . . . I'm going to break up with Mel."

Her mouth dropped. "No! You can't!"

Demetri leaned back abruptly.

That reaction was opposite of all the feelings that he'd been receiving from her.

"Why not?"

Her eyes turned to her chowder, her cheeks red. "Please tell me you aren't doing it because of me. I mean, because you're helping me right now."

"I'm *not* doing it because of that. But you've helped me realize that her and I don't fit. It wouldn't be fair to her or myself to keep it going when it isn't going to lead to anything."

She considered his words. "Do you *promise* it's not just you're afraid she'll find me? Because if it is, we can think of something else." She still didn't look at him.

"No, it's all right," he insisted. "I've been thinking about it, and I've realized that I don't have anything . . . *special* with her. She's just someone who comes around sometimes when I'm free which is almost never."

Jenny felt torn again. She wanted Demetri more than anything else, but she didn't want to do this to Mel, who already hated her.

She sighed. "Do you love her?" Her head stayed down.

"No." Demetri didn't have think about that one at all. "She and I have never been able to connect before on . . . *important* things. I don't think she understands me very well either."

A weight disappeared from Jenny's shoulders.

Demetri felt relief from Jenny. He knew now with certainly that it was of Mel that she felt torn.

"Jenny, the next time I see her, I'll—"

Ding dong!

He lifted his head. "Who could that be? No one visits without telling me first—well, except Lewis."

Jenny's heart pounded. "I have to hide!"

Demetri thought fast. "Wait, please make our dinner disappear first. I don't have time to put it away myself."

POOF!

It was gone. He exited out of his genie page and cleared his search history. "Just to cover all trails."

Jenny vanished into the bottle; he kept the lid off.

"DEMETRI, are you here?" a familiar voice called.

Jenny shuddered. *Ugh, that voice. It's still the same rattling, alto tone.*

"Um, COMING!" *Oh, good, it's Mel. We can just go ahead and get this all over with*, he thought.

He left Jenny on the desk and glanced back at the bottle briefly before leaving the room.

Jenny peered out into Demetri's room. It was fairly easy to see; everything just appeared blue through the stained glass. From the outside in, you couldn't see anything unless you peeked down the hole.

"Oh, you *are* here."

She'd let herself in. Mel had straight medium-length brown hair. Her white skin was always tanned from the salon, and light-brown surrounded her pupils. She was a couple inches taller than Jenny and was supermodel skinny. A black-and-gold party dress came well above her knees and painful expensive stilettos were her shoe of choice this evening.

"I was actually hoping to get here *before* you."

She hung up her four-hundred and fifty-dollar golden chiffon scarf by the front door. Her heels produced echo noises throughout Demetri's house. That noise had always bothered him a little.

"Oh, why's that?" Demetri walked toward her, a little uncertain on how to start.

She strut up to him confidently; a large brown paper bag in her arms. "I was going to surprise you."

"With what?" Demetri took the bag for her like a gentleman and brought it over to the kitchen counter.

"Well, if I *tell* you, it won't be a surprise." She tilted her head and raised a privileged eyebrow.

"Well, it can't be a surprise anymore because I know something is going to happen."

"But you don't know *what* it's going to be." She kissed his cheek, and then turned her attention to the bag.

Demetri stiffened at her cold touch; he hardly felt it. *OK, I need to get this over with before she tries anything more than a simple kiss on the cheek.* "Look, Mel . . . we've been . . . *seeing* each for nearly five months now, and it doesn't feel like we've come very far—"

"That's why I'm here. Are you going to partner with them?"

"Huh? Oh. Yes, I plan to." Demetri furrowed his brows.

"Great! Then you'll have more time, and we can actually spend it *together.*"

She noticed his singed hair form earlier.

"Did you get a haircut?"

"No." *Wow, she really does notice everything,* he thought. Demetri slid his right hand in his pocket so she wouldn't notice the ring too.

"Hmm . . ." She decided to drop it, only because she wanted to tell him her surprise. "I might as well tell you, like I said—that's why I'm here. I was going to set up a romantic evening here for the two of us by the time you got home!" She smiled suggestively and then pulled out a bottle of wine from her bag.

He grimaced. *Doesn't she know by now that I can't stand alcohol?* "You were?" he asked unexcitedly.

"But it can still happen even though it isn't a surprise anymore."

She began unpacking the bag.

He let out a sharp breath. "Wait, Mel. Sit down for a moment."

"Why?" She kept unpacking.

"All right, stay standing. Have you kissed another guy while we've been seeing each other?"

He had to know if she'd been faithful.

She didn't even hesitate. "Oh, yes, several times."

He hadn't expected that answer.

"Wait . . . *what?*"

Demetri had barely even noticed another girl apart from Jenny. If you didn't count his thoughts from today, he had been completely faithful in every way to Mel and all his past girlfriends too.

"Well . . ." She stopped unpacking. "I didn't know we were that committed. I mean, you never *asked* me to be your girlfriend or steady or whatever people call it nowadays. I just thought we went on dates every now and then." She turned and noticed his bothered expression. "Look, I was just . . . *lonely* sometimes. But I've put all that behind me. I think we should make more out of our relationship and see where it goes!" She flashed him a movie star smile.

Demetri didn't know what to think; she didn't even *apologize* for it. It made him feel a whole lot better about Jenny, though.

I guess I'm more old-fashioned than I thought. He began, "Um, OK. We obviously were *not* on the same page there. Which isn't surprising. I thought we were dating."

"Well, why didn't you ask me to date you *officially*?"

"I don't know. I just thought we were by the second time you wanted to see me. I didn't think I *had* to ask. *You* could've asked *me*, you know. That's a pretty common thing nowadays."

"Well, *I'm* not a feminist," she stated. "Those women have never had a *good* man in their life. The man should ask. A woman is special and should be treated like a queen."

Demetri stared at her. *At least we agree on something*, he thought.

There was another question he had. "Why did you quit working for Mr. Conroy?"

Mel furrowed her brows. "Huh? Why are you asking me all these things right now?" She stopped unpacking again; her eyes rested on a stick of French bread.

"Well, while we're being all open here, why did you quit?"

"I've told you why, Demetri." She noticed a flaw in the bread.

"Are you sure that was the *real* reason why?"

She sighed. "Fine. I guess if we're going to be more serious, I shouldn't . . . *lie*. Well, you know there was that girl who started working there soon after I did, named Jenny—" She rolled her eyes. "We had a history already, which made it worse. But clients always chose her designs over mine. So I quit. I *tried* to stay with it as long as I could, but no matter what I did, I was never as good as her. Why is this so important? Did someone at the office say something?"

"Yes, they did actually. Look, Mel, if this was going to turn into something, I think it would've by now."

She moved closer. "But you've always been really busy. We haven't really had the chance to see."

"We've spent several evenings together. I *am* going to partner with them, but with that partnership, it's actually going to take some time to get used to. It needs my *full* attention right now. I can't keep doing this—it's not fair to *you*. I can understand that you've been lonely."

She backed away. "Demetri . . ."

"Thank you for going to all this trouble"—he looked at the food she'd unpacked—"but I *still* don't have time to be a proper boyfriend to you."

"Are you saying you don't want to go on dates anymore?" She searched his eyes.

"Yes." He had no trouble saying it.

With or without Jenny, his and Mel's breakup was for the best.

She was silent for a moment. "I understand. I just thought this would *free* up your time." She let gravity slowly pull her head down.

"It's actually done the *opposite*. I'm sorry. I mean look, do you even know what my favorite color is? Or my favorite hobby?"

"Uh, of course, it's um . . ." She looked down again after a moment. "No. I guess I don't."

"Mel, we've never been able to connect or agree on *anything*. I'm honestly surprised we didn't see this sooner."

"Yeah . . . I guess we haven't, have we?" She softly crossed her arms in acceptance.

Typically, if a guy was the one to break it off with her, she'd be furious, but Demetri was a good guy and she saw his point.

He continued, "Especially when it comes to the Bible or talking about God. I mean, you and I can't even have *simple* conversations about religion."

She threw her eyes to the left and tensed her crossed arms. "I don't want to talk about God, Demetri."

"Exactly! He's the most important thing to me, and you don't even want to acknowledge Him." He could tell he was beginning to anger Mel, so he changed the subject. "You've never wanted to meet my parents either. I'm looking for the *one*, Mel. I think right now you're looking for someone to have fun with. This has been hurting both of us. I apologize for not being able to realize this sooner. I apologize for hurting you."

She sighed, not wanting to accept it.

Demetri moved forward. "Mel, do you even love me?"

She grimaced at the word and turned away. "No . . ." She loosened up a little. "I . . . think you're right. Heh, I'm pretty sure that's the *first* time that I've admitted that." She turned back to face him, "Yeah, I'm not ready to settle down. I'm only twenty-two. I wanna live a little more." She sighed. "I'm sorry . . . that this has hurt you too."

He offered her a small smile and a hug with his left arm.

Mel tensed. "You smell like vanilla."

Crap, Demetri thought.

"Have you been with a girl?" She studied him, trying to grasp on to a different emotion.

He searched his mind and then answered calmly. "It's a candle thing. It was a gift from Mr. Conroy."

That wasn't entirely false, although he was pretty sure Mr. Conroy would not view Jenny as a gift.

"Oh." She decided he was telling the truth. "It smells really good!"

I know it does, Demetri thought. He hid a smile.

"All right, then," she sighed, and came out of the goodbye hug. She gestured toward the food she brought. "You can keep this stuff."

He gave her a thankful smile. "If you're *sure*, but . . . I actually don't like alcohol, and it looks really expensive, so please share that with your next boyfriend."

"Oh, I didn't know that." She laughed.

I told you that last time I saw you and two times before that, he thought.

"Yeah, it *is* better that we break up. I can't live it up with someone who doesn't get drunk." She laughed. "We don't seem to know a lot about each other."

Demetri smiled a closed smile. *This is going better than I thought it would. Good.*

She sighed. "Well, I will get out of your hair and let you work, you ole Debbie Downer. Oh! I left my gold bracelet in your bedroom bathroom. Let me go get it real quick."

Demetri flinched. "I can get it for you."

She clopped towards his room. "That's all right. I'll get it."

He rolled his eyes and followed after her.

Once in his room, Mel noticed Jenny's bottle. "Oh. This is new. What is it?"

Demetri stood close, ready for anything.

"That's the gift from Mr. Conroy."

"It doesn't look like a candle." She raised a confused eyebrow at him.

"Well, I guess it's more of a Scentsy thing."

She leaned forward and smelled the top. "Yup. It definitely smells like vanilla in there."

From inside, Jenny covered her ears. *Ow! That was loud.*

Mel found her bracelet in the bathroom. She had always insisted on bringing over a make-up kit and several other things when she visited. Even if it was only for a couple hours. Demetri was constantly finding things of hers laying around. Her messiness had always bothered him slightly; he liked things to be orderly. She made sure to take a good look at the room while heading back to Demetri. Nothing besides the weird candle thing looked any different.

Demetri stood in front of Jenny's bottle. "All right, well . . . I *do* have to get busy."

Mel gave him a small smile. "Yes. I'm leaving now. Walk me to the front door?"

"Of course," he said politely.

Demetri thought about her echoing heels on the way to the door and how he wouldn't have to hear the annoying noise after this.

His ears were thankful.

He opened the front door for her, and she turned around at the top step and looked back at him.

"There's something different about you." She eyed him and tilted her head.

"I'm just same old me." He looked straight into her disappointed brown eyes. "I hope you find Mr. Right, Mel, but that's *not* me."

She gave him a peck on the cheek one last time and smiled. "Thanks, Demetri. You've always been a great guy. We've been stuck in a rut ever since the beginning, haven't we?"

"I believe so. Let's just give each other the chance with the life we each want and deserve."

She nodded. "I'll keep in touch!"

"Sounds good."

She began to walk away. The pebbles muffled the sharp noise of her shoes.

Demetri called out after her. "For what it's worth, I *did* have good times with you."

"And I, with you." She waved. "Bye-bye now."

"Bye."

He made sure she drove away and then he locked the door behind him.

"Is she gone?" a voice from behind Demetri suddenly asked.

He jumped and whirled around to see Jenny holding her own bottle.

"Sorry." She shrank a couple sizes with an "Oops" smile.

"You startled me, Jenny! What are you doing? She could've seen you!" He placed his hands on his hips.

"I was careful . . ." Jenny shrunk down a little more.

He sighed and crossed his arms. "You've got to be *extra* careful. I don't know what I'd do if anything happened to you!" He was almost upset. "*Please* be careful."

"I'll be careful, master," she said automatically. *Gasp!*

Her expression was as if she'd just seen a ghost.

The little devil went to work on Demetri's human nature again. *Master? Did you hear that, boy? She called you master! You know you love the sound of that! Take her now!*

"Um, I don't know where that came from." She was still wide-eyed.

"I do." He sighed. "I have *got* to be more careful with what I say. It looks like we will *both* have to work through this." He gave her a calm smile.

Jenny looked back toward the door. "She seems to have changed a little. That's good. I hope she'll be happy someday. If you really didn't love her, then you did the right thing."

"I'm glad you think so." He fixed his eyes onto hers.

Jenny turned her eyes away; leering into his was too painful.

"How do you feel?" She was almost afraid to ask.

"I feel . . . free!" He thrust his hands out both sides dramatically.

YES! *You* **are** *free! Go, take her now!* The little devil pointed at Jenny.

Jenny laughed and then looked down. "I wish *I* could feel free."

Her wish didn't come true; the cuffs were still as if they were a part of her wrists.

Demetri glanced down at his ring. "I guess that wish can't come true. I'm sorry, Jen."

She met his eyes. "You called me Jen again."

"Oh . . . right . . . I'm sorry. I know you said not to. It just . . . came out." He rubbed his neck.

She peeked up at him timidly. "It's all right. It's just . . . no one has called me Jen except you. I actually like it . . . a lot." She smiled. "I'm sorry I got upset earlier. It's hard to explain."

Demetri believed that it was hard for her to explain because earlier it had been hard to *feel.* The feelings had been a jumbled mess, just fighting with each other.

"Don't worry about it, Jen. You've been through a ton today. I can only imagine." He tried a half smile. "There must be a way for you to be free . . . if that's what you really want."

He enjoyed having Jenny here; if she got free, she wouldn't want to stay with him anymore.

"It is."

As Jenny said it, her heart tugged at her. She wanted to stay here with Demetri, but if she wasn't a genie anymore, she knew she didn't need to live with him. She'd have to go back and live next to Mr. Mitts.

Yuck! she thought.

"All right. Let's keep looking for answers, then."

He gently took her bottle.

She let him.

"I don't want it to break," he stated.

He wasn't sure what would happen to Jenny if it did, but he for sure didn't want to find out.

"If something happened to you, Mr. Conroy would *kill* me."

She laughed at his serious joke. "Yes, I believe he would."

13

Much Ado About Genies

"Here's something," Demetri said positively.

"What is it?" Jenny sat on the edge of Demetri's office chair in his room.

"Genies can only grant three wishes." He looked over at her.

She tilted her head. "That can't be true. I've already granted more than three."

"Oh, I guess you have."

He went to a different page.

"This says they can't grant just anything—no riches or something harmful."

"Wish for a treasure chest of gold, and we'll see."

He laughed. "OK. I wish for a treasure chest of gold."

POOF!

A wet, rotting chest appeared next to them. It had sandy seaweed on it and smelled like dead fish.

"WHOA!" Demetri couldn't believe his eyes; he didn't think it would work.

Jenny bent down, unfazed, and opened the lid; the lock had rusted through. Sure enough, there was gold of all kinds inside. Gold necklaces, rings, simple dishes, and ornaments. One ring in particular caught Jenny's eye. It had a pearl, diamond, and opal embedded in the band. A smaller band of gold encircled and weaved around the gems, guarding them like a coiled snake protecting itself.

She beheld it longingly. "Wow!"

Demetri felt another emotion wash over him, so he studied her. He smiled and understood this one.

"OK, this has to go back to wherever it came from. We can't be messing with how the world works."

"I agree."

Jenny suddenly received an impulse to go around to the back of the box to examine the now-open lid. She did exactly that.

"Hmm. This is a Spanish chest! This could be Incan gold!"

She glanced back at Demetri, who was closely examining the gold inside the chest.

"OK, back it goes," he said sternly.

She nodded and thought about the chest returning to whatever secret place it came from.

POOF!

"There we go."

"Good." Demetri smiled.

He stuck his right hand in his pocket casually.

"So . . . I think there are probably almost no limits to what you can do."

Jenny tried to process the new information; she looked down thoughtfully. "Oh, look, it got your floor wet. Do you want me to poof it dry?"

"No! *I'll* clean it up. I don't think we should use your powers unless we have to, and probably not even then. It might upset the balance of nature."

Her face was overcome with seriousness. "But, Demetri, we could probably cure world hunger."

"That would be great, but we can't cure the world of its problems. The world works this way for a reason. If we cure *one* thing, something *else* is going to go wrong, and whatever that is might end up being *worse*." He gave her an equally serious look.

She avoided his eyes and thought about it. "Yeah . . . you're right. No one is supposed to have this type of power." She drew in a long breath. "I just wanna get out of this mess before we accidentally *really* screw something up by saying the wrong thing. It's even scarier for me because I can *think* of something and it happens. Do you know how often I daydream? What if I daydream something bad and it happens? This is too much pressure!" She brought her bottle to his nightstand, "sat" on the bed, and hugged a pillow.

"Hey, don't worry about it. All we can do is try our best." He came and sat down by her.

She stared at the bedroom door threshold.

"Um, it's probably time for you to call Mr. Conroy."

"That's a good idea. It might make me feel better to hear his voice . . . Wait! What am I going to say to him? What about work tomorrow?"

It was Thursday.

"I can't go in like this." Jenny's sight became distorted from tears, "My old life is exactly that, old. I'm *trapped* for real now. I'm going to have to disappear . . . literally."

Demetri sat on his bed too, scooted back against his pillows, and pulled her to him. He turned her around to face him and wiped her tears with his thumbs. He held her face so he could look into her eyes for more than the split second that she typically allowed.

"Hey, if you want, *I'll* disappear too. We can just stay here forever in my bed."

She gave a small laugh through subsiding tears. "You don't mean that. You have people who depend on you and a business to run." She shook her head.

"I do too mean it, Jen. You come before those things."

He let go of her face, she looked back down at the bed immediately. "Why would you do that for me? You just met me."

Demetri lifted her chin up and lost himself in her sad, stormy eyes. "Jen, I feel more for you in just half a day than I've ever felt for everyone else combined," he admitted.

She had no choice but to actually look deep into his warm summery eyes. "You're not just saying that to make me feel better?"

Her heart knocked rapidly against her chest.

"No. I *promise*." Demetri gave her a quick kiss on the nose.

Her heart flipped.

"Hey!" She laughed. "You can't . . . just do that!"

Demetri laughed too. "Yes I can!" he said playfully.

She smiled shyly.

He gave her a somber, focused look, "Don't you know I can do whatever I want? You're mine now."

Her heart knocked louder. "As a genie? Yes. I know." She blushed.

"No, Jen." He locked onto her eyes, and she couldn't look away.

"You're mine if you . . . *want* to belong to someone." He broke the lock just long enough to glance at her orange-scented pink lips; their faces were inches apart.

This would be the third almost-kiss if he didn't do it. Jenny wanted him to kiss her; if he didn't, she would. Demetri felt a part of that same emotion from earlier. It was desire and . . . passion maybe? Whatever it was, it caused him to want her even more. It wasn't a feeling that he was able to overcome.

"Are you going to kiss me now?" Her feelings spoke for her.

"Do you want me to?" He grinned a libidinous grin.

"I . . . want you to, Demetri." She was lost in his hazy eyes again.

The little devil was on edge. *Yes! **Finally**! Go on, KISS! Feel her! Necessary steps to the corruption of her pure soul!*

Demetri didn't know anything about her past—how many boyfriends she'd had, how *they* had kissed her, but he wanted his to be the one that she would remember forever. He could already feel so many racy feelings from her that he wondered what kissing her would do to his *own* feelings.

He was determined now; he lunged forward to pin her down on the bed.

Take me, Jenny thought as butterflies fluttered in her stomach.

Her skin was alive with goose bumps and her chest sent ripples of passion throughout her torso.

She closed her eyes and waited for him to begin.

Demetri felt her surrender. He felt that he was finally free of restrictions. He studied her hair, her forehead, her cheekbones, her jawline, her neck, and then, finally, her lips.

Jenny felt his exploring eyes. Her breathing became heavier, and her skin heated up seven degrees. She waited patiently.

He bit his own lip for a moment as he leered at hers and then he leaned down the rest of the way, closed his eyes, and brushed his lips gently against hers, just enough for electricity to transfer between them.

Wow! he thought.

Her lips were a perfect fit to his.

Demetri kissed her more eagerly and lowered his body down onto hers. He supported his weight with his elbows and knees and held her head up in his right hand.

She gradually ran her hands up the undersides of his arms and then finally to his back so she could pull him closer.

He shoved his tongue in her mouth and pressed his lips firmly into hers.

Jenny's head spun. *Dear God . . .*

That was all she could think; her brain was overwhelmed by her heart's desire. The butterflies multiplied in her stomach.

"Mmm."

That's hot, he thought to himself.

He wanted to make her do it again. He moved his tongue around; it fought a battle with hers. Neither parted their lips for air, but they breathed excessively together through their noses. Their lips just wouldn't demagnetize to allow for breaths.

Finally! It feels like I've been waiting thousands of years for this, he thought. Demetri let all his weight down on her and secured his hands passionately around her waist and neck.

Her genie powers wouldn't even have been strong enough to whisk her away from his hold. He felt that he needed more . . . no, scratch that. He *did* need more!

He moved his right hand up to cradle the back of her head, and pulled her closer, making their kiss even more forceful. He slid his other hand to the center of her lower back and pressed her stomach closer too.

Jenny draped her cuffed arms around him and pulled him to her. She lost all train of thought and all track of time.

Neither had any idea a kiss could feel so right.

After who knows how long, Demetri slowly peeled his lips away and studied her.

"Don't stop," Jenny gasped, out of breath and completely drunk.

Her heart pounded excitedly in her chest and her eyes stayed closed from sexual ecstasy. The butterflies were trying to claw their way out now.

Demetri obeyed and leaned back in to kiss her. He held his top lip firmly on hers and ran his tongue along the bottom one.

Jenny kissed him back with her every being of existence. "Mmmmm!" she breathed.

He could sense her craving; it *tripled* his own.

The little devil grinned an evil grin. *Good! Now . . . time to turn up the heat.*

Demetri began unbuttoning his jacket on Jenny. He didn't stop kissing her to get it undone; he didn't have to. He knew his jacket well.

She slid it off her own arms impatiently.

He began to take his own shirt off but Jenny went ahead and nearly ripped it off for him.

Demetri gently bit her bottom lip. He pulled his face back slowly until her lip slid back to meet her other one.

Ordinarily, that might have hurt, but with all the endorphins and dopamine being released, that move of dominance made her want to submit completely.

Wow! she thought, *I love that!* She voluntarily started sliding her own shirt up.

Demetri sat her upright in his lap and leaned back against his headboard. He intimately touched her now exposed hips and slid his hands up her sides, moving to her waist, helping her bring her shirt up in the process.

When her shirt reached the bottom of her chest, he paused and shifted his intoxicated gaze down. Both of his hands found the material on either side of her breasts.

Their breathing intensified; sweat threatened.

Demetri fixed his eyes on her breasts while he slid her shirt up over her head.

Her chest moved, parallel with her heavy breathing.

He stared back into her eyes, and instead of sliding her shirt off her wrists, he trapped her hands behind her back with it.

She gave off another emotion.

Submission? he asked himself, *I guess I'll just have to find out.* Demetri pushed her back down to the bed with his bare chest and kissed her mouth again and again. *So warm!* he thought.

He maneuvered to the left side of her face and lingeringly prod his lips into the warm, soft skin of her jawline. He continued behind her vanilla-scented ear and breathed intensely. His lips ventured down her neck, still kissing her fervently.

Jenny loved everything he tried.

Demetri followed her collarbone for a moment and headed down, exploring further. Another feeling emerged. It was almost like . . . begging? He wanted to be sure. His lips stopped for a moment, so he could ask her if it would be OK to—

"Please do it!" she pleaded. Her hands were still trapped behind her back, which made her chest stick out profoundly.

He grinned the same "I hope you're ready" grin again. *Yup, begging.*

Demetri's lips magnetized to hers again while his hand drifted from her lower back up to her bra clip. His fingers skillfully unclipped it. His left hand freed her hands only so her bra could come all the way off. He demagnetized his lips just long enough to see what lay hidden to the world.

Jenny held her bra in place for a moment with her arms, opened her heavy eyes, and gazed flirtatiously into his hungry ones. She seductively traced her own skin with one hand from the left side of her collarbone to her right shoulder and curled her fingers around the straps. She sensually pulled the right strap down to the middle of her arm and did the same with her left.

Demetri waited patiently. This time *he* was the one a little too shy to look her in the eyes.

She stared at his anyways.

Finally, she crossed her arms to grab the bottom of her bra and lifted it and her arms up over her head to take it off completely.

That move caused her hot chest to press into his for an idle moment. *Oh man!* he thought.

She leaned forward and hung her arms, slightly bent, on either of his shoulders and watched as he practically drooled over her chest.

Neither of them could think straight anymore; they were living on the edge. Demetri was so hard it hurt.

He met her tipsy gaze, "If you had your bottom half right now, Jen, neither one us would be a virgin anymore."

Jenny bit her lip in acceptance and tilted her head back. "Keep going, Demetri."

Her chest allured his eyes' full attention again. *Ow! This hurts!*

He had no choice but to calm down.

Demetri sighed. *I'm still restricted,* he thought.

Jenny peaked her eyes open and brought her head back up to look at him. "Why are you stopping?" she whispered.

Jenny was dazed; she just wanted more.

He studied her dazed eyes and tried to guess what she was thinking. He heard a low, soft voice echo in his head.

Jenny pulled him close, pressing her chest into his again, and began leading the kisses.

He gave up trying to make sense of the feminine voice he heard and focused on her kiss.

Mmmmmm! Damn! he thought.

Demetri never said curse words, or even thought them, but that was the only word that came to mind. He held her in his arms again and slid one hand up her back until he reached her head. All day long he had been wanting to see what her long blond hair looked like undone. His fingers found their way around her hair clips to undo them. Her hair fell slowly; he lightly ran his fingers through it to unbraid it. After the braid was gone, he slid her ponytail holder out and watched her golden waves roll down her back.

"Your hair is *so* beautiful, Jen."

It was at least the length of her whole back.

Demetri grabbed a handful. His pain was finally unbearable.

He snapped out of it.

"Ow!"

Jenny didn't hear him; her brain had been taking a break for the past few minutes.

Demetri cringed in pain and sighed. "Jen."

Her eyes were closed in pleasure.

She opened them a tiny bit, "hmmm?"

He looked away shamefully, "I'm sorry. I shouldn't have . . . took your shirt off . . . or kissed you like that . . . or trapped your hands . . ."

The list went on, but he didn't bother mentioning it all.

I can't believe what I've just done to her, and what I would've done if she had a pelvis.

She opened her eyes and looked straight into his, "Demetri, it's ok." She closed her eyes again and started to lean back into him for another kiss.

He painfully turned away. "I . . . can't, Jenny," he sighed.

His eyes stole one more longing glance at her chest before he silently wished that they were both fully clothed again. He covered his face with his hands, breathed out hard, and turned his whole body away.

Jenny flashed him a confused expression, still out of her mind with desire.

Ow! This hurts so badly, he thought. He continued, knowing she needed an answer, "I can't because . . . it hurts me too much."

She blinked blankly a few times and shook her head a little, trying to wake her brain back up.

"Hurts you?"

He looked so tormented.

She drifted closer to him, "What hurts you?"

He couldn't find the words to say it, so he just leaned back and let her see.

"Oh."

Jenny was a little embarrassed but also felt accomplished at the same time.

"Sorry, I . . . I didn't even *think* about that," she held her right arm with her left.

Demetri felt something, and he opened his eyes and looked back up at her to be sure.

"Woah! Don't do that!" *Yup, definitely embarrassment.*

"Do what?"

"Every time you get embarrassed, you don't realize that you're pushing your . . . *breasts* together."

Her gray shirt was attractive enough as it was.

"Oh! Sorry," she gave him a guilty look, "wait, what do you mean . . . *every* time? Have you . . . been looking at my boobs all day?" She was surprised but not in the least bit upset.

Demetri sighed and stared into her foggy blue eyes, "Well, of *course*, I have. If you're going to push them together like that, then I apparently have no *choice* but to look."

"Apparently?" She tilted her head, "What do you mean?"

"I don't know, Jen," he met her eyes again and sighed, "I've never had *any* trouble keeping my eyes to myself until I laid them on you."

Her cheeks burned, "Just with me, huh?"

He felt that she really, *really* liked that; it made him smile.

"*Just* with you," he reassured her.

She crossed her arms, which didn't help the situation either.

"Oh . . . well, when? I didn't notice . . ."

He let his eyes fall, and answered to her chest with a satisfied smirk. "Like in the elevator, when I helped you in and out of the truck, when you fell on top of me, tried to help me up, bent down to touch my hurt head, basically the whole time you didn't have a shirt on when you turned into a genie, when you put my jacket on . . ."

Jenny's eyes grew wider each time he mentioned something, and she finally understood why he had acted so awkwardly back there.

Demetri continued, ". . . when you were on your countertop and I saw how my jacket fit, when you were downsizing your room—"

She cut him off, realizing that it had been all day long. "How *could* you, Demetri?" she threw him a pretend mad look.

He studied her playful eyes and raised an eyebrow. "Hey, you can't be mad at me."

She turned away slightly. "Why not? I can be mad at *whoever* I want."

He smiled even bigger and leaned close to her ear, "because I can *feel* that you like that I've been checking you out all day."

Jenny's eyes widened; she blushed brighter and started to lift her arm again.

"Oops," she dropped her arm, "fine! You caught me." She wouldn't meet his eyes again, but a smile traced her lips.

Her cheeks are cute when they're red, he thought. "Hey, there *is* actually something that I want . . . um, *need* to know."

"Yes?" she managed to peek up at him.

"Tell me, how was . . . *that* for you?" Demetri held her gaze. He already was pretty sure he knew the answer based on what *he* felt from her, but he wanted to be sure.

Jenny turned back toward him completely with no choice but to tell him the truth.

"I could barely breathe," she began, "I couldn't think about anything except how much I wanted . . . *needed* you. I felt so drunk with love that I didn't care *what* you were going to do to me next. It was so indescribable!"

Jenny's face turned grave, "I love you, Demetri."

Her heart stopped. Her eyes widened again with what she had to admit to him.

Demetri turned serious, "You love me?"

"Yes. I mean, n-n—"

She tried to say no but couldn't; she couldn't even shake her head.

Jenny *did* love him; she just hadn't wanted him to know yet.

He held her waist and dove into her eyes, "Jenny, if you *really* love me, then please just tell me."

She focused straight into his eyes again, "I love you, Demetri."

Her face turned beet red.

Demetri pulled her to him and kissed her again.

This time he was able to control his feelings, thoughts, and actions.

He pulled away and reviewed her now weighted eyes, "I love you too, Jenny. I loved you from the first moment I saw you."

She couldn't believe it, "You loved me at first sight?"

Jenny was exultant. She didn't want to tell him that she loved him at first sight too, not yet. She still wanted *something* to be a secret from him.

"Demetri, I have to tell you the truth. I can't hold anything back from you . . ."

He tilted his head slightly, "What do you mean?"

"Earlier in the truck, I couldn't lie to you. I felt horrendous, *not* fine. And just now I *had* to confess that I love you. I had no choice."

He furrowed his brow, "Hmmm. I will try to keep that in mind. I don't want to force you to tell me things that you don't want to or aren't ready for. But I *am* glad that you admitted that you love me. Most people take forever to say it."

"Thanks, Demetri."

Jenny smiled and thought to herself, *He's so considerate. That's hard to find nowadays.* She suddenly felt guilty about the pain that he was going through. Jenny's eyes fell, "I'm sorry for causing you so much pain. I shouldn't have egged it on like that."

He gave her a strong look, "That's OK. I feel a *lot* better now."

He felt something else. Concealment?

"Hey"—he looked into her eyes—"I know you're keeping something from me, but whatever it is, you just tell me when you're ready, OK?"

He kissed her cheek.

"OK, I will. Thank you."

Jenny's mind was replaying events from high school. The last time she had felt anything similar to what she just felt happened almost three years ago. She was *not* ready to tell him about it yet. She wanted to be honest but didn't want to ruin the perfect moment.

"Can you really feel *all* my feelings?"

He gave her a thoughtful look. "Something like that. It's hard to explain, but if *you* feel sad, *I* can tell, and stronger emotions overpower me or something, and it makes *me* feel that way too." He gave a small laugh. "You made a tear roll down my face in the truck earlier."

"Really?" Her blue eyes were speckled with wonder. "Wow . . . I wonder why and how that happens."

He looked down at his right hand. "It's probably this ring."

She looked at it too, and he continued.

"I was able to feel your feelings after it appeared. It . . . *connected* us somehow on an emotional level. It lets me know how you feel."

She noticed her name again.

Her heart flipped.

"See? I can tell that you like that your name is on there." He grinned at her.

She blushed and thought for a moment. "I guess you'll be able to read me like a book."

Jenny didn't know how to feel about that.

He touched her hand. "Well, if it makes you feel any better, I haven't learned *all* of your emotions yet. Girls feel emotions differently from guys because I have *never* felt such *complex* feelings in my entire life, so I'm sure it will take a while to learn them all." He searched her.

He knew she felt a little uneasy.

"Hey, we will try to have you out of that bottle before that time comes."

He hoped that thought might cheer her up a little.

"Hopefully."

Her eyes fell.

I hope he can't read my mind too, she thought.

Demetri studied her and thought to himself, *OK, wrong move. I want her to cheer up. This is going to hurt again.* Without warning, he tackled her back to the bed.

She laughed. "What are you doing?"

"Jenny, we're adults. If we wanna kiss, then we can kiss, can't we?" A suave look overtook his face.

"Yeah . . . but won't you hurt again? I mean, right now, I can't even let you . . . uh . . . never mind!" Her cheeks burned scarlet again.

Demetri leaned away a little. "You would let me . . . but we *just* met?" He tilted his head.

She sighed. "I don't *want* to do that until I'm married, but if I was going to let anyone out of wedlock . . . it would be you."

He stared straight at her, even though she wouldn't meet his eyes. "Jenny, as much as that would be so . . . indescribably and utterly *amazing*, I *also* want to wait. I mean, I've waited this long. I'm probably the oldest virgin alive."

They both laughed.

"Yeah, I couldn't believe it when you told me, but I'm really glad!" She met his eyes again.

"You should call Mr. Conroy now. It's almost five," Demetri suggested.

She took a breath in. "We kissed for nearly an hour?"

He grinned.

"You have some serious self-control, Demetri."

He nodded. "Thanks. I try."

"OK." Jenny sighed.

She knew she needed to call Kurtis, or he might do something drastic in his current state.

Demetri pulled her up with him and kissed her hand like a gentleman. "Good luck."

Jenny turned away shyly. "Thanks . . .," she whispered.

She squeezed down into her bottle to get her phone and then floated back out. She sneaked a quick look at him before she dialed number one, the speed dial shortcut for Kurtis.

Demetri watched her attentively. Despite what he knew Jenny would want, he wanted to know *all* of Jenny's feelings.

Mr. Conroy answered immediately, "Jenny! Good. Glad you called. I was beginning to worry about you! Are you OK? Did anything happen to you?"

Oh great, well . . . I guess I'll get to see if I can lie to anyone else. "Kurtis, I'm just fine. Nothing happened." *Yes! At least I'm not a slave to everyone.*

She heard Mr. Conroy let out a breath of relief.

"OK, good! He . . . he hasn't done anything *stupid*, has he?"

"No! In fact, he's amaz . . . He's very courteous. I think you will look forward to working with him if you still want to."

"Hmmm. So you think we should partner with him?"

"Yes." She smiled and shook her head.

Jenny couldn't believe how protective he was of her.

"Are you still with him?"

"Uh, yes."

She hoped that answer was OK.

"OK, well, if you're *sure* he'll be good, then . . . I trust your judgment. Thank you for today. Tell him to pick a spot for dinner tomorrow, and we can go over the details. As long as *you* trust him, I guess . . . I can trust him too."

Demetri whispered over, "Tell him I'll make dinner here at my place tomorrow night."

Jenny obeyed. "Demetri said that he would like to make you dinner at his house tomorrow."

"Oh, I suppose that's OK. I'll be able to see how he lives. Tell him I'll be there at six. Text me his address."

"OK, will do." She smiled.

"Can he *hear* me?" Mr. Kurtis asked.

"I think so." Jenny looked at Demetri.

"Move out of his earshot, please."

She rolled her eyes and moved over to the door. "OK."

Demetri grinned. *Seriously?*

"I don't like the way he was looking at you today. Did he *try* anything?"

Jenny's face warmed. *Not without me wanting him to,* she thought. "No. He's a gentleman," she insisted.

"Hmmm, *I'll* be the judge of that, but . . . as long as you're safe." He paused and then continued. "Well . . . I'll see him tomorrow then. You should be there too so you can see how business meetings work."

Jenny shot a worried glance at her nonexistent lower half. "I can't. I . . . have something really important to do tomorrow."

Her heart sank at the thought of not be able to spend time with Kurtis again.

"Oh, like what? Oh, *never mind,* as long as you aren't with *him,* I don't care *what* you're doing. Actually, yes, I *do* care. What are you going to be doing?"

Jenny held in a laugh, not sure how to answer. She didn't want to lie to him any more than she had to. "Actually, um . . . can I have the day off? It will take up all day."

"Um, of course. I don't think you've had a day off in over a year. Are you *sure* he didn't do anything?"

"Yes. I promise, Kurtis!"

"All right . . . it's getting late. When is he going to bring you back to the office? Your truck is still here."

Crap! Jenny thought fast. "Um, he did already. My truck wouldn't start, so he just brought me home. He's getting ready to leave."

"Oh, it won't? I could have given you a ride home."

"I didn't want to bother you, and besides, Demetri offered to."

I'm sure he did, Mr. Conroy thought, *a **real** man could fix your truck.* "Is that why you need the day off tomorrow because you don't have a ride to work?"

"No, something just came up."

"OK, I guess I will see you later then. Soon?"

"Yes, of course, Kurtis. Have a good evening. Thank you for being concerned about me and for tomorrow off!"

"Anything for you, Jenny." He smiled sadly to himself and hung up.

Demetri stood. "Well, I think I'm going to have to earn his trust." He walked right up behind her and smiled over her shoulder.

A strange weakening sensation rippled throughout her body.

"Yes, I think so too." She turned to face him and weakly smiled back. "I think it's going to take more than a trip over a genie bottle to earn his trust though." She let out a little laugh.

Jenny was still recovering from the wave of weakness.

"Are you OK, Jen?" Demetri grimaced. He wasn't used to whatever she was feeling right now.

"Yeah . . . I'm *great* actually." She peeked up at him quickly.

"OK . . . Well, anyways, what's his favorite thing to eat?"

"Definitely rice and kielbasa."

"Hmmm, OK. I can make that. No problem. Maybe my cooking will make him come around." He smiled confidently down at her.

She raised an eyebrow. "Are you any good at it?"

He reared his head back slightly in shock. "Am I *good* at it? I was only top of my class in culinary school." He smiled at her proudly. "I can make whatever you want." He grabbed her waist in one arm and leaned her back.

She laughed.

"Wow, you're light as air," he snickered.

"I *am* air." She smiled fraily.

He brought her back upright.

"Hey, why *did* you invite him to your place? It's not just to win him over with your *cooking*, is it?"

"I just thought you'd like to see him. You've been through a lot today, and sometimes seeing familiar faces helps, even if it's from afar. But cooking for him *will* be a lot of fun. You can help me." He smiled.

"Hmmm, fine." She squinted at him and folded her arms. "But you should know that I've successfully made cheesecake in under thirty minutes *without* using dry ice."

"You *have*? Interesting. Are you *challenging* me in the kitchen?" He crossed his arms too and squinted back.

"You bet!" She leaned forward with her hands on her waist.

"What's up on the table?" he asked.

She raised an eyebrow. "Huh?"

Demetri said it another way, "What do *I* get if I win?"

"Hmmm." She abruptly pressed herself up against him. Demetri wasn't ready for her unexpected forcefulness. Jenny pinned him against the doorframe. She looked directly into his eyes and whispered, "What do you want?"

Demetri was the one who was trapped this time.

Woah, he thought, *you can't give me what I really, **really** want right now.* He thought of her nonexistent pelvis and cleared his throat. "How about if *I* win"—he advanced forward, pushing her backward with his whole body—"you have to come and take pictures with me out in the woods?"

He immobilized her against the opposite doorframe and stared down into the churning, blue storm pools of her eyes. He noticed that for the last little while, they had stayed blue.

Jenny thought, *It's a good thing I don't have knees because they would've given out just now.*

Demetri fought off the weakness he felt again, understood why it had happened to her earlier. He grinned alluringly, which made the feeling from her increase. He fought it off so that his knees wouldn't give out from her weakness.

"Deal," she managed to say. "But that sounds like fun. You can even teach me how to take good pictures."

He raised an eyebrow. "You'd be interested in doing that . . . voluntarily? Mel always hated getting her shoes dirty and complained the whole time." He laughed.

Jenny felt so dreamy inside that she hardly noticed his mention of Mel. She smiled at him. "Demetri, it sounds wonderful."

He wrapped his arms around her. "Just don't make too much noise when I'm trying to get pictures of eagles, OK?"

His joke eased the weakness. "Hey, you act like you're going to win!" She gave him a little shove.

"I am *definitely* going to win." His eyes smiled at her.

She flashed him a sassy look. "What do I get if *I* win?"

He rested his forehead on hers. "What do *you* want?"

She sighed. "To be honest . . . I *really* just want to be a normal-looking person." She looked back down at herself somberly.

Nothing happened.

"I guess that wish can't come true, Jen. I'm sorry." He looked away, disappointed for her.

Jenny figured as much. She sighed, and a thought came to her. There *was* one thing she wanted to know and knowing the answer would take her mind off her situation.

Her cheeks began to heat up. "Hey, you asked me earlier if . . . well, *you* know." She kept her head down and continued. "But you *are* a lot older than me—"

"I'm not *that* much older," he interjected.

"I know. Our age difference doesn't bother me. I actually . . . *like* that you're seven years older." She smiled up at him.

He lifted her chin and gave her a transfixed look. "Me too."

Her arms were riddled with goosebumps, and after her heart calmed back down a little, she finally asked her question.

"Have you ever . . . felt . . . another woman's—"

"No, Jen. Just yours against my chest."

"You *haven't*?"

Demetri sounded more perfect all the time.

He pulled her closer. "I'm glad I've waited as long as I have because it was amazing!"

She had to look away now. "Why did you feel mine?"

"Uh . . . you started it." He smiled down at her. "*You* started taking your shirt off."

"But *you* were going to ask," she countered.

He sighed. "You got me. I don't know, Jen. I apologize. I just can't control myself when I'm with you."

Just doing my job. The little devil rested on Demetri's head and glanced eagerly between them, just letting things play out.

"Don't apologize, Demetri. I *wanted* it to happen, and you still haven't seen my lower half, so . . . my future husband will just have to be OK with that." She glanced up at him briefly.

The thought of Jenny being married to anyone else punched Demetri in the gut without warning.

It was painful and caused him to feel protective. He loved Jenny, and she had told him that she loved him, but she was still young, and she had been through a lot today. She might have just *thought* she loved him, especially if she was saying the term "future husband" without picturing *him* as such.

He tried to stay calm and even toned, "Well . . . for your future husband's sake, we better make sure you have a lower half."

Those were the only words his brain could think to form.

Luckily, she couldn't feel *his* letdown.

"Yes, I would like to have my legs back if possible. It might be a while before we can figure that one out . . . if we *ever* do."

Jenny closed her eyes and leaned her forehead on his chest. She was going to miss her legs a lot. She thought she looked funny as half of a woman floating around on a pillar of smoke.

Go on, Demetri, give her legs back to her. The little devil lay on his side with a foul smile as if he was in charge of all the events.

"Jenny . . ." He kissed her head while staring at the doorframe in front of him. He moved his lips gently back and forth against her forehead.

She closed her eyes.

Yes, go ahead and do it, boy! It smiled maniacally and shifted onto its elbows.

"I wish you had legs!" Demetri said, still staring at the doorframe.

14

His Song

*P*OOF!

Silver and blue smoke twisted together and surrounded Jenny.

Demetri backed up and watched intently, on guard.

The sparkling, hypnotic smoke picked her off the ground and completely consumed her for a moment.

Demetri's heart thumped loudly. *OK, this is different. I hope my wish isn't hurting her!*

The smoke slowly dissipated, and the sparkles disappeared.

Jenny wasn't ready to stand; her knees failed.

"Woah!"

Demetri kept his promise from earlier and caught her. He held her upright against him until she was able to maintain her footing.

Jenny was now wearing the full genie outfit that she had on from when she was inside her bottle, and her hair was back up in the shimmering silver veil again. She had the same dark blue top, but now her hips were dressed in a matching dark blue band with silver glitter. Around her hips were loose matching pants that cuffed her ankles. She wore small silver shorts underneath the sheer pants. Her fashionable flat shoes were shiny silver with dark blue sapphires near the toes.

"My . . . my legs!" She gawked at herself. "I could have been whole this *entire* time?" She couldn't believe it.

She had the biggest smile that Demetri had ever seen on anyone.

"Thank you, Demetri!" She flung her arms around his neck and secured him against the doorframe again.

He was glad she had her legs back. Now she could give her future husband *everything* again. Demetri felt depressed inside despite her happiness, but he wanted to let her have her moment.

The little devil's eyes grew wide with hungry anticipation. *FINALLY!*

It stood and gave it everything it had. He went *into* Demetri's head and worked with Demetri's personal devils. The devil's thoughts fully became Demetri's.

*Now I can take her to bed and relieve this pain. I know she wants me. Ten feet is what comes between having pain and having **none**.*

A glazed look overtook his eyes. He imagined it, even though he wasn't sure where it came from. Out of nowhere, every bit of the pain he had felt today came back all at once. He wasn't ready for it.

"owww!" he breathed through clenched teeth. He slowly buckled over in pain. It felt like someone just sucker punched him in the groin.

"Demetri!" Jenny bent down and caught his head before it hit the ground. "What's wrong?" She stared at his agonized, scrunched-up face with concern.

He couldn't say anything; the pain was too immense. He couldn't even say "ow" again.

Jenny laid her forehead on his and closed her eyes. "Make this pain go away." She glanced down at him to see if it worked.

The pained look on his face slowly faded.

He sighed a breath of relief and took a couple of deep breaths in. "Thank you!"

He took in a few more deep breaths and then focused back up to see an upside down smiling Jenny. His head was in her lap.

"Don't scare me like that," she scolded him.

Demetri's eyes shot open. "Believe me, I was *not* trying to scare you! You'll know with zero doubt if I'm ever trying to scare you."

"What happened?" She tilted her head and caressed his face.

He was nearly sweating. "I have no idea, but I hope it never happens again!"

The little devil came out of Demetri's head to see what was going on.

*NOOOOO! All day long was for **nothing**? You stupid, **stupid** boy! Satan* *will **torture** me for this! AGH! **I give up** on you! **This** is torture! I can't take it anymore!*

It left Demetri's personal devils behind and went to accept its fate in Hell.

Out of nowhere, Demetri began feeling more like his normal self.

Jenny offered him a gentle look. "You should go take a shower. My mom always told me to do that when I didn't feel good."

He slowly got to his feet and then helped Jenny up too. "That's a good idea."

There wasn't a door between his room and the bathroom, but the walls blocked all sight lines to the shower.

He started to walk over toward it and nearly fell over again.

"Too fast!" He grabbed the edge of his desk for support.

Jenny rushed to him and gently kissed his cheek. She thought that might help.

He instantly felt a little stronger.

"Thanks." He smiled at her. "I'll be right back."

He began walking toward the shower again but turned back, pulled her close, and kissed her intently one more time. If she didn't feel the same way about him as he did her, then he would just have to help her fall in love with him. Girls love kisses.

"You're *just* going to the shower, Demetri." Jenny laughed when he finally detached his lips. "You won't be gone *that* long."

"I like to take *really* long showers." He grinned down at her with half-shut eyes. "But I'll be as quick as I can for you."

Her eyes followed after him as he walked into the bathroom. *He has an attractive walk. It's very manly.*

Jenny sighed to herself happily. "What should I do now?"

She perked up and squeezed back into her bottle while Demetri showered.

Her eyes took in her new room.

Since I live in this bottle now, I'd better make my furniture stays in one place in case it tips. I wonder if this bottle can break? I'd hate to be in here if it ever did. Jenny stared at her bed and dresser and thought hard, *Don't move unless I say.*

She tried pushing her bed to another spot. It wouldn't budge.

Good.

She looked around her blank circular walls.

Actually, I think it would look better over there.

POOF!

There we go. That's better. Now . . . I'd like a place to sit other than my bed.

The curved couch in Demetri's room came to mind.

That would be perfect! She focused. *I'll make a matching dark blue replica of it.*

POOF!

One appeared.

She stopped and smiled at her handiwork. In that moment of silence, she heard a low melody. "What's that noise?" The low sound floated from the bathroom. She peeked up through the spout of her bottle to get a better listen.

Demetri's voice sang out, "Jenny, I got your number. I'm gonna make you mine."

She gasped. *Again?* Her heart pounded. *That's sweet.*

Jenny slid back down and sang along with him.

Her voice echoed off the glass walls.

Ow. I've got to fix this. I need curtains in here to dampen the ear-piercing echo. Let's see . . . My bottle is blue with silver accents, so let me do silver curtains. She thought about the arrangement of them in her head and closed her eyes. *They will start at the bottom of the straight tube and then follow the curved walls down to the floor. They will be just loose enough to tie them in the middle so I can still see out when I want.*

POOF!

She opened her eyes. Everything she imagined had appeared.

"Yep, silk! Wow! Down to the detail! Awesome! I wish Demetri could see what I've done in here!"

"8675309, 8675309—"

Demetri stopped singing.

Jenny grimaced, *Wow, that was loud! How could curtains make it **worse**?*

"JENNY!" Demetri yelled.

He quickly yanked the blanket off her bed and covered his wet body.

Jenny whirled around. "Ahhh!" she screeched. She fell backward onto her couch. "How did *you* get in here?" She lifted her hand to her chest and took in a deep breath. "You *scared* me . . . *again!*"

Demetri was dripping wet.

"*I* scared *you*? *You* are the one who apparently *poofed* me in here without *warning*! What about how *you* scared *me*?"

"Oh." Jenny realized what she did. "I accidentally wished that you could see what I've done in here," she said meekly.

"Oh." He took a breath in. "Um, it looks great."

"You didn't even look!" She put her hands on her waist.

He leaned his head back. "Jenny, I would *love* to come in here . . . *later* and look at what all you've done, but right now, I'm cold and wet." He wrapped more blanket around him.

She just sat there with her hands still on her waist.

He gave her a sly look. "Unless you wanna come over here and warm me up, then will you please poof me back into the shower?"

He knew she wouldn't go for it.

Oh, he wants to play **that** *game, does he?*

Jenny took in the sexy sight before her and sprung up from the couch. She slowly walked over to him, ensuring that her hips moved back and forth.

Demetri noticed and felt a strange new feeling. *Wait . . . is she serious?*

She locked eyes with him and continued walking until she couldn't go any further. She bent down close to his face.

Demetri studied her bright blue eyes.

She finally spoke. "You're getting my blanket wet," she whispered.

He realized she was toying with him.

"Well, here then, let me take it off," he shot back at her.

They were even now.

"Now that's an idea," she said seductively.

He felt that she meant it, but there was also something else mixed in, and he was beginning to figure out what it was.

15

Can You Forgive A Devil?

The little devil arrived back in Hell. The blackness consumed it, and it didn't know which way to go.

Agh, I hate this part!

An eerie booming voice appeared right in front of it.

"AH! You're back! I trust you have brought me good news."

Satan had been waiting impatiently for its return.

The little devil yelped, flew backward, and hit the scalding hot ground. "OW, HOT!" It quickly flew back up. All around it was still pitch-black. "Um . . . well . . . no . . . it turns out—"

"NO? You have FAILED me!"

"I did *all* the usual and even went *inside* his head. The closest thing I got that stupid boy to do was take her shirt off."

It cowered in fear, even though it couldn't see anything through the suffocating darkness. The blackness alone was enough to make you want to end your second death. Hell was bad enough with the constant screams of torture and terror that made your ears bleed, not to mention the ungodly amount of heat that seemed to asphyxiate you.

"THAT DOESN'T MAKE HER IMPURE, DOES IT! I NEED HER TO BE *CORRUPTED*! I CAN'T CONTROL THE WORLD WITH *PURE* SOULS! THAT'S WHAT *HE* DOES!"

Satan shivered despite the calefaction.

"I know, master. I am sorry, master. I have failed you." It hung its head, terrified, and waited for what Satan would decide next.

Satan's blackness consumed the little devil creature and took it away to be tortured with its own worst fears.

"No! Please forgive me! I don't want to be tortured again!" the devil cried out as it was whisked away.

Satan didn't even blink. "Well, I am not wasting *my* precious time with them anymore. It will be a lot easier to use a soul that already belongs to me, like Dalia's."

He laughed maniacally and went to find her himself. "I'm sure she will be *so* happy to see me again."

16

Sealing Secrets

POOF!

"Ahhh!" Demetri yelled.

Jenny heard loud and clear and cringed a little. *Sorry, Demetri.*

She poofed her blanket dry and straightened her bed back up.

He got water on my floor. "Hmmm. That other genie just snapped her fingers, and she disappeared. I wonder if I can do something like that. It hurts my brain to concentrate so hard."

Jenny felt a little light-headed. She gave the water puddle a quick, silent command and snapped her fingers. It dried up. She thought of a chocolate bar. A chocolate bar appeared on her bed.

"Sweet! So as long as I think it and *want* it to happen, it happens. Good. Now I don't have to be so stressed out about daydreaming. I daydream to *escape* reality, not to *create* one."

"JENNY!" Demetri hollered down into the bottle.

Demetri's voice was deafening. Jenny was thankful that she had just put the curtains up. She floated up and no more than grew full size out of the top of the bottle than was met face-to-face with a dried-off, angry-looking, dressed Demetri. He wore basketball shorts and a soft long-sleeved red shirt.

She shrunk a little. "Woah! Hey, I'm sorry I did that seductive stuff, but—"

"The water was *freezing*! You poofed me back into a *freezing-cold* shower!" His arms were crossed; he gave her a hard stare.

"Oops." She slunk down a little more and slid her arms behind her back. "Well, *you* wanted to go back to the shower."

"You could've made sure the water wasn't *ice-cold* though." He calmed down a little. "And *yes*, there *is* the matter of you doing your little enticing tricks. I just went through hell for you with all that pain."

She frowned sadly. "I know. That was wrong of me." She peeked back up at him slowly. "I'm . . . really sorry."

He let out a pained breath, tilted his head toward the ceiling and stared at it for a moment. "Jen"—he sighed, and then he looked straight at her—"you've caused me a *lot* of pain today, more than you realize, I think. Physically, mentally, emotionally, *physically*. It's been *very* difficult and *confusing* to deal with."

She hung her head and started to tear up.

"But"—he took his pointer finger and lifted her chin—"if that's what it takes to live with you every day . . . at least until you . . . *leave*"—his heart ached at the word—"then I'm *glad* to put up with all that pain for you." He connected his gaze with hers. "I *love* you, Jenny."

She clung to him. "I'm sorry. I'll *try* not to tempt you anymore for fun."

He embraced her with his hands around her lower back. "That *is* a pretty mean trick. I'm not as strong as you might think. One look at your body and I want to tear your clothes off and take you to bed with me."

Jenny's heart let her know it was still beating like it was supposed to, maybe a little faster though.

He continued. "It makes it even *harder* when I know you want me too." He kissed the top of her head. "The *hardest* thing is knowing that I can actually *make* you do anything I want." He pulled her away a little and delivered a mischievous grin. "All I literally have to say is . . . get in my bed and let me take your virginity away."

Jenny's eyes tensed. "Yes, master!"

She floated the rest of the way out of her bottle. Thanks to Demetri's wish, her legs came with her. She crawled onto his bed and no more than faced him when he pounced on top of her.

Jenny's voice was uneasy. "Demetri."

He gave Jenny an intent gaze. Her eyes were the most frightened that he had seen them all day.

It would be so easy just to let this wish take its course, he thought. "THAT is for the icy shower *and* trying to mess with my head."

Jenny was relieved he was just getting her back. She let out a thankful breath.

He sighed painfully. It went against *everything* in his body except his conscience, but he proceeded to wish it anyways.

"Jenny, I wish that neither of us will lose our virginity . . . until you and I are united together in the bonds of marriage."

Jenny's expression transformed from fright to shock. There wasn't much change in her facial expression, but he could tell the difference.

She didn't realize how he said it, only that he just sealed off any possibility of sex until marriage.

"Thank you, Demetri! Thank you!" She pulled his face to hers and kissed him for a long moment.

"Uh, Jen," Demetri said, withdrawing his lips unenthusiastically, "that's just making it worse right now." He gave her a painful expression.

"Oh right. I'm sorry *again.* I . . . I have a feeling that you're going to be going through a lot of pain until we learn more about all this."

He looked straight into her eyes. "All the pain in the world will be worth it if I'm helping you."

Jenny blushed. "You're too sweet."

He continued. "And besides, I want to wait too. I don't know why we keep achieving this position today. I've *never* been like this before, and I've been alone with a *lot* of women."

Jenny looked away. "You have?" she asked him. *I should've expected this with as old as he is. He also owns a successful business, has an amazing bachelor pad, is sooo handsome, and is a perfect gentleman . . .*

He sat up and held her on his lap. He didn't need to study her face to try to understand what *this* feeling was. "Jeez, Jen, did that comment really make you feel as bad as I feel now?" He cringed a little.

The feeling lingeringly throbbed in his stomach.

She kept her head down. "I guess so . . ."

He lifted her chin again. "Hey, it's not what you think. Yes, I've dated many girls but only for a short period of time because none of them were the *one.*"

She sat completely still. "Did you *do* anything with any of them?"

Again, she was afraid of the possible answers. Her heart started thumping louder and faster.

He still held her chin and gave her a comforting look. "I kissed some of them to see if it felt right. I've never dated for fun. I always did it to try to find the right one."

"Does it . . . does it feel right when you kiss me?"

She regretted asking it as soon as it left her lips.

"Jenny, if you only *knew* how it feels when I kiss you. Yes. It feels perfectly right when I kiss you."

His response gave her a surge of courage.

"Does that mean that . . . that *I'm* the one?" She bravely met his eyes.

He felt her hopefulness, but he still wasn't sure if she truly *knew* what she wanted.

"Yes. As long as you feel the same way."

He grabbed both her hands and got up off the bed. Dusk was upon them, and the lights in Demetri's room automatically dimmed accordingly. The moon shone down on them through the floor-to-ceiling windows.

"I love you, Jenny. I've never felt this way about anyone before."

"I love you too!" Jenny replied. "I loved you from the first moment I saw you."

Demetri's smile faded. "You did?"

He felt another emotion. He couldn't pin it down, but it felt like seriousness. It was good enough for him. Jenny may be young, but he believed her now.

"Yes." Jenny blushed and studied his clothed stomach.

"Wow. Love at first sight for both of us then. That's really rare . . . just like you."

Jenny blushed and held her arm again. The agonized look on Demetri's face reminded her that she couldn't do that anymore.

"Oh jeez! Here . . . let me put something different on so you're not in *constant* pain."

His brain battled his eyes; his eyes won.

"Yeah," he sighed, "it would help a lot if you wore something more modest. I don't know if you've noticed, but your shorts underneath your veiled pants don't actually cover much.

"Oh, so you *did* notice." Her eyes laughed.

He gave her a "duh" look. "Of course, I did."

"It *is* fun to tease you." Her eyes bonded with his, and she sighed. "But I know it hurts you, and that's *not* fun for me . . . and *especially* not fun for you." Jenny placed her feet on the ground and pointed to her body.

POOF!

Her original clothes from this morning appeared on her.

He leaned back onto one elbow. "Wow, you're getting good at that."

"I've been practicing." She smiled.

"Thanks . . . Those clothes are a *lot* easier to handle."

Demetri sat up the rest of the way. It was getting late. He didn't want the day to end.

"Hey, do you want a cup of hot cocoa?"

"That sounds great!" She poofed two hot cups over on the desk.

"No, Jen. I'll make you some *myself.*" He came closer. "I really just want everything to be as normal as possible. It'll be a lot easier to pretend like it is since you have legs now."

She gave him an accepting smile. "You're right."

Jenny poofed them away.

"Good. I'm glad we're on the same page. Now follow me to the kitchen, and I'll show you where everything is."

"Yes, master." She looked down, embarrassed again.

Demetri turned around with a soft look and grabbed her hand to lead her to the kitchen.

Her insides sent a heat wave to the surface of her skin.

She smiled, and unbeknownst to her, he smiled too.

Demetri truly had a gourmet kitchen with top-of-the-line everything. Jenny felt like she was in cooking heaven.

"Wow! You have a pot filler over the stove top? That's fancy!"

Demetri laughed and stood back and watched as she explored. *I guess she will just find everything on her **own** then.*

"Woah! You have a smart fridge! Do you like it?" She ran her fingertips down the screen lightly.

He smiled. "Yes, I do. Everything is smart technology in here. I use it a lot actually. It's nice, *especially* when your hands are covered in icing or something."

"You like to bake too?" She paused her rummaging for a moment to meet his eyes.

"Yes, remember? I went to culinary school."

"Oh yeah. That's awesome! I love to bake too!" She continued rummaging around in the light-toned wooden cabinets, finding out where everything was. She was careful not to move anything out of place without putting it back.

"What are you doing?" He laughed and shook his head.

"Well . . .," Jenny started as she kept reading labels of fancy ingredients, some she had never heard of, "I've got to know where everything is for tomorrow so we're even before we get started on our cooking challenge."

Jenny stood, satisfied now and walked over to him. "Don't worry, I didn't switch anything around on you." She flashed a sly look. "Or did I?"

He laughed. "Either way, I think it's a pretty fair competition now." He headed to the fridge to pull out fresh milk for his favorite hot cocoa recipe.

She watched him. "Can *I* help?"

He stopped for a moment. "Uh . . . well, I don't know. This is a *top* secret cocoa recipe. It has a special ingredient in it. Can you keep a secret?"

"Seriously?" Jenny couldn't tell if he was serious or just joking with her. "*Yes,* I can keep a secret if you're *really* worried about it." She put her right hand on her hip. "I mean, I'm going to need to know it eventually anyway."

He turned his head away and pretended to find another ingredient. "Why?"

"Well, if I'm going to be here for a while, I'll need to know how to make it for *you* someday."

Demetri smiled, even though it wasn't *exactly* what he wanted to hear. He shut the fridge door and met her eyes. "You're going to stay?"

She greeted them back, "If that's OK . . ."

"Yes, that's *more* than OK. I just was worried that you might want to leave since you have legs now." He rubbed his neck and glanced down at the dark hardwoods.

"I'm *still* a genie, and . . . I don't think I *can* leave you, master." Her eyes went wide. "I don't know why I said that again! It just came out!"

"It's probably just a master-genie bond thing. Don't worry about it." He sneaked another look at her before returning his eyes to the floor.

"Yeah, we should try to figure that out tomorrow." She thought about all the questions she had and started listing them out loud. "Why did a ring with *my* name suddenly appear on *your* finger? Why can you feel my emotions? Wait . . . I think I know why!" She looked at him with an open mouth.

"Why?"

Jenny examined the white marble counter first and then Demetri. "What was it I said right before that started happening? I said . . . it's *yours*! I, as a genie, told you that you could have my bottle, like you could have . . . *possession* of me. Then the ring and names appeared. So it created a . . . *connection* between us, where you can feel what *I* feel."

Demetri took it in. "That sounds logical . . . for the situation, I mean, but remember, Jenny, you and I had a connection *before* that happened, a *real* connection, when we first saw each other. *That's* the important one."

Her heart jumped, and she smiled.

He smiled back. "Are you ready for the secret ingredient?" He paused with the hot cocoa for a minute and walked up to her.

"Yes!"

"OK, the secret ingredient is . . ." He put his right arm around her lower back pulled her close.

The echoing feeling in her chest throbbed a few times. She wondered if Demetri could feel it too. He used his other hand to bring her head to his mouth and whispered into her ear sensually.

Jenny's knees went weak, and they failed her again, but Demetri didn't. He held her up with his right arm. She didn't slip even the slightest. He picked her up and sat her on the counter facing him. "Are you OK?"

"Yes. Thank you for catching me again . . ." She smiled shyly at him.

His counter was a little taller than hers, so she was equal height. Their eyes were level. She tried her best to maintain eye contact, but somehow being the same height made it even more difficult.

"I never would have guessed that *that* would be your secret ingredient. Hmmm, I can see it though. I promise I won't tell anyone your deepest, darkest top secret." She dramatically rolled her eyes.

"Jenny?" Demetri stopped for a moment. His arms still around her. Her legs were positioned on either side of his body, and her flowy skirt was pushed back behind her knees a little.

"Hmmm?"

He searched her eyes. "What's *your* deepest secret?"

She didn't skip a beat. "Right now, this genie thing is."

He smiled. "What was it *before* today?"

"Hmmm." She thought hard, but it was difficult to think back past today. "I'm not sure. I didn't really have . . . I didn't have . . ." Jenny sighed. "Look, apparently, I had one, but I can't remember it right now."

"That's OK, Jen. I *would* like to know someday though." She smiled at him, and he continued. "Do you wanna know what my other one is?"

She had no trouble looking into his eyes this time. "Yes. Tell me!"

His eyes focused on hers. His face was happy, but he didn't smile. "I love you."

Jenny laughed. "That's not a secret. I already *know* that."

"Well . . . no one else knows yet. Like my parents or my best friend, Lewis."

Jenny's thoughts turned to Cali.

"Oh my goodness! Cali is going to flip about . . ."

He waited a moment for her to finish, but she never did.

"What? What is she going to flip out about?"

Now she had trouble meeting his eyes. "Well, that we're . . . dating or something. Aren't we?"

He leaned back a little and smiled. "I guess I shouldn't make the same mistakes that I've made in the past. *I* think we are, but I guess I should ask you officially, shouldn't I?"

"I would like it if you did." She wrapped her arms around his neck and peeked up at him meekly.

They were in his house. He was teaching her his favorite recipe, which also happened to be one of her favorite things to indulge in. She was sitting on his counter, which he had installed with his own two hands. Currently, those same two hands were tangled around someone Demetri had been waiting for thus far. Jenny waited patiently, with her loving, mysterious blue eyes bravely leering into his.

This is perfect, he thought. He beheld her and squeezed her tighter. "Jenny, would you like to be mine? Would you like to be my steady?"

He thought she might enjoy the old-fashioned touch.

"Yes, Demetri, I would." She smiled back at him. "I will *always* be yours."

His heart smiled, and he pulled her all the way to him; her skirt scrunched up against his stomach accordingly. He kissed her intently, and he managed to keep the pain at bay.

Unbeknownst to them, dark blue and shiny silver smoke extracted itself from her cuffs and quietly vanished into his ring.

Demetri kissed her a little longer than he had planned. He reasoned since he was getting better at controlling himself, that it would be OK. But it was also partly because their lips didn't seem to want to pull apart. They didn't *want* to separate from their match. He moved his strong hands around her back slowly, and she ran her fingers through his hair. Electricity transferred again, and both their hearts beat as one.

He loved the taste of her lips. He had never tasted orange-flavored lips before, but out of all the lips he had tasted before, Jenny's were by far his favorite. It was near impossible, but he finally managed to stop kissing her. Maybe some of those prayers he prayed earlier were finally kicking in.

"Well then, I guess we're ready to make my famous hot cocoa." He helped her down. "Let me show you how."

She smiled heavily. "Do you hurt?"

He gave her a proud grin. "No, surprisingly."

"I'm glad." She gazed at his broad chest. *I love you.*

She didn't say it out loud.

Demetri cocked his head to one side. "Huh?"

Jenny raised a tired eyebrow. "What?"

He scratched his head. "Didn't you say something?"

She shook her head. "No," she said with sleepy eyes still staring at his chest.

Demetri felt another feeling come through. He smiled and lifted her back up to the countertop.

She didn't resist at all. "What are you doing?"

He leaned his forehead on hers. "Jen, you're tired. How about you just watch me this time, OK?"

Jenny was glad for once that he knew what she felt and nodded slowly.

He showed her everything as quickly as he could and then carried her to his couch in his room. The couch reclined back nearly a full one-hundred and eighty degrees, and he draped a warm blanket over her.

She gave him a sleepy smile. "Thank you, Demetri."

He smiled down at her and came back a few moments later with the hot chocolate. He sat them down in the cup holder next to them and lay next to her. She snuggled to his chest, and he handed her a cup.

"Wow . . . Demetri . . . wow." She sat up a little. "Demetri, this is wow."

He laughed. "Well . . . if you can't think of a normal way to describe it, then I guess I take that as a compliment."

By the time he had finished replying, hers was completely gone. She handed it to him.

He accepted it, wide-eyed. "Wow . . . *definitely* a compliment then. Did you even *taste* it?"

"Thanks . . . That was the best hot chocolate, hands"—she yawned—"down, that I've ever had."

He laughed a little, sat the cup down, and pulled her close to his chest.

They stared up at the moon and the twinkling stars. Everything was perfect.

Jenny soon fell asleep. She had her head on the right side of his chest, and he lay on his back with his arm around her. Demetri leaned his face against her soft updo from the genie transformation.

He wished a tiny selfish wish that her hair would come down.

His fingers gently found their way through her long hair, something else he'd never done before to another girl.

Demetri loved it.

Vanilla inundated his senses. Soon, he fell asleep too. A peaceful smile adorned their faces. Unbeknownst to Jenny, this would be the first peaceful night's sleep that she'd receive in a long time.

17

Mere Human

Dalia woke up with the cold keys in her face. She was stomach-side down and still exhausted.

Man, I feel terrible.

Her arms slowly pushed her body up out of bed and into a slumped sitting position. She remembered exactly where she was and made sure the door was still how she left it.

It was.

She rubbed her face, slid her burka back on, and grabbed the keys. Her feet balanced her as she smoothed the material down and tried to clear her head. Low voices resonated from the hall and she quickly rushed to investigate. Mimir was handing another man a bag of dates. After the man left, she drifted from the shadows.

"Well, good afternoon, Dalia." He turned around and smiled at her.

"Afternoon?" She crossed her arms. "You promised to take me to the oasis in the *morning*!"

"I tried to wake you up, but you did not budge. So, I just let you rest. We can leave in thirty minutes. It will be one o'clock, and I will be closed for lunch."

"Fine, but we better leave in exactly thirty minutes!"

Dalia observed her new surroundings and noticed all the different types of foods he had.

"What are those?" She pointed to large rectangular boxes with lights that made small humming noises.

"Those are vending refrigerators. They keep food cold all day and all night."

Her eyes widened. "*That* is power! Give me some!" She eagerly examined it and opened it up. "Brrr! It's cold in there."

Mimir laughed. "It is called electricity." He showed her where the plugs were.

"Ah! The source! *That* is what I need." She started to reach her hand to an open outlet.

He lurched forward a little. "No! It could shock you!"

"A small price to pay for the powers it will give me." She kept reaching.

Stubborn girl, he thought. "Fine, let it shock you."

ZAP!

"Oww! My hand!" She clutched it tightly.

He rolled his eyes. "I *tried* to tell you. A good portion of the people on this earth have access to electricity. It is very great but not as great as you are hoping."

She didn't respond.

Mimir shook his head and continued to straighten the produce on the shelves. After a moment, he returned his eyes to her. Her face was blank and unreadable.

"Here, let me tell you about all this food. Then you can help me sell some until it is time to go."

*Great, reduced to manual labor, some great sorceress **I** am.* Dalia existed next to him and listened about as well and as painfully as a bored pre-teen.

Mimir picked up a fig. "I think these were around back when you lived before, but they have changed a little I am sure. Have a taste to see for yourself."

Dalia remembered perfectly what a fig tasted like. She would conjure them to eat all the time when she was trapped in the vase. She took an eager bite and then quickly rejected the fig to the ground.

"Eww! What have they done to them?" She gave him a disgusted look.

Mimir laughed. "Nature has done it. And I do not know. I have never had a fig from your time to compare it to."

He started to bend down to retrieve it.

"I will get it." Dalia held out her palm.

Nothing happened.

She bore her eyes into the fig and tried again. It slowly moved up to her palm.

"Ah, there."

"That took longer than it would have if you would have just let me pick it up."

She handed it to him without meeting his eyes.

He regretfully cast it into the trash, and when he came back, she still had the same dazed expression.

He studied her. "Dalia, are you OK?"

She sighed to herself. *I am not going to tell a mere human that I am losing my power and that I feel almost completely drained.* "I am fine," she answered. "Has it been thirty minutes yet?"

Mimir didn't believe her one bit, but he dropped the subject anyhow. Dalia was the most stubborn, unhappiest person he had ever met. He had no idea how to cheer her up, not that she would probably go along with any of his ideas anyways, so he just tried what he knew.

"Almost. Here, let me show you how the cash register works." He ushered her over to it.

Dalia didn't fight it, although she would start to if he didn't take her to the oasis soon.

She looked at him plainly. "Why do I need to know how to work this?"

Mimir sighed. "It will give you something to do just until I can close up."

He explained trading, debit cards, credit cards, cash, and what to do with each when a customer pays.

Another male customer walked in and asked where the prunes were. Mimir escorted him to a shelf, and the man thanked them.

I wish Dalia would do that for once, he thought.

The man continued shopping.

"Here, Dalia, when he comes back, you try to ring him up, OK?"

"Ring him up?" She looked at him like he'd lost his mind.

"You do what I just showed you. I will be right here to help if you need it." He smiled at her reassuringly.

"Fine." She rolled her eyes. *Anything to get us to the oasis before I lose **all** of my power!*

The customer was finished and came up to Dalia at the register.

"Will that be all . . . um . . . sir?" she tried.

"Yes. Thank you."

She did what Mimir said successfully, and the customer left happily.

He hoped that putting his hand on her shoulder wouldn't be too much. She tensed but let him.

"Good job, Dalia. There, that was not so hard, was it? And you did not even need the power you keep referring to, did you?"

She gasped and flashed him a horror-struck expression. "You! You *took* my power! The bed I slept in must have drained even more of it out of me! You are trying to weaken me to steal it for yourself!" She glowered at him.

He sighed. He offered an earnest look. "Dalia, I am *not* trying to steal your power. I would not even know how to, even *if* I wanted it."

She batted his hand away. "*You* are taking me to the oasis *now!*"

Dalia would get rid of him as soon as she had what she needed.

"Fine. It is basically one o'clock." He turned the sign around that read "Out to Lunch" and opened the door for her. "May I have my keys so I can lock my shop?"

She retrieved them from her pocket and threw them at him.

"Thank you." He sighed and locked up. "This way."

He led her through the crowd.

"Has no one ever shown you kindness before?" he asked after a minute of walking.

"Leave me alone. I am *not* telling a pathetic human about my life."

He abruptly halted and whirled around with crossed arms.

She had been engraving the ground with her laser stare and ended up running into him.

He firmly pulled her into an alleyway. "You are *very* ungrateful, Dalia. *I* slept on my tiny couch last night so that you could sleep in *my* bed. I risked getting *myself* arrested just so I could help *you* out. Unmarried women are not supposed to stay with unmarried men. I am *trying* to teach you how to take care of yourself and give you a job so you can survive in this new world when all your power finally dissolves, and all the while you think I am trying to trick you, trap you, and steal your power."

He focused into her now surprised and almost frightened-looking eyes. He turned around and kept walking, a bit faster now.

Dalia didn't follow for a moment and considered what he said. *Could it be true? Or was **that** all part of the trap too?* She caught back up. "Are we almost there yet?"

Unbelievable! he screamed in his head. He didn't turn to look at her. "Dalia, I *swear* I am not interested in having power, nor am I working for or with anyone who is. I pick up my own stuff when I drop it, and that is how I like it."

She tried to meet his ticked-off eyes. "Why should I believe you?"

"Why should you *not*? I have not done anything besides *help* you. I do not want to harm you."

She mulled it over.

Everything he said could make sense, and she hadn't been trapped inside the store or the room.

"Fine. So what if you *are* telling the truth, *why* did you help me? You do not even know me."

"I just saw a half-naked woman standing in the street and knew she needed help. Is that a crime?" He glanced back at her briefly.

"Well, then to answer your question, no, I have *not* ever had someone show me even one ounce of kindness, and then when I thought someone finally did, he *trapped* me in a container. So I am *not* sorry for *not* trusting *anyone*, including *you*!"

She wasn't angry, just forceful.

"I understand, but I am not him. *I* would not hurt you, and if you will let me, then I would like to help you without you thinking I have an ulterior motive."

"Why?" She looked at him, her eyes a little softer.

"I do not know. Because when I see someone who needs help, I help them."

Dalia sighed.

Her heart didn't want to trust anyone, even Mimir, but she realized that she had made him upset. Not that she really cared, right?

She tried to be a little better. "Well, if what you say is all true, then . . . thank . . . you, Mimir." She nearly gagged.

Finally! he thought.

He turned around without warning again, and this time he caught her when she ran into his arms. Mimir held her with both hands for a moment while he stared down into her dark, troubled eyes.

"You are welcome, Dalia."

Her eyes went wide, and she could feel her heartbeat pulse throughout her whole body. She felt light-headed and was glad that all the strange feelings ceased when he let go and gestured toward a pathetic excuse of an "oasis."

He moved out of her way. "Here we are."

She shook her head to clear it. *This is not the same one.*

Dalia had always practiced at a specific one back then. She figured if anywhere on this earth still had mystical power, it would be there.

She sighed, more frustrated than disappointed.

Mimir said that this was the closest one, and she wasn't sure how much longer her power would last. She gave it a chance and picked a stone to quietly try a spell on.

Nothing happened.

She tried two more times with clenched teeth.

"Agh!" She stoned the innocent water with the rock and a few more that she found close by.

"What is wrong now?" Mimir cautiously came up behind her but refrained from singeing his hands on the simmering volcano before him.

"Satan," she spit bitterly, "he is the one who trapped me! Maybe if I had not made a deal with him, I would still have my *old* powers."

Dalia sensed a familiar evil presence.

"Speak of the *devil*." She turned around to look upon an old wise man. "Using your old disguises, I see." She crossed her arms tightly.

"Hello, *Dalia*. Well, you *did* call, didn't you?" He sauntered up to her with a wicked grin.

She tensed. "Stay back! Just give me my power back!"

"Stupid girl!" Satan grinned.

Mimir stepped between her and Satan.

Satan assessed Mimir. "Ah, what do we have here? Are you really *attempting* to protect a *soulless* being from *me*? There's nothing left to protect; I already have everything that matters!"

Mimir tossed his confused eyes at Dalia for a moment and then returned them to Satan. "She is not soulless! You cannot torment her any longer! No one is past forgiveness!"

Satan stared daggers at him. "Dalia is. I have her soul," he glared back at Dalia, "she gave it to me."

Mimir stepped back a little and then turned to Dalia. "Is he telling the truth?"

She nodded plainly with emptiness.

Satan ignored Mimir. He didn't even try to convince Mimir otherwise about forgiveness.

His eyes stayed on target. "I gave you *unmatched* powers when you were trapped *inside*, but now that you so cleverly. . . *escaped* . . . the remaining power is draining fast. You will only be able to perform just a few more *little* tricks."

"Like what?" Dalia was steaming.

"Like make a few more things disappear and appear. It takes less power to take something existing and make it appear somewhere else than it does to conjure new substance from nothing. Now that you are *without* the vase, given a little time, you won't have *any* power at all." Satan pointed up. "*He* has taken away such powers. There is no longer any place for it in this modern world."

"No!" She couldn't lose her power for good.

Her hands found their way to her temples and her knees found the hard earth.

Satan faked concern. "Don't fret, dear. I can *help* you now that you've helped *me* find you again."

Her eyes narrowed into his. "Why would I want *your* help again! You imprisoned me and left me to *rot*!"

"*I* was not the one who wished you to be lost! Until *today*, I haven't been able to *find* you. That wretched boy's wish was for you to be *lost* nearly forever. I was going to help you achieve world domination had he not interfered!"

"Well, you *failed*," she stated plainly.

"Really? I hadn't *noticed*!" He raged. "Do you want help or not?"

She scanned him and slowly stood. "What is your plan?" she asked warily.

He gave her a smirk. "If we can get you back inside the—"

Dalia exploded, "NO! I am NOT going BACK in! It took me *thousands* of years to escape! If I had not tricked that *Jenny* girl, I would *still* be trapped!"

Satan continued anyways. "If you get back in, ONE wish is all it will take to achieve what you want! Then you can trap someone else in there and be 'free!'"

"Dalia . . .," Mimir mumbled uneasily.

She ignored him. "Could I wish for my powers after I got out?"

"No. I told you there isn't room for power like that in this world anymore, thanks to *Him*!"

She squinted at Satan. "So, I can only have powers if I am trapped?"

"You can't have *everything*, *even* when making deals with *me*. So what will it be?" He tapped his foot impatiently.

Mimir turned to her. "No! Dalia, come with me. I will show you this new land, and I can protect you when you lose all your powers. Please, Dalia, let me help you."

She studied Mimir.

He was inches away, gazing into her torn eyes.

"Please. For me?" he tried.

She glanced back at Mr. Evil for a moment and then returned her eyes to Mimir.

"Fine," Dalia stated.

She turned towards Satan and grinned wickedly. "Deal."

18

Am I Dreaming?

$\mathcal{J}$enny woke up the next morning in Demetri's bed. At first, she didn't remember where she was. Then slowly, some of the events of yesterday replayed themselves. She enjoyed all the highlights again.

*Wow, it **wasn't** a dream! I . . . I actually feel good—no, make that **great**—this morning!*

She sat up with a rested smile, realizing then that she was in Demetri's bed.

This . . . isn't where I fell asleep last night, was it? She gasped. *We didn't sleep in bed together, did we? Please no, please no!* Her eyes went wide with worry.

Her conscience pricked her.

Demetri walked through the threshold of his bedroom door carrying a breakfast tray. He had felt her wake up.

"Good morning." He stood near the doorway with an amused smile. "Your hair is messy."

"What?" She quickly ran her fingers through her hair and parted it to the side, embarrassed.

Demetri laughed. "Hey! I thought it looked cute."

Jenny blushed. "Uh . . . thanks. Um . . . how did I get in your bed? We didn't both sleep here did we?"

Her brain was still waking up; she hadn't slept that good in a really long time. Despite her mind's grogginess, her conscience was wide awake and alert, waiting for its answer.

He shook his head gently. "No, Jen. We fell asleep on the couch, and when I got up this morning, I carried you to my bed so you'd be more comfortable."

Jenny felt relieved.

Sleeping together on the couch is a little more OK than sleeping together on the bed but still not preferred, she thought.

He sat the tray down on her lap.

She didn't have to look at it to know what it was. It smelled amazing. *Mmmmm, breakfast.*

He sat across from her.

"You"—she met his eyes—"did all *this* . . . for me?"

Her eyes confirmed what her nose knew.

There were hot scrambled eggs, waffles with syrup, strawberry yogurt, sausage, cranberry juice, *and* orange juice.

"Yeah." He studied her with a small smile.

"This was so thoughtful of you. Thank you, Demetri." She felt embarrassed, looking into his eyes, and she was sure her cheeks were still red from the apparently "cute" bed head compliment.

He also thought Jenny looked cute when she was embarrassed, but he didn't want to tell her because he wanted the embarrassed feelings pulsating from her to stop.

"You're welcome. I just wanted to make sure that you had a good first night here since this is all so new."

"I did," she looked down, "actually, I don't know if I've *ever* slept this good my entire life. I feel so rested."

Demetri laughed. "Well, good. I'm glad."

She furrowed her brows. "I usually don't sleep very well. Almost every morning, I wake up with a little bit of a sore throat. Hot cocoa helps."

"Hmmm"—he raised an eyebrow—"do you have insomnia?"

Jenny shook her head no and sighed. "I sleep really heavily, but I feel pretty bad when I wake up despite the fact." She gave him a small 'What can you do?' smile.

Demetri smiled at her. "Well . . . I'm glad you got a good night's rest for once then."

He started for his fork.

"Wait," Jenny said, "we should really . . . um . . . *pray* first. I forgot to yesterday when we ate, but I do try to remember as much as I can."

He stared at her for a moment, surprised, then snapped out of it. "Oh yes, you're right. I *do* have a lot to be thankful for." He smiled at her. "I actually normally pray as well, but . . ."

He didn't finish, and he hid his eyes.

"But what?" She leaned her head closer, trying to meet his, for once, uncomfortable eyes.

He let her meet them. "Things have just been going so good I didn't want to *ruin* it . . ."

Jenny was beyond confused. "How would praying for something *ruin* the situation?" she nearly laughed.

Demetri tried to explain, "When I normally bring it up . . ." He sighed. He just didn't feel like telling her right now.

She offered him an understanding smile. "Hey, just tell me when you're ready, OK? No rush."

He felt relieved. "Thanks, Jen. That means more to me than you can possibly know."

They both bowed their heads and prayed silently.

"Amen," they both said out loud at the same time.

They let out a quick breath of laughter.

"You and I have a lot in common," Demetri said. "We have the same type of truck, the same passcode—"

"I know! That is *so* crazy!" Jenny took her first bite and then quickly went in for another.

"You also love . . . God too, right?" he asked it carefully.

"Yes. I read the Bible regularly, and I give part."

Demetri's smile slowly faded. There was a subtle change in her mood that he just barely noticed; It felt like a small wall rising between them. He wanted to ask which church she went to but didn't want to push it. He'd found that religion is one of the most delicate things to talk about and things were going so well.

He continued. "Cool! That sounds awesome!" He decided to speak his thoughts. "I can barely believe this is all real. I mean, I had to pinch myself when I woke up next to you this morning."

He felt the wall come down and . . . relief resonate.

Good, he thought.

Jenny smiled. "I could barely *think* when I woke up. It took me a minute to even figure out where I was." She shook her head and chuckled at herself. "Demetri, this is the best breakfast I've ever tasted. You're an *amazing* cook!"

He smiled at her. "Thank you. I found myself a little nervous honestly, wondering if you would or not."

She raised her eyebrows at him. "You *don't* need to be worried. This is *too* good."

"It must have *been* because you've eaten it all. I haven't even had two bites of mine yet." He laughed.

"Mmmm, and how did you know that I like cranberry juice?" She took a drink.

"Well, I figured anyone with strong enough taste buds to be able to enjoy clam chowder would have strong enough taste buds to endure the sour taste of cranberry juice." He smiled.

"Well, you were right," she said before downing the last of it. "Thank you again, Demetri. This was all so sweet. I'll clean up."

"I already did that except for the tray here."

She looked at him with a surprised expression. "Wow. OK, this *has* to be a dream. No man cleans up after he destroys the kitchen. My dad never cleaned up after himself without my mom having to tell him five times."

She reflected on the memory for a moment. What used to be an unpeaceful situation, what with the yelling and mess, had turned into a comforting memory.

Demetri's voice snapped her out of it.

"Well, I guess you can thank culinary school for that. I've been trained not to work in a dirty environment. It ruins the enjoyment of cooking for me."

"You're too good to be true." She smiled a thankful smile. "Maybe *I'm* the one who hit my head, and *I'm* the one dreaming."

He laughed. "This is all a gift from God, Jenny."

She grinned knowingly.

He wanted to explain anyway, "Yesterday I woke up thinking about how boring my life was getting. Just working all the time and the same thing over and over. I was starting to give up on everything. So I prayed . . . uh, never mind." He looked away and rubbed his neck again.

"What did you pray for?" Jenny looked at him seriously now.

"I would . . . rather not say." He slowly looked back up at her. "Let's just say that my prayers were answered."

Jenny would normally keep persisting, but she couldn't bring herself to do it this time.

"OK, I understand." She smiled at him gently. "Now finish eating while I get dressed and do my hair."

"Thank you, Jenny. I knew you would understand."

Demetri felt so comforted having someone whom he could *finally* share spiritual things with. He'd never felt like he could do that with anyone else before.

*She's **definitely** a gift from God,* he thought.

Jenny carefully got out of bed, minding the tray, and turned back to him suddenly.

She gasped, "I *can* see Kurtis today! I can have dinner with you guys too!" She beamed up at him.

He placed a forkful of egg back down on his tray. "Uh . . . Jen?"

"Yes?" she chimed brightly.

"I'm not . . . sure if that's a good idea yet," he started.

"What? Why?" Jenny's face morphed from excited to confused.

"What do you think he will do to me when he finds out you skipped work to be here at my house all day?"

"Oh, Demetri, is that *all*?" She smiled a "*Really?*" smile at him with one raised eyebrow.

"Is that *all*?" he moved his head back. "He might do something *crazy* to me!"

"Kurtis will love you!" she insisted.

He looked at her in all seriousness. "Well, once he finds out you've been here all day with me *alone*, he isn't. And he's *not* going to be happy that you and I are a couple now."

"Hmmm."

Her mind worked double time.

"Look, he's like a father to me. He will love you because *I* love you. It might take a while, but I *know* he will come to trust and accept you. This dinner would be a good start."

He furrowed his brows. "It's still a business dinner, Jen. We need to go over details of this merging or partnership or whatever it ends up being, and we won't be able to do that if he's trying to pepper spray my eyes the whole time."

"Oh my goodness, you heard him mention my pepper spray?" She laughed.

"Yes, I did. And I *still* don't think it's a good idea for you to join us *this* time. We should just give him some time to get used to me and actually *like* me before I try to tell him"—Demetri used a silly voice—"'This has been a splendid partnering opportunity, sir. Oh, *by* the *way*, Mr. Conroy, I'm not talking about the business partnering. I'm referring to your daughter figure who has been living with me out of wedlock. I've even seen her breasts already! Oh, and we're dating too, even though I didn't ask for your permission.'"

Reality began to sink in with Demetri; it wasn't a pleasant feeling.

Jenny blushed brightly and chuckled. "We aren't telling him that stuff, except for maybe the dating part." She tilted her head. "Look, he *did* want me to come tonight. If you eat alone with him, he might drill you with imposing questions, and I wouldn't be here to defend you and insist to him how great you are."

She had a point. Mr. Conroy already knew that Demetri was interested in Jenny and Demetri knew it.

He sighed helplessly. "I'm not going to be able to change your mind, am I?"

Her determination . . . or stubbornness was clear to him.

"No, you're not." She flashed him a victorious smile. "So you might as well stop trying."

He didn't want to have to accept defeat, so he countered with a mischievous smile. "You *do* know that I can just tell you to stay in your bottle the whole time, don't you?"

"Yes, but you won't." She crossed her arms, still victorious and unfazed.

He kept his mischievous gaze for a moment and then smiled defeatedly. "You're right. I won't." After a moment of consideration, he said, "Fine, you win. But you'll see that I'm right about later though. He isn't going to be happy if you go ahead and tell him about us. And, he isn't going to like that you'll be here helping with dinner before *he* even gets here."

Jenny sat next to him on the bed. "He needs to know. He and Carrie are the closest thing I've got to family."

"Is Carrie his wife?" Demetri asked.

"Yes."

"Well"—Demetri sighed—"maybe we should have her over then too. If *she's* here, maybe he won't be as apt to get upset. Plus, I'd like to meet your mother figure. Maybe I can at least get *her* to like me. The last thing I want is for *both* of your 'parents' to not trust me."

Jenny's heart smiled deeply.

"OK, I'll call him and see if he still even wants me here tonight. Will that make you feel better?" Jenny smiled at him hopefully.

"Yes, it would. Just don't let him know you're here right *now*. It's eleven thirty-five. If he asks what time you're planning on being here, tell him five and that you're helping me make dinner. That way, if he shows up early and catches you here, he knows there's a reason for it."

Demetri's mind usually worked quickly in stressful situations.

"OK, good idea."

Jenny started heading for her bottle. "I'm going to get ready, and then I'll call him."

"Wait . . . Jen?" Demetri met her eyes softly. "Will you leave your hair down, please? You . . . have the most *beautiful* hair I've ever seen."

Jenny's cheeks burned. "Um . . . yes, I will."

"Thanks." He turned back to his breakfast.

She stood still for a moment longer and looked at him fondly. "Demetri?"

He looked back up at her. "Yeah?"

"Thank you."

He smiled.

The thank-you was for everything and he knew that without her explaining. He watched her as she disappeared into her bottle.

19

Quick Change

Jenny rummaged through all her clothes in her chest-of-drawers. She took a step back and wondered what Demetri would want her to wear for dinner. For some reason, that was all she could think about.

*I can't think about anything else! Why do I care this much? It must be a genie thing. I feel like I need to . . . **please** my master or something.*

It still sounded kinky, and her uncontrollable imagination turned her cheeks pink. She was glad that he couldn't read her mind. Actually, she wasn't for sure that he couldn't.

Her cheeks transformed to red.

Jenny sighed. "OK, focus," she ordered herself.

She had no idea what he liked as far as clothes on a girl went. She decided to just go up and ask; that way, she could get somewhere. Her reflection in the mirror stared back at her until her cheeks faded back to normal beige. Up the tube she squeezed to appear beside the desk.

Jenny just blurt it out. "What do you want me to wear tonight?"

He jumped a little and then turned to look at her.

"NOT THAT!" he spouted.

She put her hands on her waist. "Well, I *know* I'm not going to wear what I wore yest . . ."

Her hands discovered bare skin instead of her work blouse.

She gawked at herself. "AHHH!"

Demetri sensed her surprise; it let him know that she didn't put on her genie outfit on purpose.

"I didn't . . . How did this . . ." She looked to him for an answer.

He tried to meet only her eyes. "Jen, it's probably just a genie thing. I'm sure it will only happen when you . . . use your bottle for the first time each day or something."

It was all he could think of. He hoped it was enough to satisfy her so she wouldn't linger around half-clothed.

She considered it and accepted his answer. "OK."

Even though she didn't understand it, just knowing that Demetri was so confident in his answer made her feel better.

"All right"—he looked away—"to answer your question, anything you pick out and want to wear tonight will be fine with me. I'm sure you look great in *anything* you wear." He turned back to smile at her and again tried really hard to look at just her eyes.

"That's sweet, Demetri."

She managed to refrain from putting her left hand over her right arm.

"I'll go get dressed now."

"OK, I'm almost done eating. Then we can go do something until dinner, OK?"

"Sounds good."

Jenny disappeared into her bottle again and finally decided on a purple dress. She began to take off her genie clothes when she realized that she didn't shower yesterday.

*Do genies **need** to shower?*

She wasn't sure, but even so, she felt like she should.

Jenny sniffed her shoulder. *I still **smell** good . . . I think. I don't want Demetri to think that I smell **bad**, but I don't even have my shower stuff. It didn't really sink in that I would be . . . spending the night.*

She thought about what Demetri said about trying not to use her power for small stuff.

*Oh . . . just **one** instant clean won't hurt.*

POOF!

Instantly, her hair was washed, and her clothed body was clean. She felt a lot better.

Good. He doesn't have to know anyway.

Jenny realized that the dress she had picked out was not dinner worthy.

It was an important dinner. They would be discussing business. She might tell them that she likes Demetri.

Ugh, I don't have anything to wear.

An idea popped into her mind.

Oh, just one more time. How about a red zip-up dress with a high collar and four-inch shoulder sleeves? It needs to fit my figure and come down below my knees a few inches.

She closed her eyes and smiled expectantly.

POOF!

The dress appeared on her body in place of her current attire. She willed a floor-length mirror to appear at the left side of her dresser and commanded it to stay put too.

Wow, I love this dress. It's awesome being a genie!

That was the first time she had thought that since turning into one. Jenny brushed her hair out thoroughly, parted it on the left, and pinned it to the other side, forming a little poof starting at her forehead. She let the rest of it hang down. Her hair consisted of natural blond waves; a few of them were surfing worthy.

*OK, I'm ready. Hopefully, this outfit **stays** on me and Demetri is right.*

She squeezed back up the bottle and appeared full size in front of Demetri.

He'd just finished eating and stood with the breakfast tray in hand.

Jenny beamed at him. "Do you think this is OK for dinner tonight?"

CRASH!

Time slowed.

The metal tray echoed metallically against the hardwoods. The porcelain plates shattered from impact. The glass cups fragmentized and scattered in all directions.

Demetri stood there frozen.

Completely captivated.

Dazed eyes.

Mouth open slightly.

Jenny had watched the tray slip from his fingers and hadn't noticed his expression. She immediately touched her knees to the floor carefully and began finding the larger shards.

"Oh . . . I don't think anything survived."

Demetri finally snapped out of his trance and bent down too. He gently grasped her hands.

"Jen, let *me* get this, please," he said softly.

She *had* to stop helping him. She balanced on her wedges with her knees together. "But—"

"*I'm* the one who dropped it, and you're dressed too nice to do something like this."

She tried to meet his gracious eyes. "Demetri, I *want* to help you."

He glanced at her briefly. "I'm already done. I just have to vacuum the smaller pieces, and you don't know where my vacuum is."

She sighed and tried a little humor. "I thought *I* was supposed to be *your* slave. This is the third mess you've cleaned up since *yesterday*." She stood up and crossed her arms with a helpless half smile.

Demetri stood too and sat the tray on his nightstand for a moment. "Jenny, you are *not* my slave, nor do I *ever* intend on treating you as such." He gazed into her playful eyes with soft, caring ones and came very close.

Her body weakened, but his gaze held her upright.

That's when Demetri noticed that something was different about her. He studied her face and then her neck and leaned into it suddenly.

Jenny's eyed widened; she would've fallen had he not already prepared for that.

He held her as he frisked her neck with his face.

She smiled and squirmed because his gentle movements and breath tickled.

Demetri received his answer but nuzzled a little longer anyway. She didn't smell like vanilla anymore.

He eyed her. "What did you do in there?"

Uh-oh, she thought. "What do you mean?"

Jenny batted her eyes away quickly and hoped that a question would be enough to answer a question from her master. It seemed to work for a short time.

He crossed his arms. "Jenny, *tell* me what you did."

"Yes, master. I looked through my clothes, came back up to ask you what you wanted me to wear, looked through my clothes again, realized that I didn't have a shower yesterday, poofed myself clean—"

Demetri was shocked at the specificness of what she *had* to say to him, but he interrupted her when he heard that she had used her new ability again for something so small.

"Jenny, I asked you to try—"

She didn't let him finish. "I know, I know." Her eyes fell as she sighed.

"I was just too scared to ask if I could take one. *Plus*, I don't have my shower stuff. I would've had to poof it here."

"Jen"—he presented a soft expression again—"my house is *literally* your house now, so please use anything you want or need. Don't be afraid to ask."

He ordered it because he wanted to make sure she had what she normally did to be comfortable.

"Yes, master."

Jenny didn't freak out this time. She was getting used to calling him that. It was as if she had to.

"Please don't call me that. As much as I like it, I don't want you to feel like you need to serve me or obey every word."

"Sorry, master"—she looked at him apologetically—"I think I *have* to call you that."

He sighed. "OK." He tilted his head a little. "Hey, I *really* like the vanilla. Would you want to put some more on for me?"

He worded it carefully, so she'd have a choice.

"I would love to, mas—uh—Demetri." She fought through it. "But to be honest, I'm not sure what exactly I use that smells like vanilla."

He raised an eyebrow. "What? How do you *not* know something like that?"

She tilted her head and gave him a small apologetic smile. "I don't know. I don't wear perfume, my lip balm is orange-flavored, I don't wear hairspray usually, and it's not vanilla-scented anyways. I don't . . . Oh! I know what it is!" She looked at him happily.

"You do? Great! What is it?"

"Cali got me some vanilla shampoo and conditioner for Christmas last year, and I finally started using it last week."

He laughed. "Jen, it's *almost* Christmas again."

"I know. I had stocked up on the old stuff I used right before she got it for me."

"OK, where did she buy it?"

"I'm not sure . . ." She looked into his eyes. "Hey, I promise I'll take regular showers, but can I please poof the stuff in my bathroom over? I don't want to have to deal with Mr. Mitts again, and if you go and get it, he *will* be able to say that you're carrying things out that you didn't come in with."

Demetri couldn't think of any other options. He decided to give in, but not without conditions.

"Fine, but *only* because I don't want Mitts bothering you anymore and *only* if you take a shower the right now and use your vanilla shampoo and conditioner."

"Yay! Thanks! Uh . . . where should I put everything? I don't have much room in my bottle." She laughed a little.

He smiled. "You can use my bathroom . . . or I can give you your own room with its own private bathroom. I have two guest suites upstairs. You can pick one out if you want."

Jenny thought about having her own *real* room here, but something kept her grounded. She didn't want to be that far away from Demetri.

She met his eyes. "Would it be OK if I . . . share yours with you? I don't have a lot of stuff. It won't cover the entire sink or anything."

"Yes, Jen. That's *more* than fine."

He was glad she wanted to share. He didn't know what it was, but he didn't want her to be that far away from him, even if it *was* in the same house.

"OK, thank you."

She walked into his bathroom and analyzed the layout. A wooden bench against the wall met you when you walked in. To the right, against the back wall, was a stand-up shower with a large glass door. It had a tinted outside window about shoulder height, so you could view the woods while you showered. Directly to Jenny's right was a huge dark brown double vanity. To her left against the other wall was a toilet closet, and to the right of that was a big corner tub. It too had a tinted window and a beautiful view.

Wow, Jenny thought.

POOF!

All the things she needed appeared on the vanity. There wasn't a lot, so it didn't take her but a minute to find a place for everything. She came back out to Demetri, who had just finished vacuuming the glass.

"Am I supposed to take a shower now?"

Her instinct was to ask for permission. She waited patiently for an answer.

"I would like it if you felt comfortable enough to."

He tried not to command her to do anything.

She glanced back at the bathroom. "There isn't a door."

"I won't look, I promise."

Jenny knew he would keep it.

He smiled at her. "I need to make a few calls anyway, OK? If you take one now, it will give me a chance to check up on everything."

"Sounds good." She returned his smile and proceeded to the shower.

"Oh, and please wear the same dress. You look great in it." *A little too great,* he thought.

"Yes, master." She rolled her eyes in acceptance and sighed. "Just get used to it, Demetri. I have no *choice* but to say it to you at least every now and then, almost like a reminder . . ."

"It's OK. To be honest, I *actually* like it."

Demetri left the vacuum for now, shut the bedroom door to give her some privacy, and went to the living room to attend to his business.

Jenny undressed and then tried to slide her cuffs off again. They wouldn't budge. She could twist them, but they wouldn't move up or down her arms even an inch.

"I wish these would come off so I can at least take a shower."

They were still there.

She stared at them hopelessly. *Oh well, this will just take some getting used to as well.*

Jenny hopped in the shower and washed her hair with the infamous vanilla shampoo and conditioner.

This is going to make him so happy!

Demetri's shower had an all-glass wall where you entered, and up against the wall were light-gray subway tiles with dark blue accent tiles as a top border.

He has good taste, she thought.

She stepped out, dressed again, and then smelled her hair.

Yup, vanilla.

Jenny wrapped her hair up in a towel to absorb what was left of the water, and then let it air-dry. She applied her orange lip balm, and even though her hair was damp, she put it in the same hairstyle as earlier. The mirror revealed her appearance.

*Well, at least I don't **look** any different. This genie thing isn't so bad. If I hadn't turned into a genie, I wouldn't be here with Demetri.* "Demetri!" she gasped.

Loneliness consumed her. Jenny hadn't felt this alone since her parents died. She quickly made sure everything was clean, out of respect, and then practically ran out into the living room to be with Demetri. It had felt like a month since she last saw him. Apparently, he felt the same way because as soon as she opened the door, he hung up on whoever he was talking to and met her halfway.

"Jenny!"

He hugged her eagerly and felt her emotion change from loneliness to relief and comfort. Demetri knew it was loneliness because he'd felt it as soon as he shut the door earlier, and with each passing second, the feeling worsened. He'd barely been able to focus on his calls.

"I don't think we're supposed to be apart for very long," Jenny guessed.

"I think you're right. You were gone for thirty-five minutes!"

He calmed down a little, smiled at her, and hugged her again tightly. He didn't let go this time.

She peered out at the beautiful living room view with her head on his chest. "Do you think it's a genie thing or . . ."

Jenny just wanted it to be because he was her soul mate.

"I don't know, Jen . . . probably. I think normal couples can take a shower separately and not feel like their heart has been ripped from their chest."

"Is that what it felt like for you?" She looked back up at him.

"As soon as I shut the door." He kissed her forehead.

Jenny smiled, and her heart fluttered. "Do you need to call whoever that was back?"

He sighed. "Yeah . . . I should."

20

Confession

"You should call Mr. Conroy now, OK?"

"OK," she obeyed. "What's your address? I need to text it to him."

He kept his arms around her.

"It's 84 Willow Tree, Private Drive."

"OK, already got it memorized."

She slowly peeled herself away to retrieve her phone.

His eyes followed her.

"Jen?"

She stopped and turned.

"Try to be as quick as you can, please?"

Demetri couldn't think of a way to word it where it wasn't an order. He really didn't want to feel that alone again anyways. It was almost terrifying.

"I'll try, but it *is* Mr. Conroy."

She felt sad being separated from him again, but Mr. Conroy could *not* know that she was here right now, and Demetri had to make a call. She drifted down into her bottle and dialed number one.

"Hey, Kurtis. It turns out I'll be able to join you guys tonight. I hope that's still OK." She thought to herself, *It's going to **have** to be OK because I can't be apart from Demetri for much longer than thirty minutes without it threatening my sanity.* She continued. "I'd like to see you."

"Oh, what about your plans or whatever you had going on?"

"Turns out it won't take all day."

"Um . . . agh . . ." He sighed. "Look, Jenny"—he rubbed his eyes—"I'm sorry about how protective I was acting yesterday. I beat myself up for not doing a background check on him before sending you out *alone* with him."

"Oh, Kurtis . . ." Jenny understood now. "Hey, it's OK. Everything went great! You don't need to worry!"

"But I *do* need to worry, Jenny, your parents are gone. Carrie and I are all you've got left. David and Jane were our closest friends. When they passed, we were *devastated*. We promised ourselves we wouldn't let anything happen to you. Plus, I had that bad feeling about yesterday, but . . . maybe that was just your truck. *I* couldn't get it to start either."

She didn't know what to think, but she wasn't surprised that he checked. She'd been sure to think about the fuel filter getting clogged up. It needed to be replaced anyway. It was a relief that her wish had worked even though they were miles away.

"Well, let me come to dinner, and you can see for yourself that I'm OK."

"That *would* make me feel better about everything. After we got off yesterday, I *was* looking forward to talking with him alone first though. I had a few things I wanted to get straight with him about . . . um . . . *business*."

Right, business, she thought.

"But making sure you're OK is more important, so yes, please come tonight."

"Why don't you bring Carrie too? I'd love to see her!"

"Hmmm, I suppose I could do that. I'm sure she'd love to see you as well. It's been a while."

"All right, sounds great! I'll text you his address after we get off."

"OK, when are *you* going to be there?"

Oh boy, Jenny thought. "I'm going to offer to help him make dinner, so five."

"Oh . . . are you sure that's a good idea?"

"Yes, Kurtis. I trust Demetri. He has a lot of integrity. He's great!"

"Integrity, huh? Wait . . . what do you mean by *great*?"

"I . . . just mean that he's a really great person to be around." She tried to change the subject. "Are you *sure* it's still OK with you that I come to dinner?"

Thankfully he dropped it.

"Fine, yes, yes." He sighed. "I can't put my finger on it, Jenny, but there's something different about you. I can't explain it, but I just *know* something is different."

Jenny's eyes widened. *Wow, he **is** good. Maybe this sixth-sense of his is how he became so successful in his career.*

Mr. Conroy continued. "Is he going to pick you up then?"

"If he can't, I'll let you know, don't worry. See you tonight, Kurtis. I can't wait to see you both!"

"See you, Jenny. Remember the pepper spray."

*This again . . . Seriously? **I am** an adult after all.* "Yes, Kurtis, I promise I'll remember."

"Good." He hung up and started talking to himself. "*Great.* I guess I'll have to drill him for questions another night. I just *know* something's up. I *need* to get to the bottom of it!"

Jenny zoomed out of her bottle with a huge grin. "I still get to come to dinner!"

Demetri had been waiting impatiently outside her bottle.

He raised an eyebrow. "So if *he* would've told you to not come, would you've listened?"

"Nope."

Her huge smile stayed. He could have sworn that he saw an angel halo appear above her head for a moment.

Demetri bent down and began wrapping up the cord on the vacuum. "Well, at least I'm not the *only* one that you're not listening to about dinner."

She laughed. "So I guess you're kind of a klutz like me, huh?"

He gave her a puzzled look. "What do you mean?"

"The tray." She tilted her head. "Did you not have a good grip on it?"

Demetri averted his eyes and stood angled away from her.

"It slipped."

Jenny remembered his nice dishes.

"I'm sorry everything broke."

He smiled. "It's only dishes. I have more."

She followed him.

"So where *does* the vacuum go?"

He laughed. "Why do you want to know that?"

"Well, if I'm going to stay here, I need to help out too. In fact, I should probably know where *everything* is."

Demetri grinned and led her to a storage closet by the main floor bathroom. He put the vacuum away and then turned his head toward her.

"Yeah, this is the third mess of *yours* that I've had to clean up."

He wrapped his arms around her lower back and gave her a kiss on the forehead.

Jenny leaned her head back a little. "What? You're the one who dropped the tray!" She raised an eyebrow.

"But *you* made me." His grin turned playful.

She backed up and crossed her arms. "*I* didn't do anything."

He put his hands on his hips. "Jen, you're the one who decided to put on an attractive red dress."

She stood still. "You . . . dropped the tray because of the way I looked?"

His eyes swept the floor for a brief moment and then returned to hers. "Yes."

Jenny's cheeks warmed her face. "Oh."

He came forward and put his arms back around her. "Yeah . . . 'Oh'."

She tilted her head down. "Sorry . . ."

"I'm just teasing you, Jen. Of *course*, it was my fault."

She kept her focus down, still too embarrassed to look up at him.

"Hey, my eyes are up here." He laughed.

"Hey! I wasn't . . . um . . . never mind." Her face grew warmer.

"I'm just playing with you, Jen. Hasn't anyone *teased* you before?"

Her smile disappeared. The emotions he felt next spoke for her.

"Oh hey . . . I'm sorry." He furrowed his brows. "Do you want to talk about it?"

She shook her head. "No . . . not right now," and her eyes fell again.

Demetri lifted her chin with his right hand. "OK, I *do* want to know about it, but just tell me when you're ready."

She gave him a grateful smile.

He wanted to get her mind off whatever it was. "Here, I'll take you on a tour now."

She blocked memories away. "Did you complete all your important *boss* things?"

Demetri smiled down at her. "The rest can wait."

That bothered her a little.

"Are you sure? I mean, I've already *completely* turned your life around. Don't let me affect your business, please."

"Jen, don't worry about any of that. Now I have a future *worth* thinking about, so believe me, I'm not going to let anything happen to my business."

That made her feel better.

"What's upstairs?" Her eyes traced the metal stairs with airplane cord rails all the way to the top. "Awesome! I love the design of the stairs."

He grabbed her hand. "C'mon, I'll show you."

Jenny let him lead her up the open stairs. She looked around when they got to the top.

Her lungs filled with air in awe.

Demetri switched the lights on.

They stood in the middle of a gallery of photos of different shapes and sizes. They were all in sleek black picture frames with white or black mat boards.

Demetri took in her expression; It made him smile. There were no windows in this main area, only soft display lights.

"Demetri, these . . . are amazing! Did *you* take all these?"

She walked around slowly, appreciating them all.

"Yes."

He could feel how genuine her emotions were towards his photos. None of his other girlfriends had been very interested in his photography hobby. He stood back and watched her. Jenny really liked one in particular. It was a unique angle of piano keys on an ebony colored grand piano.

Her eyes shifted towards him. "Do you play the piano?"

Demetri tilted his head. "Sort of. I don't have one, but I took lessons when I was younger. When I'm around a piano, I play what I know. I like to keep in practice when I can."

Jenny rushed to him in excitement, "I can help you! I play!"

He gave Jenny a gentle grin. "I look forward to it."

She calmly took another look around the room. "Demetri, these photos are all *so* incredible! Can you teach me how to take a picture like you? Please?"

Her eyes pleaded with his and her smile was hopeful.

He laughed. "Yes, I'd really like that actually. Let me show you my editing software in my equipment room." He gently took her hand again and led the way. "I'm glad you like them because Lewis owes me twenty dollars now."

"Lewis . . . he's your best friend, right?"

She scanned more pictures in the hallway as they walked past.

"Yes, and he made a bet with me quite a while ago saying that I'd never find a girl who would be interested in my photography." He looked back at her and smiled. "I've never been able to forget about it because every time he found out that one of my girlfriends wasn't interested, he'd remind me."

Jenny smiled.

"In here," he said.

"Woah!"

This was definitely the most disorganized room in the house.

"I apologize for the mess. I haven't had time to clean it up."

Jenny laughed. "I thought you were Mr. Perfect," she joked.

He laughed modestly. "Far from it. Take a look around."

Older cameras and newer ones neatly adorned the shelves, but frames leaned all over the walls. Mat board cutouts and box cutters riddled a sturdy table in the middle of the room. Cans of orange mounting tape were knocked over here and there as if they had been in a fight. A couple of larger photographs hung on the far wall. A silhouette of two people kissing in front of a sunset made up the first one. It was as if the couple was standing on top of a mountain because perfect sunset surrounded them. Their silhouette was so dark it looked like someone cut them out of black paper and pasted them there. Though you couldn't see their faces, you could tell that it must have been a kiss between two people who were meant to be with each other. It was the most romantic photo that Jenny had ever seen.

She loved it, and it caused her to want it to be her and Demetri in the photo.

Another photograph that caught Jenny's eye was a yellow lab puppy in a playful position. Its eyes were warm brown, and its tongue hung out. The detail was immaculate. The puppy was completely in focus, and what little there was of the background was blurred. You could see the healthy wet of its nose and the excitement in its eyes. It would make any non-dog lover think twice about loving dogs.

"Demetri, these are . . ."

She was too awestruck to finish.

"I just finished those two for someone. They are a gift."

"Wow, I'm just speechless!"

Those were the only words her mouth could find.

"Well, besides my parents, you're the only one who seems to care this much."

She furrowed her eyebrows sadly. "Mel didn't care?"

"No." His eyes fell briefly but quickly returned to Jenny's apologetic grayish-blue eyes. "Pictures aren't *exciting* enough for her." He gave her a small reflective smile.

Jenny let out a quick breath of disbelief and then looked at him softly.

"Well, *I* love them! There's *tons* of excitement in this puppy one. I love taking pictures, but I don't know anything about the camera settings. But despite the fact, I still think I'm pretty good at it."

"I'd love to teach you the camera features."

Demetri ushered towards his computer and a chair for her so he could teach her a little about editing. She listened eagerly and absorbed it all. He took a DSLR and taught her some tips and tricks for taking photos in daylight.

Jenny grew impatient. "Can we go try now? I learn better if I can actually do it. I'll just forget if I don't practice."

"Really? You want to go even before our bet begins?"

He was surprised. Usually, getting a girl to go take pictures with him was as hard as capturing a hummingbird's wings without a feeder for bait. Not impossible but difficult.

"Yes! Please? Just for a little while?" She batted her puppy eyes at him.

"Jenny, you don't have to beg or ask *me* twice to go take photos. Let's go!"

Demetri grabbed another DSLR for her and two new batteries off the charging pad. He draped one camera strap around her neck and let her put the battery in hers. They were as two kids in a candy store and practically raced downstairs and outside the living room glass door exit.

21

The Devil's Deal

Not too far away, Satan and Dalia appeared in the woods and started watching them. Dalia felt awful from having to teleport back here again. She wasn't sure how much longer what little power she had left would last.

"Ohhh, I feel like I am going to throw up. At least I no longer have to wear that stupid burka anymore. I *hate* that thing!"

Satan was instantly annoyed. "SHHH! You're going to give us away!" he hissed.

A white-faced Dalia stumbled over next to him and tried to focus on the blurry sight before her. "How does she have legs? Did she escape too? We can just go grab the vase now!"

She felt a little better with the hope that her power was in reach.

"No, you imbecile! She still has the cuffs on, and that boy now has a ring as well."

"He is *not* a boy. He is a *man*," she said dreamily, "and quite the *man* at that."

Dalia leered upon him, thinking she would keep him around when she got her powers back. Ogling Demetri made her feel much better.

"What does a ring have to do with anything? He is not getting. . . *wedded* to her, is he?" Dalia wanted him for herself.

Satan let out a low vicious chuckle. "That *ring*, Dalia, means that if she suffers, *he* suffers."

"Well, she is my competition, so we need to *break* that bond, so that he will not feel pain when I wish her to be tortured."

"Do what you wish with her . . . wait . . . ha-ha, wish . . . get it?" He turned only to meet her unamused face and just rolled his eyes.

"I am going to wish that she never existed! That way, I can be sure that he is *never* able to find her *or* fall for her ever again!"

Satan pondered the thought. "Yes . . . that is *very* thorough. I am *impressed*, Dalia."

She smiled boastfully to herself, satisfied, and then glued her eyes to Demetri again. Dalia painfully watched as Demetri showed Jenny a strange little black device and stood close to her.

Too close.

Dalia crossed her arms. "ugh! Why does he have to be so close to her?"

Her anger grew each time Demetri found another excuse to touch Jenny.

Envy caused her to shake. "That should be *me* in his arms!"

Satan selfishly enjoyed every bit of what was happening.

An eager smile plastered his lips. "Let's go offer them the deal."

Dalia's legs stood her up but then hesitated. "Why do you not just have *her* do it? She *already* has the power."

He rolled his eyes again in disgust that she had finally thought to ask that question. He offered her a smile of manipulation. "I want to work with *you*, Dalia," he lied. "I feel *badly* that you've been locked away for *so long*. I want to make it up to you."

She considered it and decided that was a good enough reason.

"All right then," she complained impatiently, "what are we waiting for?"

They came out from the left side of Demetri and Jenny. Dalia made sure to wag her hips for her lover boy.

Demetri's defensive instinct noticed movement on their left; his eyes darted to assess the possible danger. The genie girl and some old man were slithering toward them. He positioned himself between the threat and Jenny.

Demetri stood his ground. "Jen, she's back."

Jenny lifted her face from the camera's viewfinder to see what he was talking about.

Her eyes froze open.

She set the camera on the patio table next to them and stayed behind Demetri.

Satan sneered, "How *precious*, Demetri."

Demetri stared hard at the strange man before him. "How do you know my name?" He held Jenny behind him with both hands.

Dalia sauntered up close, still wagging her hips. "Demetri? What a *sexy* name. Hello again, you big hunk of man."

Satan rolled his eyes.

Dalia ran her left pointer finger along Demetri's chest; Jenny was still behind him. "Are you tired of the *dumb* blonde yet?" She shot Jenny a snarky look and then returned her gaze back to his eyes. "I will let you be my master too, darling."

"Stay away from him!" Jenny tried to position herself between him and Dalia now.

He didn't let her move. "Don't let it bother you, Jenny," he stated tensely.

POOF!

Dalia's advances no longer bothered Jenny.

Demetri needed the bit of jealousy and fear radiating from her to stop. He wanted to be on top of his game; distractions weren't helping.

He met Dalia's swooning eyes. "I will *never* be tired of Jenny. Get *back*!"

Her sexual wiles didn't affect him. Dalia swayed over to join Satan again. She hoped Demetri had noticed her walk this time.

Satan snuck an acrimonious look towards Jenny. "Jenny the Genie! That's very. . .*fitting* actually!"

Demetri stiffened. "What are you talking about, crazy old man?"

He sneered rancorously upon Demetri, "Oh, come now, let's not play the 'I don't know what you are talking about' game. I know all about how you two have almost sacrificed your pureness to each other. A perfect *waste* of my best devil! I know *everything* about you two! *Everything*."

He left the part out about them being two of the most difficult people that he had ever tried to influence.

"*Who* are you?" Demetri asked sternly; it was more of an order than a question.

"Ah tah tah, Demetri. You can't order *me* around like you can *Jenny*. I am the one in control here."

"You didn't answer my question."

Jenny's heart sped up as she clung tighter to Demetri. She sensed that the being in front of them wasn't all human; or maybe *too much* human.

An enormous feeling of caution overflowed her conscience as the man turned to steal into her eyes again.

It can't be . . . can it? she thought. She peeked out behind Demetri's arm a little bit more.

Satan spoke to Jenny, "I can tell you how to become normal again. It's *very* easy. It won't take long."

"Who *are* you?" Demetri demanded at the same time Jenny asked, "How?"

"OH . . . it seems we have a bit of *difference* in interest here." He grinned malevolently. "You, Demetri, can *command* her to do *whatever* you want, yet you let her walk around in *normal* clothes instead of the seductive genie wear, and you're currently *wasting* your time out *here* taking. . . *pictures!*" He had grown angrier.

Demetri didn't respond. He still had no clue how this annoying old man knew so much.

"C'mon, Demetri"—Satan stared directly into his soul—"I *know* how hard it's been for you to restrain yourself from wishing that she would . . ." He sent the rest of the message directly to Demetri's amygdala.

His eyes grew wide. "NO, I HAVEN'T!"

All Demetri's muscles tensed up. A couple of short, fast breaths escaped while trying to fight off the images Satan revealed to his brain. His head suddenly was thick with sensual grogginess; his eyelids became weaker. He fought through it and tried to think about something else.

Satan was nearly offended. "You can't *lie* to *me!*" He was satisfied though, with Demetri's reaction. He hoped that it be engraved enough that once they left, he would lose control and just end the purity already.

"Well," Satan continued, "she wants to be *normal*, but what does her *master* want? Remember, Demetri, what *you* say *goes*. Period."

Jenny wondered what Satan had done to Demetri's mind. She could sense that pain he was going through at the moment, and she knew that he was warding it off as best as he could. She focused and tried to push innocent feelings of love into him. Her mind thought back to his pictures and how happy he looked when she had shown her interest in them. Her next thought was how happy it had made her when he grabbed her hand the first time. His hand had been so warm and gentle, so loving and kind. Slowly, she felt Demetri's tenseness turn to tenderness.

His breath was steadied. He turned to smile at her thankfully.

Jenny reached up and rubbed a couple of beads of sweat off his forehead with her right hand and offered him a supportive smile. She kissed Demetri's shoulder and reassured her mind and heart, thinking, *He would never do anything to me that I didn't want him to.*

Unbeknownst to a confused and simmering Dalia, Satan was enjoying watching his creation work for the first time like it was supposed to, well, *kind* of. If only the two involved were more interested in something besides morals and boundaries. But he took what he could get for now.

Demetri could almost think normally again, thanks to Jenny. He stared daggers at the man in front of him.

"How did you *do* that to me?"

Satan answered vilely, "Oh Demetri, those are all the thoughts you've been fighting off. I just let them *out* to play."

Demetri examined him warily and decided to focus on Jenny. He weighed his two options. He wasn't for sure what *he* wanted, but if Jenny really wanted to be free, then he would help her get free.

Satan grinned, satisfied. "Good boy. I will show you how."

Demetri narrowed his eyes. "Did you just read my thoughts?"

"Yeah . . . he does that." Dalia was bored. *Why is he taking so long?* she wondered. *Just get this over with!*

Demetri scooted Jenny behind him completely again. "We aren't doing *anything* until you tell us *who* you are!"

"Very well . . . since you asked so *nicely*. I am the *devil*, Satan *himself.* You may take all the photos you wish, but if you want an autograph, well . . . for that, I'm sure we can come to an agreement or shall we say . . . a *deal*!" He brought his fingertips together and stood a little straighter.

Jenny froze. She couldn't believe that the devil was standing right in front of them. She was *really* scared now and closed her eyes to pray mentally.

Demetri raised an eyebrow. "Yeah . . . whatever. Just tell us *why* you're here."

"Well, I want to make a *deal.* You give me the vase, and I will show you how to set Jenny free."

Demetri tilted his head a tad. "The vase? You mean the *bottle*?"

Satan refrained from rolling his eyes again. "Whatever you want to call it. Yes!"

"We already *know* how. We just need a person to take her place."

Satan's eyes grew wide with evil happiness. "Well, what a *convenient* coincidence. I happened to have *just* what you *need*. *Dalia* here will take Jenny's place." He ushered toward her with his persuasive hands.

Jenny opened her eyes and found Dalia's. "How long were you in there? It was buried pretty well in the middle of nowhere."

Dalia's eyes didn't want to accept the invitation of Jenny's concerned ones, but she gave in against her will. "I lost *count*, easily six thousand years . . . or more." She crossed her arms defensively.

Jenny gasped, "That must have been terrible! Why in the *world* would you want to go back in?"

Dalia shot her a nefarious look. "I do not need *you* feeling sorry for *me*! You are just a *dumb* little girl who cannot give her master what he wants, or *needs!*"

Demetri fought to bottle his anger. "Jenny, *forget* what she just said."

POOF!

She forgot instantly and went back to a soft feeling of compassion.

He only commanded it because he felt how deeply Dalia's words hurt Jenny. He needed his head to be clear.

Demetri turned back to the "devil" who had just rolled his eyes at Demetri's protectiveness.

"Why do you want *her* in there instead of Jenny?" Demetri demanded.

"Questions, questions! Why all these questions? Do you want her to be *free* or *not*?" Satan suppressed how hideously overjoyed he was with the effectiveness of Demetri's command. Even if it had been to *help* someone.

Demetri eased up a little on his protective stance and turned to look at Jenny over his shoulder, "Jenny?"

She meekly lifted her head.

His gaze and voice softened, "Do you want to be free?"

Her eyes were worried and her mind unsure now given the new situation. No matter what she wanted, the bottle could *not* fall into Satan's claws. "I . . . I don't know honestly."

He kept his soft eyes but pushed his brows together, "Why are you torn between your freedom and the bottle?"

She couldn't lie. "I want to stay here with you," she admitted, "if I'm not a genie, I really *shouldn't* live here with you."

Satan grinned proudly. *It will be interesting to see how long it takes them to discover the **rest** of the bottle's secrets. I do **very** good work.*

Demetri turned to face her a little more, "Jenny, you *can* live here with me. I *want* you to stay." He placed his right arm around the small of her back.

Satan extended her a pretend caring look. "Yeah, Jenny," he said mockingly sweet, "living with a man out of wedlock *is* OK! You should really get to know the person and how they live *before* you marry anyways."

She ignored him and painfully looked up at Demetri, "If my parents did *anything*, they instilled the Bible's moral values in me. One of which includes *not* living with a man unless married to him. If I did that, *without* being your genie, I would be letting them down, and it would be letting God down too." She looked down, "I already feel like I've let them down by staying here last night. I can't. I'm sorry."

Satan exploded. "That's *enough*! Why does everyone always bring *Him*"— he shuddered—"into this?"

Demetri answered, "Who? God?"

The devil flinched and growled.

It was time to move things along. No matter how much he wanted to stay to see how his creation worked, he couldn't let Dalia get suspicious of his real plan.

He steamed, "Do we have a *deal* or not?"

Demetri understood what Jenny said. His parents instilled moral values into him too. If it wasn't for that, he wouldn't be the man he is today.

A strong but soft voice came to Demetri. "Don't."

Demetri was petrified with fear and comfort at the same time. He understood now that this man *was* Satan.

He looked into Jenny's eyes, "I'm sorry, Jenny. We will find another way." He turned back to Satan, "No! Jenny stays a genie!"

He instantly felt overly relieved. It must have come from Jenny.

"You *stupid boy*!" Satan raged for added effect.

He tried to stalk up to Jenny, but Demetri pulled her completely behind him again.

*I can't believe my evil creation has been **this corrupted**! It has been corrupted in a **good** way. YUCK!*

"LEAVE," Demetri said forcefully, "oh, and thanks for your temptations yesterday, but you failed!"

He shuddered with genuine malice, "AGH! I DO *NOT* FAIL! YOU TWO THINK YOU ARE ON *HIS* SIDE? WELL THEN, HOW ABOUT I HELP YOU FEEL A LITTLE *CLOSER* TO *HIM*? MARK MY WORDS, YOU TWO WILL BE SEPARATED AND FEEL AGONY LIKE YOU NEVER HAVE BEFORE! YOU. WILL. *SUFFER*!

With the last word lingering in the air, Dalia and Satan both vanished.

Demetri turned and pulled Jenny close with both arms until he knew for sure they were gone.

Their hearts beat rapidly as one.

Jenny clung to him; face buried in his chest.

Demetri tried to fathom everything she was feeling right now. There were so many emotions flooding in, not to mention his own. They kept swirling together like the smoke that comes from the bottle. He felt like he was going to pass out, but that might also have solely been because they had just seen the devil in disguise.

"We should go back inside now," he offered.

She couldn't move.

He gently lifted her up from her knees and lower back and carried her inside. He sat down on the living room couch with her in his lap.

Jenny kept her face buried in his chest.

Demetri held her tighter. *I won't let anyone or anything hurt you, Jenny,* he thought.

22

Plans

Satan and Dalia appeared inside Jenny's house.

"What is this place?" Dalia asked.

"This is Jenny's house. She is staying there with Demetri, and you need is a place to survive. You're *not* staying with me."

He concealed the fact that he didn't want her staying with Mimir either. Mimir was a good man and the last thing Satan needed right now was for Mimir to change Dalia.

She crossed her arms. "Why did you not just go grab the bottle?"

"It has to be Jenny's *choice* to give up her powers. You cannot force it or wish it. It would *not* have done any good. The rules are set, and they can't be altered because that kind of power doesn't exist anymore."

"Ugh. What is your plan now?"

She collapsed on the couch. A third teleportation left her feeling like she had been beaten up.

"This is *all* part of my plan!"

He went to the window and peeked carefully through a blind. Mr. Mitts was next door hunched over his soup, staring at Jenny's house intently.

Dalia curled up in pain. "To *fail* is part of your plan?" she croaked out.

Satan rest his annoyed eyes on her and drifted forward. "The *next* person who says I have *failed* will receive a personal *gift* of ten devils to . . ."

He paused and looked back through the blinds at nosy Mr. Mitts. He kept more thoughts to himself. *There's an idea. Leonard Mitts over there could be quite useful for my plan.*

Dalia grimaced from his simmering. "Calm down. It was not my intention to scratch your scales." She held her head and continued fighting off the throbbing pain.

"*Scales?* I do *not* have scales!" He looked at her in disgust. "Despite my disguise . . . and the usual heat . . . I have *flawless* skin." He looked proud.

"Sure," Dalia smirked, while taking in his imperfect old man body.

The painful laugh was worth it to see his annoyed reaction.

He glared at her. "I do *not* look *anything* like what the world depicts me as! I was . . . *His*"—he quivered—"*most* beautiful angel. I am the *most beautiful* thing you can imagine, girl! Not that I would encourage you to read the Bible or anything, but it does talk about *me* in *several* places. You can read *those* parts."

"The Bible? What is that?"

"Ugh!"

He eyed Jenny's small desk in the living room knowing that she kept exactly seven Bibles in it.

She just has to have an extra one around for anyone who needs one. Yuck! The revolting thought pranced around in his mind.

He opened the drawer and picked one up with two fingers in disgust and plopped it down beside her.

Satan crossed his arms. "And no. Touching it will *not* send me up in flames either!"

"I was not going to ask. I don't even know what it is." She managed to sit up.

"Here, Ezekiel 28. Read it. I am *not* going to."

She read the chapter, "This *English* is so confusing, but I understand. Hmmm, the most beautiful one, huh?"

"Yes." He gave her the look of a seasoned braggadocio.

Hmmm. Then you must be more handsome than Demetri, she thought as she tossed the Bible aside carelessly, slowly stood, and began advancing towards him.

Satan stood his ground and focused into her mind. "Don't even *think* about it!"

"Ugh, I *hate* that you can read my mind!" She crossed her arms too. "I am sure you have watched everyone consummate before. Do you *not* want to feel that way toward someone? Do you not want to be *loved*?"

"NO! There is only room for *me*! I am *not* going to be held down by *anyone*! Sex is *His* thing. *Lust* and *adultery* are mine. Go get married to another first and *then* we'll talk."

She was hopeful. "Really?"

He threw his hands up in aggravation. "NO! *I* corrupt people. People don't influence or corrupt *me*. I don't want *sex*! That is *His* gift for mankind between a man and a woman."

Dalia rolled her eyes. "You cannot enjoy power without having someone to share it with. It gets boring after a while. I *already* tried it. That is why I want to rule with Demetri." She sat back, pulled her legs to her chest, and rested her head on them. "And do not think that I did not notice your wording. It is not just about you. We are in this *together*."

He gazed down on her. "Of course."

Dalia changed the subject due to her migraine. "So . . . God is pretty powerful, right?"

Satan glared. "Are you *trying* to make me angry, because it's working!"

"I just meant can God take away this pain I feel? It is unbearable."

"NO! *I* will help you. No need to go to *Him*! Here . . . I extracted some of my old power away from Jenny when I got close."

"You did?" She shot up. "But how? You did not even touch her."

"I made that *bottle*, as they call it. I know *all* of its secrets. Now *stop* doubting me." He held his hand over hers and transferred some. "I am not giving it *all* to you, only enough to last you for a little while. I can't have you betraying me, can I?" He looked at her harshly.

"You would know if I had thoughts of betrayal. Thank you."

"I don't want your *thanks*! I want your *service*! I want your undying loyalty," he yelled.

Gradually the strength returned. "Fine," she stated casually.

He grinned, satisfied.

Dalia drew in a thankful breath. "Yes, that is *much* better! Where is a mirror? I want to see myself. Wait . . ." Her lids went heavy with satisfaction.

POOF!

A floor-length mirror appeared against Jenny's wall. She was glad to have such powers back. She spun around and judged herself. "Yes, I still look sexy."

"Yes . . . you do. Admiring yourself is *always* a good use of your time. All of your *good* qualities come from me."

She grinned admirably, still looking at herself. "Like what? My gorgeous coal-colored hair? My deep, engulfing eyes? My sexy body?"

His hand dramatically found its way to his forehead in disgust. "NO, you idiot! *I* didn't give you *those* things. But you can *enjoy* them because of me."

"What do you mean?" she asked, still admiring herself.

Satan lit up. "Vanity! Keep going. It disappoints . . . *Him*."

She obeyed. "You sure do spend a lot of time thinking about God for hating Him so much."

"I don't have to explain myself to you! I have told you too much already!" He appeared behind her.

Dalia kept admiring herself. "If we are going to be in this together, I want to—"

"UGH! FINE! STOP TALKING ALREADY! Revenge, Dalia! It's simple! You should know *all* about that; or have all those thousands of years made you . . . *soft*?"

"No! I am as evil as ever! Being trapped for that long makes you bitter. Although I do have to say that most of the bitterness *was* toward *you* for trapping me."

She pried her eyes away from her reflection long enough to view his reaction. He was only a foot away; she moved closer.

He disappeared and reappeared by the living room entrance with his arms crossed. "Nice try . . . and I have told you, *I* was not the one who wished you to be banished."

"I know. So, what now?"

He drifted over to the blinds and carefully peeked through again. "Come here, Dalia. Slowly now so he doesn't notice. I will show you what I'm best at."

She grinned meanly and did as she was told.

Satan sent his devils to conspire with the existing ones in the unsuspecting weaselly mind next door. They observed unnoticed as Mr. Mitts became restless and began to pace. Satan used the devils to reveal to Mitts about the new and improved Jenny. He threw in that Demetri was controlling her against her will. Mitts steamed, along with his soup, in anger and waited impatiently for her return. He simmered together a plan that would remove Demetri from the picture. But the best part? He would finally get Jenny for himself.

Satan mentally approved of his plan and turned to Dalia. "Now . . . we wait."

She crossed her arms. "I thought you said that being patient brought you closer to God or something like that?"

He shot her a sly look. "I do *evil* things while *I* wait. There are billions of souls on this earth to corrupt and deceive, Dalia. I'm constantly busy."

23

Secret's Out

Jenny's teary eyes met Demetri's. "That was Satan. He's going to *separate* us! You know how it feels when we are apart!"

She was still in his arms. He was fighting to win the battle over her overpowering emotions and the raunchy thoughts that Satan had embedded into his brain.

"Jenny, we'll be careful, and I'll be *right* next to you every second of the day and night."

His words comforted her. She stayed in his arms for a while.

He pressed his lips into her forehead for a long second. Suddenly, someone burst the front door open.

Demetri stood and had Jenny behind him again before the door even finished opening.

"Demetri! Is it true?" an excited voice asked.

Jenny poked her head around Demetri. A man she didn't recognize was shutting the front door behind him. He was a little taller than Jenny and had bright blue eyes. His skin was an even mix of coal and mahogany. His hair was curled up little balls that lined his head strategically in a pattern. He wore a big smile, a blue shirt, and jeans with a belt. His wore slick-looking black work shoes.

Demetri was too relieved to be upset. "Lewis! Dude . . . at least *knock*, will you?"

"*Why?* I *always* come in like that. Are you in the mi'l of some—?" He noticed Jenny peeking out from behind Demetri. "Oh, ho ho, I can see that you *are*. *Dude*, is she *hidin'* behind you? Man, *how* have you already got another one? You have *all* the luck! Share some wif ya, bro, no?"

He talked fast, but Jenny understood every word. She smiled, relieved.

Demetri tilted his head to the side a bit to look at Jenny. "Jenny, this is Lewis. He is harmless . . . *most* of the time." He crossed his arms and raised an eyebrow at Lewis.

"Aw, man, don't give her the wrong idea about me. I'm Lewis." He gifted her a big smile with his face turned flirtatiously away a little. "It's nice to meet ya." He started across the room towards Jenny to shake her hand. "Man, you must be pretty special for Demetri to break up with Mel."

Jenny slowly came out from behind Demetri and reached out to shake his hand. She moved her hair behind her left ear and gave him a kind smile.

Lewis's feet stopped in their tracks and gave her a once . . . make that a *twice* over. Her red dress made her cheeks glow pink, or maybe she was nervous. Lewis couldn't tell, but he loved the extra color.

"Demetri! *Man*, where did you find *this* one? I been looking for *you* for a *long* time, girl."

Jenny's cheeks blushed brighter, and her shy smile doubled.

His eyes never left her face as he closed up the space between them to shake her hand.

The next words were for Demetri. "Thanks, man, for findin' her for me. *You* are the *best*. Remind me to get you something *good* for Christmas this year, OK?" He hadn't let go of her hand yet from shaking it and started walking back toward the door with her.

Demetri already had her other hand, and she was pulled between them for a moment.

Lewis looked back. "Aw, c'mon, man, not fair! Let me have this one. If you found her in less than one day, I'm sure you can go out and find another girl."

Demetri pulled an amused Jenny to his side and placed both arms around her. "Sorry, Lewis." He smiled. "*This* one is mine."

Lewis typically pulled something like this.

Jenny glanced up at Demetri and smiled.

Lewis fixed his eyes on Jenny again. With a wrinkled face and one eyebrow raised, he asked, "Are you sure you want to be with *him*? I can tell you some stories to make you change yo mind."

"Hi, Lewis, it's nice to meet you," she finally said.

"Hi Jen-Jen, I'm just playing wif you by the way." He smiled and gave her the gun hands to top it all off with.

Jenny laughed again.

"So, dude, it's true then, huh? You broke up with Mel. Wow, you guys dated for like eva, man. Like almost five months, was it?"

Five months was a long time for Lewis, who usually only dated the same girl for a couple of days.

"So anyways, I don't want to take up any more of yo time 'cause I can see y'all *busy*, but she asked me if I wanted to go out on a date with her, and I was like, girl, you datin' my man. I ain't gonna do that to him. Then she said that you guys split. So I came to see for myself before I made any promises, and I can see it's true, so if it's all right—"

Demetri interrupted him, "Dude, you already know what you're getting yourself into. If you really want her, she's yours. But look, *only* if you don't tell her about Jenny, OK?"

"What? Why man? You don't want her to know that you found someone already? I can understand that."

"Jenny and Mel have a past, and I don't want to bring it back up so soon. Just give it some time. You can keep it a secret, right?"

"Yeah, man, no problem here. I won't tell."

Demetri sighed doubtfully.

If it came to a girl, Lewis never stopped talking. He knew that Lewis, despite good intentions, would give it away.

"Look, Lewis, this is more serious than you think. If you wanna go out with Mel, go for it. But make your first date for at least a week out, OK? And don't spill the beans about Jenny *before* then *or* after if you can help yourself, all right?"

"Ah, man, really? Imma have tuh cancel my date tonight."

"Lewis!"

"Oh, D., I knew you would be OK with it. Don't worry, I'll call her and move it back. Yeah, you know better than anyone how I get with girls. I come out and tell them everything, don't I?" He tilted his head and looked away. "All right, a week out, and I promise I'll try my *best* to not say anything after that too, OK?"

"Great! Thanks, Lewis. You're welcome to stay. I'm sure Jenny would like to get to know my best friend."

Her feelings spoke to Demetri for her.

Lewis twisted his mouth into a large smile. "Have you guys had lunch yet?"

"No, what time is it?" Demetri asked.

"It's 1:30. Let's just eat here. I brought green bean casserole. It was a preemptive thank-you gift for letting me go out with Mel." He smiled a cool smile at Demetri.

"Of *course*, you did." Demetri rolled his eyes.

He and Lewis didn't have a lot in common, but their opposites-attract personalities made Lewis the best friend that Demetri ever had. It was exactly like Lewis to prepare for every situation, no matter how small, which was one of the best qualities that Demetri thought that Lewis had, so he couldn't bring himself to be upset about it.

"I have some steaks that are thawed. It won't take long to fix them up. Meanwhile, you can tell Jenny all the embarrassing stories you want about me."

"Girl, you *hear* that? He just gave me permission to *embarrass* him. That has *never* happened before. He must *really* like you." He put his arm around Jenny and escorted her to a barstool so they both could watch Demetri cook.

"How do you figure?" Jenny wondered.

"Usually, my man over here don't want no one to know nothing about him, so the fact that he wants me to tell ya 'bout our times together and get to know *me*, his *best* bro, means he's *definitely* into you. It's like meeting the parents, but *more* important. You feel me?"

Jenny raised one eyebrow at him and gave a cool smile. "Yeah, I feel ya, bro," she answered calmly.

Lewis's eyes popped. "BRO! Are you *sure* you don't want to take Mel back and *I'll* just have Jenny here?"

"I'm *sure*, Lewis," Demetri called over his shoulder from the stove top.

"Dude, I ain't *never* had a girl answer me back like that . . . I like it." He smiled at her.

Jenny gave a small laugh. "Lewis, how long have you known Demetri?"

She positioned her right elbow onto the counter and her hand on the side of her head comfortably.

"Girl, I can tell you *everything* about him! We grew up together. We even went to the same school."

He put *his* elbow on the counter and put his left hand on his head.

Jenny felt very comfortable around Lewis. She felt like she could say anything, and he would think it was cool or funny.

She dove right in. "Awesome, sooo . . . who was his first crush?"

A big smile appeared on his face. He gazed off into the distance over Jenny's head for a moment as if he could see back to the past.

"Maddie West, sixth grade," he answered.

Jenny felt like he had a very detailed account of everything memorable about him and Demetri by the way he answered so quickly.

Lewis continued. "He just liked her because she had the 'most piercing blue eyes you have ever seen.'" He threw his eyes over at Demetri. "Then he actually dated her in high school a little bit."

Demetri revealed a small thoughtful smile. "Yeah, and then again a couple of years ago."

"Oh yeah, that's right!"

Jenny didn't want Demetri to know that had bothered her. She tried to conceal the feelings in an imaginary bubble.

Lewis returned his eyes to a slightly troubled-looking Jenny and decided to change the subject.

"Yo man ova here matured early. He was always the *classy* one that held the doors open for everyone. You know that kid. Every school has one. *I*, on the other hand, was the *cool* kid. I threw paper airplanes into the trash cans while the teacher was teachin' on the board."

Jenny's troubled expression transformed into an amused smile; she forgot about Maddie.

Lewis understood that he hit the jackpot and continued. "I also skipped class sometimes to go play spy. The principal, Mr. Ross, was the evil mastermind and all the teachers were his brainwashed slaves. Those were fun times. Another thing I used to—"

Demetri interrupted him, "Lewis, I thought you were supposed to be telling Jenny about me."

"Hey, bro, you said I need to stay so she can get to know *me*. Now stop yo interruptin'. If you get to keep her, at least let *me* have a few minutes wif her." He turned back to Jenny and continued. "Yeah, we became friends because he stood up for me in first grade and convinced the teacher that I just needed a good friend, and *then* I would behave." Lewis laughed. "I don't know how he did it, but she let me off the hook, and we've been friends eva since. He has bailed me out of a *few* situations." Lewis laughed. "Which is totally ironic."

Jenny was about to ask how come but Demetri spoke first.

"Yeah, the problem with Lewis is that he is too smart for his own good."

Lewis boasted an accomplished expression. "Yeah, girl, you lookin' at straight As right here."

Demetri rolled his eyes. "I don't know how he managed it with as much skipping and partying as he did."

"I was just lucky. But apparently, my luck has run out because I ain't hitched yet, and I'm almost twenty-eight. All I want is a girl I can connect wif, ya know? Do you and D. connect?"

Jenny smiled at him. *You have no idea,* she thought. "Yes, Lewis, we connected from the first moment we saw each other." Between Demetri's comfort and Lewis's exciting personality, she had completely forgotten about Satan's appearance. She felt great.

The appetizing scent of steak drifted over to Lewis. "Well, I can smell that those steaks are almost done, so imma go get my casserole. Hey, did he tell you that I'm a better cook than he is?"

Jenny's eyes were full of surprise. "*If* that's true, then your casserole will be the *best* thing I have ever tasted!"

Lewis gave her a pretend serious look. "All right, you don't let him talk about me while I'm gone, OK, Jenny?"

She laughed. "OK, Lewis. Nothing bad or I'll stick up for ya. Promise."

He shook his head, gave her another smile, and said, "My *girl,*" and then went to fetch his casserole.

Demetri leaned over the counter on his elbows across from Jenny, "I think his *casserole* is better than mine, but *my* steak is better."

"Ah-uh. Careful. I promised him *no* bad talk."

She got up and helped Demetri set the table.

"I really like him, Demetri. He's a great friend. I can tell."

"I am glad you like him. He really likes you too, probably a little too much. I have never seen him persist with a girl like this. Let's just say if *I* hadn't asked you out yesterday, he would have dragged you out of the door by now to go on a date with him."

Jenny laughed. "I believe it." She stopped for a moment and touched her body to his. "Don't worry, Demetri, I love *you.* But he *is* a great person to be around. I feel like I can tell him *anything,* and he would respect it and not think of me any differently."

Demetri furrowed both his brows. Jenny's voice echoed gently in his mind. It sounded angelic as if he was in a dream. He knew Jenny felt uncomfortable enough with him being able to tell exactly how she feels, but reading her mind? He thought he had imagined it yesterday.

Oh no, he thought.

He heard everything she said in her head clearly.

"Jenny, we are *not* telling him . . . not yet. Trust me. Let's wait until he has moved on from Mel. It shouldn't be more than a couple of days. *Then* maybe we will tell him."

Jenny wondered how he knew what she was going to ask, but didn't have time to ask.

Lewis had just shut the door. "Tell me what?"

She thought fast. "Tell you that we are going on a picture-taking quest later tomorrow. You can join us if you want."

"Uh, yeeaah . . . no, thanks. Wow, D., did you really find one that likes pictures as much as you?"

Jenny's thoughts had ceased from echoing around in Demetri's head.

Good, he thought. *Maybe it won't happen again.* He answered Lewis, "I don't know if she likes them as much as *I* do, but she is *definitely* interested."

"Wow, you might really be the *one* for him. I *hope* you are. I feel sorry for the guy. All he talks about is finding the 'one'. I always tell him that if he finds a girl—"

Jenny finished for him, "That is interested in photography, then she is going to be the *one.*"

"Oh, so he told you about me, huh?" Lewis said with a smile, "good."

He sat his casserole on the breakfast table.

"He also told me that you owe him twenty bucks for that bet."

"Aw, man, I was hopin' he wouldn't remember. All right here, a bet is a bet." He pulled his wallet out and handed Demetri a twenty.

"Thanks, Lewis. Nice doing business with you." Demetri smiled at him, took the money, and patted a playfully annoyed Lewis on the back.

Lewis noticed the table was already set. "Man, you guys work fast."

Jenny smiled at him.

He furrowed his brows and studied her for a moment. "How old are you, Jenny, if you don't mind me asking?"

Jenny bit her lip nervously and then answered, "I'm almost twenty-one."

Demetri pulled out a chair for her across from Lewis, and she sat.

"*Woah,* girl, you young to be datin' a twenty-seven-year-old. In two weeks, D. will be twenty-eight." He held up his hand toward Demetri for a high-five. "My man!"

Demetri took part in his high-five offer and rolled his eyes. "It's not *that* much younger, Lewis. I know couples who are farther apart."

"No, man, it's *cool*. Love is love. I hope *I* can find someone someday. I don't care how old she is. I just want real love, man. Hey, wasn't Mel also really young?"

Jenny answered him, "Yes, she's little more than a year older than me actually. Her parents put her in kindergarten a year late."

Lewis shook his head at Demetri in pretend jealously. "How do you keep findin' all these young girls, D.?"

Demetri just grinned and sat next to Jenny. He scooted his chair as close as he could.

Lewis raised an eyebrow at them. "All right, y'all, we are tryin' to eat here. No more makin' goo-goo eyes at each other."

Demetri rubbed his neck and looked back at Lewis.

Jenny looked down, embarrassed too. "All right, let's pray so I can judge both of y'alls cookin', OK?"

Lewis smiled again. "OK, but hey, be honest now. Don't go easy on me just 'cause I'm cute." He winked at her.

She laughed and shook her head, "All right, Lewis, I promise."

Demetri led a prayer out loud, and they all said "Amen."

Lewis calmed down a little and sighed. "I'm sorry, Jenny. I'm not tryin' to take you away from Demetri. You know that was all just me playin' with him, right?"

"Yeah, I know, Lewis. It's flattering." She gave him a reassuring smile.

"Good. It's just. . . I pray and pray for God to bring a girl in my life so I can settle down and have a family. I'm tired of waiting. I've had my fun. I've got a car, a steady job, and an apartment. I just need me a woman and some kids now. I'm getting old."

"Hey! We are the same age, Lewis. We aren't *old*."

Jenny laughed. She felt bad for Lewis and tried to think of any single women for him. Cali had been with Stefan for nearly a month, and it seemed to be going well. No one else came to mind.

She tasted Lewis's casserole first. "Mmmm, wow. This is *great*! Lewis, your casserole is exceptional!"

He flipped his wrist at her dramatically. "Aw, shucks, girl. You makin' me blush."

Demetri's steak was next. "Wow, Demetri, this steak is *perfect*. It's just the way I like it, not too chewy but not too hard. And what did you use to season it? I can't pick it out."

"Another secret ingredient." He winked at her. "I'm glad you like it."

"Thank you, both. This is so great. If you come over again, Lewis, you have to cook something because my taste buds wouldn't be forgiving if you skipped out on them."

"A'ight, will do. Thanks."

The rest of their dinner was filled with good laughs. Lewis teased Demetri, and Demetri let him have his fun. Jenny loved watching them. They had a wonderful friendship. After they were finished, Jenny started cleaning up.

"You guys cooked. I clean, OK?" She eyed Demetri specifically.

"Um . . . OK, Jen." He smiled back politely. "Thanks."

Lewis smiled at her too. "Yeah, thanks, Jen."

Demetri quickly captured Lewis's eyes. "Only I call her Jen, Lewis."

He tilted his head a little and complained. "What? Why? That ain't no fair."

Demetri's voice was firm. "Because I said, OK?"

"Well, why don't we ask her, huh?" Lewis gave him a competitive smile.

"All right, you two . . ." She looked softly at Demetri. "I don't care if he calls me Jen, Demetri, but if it bothers you, then he can call me something else."

Demetri sighed and hesitated. "Oh . . . go ahead, Lewis. I'm sorry, I'm just—"

"Dude, no need to explain yo self. You just being protective. Nothing wrong wif that. I will try to call her Jenny as much as I can help myself, OK?"

Demetri punched Lewis's shoulder gently. "Thanks, man."

"Hey, D., what happened wif you and Mel anyways? I thought things were OK again. Is it OK with you, Jenny, that we talk about this? I just wanna know what I'm gettin' myself into."

"Yes, Lewis, of course. You deserve to know everything about Mel."

Jenny really didn't want someone as nice as Lewis to date Mel. If they got together, then she would have to see a lot of Mel again. According to Demetri though, she had changed, so maybe it wouldn't be so bad if Lewis ended up dating her for a while. Demetri told him all about Mel and what had happened, and Lewis took it all in.

"I'll give it a shot with her," Lewis decided.

They talked for a while longer, and pretty soon, Lewis had to go.

Demetri snapped his fingers. "Oh wait! Let me run upstairs and grab the bracelet that Mel left in my equipment room. She always left them everywhere. You can give it to her, Lewis. I'm sure you will see her before I do."

"I can get it for you, Demetri." Jenny started to head for the stairs.

He smiled. "No, you stay put here with Lewis. You're both guests. I'll get it."

"Yes, master." Jenny quickly put her hand over her mouth. *Oops!* she thought.

Demetri turned back around for a moment with wide eyes.

Lewis's eyes were equally as wide. "WOAH, MAN! I can *definitely* see why you chose *her* over Mel. You couldn't get Mel to say that if you *paid* her! *My man!*" He held up his hand for another high-five.

Demetri nervously gave him a high-five. "Heh . . . I'll, uh, be right back."

He practically ran upstairs.

Jenny held her right arm, embarrassed, and looked at Lewis. She couldn't move and she wasn't for sure if Demetri realized it or not.

"Jeez, girl, all right, you comin' wif me. Give me *one* chance and then you can pick between me and him, OK?" Lewis grabbed her left hand and jokingly tried to pull her towards the door with him.

She didn't budge.

"Wow, you're strong, girl! Don't worry, I was only kiddin' again . . . mostly."

Jenny's lips pursed into a worried smile, hoping he wouldn't get suspicious that she couldn't move. Demetri sprinted back downstairs.

"Here, Lewis. She really has too many bracelets. Hopefully, I don't find anymore. I think she leaves them laying around on purpose." He rolled his eyes.

"A'ight, thanks, man. I'll see you later. Bye, Jenny. It was great meeting you. Take care of my man here, OK?"

"I promise, Lewis, and it was great meeting you." She smiled at him, still stuck.

Demetri took her hand and offered an apologetic smile. She looked gently up at him, as he led her to the door. Jenny was able to give Lewis a side hug.

"You got yo self a good one, D., I'll see you later, bro."

Demetri gave him their special bro hug, where they bumped chests and pat each other on the back three times.

He met Lewis's eyes again. "Remember what I said about waiting at least until after next week, OK?"

"Yes, Sergeant, sir." He saluted Demetri and winked at Jenny.

Demetri rolled his eyes again and saluted him out the door.

24

Master

Demetri changed his passcode so that Mel wouldn't be able to burst in here for whatever reason like Lewis had. He would tell Lewis the change in a week or so. The passcode automatically applied to all entrances.

He felt a familiar emotion radiate from Jenny and turned around to meet her eyes to see if it would increase. It did.

Demetri slowly walked toward her and scooped her up in his arms. "C'mon, Jenny, you can't be teasing me like that."

Jenny smiled at him angelically. "What do you mean?"

He rest his forehead on hers. "I can feel your *desire*, Jen. It's almost unbearable."

Her heart ached. "I just . . ." She closed her eyes, foreheads still touching.

"What is it?" He closed his eyes too and took her to the couch and sat with her in his lap like earlier.

"Look, Demetri, I don't know if we're supposed to be together. I'm not sure if our attraction is just because of this genie stuff, and I know I'm still young, but the way you make me feel is unlike *anything* I've *ever* felt before. I didn't know it could *exist*."

Her eyes smiled heavily, and she bit her bottom lip attractively. Jenny proceeded to get up off his lap and face him. She slowly slid her tight dress up to miniskirt height.

Demetri stared at her legs, which he hadn't got a good look at yet.

He tried to block everything out, and he might have succeeded had Satan not engraved erotic scenes of Jenny in his mind every time he closed his eyes. Now that Lewis was gone, he couldn't fight it.

He gave a quick prayer. *Dear Father, please help me. Amen.*

Demetri's heart rate increased dramatically, his head filled with her eagerness, his mouth dried with her thirst, his heart was overcome with her yearning, his stomach consumed with her appetite. His whole body fought against the battle of her thoughts but inevitably lost the war.

Jenny locked eyes with him and moved one knee to the right side of his lap and then her other to the left side in a straddling position. Both of her hands eased themselves to either side of his neck and moved their way up until they reached his face. She brought her face to his and locked their perfectly fitting lips together. Her hands then found her their way through his hair.

His arms quickly found their way around her body. He ran his hands along either side of her waist, slid them around her back, and pressed her to him as tightly as he could without hurting her.

Jenny's desire overwhelmed him completely, and he couldn't think straight anymore. Among his own thoughts, Satan's, and Jenny's, there was no chance.

Oh man! he managed to think, still kissing her.

He explored her thighs hungrily. They were so soft. He grabbed one of her ankles and moved it underneath his leg and grabbed the other one and did the same so that she would be trapped.

Jenny's entire insides felt like a gymnastics face-off.

"Yes, trap me."

She leaned her head back for air. Demetri drunkenly turned to her neck, grabbed the back of it, came forward, and gently bit it.

"Mmmm." She closed her eyes and bit her lip in sweet pleasure.

So she likes it a little rough? Good.

He bit again in a different spot, breathed hard, and held her tighter.

Her genie instincts came out without a choice. "Mmmm, yes, master."

It felt like such a natural thing to say to him now. It didn't even bother her anymore.

Yes, he thought.

Demetri kissed her lips now and stood. He carried her to his bed with his eyes still closed and trapped her there with his body. He bit her lip again the way she liked it and then kissed her roughly all over her neck.

Jenny's desire increased again.

Demetri's shirt disappeared. He didn't even flinch from Jenny's apparent wish.

Her dress disappeared too, and he commenced gently biting her everywhere he could—her stomach, her sides, her collarbone, her arms, her neck again, and then back up to her lip. He stopped for a moment to look at her body. It hadn't been this exposed before. He was so hard, and he wanted her so badly. He leered into her amenable, steamy blue eyes and began sliding his hand around her back to unclip her bra.

His cell phone rang.

He let it ring and continued.

It started to ring again.

"Agh!" He searched helplessly into Jenny's eyes and sighed. "I should get that." He kissed her lips. "Don't move." Then he got up to answer his cell on his desk. "What's up, John?"

He headed toward his bedroom window so he could *try* to think clearly. He furrowed his brows and rubbed his eyes at the same time with one hand. "I won't be able to do that today. I can do Monday, late afternoon."

Jenny lay there in Demetri's amazingly comfortable bed, trying to catch her breath. She couldn't even turn her head to look at Demetri. She was able to start thinking a little clearer.

What am I doing? I don't know what came over me. I can't believe I did this to him again!

She sighed and thought of her dress being back on.

Demetri hung up his phone, plopped it on the couch and turned back around. "No, no, no, no, NO!"

He ran over to the bed and positioned his body over hers. She lay there completely still and clothed.

Demetri sighed. "You can move, Jen," he mumbled.

She couldn't meet his disappointed eye, "I'm so *sorry*, Demetri. I couldn't help myself. It just . . . I don't *know* . . . That was *all* I could think about."

He lay down too and shifted onto his elbow beside her, "Jen, if I hadn't had gotten that phone call, we would have seen how strong wishes can be."

She knew what he was talking about, "Demetri, I . . ."

"It's OK," he looked down. "I guess . . . I'm glad I got the call." He put his hand on the right side of her face. "Jenny, I *want* you. My whole body yearns for yours," he admitted, the expression on his face painful.

She closed her eyes and leaned into his hand. "I want you too, master."

Again, it just came out naturally.

Demetri was used to it now and had accepted that he would just have to be OK with it.

He shut his eyes and took a breath in. "Jen, we *can't* let ourselves get into a position like this again."

She lightly ran her fingers through his hair. "But your wish will protect us."

He looked up at her. "Jen, my wish *might* protect us, but I'm not even 100 percent sure that it will, and if we keep only going halfway, I might do something that . . . I don't want you to see."

She looked at him, concerned now. "Like what?"

He didn't want to say it out loud. "Jenny, you drive me *crazy*."

Her eyes fell.

Demetri felt her sadness.

"No, Jen, I mean . . . *sexually*."

He felt her relief, and understanding maybe?

"I know . . . I'm sorry," she offered, "but I just couldn't help myself. He was here for almost three hours. I *had* to have you hold me."

"I know. I felt that way too. This is just going to take some time to get used to it. I'm sure in the future, we'll learn to control it better," he held her cheek, "we can't be doing this in public after all, and with the way you make me feel, Jen, I don't care who watches." He grinned at her playfully, trying to lighten the mood.

"Me either. It's a little scary if you think about it. We should practice," she returned the playful look.

"*Practice?*" He pulled his head back a little, "Jenny, if we practice trying to *not* rip each other's clothes off or make them disappear—" He gave her a look.

Jenny smiled a small "Oops" smile and sunk down a little.

"Yeah, I noticed, Missy, and you're in trouble," he smiled at her.

She gave him a meek expression and put both hands behind her back, which made her chest stick out some.

Too bad I can't punish her like I'd like to, he thought while staring at her chest. He continued, "—then I *would* lose it. We just have to try to control this *before* it gets to the point of no return, OK?"

"OK," she said, her chest still eye level with his face.

"Geez, Jen, I can't even have a serious conversation with you. Agh!"

He put both hands behind his head and looked up.

"What's wrong?" She brought her hands back to her sides.

"I just . . . can't even *look* at you without getting excited. Maybe you should put a different dress on." His face wore an agonized expression.

Jenny held his face for a moment, "Like this one?"

POOF!

He looked up, not in the least bit upset that she used her power.

She sat on her calves, facing him. This dress was a low-cut tight black one with a pencil-type skirt. It made her face look attractively pale and made her eyes grayer.

He studied her now gray eyes. They lured you in and appeared to be full of secrets.

"Absolutely not!"

If anyone else saw them, he was sure they wouldn't be able to look away.

POOF!

This one was dark blue with a beaded two-inch Egyptian-style collar that connected to the dress at the top and back and covered everything save for a split where her cleavage was. Under her breasts were a matching beaded band that wrapped around her body. The rest hung loosely. Her face was full of color and her eyes overly noticeable. They were now a rich sapphire blue, and her hair seemed lighter. She looked like she was ready to strut down the catwalk.

"Um, no." He thought to himself, *It's too fancy, and she still looks too attractive.*

She sighed.

He met her shy eyes with a soft smile. "Try something not as tight, and covering and . . . purple."

It was the first color that popped into his mind; hopefully, it wouldn't make her look extra noticeable.

Jenny thought for a moment. "How about this one?"

She poofed a third dress.

It was royal purple, covered her chest, and had cupped sleeves. It had a silver link at the collarbone that connected the tops of the dress. The silver matched her cuffs. The middle shaped her body but didn't cling to it. The bottom was flowy and dropped past her knees. He studied her face last. Nothing stood out too much. Modest but still beautiful.

He sighed a breath of relief. "Perfect. You still look great, but now you are *bearably* sexy."

Jenny smiled. "Third time's a charm."

25

Interrogation No. 3

Demetri smiled too and peered back up at her. "All right, I'm sure it's almost five, and I wouldn't be surprised if Mr. and Mrs. Conroy showed up early."

"Me neither. Let's get started. After all, we have a competition to start." She smiled playfully at him.

Demetri fetched her an apron to protect her dress. He tied it in the back for her. "I am going to go put something nicer on as well."

"All right. I'll get the ingredients we need."

"OK, be right back."

Jenny found the ingredients first and then located all the pans they would need. It was so awesome to be able to work in a kitchen this size. The kitchen was organized as parallel lines, one being a massive counter in the middle with a raised bar for the whole length of it to seat six people. If you were sitting at it, the fridge was to the left against the wall, to the right of that was counter space and then the oven, and then more counter and cabinets all the way to the wall. The round breakfast table was to the right and behind you a little with a large window to see part of the driveway and garage. The dining table was on the left side of the kitchen, and you had to pass the front door to get to it. You could see the amazing living room view from the large floor-to-ceiling windows.

We will get to watch the pretty sky as the sun sets tonight, she thought. *As long as everyone is getting along.* Suddenly, she felt extremely nervous.

Demetri came quietly up behind her and placed his hands around her eyes. "You ready to see what *I'm* wearing?"

He felt very nervous asking her, and he wondered if it was his emotions, or hers, or both maybe?

She turned around to face him. Her head came forward a little in surprise. She scanned him over a few times.

"Demetri, you look . . ."

He waited for an answer. He felt like he was going to start sweating if she didn't say something soon. *I have never cared about what my girlfriends have thought of my attire in the past. This has to be her nervousness.*

"I didn't know it was possible for you to look more *handsome* than the first time I saw you." Her cheeks burned red as she shied away.

He felt relieved and tried pushing away her girly emotions so that his own cheeks wouldn't turn red.

Demetri wore a black dinner jacket, matching slacks, and a tie decorated with a little royal purple. His cufflinks were silver, and they matched his ring and her cuffs.

She grabbed him an apron now and tied it around him.

He smiled. "Yeah, I don't wear these in front of Lewis. He makes fun of me so much that I can't even concentrate on cooking.

Jenny laughed. "Lewis. What a character. He is kind of goofy but smart too, a lot like Cali actually."

Demetri smiled.

She returned his smile. "All right, let's get started. I've already gotten everything we need."

He watched her for a moment. He realized that no one had ever helped him cook in his kitchen before, not even his mom or Lewis. He didn't know how to feel about it.

Jenny headed over to the stove and pulled out a drawer from the tall pantry cupboard with an electric can opener on it to open the cans. She opened all the cans of beans and chilies and slid the drawer back in and closed the cupboard.

She hadn't realized that her hand had almost knocked over an open can. Demetri's eyes gradually widened as he realized just how hard this would be for him.

Jenny poured all the cans in the pot at once and then started slicing the kielbasa.

Even if it was precooked meat, that was a huge no-no in his eyes.

"Aren't you going to get started?" Jenny asked without looking over at him.

It was a good thing she didn't because the expression on his face was haunting as he watched her almost bump the hot pot with her elbow as she straightened her apron.

"Um . . . yes," he answered. *This is nerve-racking. She has almost burned herself, completely violated one of the most important rules in cooking, and nearly caused the domino effect with the cans all in less than five minutes.*

Demetri sighed and decided to just power through it. Without Jenny knowing, he saved her from ruining her dress three times, burning herself twice, and causing a complete disaster once.

Jenny's shy expressions from meeting his eyes and the happy feelings from being with him that radiated from her kept Demetri calm.

Her happiness made all the stress worth it.

They each made a batch and would have Mr. and Mrs. Conroy be the judges.

The doorbell rang.

Demetri was right; they did show up early. Twenty minutes early. The food was already finished, but they still had to set the table.

Jenny stopped in her tracks and suddenly Demetri felt nervousness wash over him again.

He came up behind her. "Hey, don't worry."

He slid his hands around her waist and touched his body against the back of hers. Her head fogged up for a moment; she closed her eyes.

Demetri laughed. "Now I'm telling *you* not to worry, but seriously, if you get nervous, it will make *me* more nervous than I already am. Then I may say something ridiculous." He kissed the back of her head and went to go open the door.

Jenny smiled as best as she could and took a few breaths in.

I really want them to like Demetri.

He smiled to himself and then opened the door to reveal a beautiful smiling middle-aged woman with shoulder-length brown hair and big green eyes. She wore a long black evening dress with a white wrap. Next to her was a stiff and expressionless Mr. Conroy, who wore a matching black suit like Demetri but with a red tie that matched Mrs. Conroy's accent pieces.

Mrs. Conroy took a good look at Demetri. Her voice was weathered but sweet. "You must be Demetri! It is so nice to meet you!" Her eyes smiled up at him.

The sound of her voice caused him to grin from ear to ear.

"Good evening, Mr. and Mrs. Conroy! Please come in!" He stood back and held the door open for them while they stepped inside, "It's nice to meet you too, Mrs. Conroy."

A warm smile radiated from her as she walked in.

"Wow," Mrs. Conroy said, "Demetri, I think you have the most beautiful place I have ever seen!"

Mr. Conroy went straight up to Jenny and hugged her.

So far so good, Demetri thought. "Thank you, Mrs. Conroy. May I take your wrap?"

"Why, yes, thank you, and please call me Carrie." She gave him another big smile and let him help her slide her wrap off.

"Carrie it is then." He hung it by the door. *At least Carrie seems to like me.*

Mr. Conroy turned his head back over to them. *I can't believe Carrie has already given him first-name privileges.* He turned to Jenny again and gave her another hug, just to be safe.

She hugged him back warmly. "Kurtis, I'm fine, *really*."

He whispered to her, "Do you still think we should partner with him because we can call this *whole* evening off if we need to?"

Jenny's eyes burst open. "Everything is still great!"

He sighed. "OK." Mr. Conroy noticed her cuffs. "What are these? When did you start wearing jewelry?"

Jenny thought fast. "Cali bought them for me. I thought I'd wear them for a while. They are actually quite comfortable."

Thankfully, Demetri rescued her. "It's nice to see you again Mr. Conroy."

"Wish I could say the same," Mr. Conroy mumbled to himself. He forgot about the cuffs and turned to Demetri, who was walking over to shake his hand. "Yes. Nice place," he said, monotone.

Demetri reached out his hand, and Mr. Conroy accepted it with a smirk and squeezed harder than he knew he needed to.

Demetri's eyes focused as he held his own. He knew he could crush

Mr. Conroy's hand, but he didn't want to start anything. He could sense Mr. Conroy's irritated disappointment as they let go at the same time.

"Thank you, Mr. Conroy. If you and Carrie would like to go ahead and have a seat wherever you like, Jenny and I still have to get drinks and finish setting the table."

Carrie headed for the couch, but Mr. Conroy went ahead and escorted her to the table instead and pulled her chair out.

Jenny asked them what they each wanted to drink.

"Scotch, please, Jenny," Mr. Conroy called over.

She tilted her head back at Demetri.

"I actually don't keep any alcohol here, sir," Demetri answered.

"Huh? You don't? Well then . . . water, please." *Crap. Well, I'll have to find fault with something else about him because his house and his drinking habits certainly aren't ones.*

"Yes, sir. Water it is. And for you, Carrie?"

She sat down in the chair that Mr. Conroy had pulled out for her. "Water as well, please."

"Certainly."

Carrie watched Demetri and Jenny as they moved around in the kitchen together. She noticed the way he looked at her when she handed him a glass or how she watched him when he was filling them up. They worked like a well-oiled machine together and had everything ready in a minute or so.

Mr. Conroy watched them too but just to make sure Demetri didn't try anything.

They each brought over their version of the main course. Demetri pulled out a chair for Jenny and then sat as close to her that he thought Mr. Conroy would be OK with. Mr. Conroy eyed him.

Carrie broke the tension. "This looks so wonderful! Thank you both." She glanced between the both of them again just to confirm her deductions.

"We hope you like it," Jenny offered, specifically eyeing Mr. Conroy.

"Thank you," Mr. Conroy mumbled.

"Shall we give thanks?" Demetri asked.

"Yes," Mrs. Conroy answered eagerly.

Mr. Conroy widened his eyes. *Great. He's just Mr. Perfect, isn't he?*

"Would you like to do the honors, sir?" Demetri asked Mr. Conroy.

"No, you go ahead. This is your home."

It was the most normal thing he had said to Demetri so far.

Demetri gave thanks, and they all said, "Amen."

Jenny and Demetri each uncovered a lid at the same time to reveal dinner.

"It's your favorite, Kurtis. Demetri and I have a bet. Whose ever tastes better wins."

"Which one's yours, Jenny?" Mr. Conroy asked.

"Can't tell you." She smiled at him. "You'll have to judge without influence."

Carrie grabbed a spoonful from the dish sitting in front of her. "That was a neat idea. What happens when one of you wins?"

Mr. Conroy eyed Demetri. "Yeah, what do *you* get out of it?"

Demetri returned his hard gaze. "Either way, Jenny goes on a photography hunt with me. I guess the only thing to lose here in this bet is just the title 'best maker of spicy rice and kielbasa.'"

"Hmmm, so you get a *date*," Mr. Conroy stated through clenched teeth, still eyeing Demetri.

Demetri offered him a small smile. "Um, I wouldn't view it as a date. More of a tutoring. She wants me to teach her camera features."

Mr. Conroy's right knuckles turned white from gripping his fork too hard. He tried to calm himself down. "What do you take photos of?"

"Everything. Nature mostly. I've done a few weddings and engagements too. I have a gallery upstairs."

"Hmmm, do you have any *other* hobbies?"

"Not really anything I consider a hobby."

Carrie watched Jenny the whole time Kurtis drilled Demetri.

Demetri began, "So I guess we should start discussing some sort of business arrangement."

"No, we can do that on Monday. I would like to have a . . . *nice* evening here with everyone," Kurtis responded.

Mr. Conroy had decided that he wanted to get to know Demetri for himself before making any business deals.

"Jenny," Carrie asked, "did you know Demetri before yesterday?"

Jenny could feel her face turn a little red. She hoped that it wasn't red enough for anyone to tell. She sneaked a quick glance at Demetri before she answered.

"Uh, no, Carrie. We just met yesterday."

"Interesting." She gave Jenny a soft smile. "So, you've only been courting for one day then."

Mr. Conroy choked on his food.

Carrie helped him.

Demetri and Jenny's eyes burst open.

The words in Demetri's mind became clearer.

Demetri sighed and accepted what she was thinking.

Mr. Conroy finally stopped coughing and tried to compose himself. "Carrie! Why in the world would you assume something that like? That is utterly—"

"Yes . . . we have," Demetri answered in a strong voice.

He wasn't ashamed for dating Jenny, even if it was within the first day they met.

"WHAT?" Mr. Conroy pleaded to Jenny's eyes, wanting a different answer.

Jenny shifted closer to Demetri. She watched as Mr. Conroy got resituated and then began to gawk at her as if she were a ghost.

She waited for someone else to say something.

Carrie finally did. "Well, that's *wonderful*. So, tell me, how did it all happen?"

Jenny bravely returned her gaze to Mr. Conroy. "Kurtis . . . *please* say something."

She couldn't stand not knowing what he thought. She wanted him to like Demetri.

"You mean . . . you mean, you guys are really *dating*? After *one* day?" He looked almost betrayed.

Demetri felt how much that look hurt Jenny.

"Yes, Kurtis, we are," Jenny said normally despite her emotions. "What's the big deal? I can date whoever I want, can't I?"

"I mean . . . when you put it that way, I guess you can. I mean . . . no . . . *no*, you *can't*. You can't date someone you just *met*! Especially not potential future *business* partners. Jenny, I told you to focus on the mission. *He* was *not* the mission."

Mr. Conroy tried to contain himself, this was dinner after all, but with each second that passed, it was becoming harder and harder.

"Kurtis"—Carrie put her had on his shoulder—"they can date if they want. You asked me on a date after the first day we met."

"Yeah, I asked you out on one date, but I didn't ask you to court me until three weeks later!" he exclaimed, dumbstruck.

Jenny had never been a witness to this side of Kurtis before.

"Dear, the point is you knew *I* was the *one*. It took you three weeks to gather the courage to ask me to be your steady." She smiled at Jenny and then turned back to Kurtis. "That should tell you something about Demetri's character. Jenny is a *wonderful* girl. He obviously snatched her up as soon as he could because he could see how great she is."

Demetri glanced nervously between the both of them.

Jenny quietly scooted closer to him again.

Mr. Conroy stood. "This must have been why I couldn't shake my funny feeling yesterday. Carrie, how on God's green earth did you know they're dating?"

"Kurtis, sit." She pulled him back down. "If you would've stopped giving Demetri the third degree all evening, you could have figured it out."

"What are you talking about, Care?"

That was his nickname for her. He couldn't believe that she was so OK with all this.

She crossed her arms. "You could have watched them for just *one* minute. They can't take their eyes off each other. They color coordinated their outfits and Jenny knows where everything is in the kitchen. They move so in sync it's like they can read each other's minds."

Demetri stiffened noticeably. *Well, I can read hers*, he answered in his head.

Jenny's cheeks turned red again. She scooted even closer to Demetri. She was touching him now and instantly felt better. It had seemed like forever since they last touched. She almost leaned against him.

"What? That doesn't make any sense! Look, Jenny—" He turned and finally noticed how close she was to Demetri. He forgot what he was going to say and instead said, "Get away from her!" He shot back up out of his chair, "she's . . . she's too *young*. She doesn't know what she's doing yet." He put his hands down on the table firmly.

"*Kurtis!*" Carrie stood too and put her hands on her hips. "You are acting *ridiculous*!"

Demetri held Jenny's hand under the table tightly. He was a little worried that Mr. Conroy might try to drag Jenny out of his house, and he also wanted to comfort her.

Jenny drowned everything out. That was the first time he had just held her hand. The world disappeared, and she leaned against him completely. She had a peaceful dreamy look in her half-shut eyes. Slowly, she heard

Mr. Conroy saying her name. He had said it four times already, louder each time, before she was finally able to snap out of it.

Jenny stood suddenly, "What?" Her hand still holding Demetri's.

Mr. and Mrs. Conroy noticed their hands.

Jenny met their eyes and continued. "Kurtis, he and I had a connection right from the start. You were there. You noticed it too! And I'm well above adult age to be able to date whoever I wish. It isn't a crime to give a connection like that a shot."

She sat back down and leaned her head on Demetri's shoulder again. She needed to be close to him right now. It was as if she would dissipate if he wasn't there to keep her whole. Jenny glued her eyes to the table. Guilty feelings started seeping in. Never had she talked to Mr. Conroy like that before.

Mr. Conroy stared at them both. He'd never heard Jenny talk so forcefully.

"Mr. Conroy," Demetri tried, "I love Jenny."

That was all he said.

It was all he needed to say.

He either accepted it or didn't.

If it meant no business deal, so be it. Jenny was more important.

Mr. Conroy took in a deep breath and locked his eyes on Demetri's. "How old are you?"

Demetri sighed and let his mind do the talking. *What, this again? He must be who she gets it from.* He answered Mr. Conroy, "Let me guess, you want to ask me a ton of questions to see if I'm worthy enough for Jenny."

He said it as more of a statement than a question.

"Something like that. Yeah." He allowed Carrie to pull him back down into the chair again.

"All right, in half a month, I'll be twenty-eight." He let go of Jenny's hand to focus, and she proceeded to wrap both of hers around his right arm. He put both hands together in a fist, rest his forearms on the table, and stared equally as aggressive back at Mr. Conroy. Jenny still rested her head on the side of his shoulder and stared at the table. Mr. Conroy tried to ignore her clinginess.

"Twenty-eight? Carrie, he is *seven* years older than her."

"Kurtis, you're *five* years older than me. My grandparents are fifteen years apart. Now calm down."

He sighed. *Carrie obviously isn't going to be any help in this.* He looked back at Demetri. "How many women have you had sex with?"

Carrie nearly stood in protest. *"Kurtis!* That's *none* of our business! Don't answer that, Demetri. He doesn't need to know."

"It's all right, Carrie," Demetri assured her, never breaking eye contact at his question. He'd half-expected it. He understood where Mr. Conroy was coming from; if he had a daughter, he would want to know the same thing of her boyfriend. "None, Mr. Conroy. My parents raised me to wait until marriage."

Mr. Conroy mulled over the new information in his head. *Great. Is there anything **not** perfect about this guy? If there is, it's my job to drag it out of him and reveal it to Jenny.* "Do you expect me to believe that? You're twenty-seven. Do you know how much self-control that would take?"

"Yes, sir, as a matter of fact, I *do* know how much self-control it takes," he said, referring to Jenny.

He'd only been tempted to close measures one other time.

Maybe I can find fault with his past. Mr. Conroy decided to start with Demetri's intellect. "What were your grades in school?"

"All As and the occasional B in science when they spent a semester on evolution. I wouldn't listen to it. And all As in college."

Kurtis kept with his firm stare amongst yet another letdown. "What did you study?"

"Film, photography, design, culinary arts, construction management, blueprinting, piano, business management, diesel mechanics, and I ran track."

Mr. Conroy wanted to roll his eyes. "What did you do in your free time?"

"Homework, study, run, piano, or my dad taught me about his business, which is mine now."

"How many girls—"

"Kurtis, that is *enough* interrogating," Carrie said, "Demetri can date Jenny if she wants him to. She doesn't need our permission or anyone else's." She gently put her hand on his arm. "She's grown up now, Kurt."

He absorbed what Carrie said but didn't acknowledge it. All his questions had just made Demetri look better. He tried a new approach. "You say you *love* Jenny? You don't know anything about her. Did you know that she was bullied in school? That she had a baby brother that died in childbirth? Or how her parents died?"

"ᴋᴜʀᴛɪꜱ!" Carrie stood this time. "Do *not* bring up such painful memories. We are trying to have a good time. All that stuff is in the past, and it needs to stay there. Jenny needs *help* moving past all that, not help being *reminded* of it." She looked over at a zombielike Jenny. "Oh no! Jenny? Can you hear me, dear?"

Jenny stared off into space. Threatening memories slowly crept their way in, and this time, she couldn't run.

26

Memories

Jenny sat with her parents in the living room. They'd just finished eating dinner and were in the living room spending family time together. Jenny's parents had always made sure they took time to talk about how things were going in school.

She'd just told her mom that the new school year was going well, and that she had showed the new kids around that day.

"That's good, Jenny. They need a good friend to help get them acquainted," her dad said. He smiled proudly at her.

Her mom sat next to her and put her arm around her back for a moment and pulled her close. Most girls Jenny's age wouldn't have wanted that kind of affection from their mom, but Jenny loved it. They were getting ready to read a chapter together in the Bible. Jenny looked over at her mother's overly pregnant belly.

"Mom, I want to see Jacob when he's born. Please let me be in the room with you and Dad when he comes."

Jenny's mom moved her arm back to her own lap and started twirling her long blond hair. "Honey, for the last time, your father and I don't think that's a good idea. It's a pretty painful thing to go through, let alone watch. We don't want you to have nightmares."

Jane remembered how difficult Jenny's birth had been for her and had been worried about this one coming up any day now.

"Please, Mom! I won't have nightmares. I'll have to go through it too someday."

Jane looked over at David who sat across from them. They'd already had this same discussion about seven times already; he sighed, defeated. Jane turned back to Jenny. "Well, OK . . . but you will sit on the other side of the delivery room, OK?"

"OK, thank you, Mom!" Jenny gave her a hug.

She was seventeen years old.

*　*　*

On October 13, 2015, at three in the afternoon, Jenny waited curled up on the sofa in the corner of the delivery room. The moment her mom's body had begun shaking uncontrollably with contractions, she regretted her decision to watch her brother's birth. Something kept her from moving or she would've bolted out the door to wait in the waiting room along with Mr. and Mrs. Conroy. Mr. Conroy hadn't liked the idea of her being in the delivery room either. Jenny decided to hide behind a pillow. She couldn't bear to hear her mom be in so much pain. Finally, her mom's screams faded into little baby cries. Jenny perked up a little.

"Jacob is here!" she mumbled excitedly to herself.

His beautiful, innocent little cry suddenly ceased and interrupting the deadly silence was the heart rate monitor's long beep. After that came loud voices from the doctor and nurses and her dad's shaky voice, "Jane? Jane! JANE!" This was more than her father could handle.

The next time Jenny opened her eyes, the world slowed as if it wanted to give her as much time as it could.

The noises haunted her.

Her dad's body trembled beside her mother's lifeless one as he helplessly clenched his chest. His breath came in loud, crisp gasps. He willed himself to meet Jenny's eyes. She was by his side already.

With the last of his strength, he kissed her forehead.

With his last breaths, he told her, "Jenny . . . we love you. Go to . . . Kurtis and Carry. God . . . will take . . . care of you if you. . . let him."

He collapsed onto the floor next to her.

Jenny caught his head. "DAD! Dad, no! Help him, please!"

Two nurses finally gave their attention to her father.

Jenny couldn't see straight through all the tears. She looked up at her mom's limp body on the bed.

"I need more help in here! Take her out," the doctor ordered over the sound of the monitor.

It was still announcing death.

"MOM! Mom . . ."

A nurse moved Jenny away from her father. Jenny turned to grab her mom's hand. It was still warm. A different nurse quickly began ushering her outside the room. She looked back one last time at her parents. Nurses were trying to bring them back to life. Jenny caught a glimpse of her little brother's completely still body on the warming table. Someone was trying to save him too. More staff rushed into the room as Jenny and the nurse left.

The images haunted her.

All the colors ran together: white sheets, black and tan skin, white smocks, red blood, white floors, gray equipment, white walls. Clear tears smudged everything before the blackness of her eyelids took over.

The tears wouldn't spill over.

The nurse guided her down the hall into the arms of Kurtis and Carrie. Jenny clung to Kurtis in the empty gray waiting room as Carrie rubbed her back in attempted comfort.

Again, tears didn't spill.

Her mom had worried about her being traumatized about her brother's birth, but Jenny would've been traumatized either way.

She had lost everything all at once.

Still, no tears.

Jenny prayed a long, long prayer that afternoon.

They waited until someone came to sound the final death note. Carrie went to retrieve David and Jane's belongings, and then they left. Mr. Conroy took Jenny home while Carrie followed in her parents' truck. They helped her pack.

Jenny walked through her childhood home in a trance.

She stopped at the first room, her brother's nursery.

He'd never use it.

Never would she know what it was like to be a big sister. Never be able to help him out when he needed it. Never be able to watch him learn and grow.

She walked past the second room, her parents'.

They'd never sleep there again.

Her parents would never see her eighteenth birthday coming up in February. Never see her graduate the following May. Never see her get married someday.

Jenny's room was the third and final room.

She collapsed but Kurtis caught her before she hit the ground. He held her close.

Tears finally spilled over uncontrollably.

Jenny moved in with them and tried to resume a normal life.

She never missed a meeting service on Sunday or Wednesday after that. Kurtis and Carrie began going with her to make sure she'd be ok.

Despite Jenny's constant praying, she was too mortified to talk about it at school. She didn't tell anyone at school and acted normal to save face.

Only one person saw through that convincing mask.

27

Knight In Shining Armor

Demetri felt increasing pain from Jenny; it built and built. He wrapped his arms around her.

She stared off into space.

Demetri studied her blank eyes. "Jenny! Wake up!"

Mr. Conroy came around the table. "She isn't sleeping. Stop holding her! You'll make it worse!"

Jenny suddenly exploded with tears.

It was a good thing that Demetri was already sitting, or he would have collapsed from the sudden immense sadness.

Demetri drew in a couple of deep breaths, scooped her up, and carried her to the couch. His arms held her close. He felt so upset himself now that he started tearing up. He tried to fight through it.

"What you said, Mr. Conroy, has made her very upset." He turned back to Jenny so that they wouldn't notice his tears spill over. He wiped hers away and then his.

Her eyes were glazed over.

Carrie came over and sat beside them. "Jenny dear." She put her hand on her head and brushed the hair out of her face. She gave Demetri a warm smile. "You *really* care about Jenny, don't you?"

He said yes but it came out as a whisper.

She still heard it.

Carrie noticed the glaze over Jenny's eyes and sighed sadly. "She must be having a flashback to when her family died. We normally don't . . . move her or anything, but . . . she seems to be OK in your arms."

Jenny blinked subconsciously about three times a minute, not able to realize what was going on around her. Or maybe she just didn't care.

Carrie kissed Jenny's cheek and explained what happened to Demetri.

Demetri held her even tighter. She was still in the same condition by the time Carrie finished. He couldn't stand to see her so paralyzed. He leaned his head down, in front of Mr. and Mrs. Conroy, and kissed her.

His lips stayed there for a moment.

Slowly he felt Jenny being pulled back into reality.

He let up, rested his forehead on hers, and waited until she opened her eyes and looked around.

"What happened? Carrie? Oh . . . things aren't going well, are they?"

No one said anything.

Mr. and Mrs. Conroy were surprised she came out of her state so quickly and normally. Usually, she came out of them in uncontrollable tears.

Jenny sighed. "You were right, Demetri, maybe I shouldn't have come tonight and we shouldn't have told them yet." She stayed in his arms.

Mr. Conroy came over. "You mean, you didn't *want* to tell me about this?"

She didn't even look at him. "I wasn't planning on telling you so *soon*."

Kurtis was calm now, and his voice gentle, "You should feel comfortable enough to tell me *anything*, Jenny."

She turned her head to meet his eyes. "I love you and Carrie, and you both mean the *world* to me. Ya'll have probably done more for me that I even know about, but if there was ever going to be a time where you were going to support me, please let it be now. I know what love is. I know what it feels like, and I *do* love him."

Mr. Conroy sighed. "I'm sorry I pushed you over the edge, Jen-Jen. I'm *truly* sorry."

He took her right hand in both of his and kissed her fingers.

"I realize that I'm the one who hurt you tonight. You've been hurt more than anyone I know, and you're still so young. If I'd paid attention, I could've saved us from all of this."

Jenny gave him a thankful smile.

Mr. Conroy got back up and sat across from them.

Carrie went to sit on his knee. She draped one arm around his neck. "Kurtis, give him a chance, OK? I really like him and I think he's great for Jenny."

He drew in a long breath. "Fine. I apologize, Demetri. I'll give you a chance with Jenny. But she better not get hurt any more than she already has."

"Sir, when you told me to look after her yesterday, I promised you that I'd watch after and keep her safe"—he turned back to Jenny's blue eyes—"and that's what I'm going to do."

Jenny turned her eyes to Carrie's. "I'm OK now. Did I . . . space out again?"

"Yes, dear, but it's OK now. It's been a while, hasn't it?"

"Yes, it has. I don't think I've had one since . . ." She glanced at Mr. Conroy, who'd stiffened.

He knew what she was referring to.

His face ridged now.

Jenny sighed and managed to bat away different memories. She didn't want to get Kurtis riled up again.

Her feet found the ground and she led Demetri back to the dinner table. "I'm hungry."

Mr. and Mrs. Conroy followed and reseated themselves.

Jenny nodded towards the beans and kielbasa. "So, which one did you guys like better?" she asked with a sort of sad smile.

Mr. and Mrs. Conroy both said that they liked the one that sat in front of Jenny just a little bit better.

Demetri gave her a small grin.

Jenny flashed him a big smile feeling a lot better. "You win!"

"What?" Mr. Conroy asked.

Jenny explained, "The one that I brought over was Demetri's. The one that he brought over was mine."

Carrie raised her eyebrows, "Well, Demetri, you are quite the cook! Jenny usually makes this for Kurtis on special occasions, and it's always *beyond* fabulous, but yours *was* just a little better."

"Cooking classes. If I teach Jenny a few tricks, then I'm sure hers would be better than mine."

He smiled into her eyes and took her hand underneath the table again.

Jenny's whole body went numb; it was a good numb this time.

"Hmmm," Mr. Conroy started. "Well . . . it was *slightly* better. Thank you, guys, for making it for me. It *is* my favorite."

He finally noticed the look in Jenny's eyes when she looked at Demetri.

A defeated sighed escaped his lips. "Demetri, I know I've acted . . . badly. If you want to forget about the business deal, then I understand."

"This hasn't changed a thing for me, sir. I *expected* this. Well some of it. It's *actually* going better than I thought it would, all things considered."

A slight laugh escaped Mr. Conroy's lips. He offered Demetri friendly eyes for the first time.

Demetri was taken aback for a moment. Not because of his kindness, which was long overdue, but because his eyes . . .

Mr. Conroy interrupted his thoughts, "How far do you think your relationship with Jenny is going to go?"

"I intend to take it all the way, sir, as long as she wants the same thing. But I'd really like her parent-figures to be OK with us being together."

Jenny smiled up at him.

Demetri had to fight off gooey girl feelings again.

His manliness nearly shuddered.

"Well, no matter how long you guys date, I guess I'll try not to give you the third-degree *every* time. Jenny, I can see now that he makes you happy. I've . . . *never* seen you this way actually, and we've known you since you were born."

Carrie met Demetri's honored hazel eyes with her gentle green. "Kurtis just doesn't adjust to new things very quickly. He takes his time."

Demetri smiled back at her and then at Mr. Conroy. "It's OK, really. If I had a daughter, I'd be super protective of her too, especially if she showed up out of the blue with a boyfriend. I understand completely, and thank you for giving me a chance with her."

"I'm glad you see it that way too, Demetri. David and Jane entrusted Jenny to us and even though she's on her own now, we both still feel responsible for well-being."

They were actually able to enjoy the rest of the evening.

Carrie's eyes smiled at everyone, "Well, shall we start cleaning up?"

They all pitched in, and it didn't take long with four people to get everything put away.

A small weight that Demetri hadn't realized he was carrying lifted from his shoulders after his kitchen was clean again.

He smiled, satisfied.

Jenny embraced Kurtis and Carrie at the same time. "Thank you. I *do* want you guys to be OK with this," she reiterated again.

Carrie pulled her into a one-on-one hug. "Don't worry, Jenny, we both want to support you in *all* your decisions. You're a bright girl, and I think you've made a good choice with Demetri."

Mr. Conroy gave Demetri a firm, but kind look. "Well, if you intend to take it all the way, then we're for sure coming up with some sort of business arrangement because now I have to keep my eye on you."

That statement was not meant to be an expression and Demetri knew it.

Mr. Conroy walked over to give him a farewell handshake and then pulled Demetri into his chest. "Demetri, I don't think you fully understand what you've gotten yourself into, but Carrie and Jenny are the only two things I've got in this life besides my business. So, if you hurt Jenny, you'll hurt Carrie, and that will hurt my business. So just be smart."

"Understood, Mr. Conroy."

Mr. Conroy pulled him in again. "Oh, and the 'go all the way' stuff better only be referring to staying together, nothing more. I can shoot the beak off a finch from three-hundred yards. Got it?"

Demetri's eyes widened, "Yes, sir."

Carrie came over and gave him a full hug, "I have a feeling we'll be seeing a lot more of you, Demetri. That'll be nice."

Demetri cleared his throat from Mr. Conroy's threat, "I look forward to seeing you again, Carrie. Oh, Mr. Conroy, I think Jenny should be present at the business meeting as well."

He didn't want to freak out in front of Mr. Conroy as a result of being away from her too long.

Mr. Conroy threw his eyes over at Jenny, and she perked up some. "Yes, Jenny, please come. You need to be at all of my business meetings from now on anyways."

"Thank you, Kurtis . . . Oh, and about the other stuff too!"

He gave her a given-up look and shook his head, but he also smiled.

Carrie turned to him. "Kurtis, it's getting late. We should head home now."

"Wait. Jenny, do you want me to call a mechanic out to look at your truck?"

Demetri stepped in. "I'm confident I can fix it, Mr. Conroy. I just didn't have my tools the other day. In fact, I'll go get them and take Jenny to her truck right now."

*Oh, so he **can** fix trucks. Great. He really is 'Mr. Perfect'.* Mr. Conroy wanted to roll his eyes but refrained. "Of *course*, you can. Is there anything you *can't* do?" he asked.

Jenny laughed inside her head. That'd been exactly what she had asked herself yesterday.

"Yes, sir, there are plenty of things I can't do. But fixing trucks and taking care of Jenny, I can." He smiled at both Mr. and Mrs. Conroy confidently.

"Well, we will see. All right, we'll get out of here. Thanks again. See you both on Monday at seven o'clock sharp in my office."

They left.

Demetri shut the door after they had driven away and locked it.

* * *

"Kurtis," Carrie began with her arms crossed as they drove away, "I want you to be fair to Demetri. I really like him. He's *perfect* for Jenny."

"OK, OK, don't say it like that," he added quickly. "We'll see if he's 'perfect' for her."

"All I'm saying, dear, is that on Monday, don't expect a lot out of him, please. I have a feeling that he won't be able to pay attention too much if Jenny will be there too."

"So I've noticed." He sighed. "Fine, dear, but *only* for Jen-Jen. She'd never forgive me if I didn't give him a fair shot, so *believe* me, I will."

"Good." She turned back to the front and looked thoughtfully out the window. "This business deal came up at a convenient time, didn't it?"

He kept his eyes forward. "What do you mean, Care?"

She pursed her lips in thought. "Well, you're trying to hand the business over to Jenny, and Demetri is wanting to make ties with it. They'd be able to work side by side with their little empire." She smiled. "Wouldn't that be sweet?"

He sighed again and accepted the possibility. "Hmmm, maybe it's a sign."

Mr. Conroy tried to think clearly. He hated when his emotions got involved; they clouded his judgment. Being away from it all now, he could see Carrie's point. It would be a good thing to merge the business with a company as successful as Demetri's. It would ensure Jenny's future.

But that still didn't make it OK, not yet. Not until he got to know

Demetri more for himself. Since he could think straight now, he thought he'd better get started on some research before he made any deals.

"Kurtis?"

"Huh? Oh, yes dear?"

"When are you going to tell Jenny?"

Mr. Conroy sighed. "I don't know, Care. I don't know."

She held his hand. "I think it would help her if she knew the truth."

Or it could make things worse, he thought to himself.

He stared off into the uncertain darkness all around them.

28

Obeying

Jenny ran to Demetri and clung to him with both arms and both legs.

"Woah, Jen!"

Demetri quickly wrapped his arms around her so she wouldn't fall.

"See? I told you that they would love you!" Jenny beamed.

"Hey, missy, it wasn't exactly smooth sailing, and I'm not so sure Mr. Conroy 'loves' me quite yet." He held her in his arms and rested his forehead on hers.

"They're gone now," she said quietly with a yearning smile.

Demetri furrowed his brows and looked away. "No, Jenny. Not again." He sat her down and kissed her forehead. He felt her disappointment. "I'm going to go get my tools. Come with me."

"Yes, master." She happily began following him.

"Crap." He turned around. "I'm sorry, Jen. You don't have to come if you don't want to."

She met his eyes and smiled. "I *want* to come with you."

He grinned and grabbed her hand to lead her to the garage.

"OK, so I need a fuel filter, right?"

"Yes. Wait . . . how did you know?"

Demetri stopped rummaging for a moment but didn't meet her eyes. "Um . . . I heard you say it."

That was the truth.

"Oh, I must've mumbled it without realizing it."

He searched for another moment and then pulled one out.

Jenny was surprised. "You have one?"

"We have the same vehicle, remember? I'm going to replace it for you." He glanced at her quickly and grinned before searching for a bright headlamp.

She watched him as he dug around some more. "You actually know how to do that?"

"Yes, Jen." He stopped searching for a moment. "My dad taught me how to fix the inside and outside of my truck and a few other vehicles as well. He was a mechanic all his life even after he and Mom started their business. You really should have *some* knowledge of mechanics to own a construction company."

He had everything he needed now. Jenny didn't know what to think other than she loved finding out interesting little things about Demetri. He just got better and better.

"All right, um . . . wait. Let me change. I'm not going to fix your truck in the dark in my nice suit."

Jenny followed him all the way to his bedroom. "I need to change too probably. What should I wear?"

He took off his dinner jacket and hung it up. There was a hidden closet in the walls to the right of the door in his bedroom.

That's awesome, Jenny thought.

Demetri had to stop himself from saying 'thank you' out loud.

"Um, you should wear . . ." He stopped for a moment and looked her over. "That gray T-shirt again or something similar and jeans."

He loved the way the gray shirt had looked on her, and he wanted to see what she looked like in jeans. She had only worn skirts or dresses, except for her genie outfit where she didn't have a choice in the matter.

"Um, I . . ." She looked down at her legs and then to the side.

"What is it?"

He had a shirt on now and was walking into the restroom.

"I don't *own* any jeans." She waited for his reaction.

He turned back around and stared at her. "How do you *not* own any jeans?"

"I just . . . don't." She reflected back to specific memories and smiled a little. "They shape my legs . . . um . . . really good. They aren't really modest in Der—um—*my* opinion."

"Well, that's what I'm wanting to—" He stopped himself and rubbed his neck.

Jenny was more specific. "Guys stare at me when I wear them. I feel uncomfortable when strangers can see the shape of my body so easily."

He lifted her chin to look into her eyes. "Can you just wear some for me tonight? It's dark out. You'll just be with me. As long as you don't mind this stranger staring at you."

She tilted her blushing face a little. "I'll have to use my powers."

"Fine. I just wanna see you in some jeans."

Demetri walked back into the bathroom and changed out of his dress pants and put on *his* jeans. He wore a white tank shirt that really showed off his arms. They were not built like a wrestler's, but they were definitely toned.

When he walked back out, Jenny noticed immediately and stared. She'd only seen him without a long-sleeved shirt once, and her mind was on *other* things.

Wow, she thought.

He stood there with his muscled arms crossed. "Hey, you're the one who has powers, and I still beat you?" He cracked a smile at his own joke.

With his arms crossed, you could see the detail of each muscle.

He noticed gooey girly feelings trying to pound their way in again.

"Are you OK?" He came forward quickly. "What's wrong?" He held onto her shoulders.

"Um . . ." She couldn't speak. She examined his arms and then reached up to grab them. "Hello. Where have you been hiding?" she asked his muscles.

Demetri raised his eyebrows. "Seriously? You just gave me a heart attack because you're attracted to my arms?" He stared at her, "So that's what the weird feelings in my stomach were about? What do you call that? Weakness or something?" He smiled playfully.

She grinned at him and wrapped both hands around one arm and then lifted both feet off the ground.

Demetri balanced the sudden weight shift. "Woah!"

She dangled from his right arm.

He peeked down at her. "A little warning next time, please?"

Her feet found the ground again.

"OK, I'm going to do it to the other arm too."

"What? Why?"

"It has to be even," she explained as she hung from the other one.

At least I was prepared for this one this time.

He hardly moved from the weight shift.

Jenny let herself down.

"OK, you've had your fun. Now, will you *please* get dressed so we can go?"

She put herself in between his arms and wrapped them around her.

Demetri looked down into her mischievous eyes. *Are they gray? Are they blue? I'm not even sure anymore.*

"I *am* ready, master," she said with a huge smile on her face.

"What?" He backed up a little. "Oh."

She wore a mid-length dark-blue shirt that hugged her skin and had two little white buttons in the front. It showed her cleavage a little and shaped her other curves too. He looked down farther and saw dark-blue jeans wrapped around her legs. They clung to her hips, thighs, and knees and started bowing out at the calves. Her jeans covered the laces of her white and light-blue streaked tennis shoes.

He stood back farther.

Damn, he thought. "Turn around . . . slowly."

Her cheeks turned red, and she obeyed. Each slow step, the jeans accentuated the way her hips moved. He hadn't realized before how long her legs were.

Daaamn, he thought again.

She completed her turn, held her own hands nervously, and looked down. Her cheeks were on fire, and her heart felt hot with burning sensations.

"Walk to the door then back to me." He watched her hips move. "Yeah, Jen. You are *not* allowed to wear these where people can see."

She held her right arm and looked up at him. "Why not?"

He crossed his arms. "Because I said."

She looked back up and hugged him suddenly. "Yes, master."

Demetri hugged her back and tried to refrain from grabbing her butt. "You are . . . *beyond* hot in jeans. I don't want anyone else to see. I understand why you were uncomfortable in them."

He felt happiness radiate from her.

"You're not uncomfortable that I just made you do that, are you? I don't feel any discomfort from you, but I just want to be sure."

She smiled. "No. It didn't make me uncomfortable, master."

"All right, good. Now let's go fix your truck."

"Let me get my bottle. I want it to be safe, and I have a feeling that something bad will happen if I get too far away from it."

"Let's hope we never have to find out," Demetri said, remembering Satan's promise.

They walked back to the garage, hopped into the truck, and headed towards town.

A thought came to Jenny. "Where should we put my truck? I mean, it shouldn't be at your house. People need to think everything is normal."

"Well, I guess that just leaves your house then."

"All right. Yeah, I mean, I guess I need to keep it in the garage. That way, Mr. Mitts doesn't know if I'm home or not. He has been known to call into Kurtis and check in with him. The little tattle teller." She crossed her arms.

Memories haunted her again.

Demetri noticed. "What has he told on you for?"

He was intrigued. He remembered what Mr. Conroy whispered to him and realized he still didn't know much about Jenny's past.

29

Jenny's Past

"Well . . ." She took a breath in. "After my parents died, I moved in with Kurtis and Carrie. Then once I turned eighteen, I moved into the place I live now. I was still in school, and Kurtis hated the idea of me living alone, but I felt like I was being a burden. My best friend . . . Derek, watched out for me all the time. I knew he thought of me as more than just a best friend though because he asked me to hang out with him after school all the time. One day, soon after my family died, I told him yes. I just wanted to," she stopped for a moment and started talking to her window, "*feel* something besides pain."

"What happened?"

Demetri could feel fear sneaking in, although it could have just been his own. This time, emotions and colors swirled around and mixed together. It was very difficult to try to determine their meanings. There was a certain emotion mixed in that he wanted to figure out, but he just couldn't quite put his finger on it at the moment. Trying so hard to understand began to give him a headache. He turned his energy towards blocking her thoughts and just let her tell him.

"You won't look at me the same . . ." She held both arms and rested her head on the window.

Demetri was so perfect in her eyes. She felt unworthy to be with him. They'd arrived at Conroy Renovations. He pulled in next to Jenny's truck.

"Jen," he unbuckled their seat belts, scooted over to her side, and scooped her up. "Jen, I love you unconditionally. If you tell me, I will love you *more* for sharing your heart with me, no matter how battered it is."

Jenny slowly looked up at him and kissed his warm lips. She held his head and then pulled away reluctantly.

Demetri felt her yearning turn into pain.

She closed her eyes. "That day, he saw me in the hallway in between classes. I was coming back from the restroom. No one was around. He was waiting for me . . ."

RESCUE

Derek slid out in front of Jenny and grinned from ear to ear. He knew Jenny well and locked eyes with her before she could look down.

Her heart sped up as she stared back into his loving brown eyes. She tried to keep her breathing under control.

Jenny moved her left hand over to the middle of her other arm.

He maintained his hold on her nervous eyes and began slowly walking forward. He cornered her into the lockers and leaned close.

"Jenny, I *want to* take you out. We will go wherever *you* wanna go. We can do whatever *you* want to do. Let's just hang out somewhere other than this infernal drama trap of a high school."

He moved his hands to her hips.

All the pain she had been feeling completely disappeared.

* * *

Demetri felt that weakish feeling again.

Jenny continued with the recollection.

* * *

"D-Derek, I . . . I told you I don't feel like going anywhere," she stuttered as her cheeks warmed her body temperature.

He kept his hands on her hips and pressed his body against hers.

She was flat between him and the lockers.

Derek closed his eyes and kissed her forehead.

Jenny's head spun.

She didn't push him away.

* * *

Demetri felt it again.

His temperature rose. He breathed a little heavier. Not with pleasure. With anger.

* * *

Derek gave her a smooth grin. "Let's just go back to your place then."

He calmly leaned his head down and deliberately kissed her warm dead lips.

She didn't shut her eyes at first. Then, after a moment, she gradually closed them and forgot about everything.

Derek hadn't kissed her so openly before. It always happened in the back of the library.

The hallway was still empty.

Derek slid his hands around her back and pulled her nervous body even closer, if it was possible.

Her feet next to his, her legs against his, her stomach and chest smashed against him.

Her body began to calm.

She wrapped her trembling arms around his neck. Her head spun as she navigated her fingers through his light-brown hair.

Her arms stopped trembling.

As soon as she started kissing back, he backed away. Only she didn't want him to.

"There will be more of *that* waiting for you tonight, if you want." He kissed her right cheekbone. "I'll come to your place. If you want me to come in, I will. If you want me to leave . . . I'll leave."

He kept his gaze on her heavy bluish-gray eyes as he backed away and disappeared into one of the only classes they didn't have together.

Jenny slid her back down the locker that was supporting her.

She sat on the floor for a moment.

Her eyes locked on the classroom door that he disappeared into.

It hadn't felt quite right, but it felt like something.

That was all she had been wanting.

Something was better than nothing.

After a moment, the pain returned.

*   *   *

The feeling happened again.

She met Demetri's eyes, feeling his tenseness. "He isn't as good of a kisser as you are."

Demetri tried to stay calm. He wanted to hear where it was going, even though he didn't like the direction it was heading.

She continued.

*   *   *

Jenny waited nervously at her kitchen bar. School got out at 3:00 p.m.; it was 3:30 p.m. She lived about fifteen minutes away and wondered what was keeping Derek. She thought he might've changed his mind, and she found herself disappointed.

She gave herself a pep talk. "It's probably for the best. I mean, I know that wasn't our first kiss or anything but—"

A knock resounded at the door.

She knew instantly it was Derek because of the way he knocked.

They had a special knock.

She turned to hold her eyes to the door and took a couple of breaths.

"Calm down, Jenny," she commanded herself. "It isn't like we're going to have sex or anything. He just wants to . . . hang out . . . *right?*" *AGH! Why am I so nervous? He's my best friend! This should be the easiest thing in the world! I see him every day! Why should him coming to my house be any different?*

Jenny bravely willed herself to the door and found the courage to turn the knob.

This time she didn't give him a chance to lock eyes with her and tilted her head away.

He stood there, leaning against the doorframe.

"Well . . . do you want me to be here or not?"

At the sound of those nine casual words, her heart shook her whole chest.

Jenny couldn't find words to speak. Her throat was too dry. Instead, she found the strength to open the door a little wider. She stayed behind it and reached her right arm out to gesture for him to come in.

He accepted the invitation with a side smile.

She slowly shut the door, turned her body to lean her back against it, and watched him.

Derek sat a brown paper bag down on her counter and took in Jenny's house for a moment. He came back over to her.

Instead of saying anything, he locked eyes with her the split second she looked up at him. He grinned.

Her heart pounded.

He leaned forward slowly.

Her eyes grew wide.

He kissed her lips.

This time she *did* slide down to the floor.

Slowly.

Derek kept distance between them and slid his hands down the door on either side of her until they both reached the floor.

The back of Jenny's hands found themselves near her shoulders against the door as they both let gravity pull them down to earth.

Derek kept his lips glued to hers the whole time. He had to bend down on his hands and knees to continue kissing her.

Jenny moved her hands to keep her skirt together in the front since her legs had managed to find themselves on either side of him. Her arms in that position unintentionally held her breasts together.

Derek didn't notice. He still had his lips connected to hers and his eyes closed.

Against the will of most her nerves, she turned her head away.

"What do you want to do, Derek?" She looked down and closed her eyes so he wouldn't notice how scared they were.

He studied her face with his eyes half-shut. "Whatever you want. What do *you* want to do?"

"I just . . . want to forget the pain . . ."

A tear slid down her face, and he wiped it away with his right thumb and then stood.

He walked over to the counter and took a brownie out of the bag he brought. Then returned to her and bent back down.

"Here, Jenny. This will help you forget." He looked deep into her hurt and frightened-looking eyes and remembered all the times he had asked her if she wanted to talk about it. She had always told everyone else no.

Derek was the only person who could get close to her.

Especially *this* close.

Jenny took a bite, not realizing what was in it. The last brownie she had eaten had been one that she and her mom had made together.

Derek helped her up and walked her over to the couch. He pulled her to his lap and held her like he always did when she needed it.

"You feel safe with me, don't you, Jenny?"

She nodded and leaned into his chest.

He held her.

Soon, she started laughing for no reason, and Derek saw that smile that had been hidden for too many months now.

He smiled too. "There you are, Jenny. I've missed you."

She tried to focus into his warm brown eyes. "I love you, Derek!"

Happy laughs found their way out of the dungeon of sadness they'd been locked up in.

She clung to his neck. Jenny turned to straddle him and leaned in to kiss *him* this time.

Her happiness was his happiness.

*   *   *

Jenny stared blankly back out the window. "I'm lucky he didn't try to take advantage of me because I'm not sure if I would've . . . told him no."

The feeling happened again, and then Demetri felt a flicker of that something else too. He wasn't for sure but . . .

"Wait!" Demetri took a breath in. He looked at her sternly. "You still have feelings for him."

It wasn't a question.

Jenny turned her head abruptly back to Demetri. "What? No, I do—"

He felt surprise from her.

She couldn't even finish her sentence.

"Jenny, don't tell me you don't when I can *feel* your feelings. Every time you talk about him, you felt a weakness feeling or, or, or yearning or something."

She looked down. "Demetri, it is a complicated thing for me to talk about. I don't know *what* I feel for him. He's my best friend . . . or, was . . . but he made me feel safe and helped me forget. You really should know the rest . . ."

He sighed. "I'm sorry . . . Continue, please . . ."
She did.

* * *

It was dark outside now, and the living room lights were dimmed.

Jenny momentarily detached her lips only long enough to mumble, "Derek."

"Hmmm?" he asked, not removing his lips.

He held her tightly across his lap.

Jenny pulled away a little. "I don't think I'm high anymore."

Derek felt high now from kissing Jenny. He could barely open his eyes.

He asked slowly, "Well . . . how do you feel now?"

She smiled really big at him despite her drunken eyes. "I feel great!"

"Good. No pain?"

She shook her head happily.

He smiled at her and then looked down. "Do you want me to stop kissing you now?"

She blushed and then gave him a kind smile. "Kiss me, Derek. It's OK."

He looked back up into her blue eyes. He wasn't sure if he heard her right.

"Really?"

"Yes." She met his eyes and locked hers to his this time.

"Does . . . this mean that you want to be more than best friends?"

She thought for a moment and then nodded.

Derek smiled ecstatically and then brought her closer to him.

He kissed her gently. He didn't want to blow it.

He held her a little tighter. He didn't want to hurt her.

He finally felt loved.

He didn't want to lose it.

* * *

"Anyways, he didn't leave until about one o'clock that morning. We just kissed and talked all night. I didn't even care that he'd gotten me high. I actually was able to think about something besides my parents and brother for once. It was a nice change. I'd done so much praying, but it'd only helped a little bit. He came over quite a few times after that."

Demetri felt so torn up inside, like someone had come at his heart with a knife and slashed it a few times. He couldn't stand the way Jenny felt every time she talked about an intimate moment with Derek. The only thing that kept him sane was her feelings of guilty happiness. They overshadowed his. He wasn't sure how much more destructive slashing and then immediate healing his heart could take from the way Jenny felt.

She continued. "The last time he came over was when Mitts told. Derek knew about Mr. Mitts, and he always thought to park a little way down the street and then walk. But Mr. Mitts must have been up for a late-night snack or something and noticed my living room light on. I had the blinds shut. Don't worry."

"It's not the blinds that I'm worried about right now, Jen."

She sighed and kept her head down. "Anyways, he called Kurtis. I don't know how he had Kurtis's cell number, but Kurtis rushed over and found us tangled up on the couch . . ."

"OK, STOP! I-I-I can't take it anymore. Look, I'm just going to go fix your damn truck now, OK?"

He slid out from underneath her and grabbed his bag.

Jenny got out after him and followed. She felt so guilty now, even though it had happened nearly two years ago.

Demetri hooked a battery-powered flashlight to the hood and started changing the filter.

"Demetri, I—"

"Jenny! I need to focus for a minute."

She backed off slowly and leaned against her driver's side door.

Do I still have feelings for Derek? What am I saying? I haven't seen him in so long!

She thought back to the first time he came over again. It had affected her so greatly that she remembered almost every detail.

KISS, DON'T TELL

After a few more minutes of kissing that first night, Derek decided to be brave. He timidly touched his tongue to hers.

They'd never ventured that far before. It'd always been more innocent. It surprised her, but she accepted his tongue with hers. After a while, Jenny finally broke the kiss. Her cheeks were bright red.

"Derek?" she asked with her face down.

He tilted his head and tried to meet her shy, reclusive eyes.

"Yes, Jenny?"

"Why are you here?" she wondered out-loud, head still down.

He furrowed his brows. "What do you mean?"

"I mean, you're *always* there for me. Why?" She managed to meet his mellow eyes.

"Jenny, I love you. That's what you do for people you love . . . I think. Look, I just know it's what I'd want if I was in your shoes."

She gave him a thankful smile, "I don't know if I've ever thanked you before. So, thank you, Derek."

He fixed his happy eyes onto her drowsy ones. "It's nothing, Jenny. I just want you to be safe and know that you're still loved."

He hugged her tightly, and she rested her head on his shoulder and hugged him back.

"Derek, it's *not* nothing. It means the world to me. You're so considerate. I don't deserve you," she said, her head in the crick of his neck.

He closed his eyes, "Jenny, I'm the one who doesn't deserve you."

She came up from the hug. "Can I make you dinner, Derek? I'd like it if you stayed a while."

His head came forward from astonishment. "You really want me to stay?"

She tilted her head. "Why's that so hard to believe?"

He looked down. "I don't know. It's just . . . every time I cheer you up, you're ready to go on about your day, until the next . . . Well, no need to bring up bad memories."

Jenny hadn't noticed that before, but she thought back to all the times he'd been there and realized he was right.

She sighed. "You're right, Derek. I'm *really* sorry. Let me make it up to you. I don't want you to think I'm ungrateful. If it wasn't for you, I don't know where I'd be right now or what . . . would've *happened* to me."

"Hey"—he brought her closer to his face, and her heart sped up—"don't think about that incident anymore. Just focus on the *now*. Now, what are you willing to make me for dinner?"

"I'm willing for whatever *you* want, Derek," she said softly.

Her cheeks blushed at the double meaning it could've had.

His face turned red too. That wasn't what he wanted from her. He gulped and then cleared his throat. "Uh, can you . . . make hamburgers?"

She smiled and began to get up off his lap. "Two hamburgers coming up, just for you."

He held her for a moment.

"Jenny?" He looked into her mysterious blue eyes.

"Yes, Derek?" Her heart sped up.

"I just want to make sure you're happy." He gave a meaningful smile.

She smiled back softly. "*You've* made me happy, Derek. I'm sorry that I haven't always made that known to you."

He pulled her into a hug and then stood with her in his arms.

"Your happiness makes me happy, *baby.*"

Something tugged at his conscience when he said it.

He ignored the feeling and hoped the sudden new term of endearment wasn't overstepping any of her boundaries.

Her heart pounded loudly on her chest, she kept her head down in shyness. She wasn't sure how to feel about her new nickname.

Her conscience spazzed.

Her brain and heart told her to ignore it.

Jenny smiled happily and made Derek hamburgers.

*   *   *

Demetri was almost finished. He was so distraught and hurt that it took him longer than normal. Jenny's emotions were a *serious* distraction. He tried again to figure out what they all meant.

*Regret? Love? Indecisiveness? Thankfulness? Endless wondering? AGH! I don't know **what** she feels! I know that she loves me, but I can feel that she loves him too. But love for him feels . . . a little different. AGH! It makes it hard to hate him when I can feel her love for him!*

Demetri shuddered. He was too upset to try to decipher it all. Her confusing thoughts coursed through his brain.

"There. Finished," he stated plainly as he placed both hands on the truck. A big breath came bellowing out. He removed his gloves to put them and everything he had used away and then he shut the hood.

Demetri studied Jenny leaning against the door. She hadn't seemed to notice that he was done. He turned away from her and the truck and put his hands behind his head.

His eyes searched the night sky.

The sudden weight of everything caused his knees to fail him.

How convenient, he thought sarcastically. *I was going to pray anyways.*

Jenny finally snapped out of it and wondered where he went. She came around to the front to find him on his knees. She wasn't sure what he was doing at first. His broad, built figure was so attractive in the parking lot lights. He was almost a silhouette. Jenny slowly walked over to stand behind him and then bent down to her knees too. She didn't know what Demetri felt, but she could see he was in pain. She leaned against him with her arms around his shoulders, even though they weren't long enough to encompass his torso.

He let her, even though he wasn't done praying.

They stayed there for a while.

Finally, he lifted his head and sighed.

"Jen, I love you, but if you have even the slightest feelings for someone else, then you *need* to decide *who* you want."

She clenched her eyes shut. "Yes, master."

He sighed. "Your truck should run now, but I saw a couple of other things that I would like to clean and replace for you later. Go test it out."

It was an order.

He wanted to be alone right now. He stayed there on his knees while Jenny got up and started her truck.

It started right up.

Jenny gave a small smile. Demetri's figure was illuminated from her headlights. She stared at him. She didn't feel very good. She turned the truck back off and then noticed the flowers in her passenger seat this from this morning.

I'd really like to know who keeps leaving me flowers. These ones need water. They're dying. She sighed. *I wonder what Derek is doing and where he is. I hope he's OK. I guess it's going to be harder than I thought to forget about him. I can't do this to Demetri. I thought I could put Derek behind me, but . . . I guess not . . .*

She closed her eyes and rested her head on the steering wheel. When she opened them back up, he was standing with his head down at her side.

Her body jolted out of fear.

He met her eyes.

"You scared me," she whispered.

"I'm sorry."

He felt strange apologizing to her. Jenny had no idea what she had just put him through mentally.

She reached out to touch his blond curls and brought him close. Her face was only a little taller than his while she sat in the truck. She wrapped her legs around him and grabbed either side of his face.

"Demetri, I realize that I've hurt you . . . *again*. I'm hurting you continuously, which, in turn, hurts me. I can't keep doing this to you."

He was trapped in her hold. He looked up sadly into her eyes with no strength to break away.

Her battered heart broke a little with the look he gave her.

"Jen, I can deal with the pain. Pain and suffering help you to be humble. If you deal with it properly, it can bring you closer to God. That's what *I* try to do with it. Our pain brings me closer to God, which makes me love you more. Don't worry about me."

She stared into his eyes for a moment and then closed them. "How are you so perfect? You shouldn't be real." It came as a whisper.

He smiled and felt a little bit better. "Jen, let's take your truck to your house. I'll follow you, OK?"

"OK." She didn't want to let go of him. "I . . . I still have some feelings for Derek, but he was my best friend, and he helped me through the toughest thing I ever went through. He's a good guy, and I'm thankful for him."

Demetri could feel that she felt genuinely about what she just said, but afterward, there was a little flicker of something, and he still wasn't sure what it was.

"Jen, it's OK." He sighed. "If I ever see the guy, I'll be sure to thank him for helping you. I understand that he was good for you at the time. You needed someone. I just want you to be happy, and if that means taking a break so you can figure everything out, then that's OK. If he helped you overcome all that, then that was no small chore by any means. For that, he deserves a chance with you if you like him too. I'll . . . be here when you need me or . . . *if* you want me again. Don't feel like you are obligated to stay with me because we *just* got together."

It was a mouthful and a knife to the gut, but after praying, he knew that was what he needed to say.

She looked wonderingly into his eyes. "You would let me do that if I needed to?"

He stared back and painfully said, "Yes, Jen, I would." He tilted his head back down.

Jenny smiled.

That made her love Demetri even more.

30

Submission

Jenny brought his face to hers and touched his forehead. "I don't need to think about it. I want *you*, Demetri Dayton."

Jenny hadn't said his full name to him yet. It made his insides flip out, in a good way. But that might have been because Jenny's insides had flipped out too.

She pressed her lips into his, closed her eyes, and tried to push her emotions onto him so that he would feel the same way that she did.

It must have worked because he instantly grabbed her thighs, walked backward, and turned to pin her against the truck.

He returned her kiss with complete devotion.

Jenny felt along his muscled arms with both hands and then ran them back up to his head. She loved his blond curls. They were so soft and fun to run her fingers through.

He kissed her mouth more intently than he had yet and then briskly began kissing her cheeks, making his way down her neck.

His heart felt like it had a small part repaired.

She made a low "Mmm" and closed her eyes.

He stayed around her neck area and kissed it so forcefully that he was sure you would be able to tell in about five minutes.

Jenny made more low sounds; it drove him crazy.

Demetri stopped for a moment to search her eyes. He whispered in her ear, "I *can't* live without you, Jen."

"Then don't."

Demetri stopped abruptly.

It was too dark outside to tell, but she was sure that he had another pained look on his face.

"AHH!" His eyes searched the stars. He gently sat her down and then picked up a rock and threw it farther into the empty parking lot.

"AGH!"

He put his hands behind his head and walked away swiftly and then came back to a concerned-looking Jenny still leaning against her truck. He smashed his body against hers. His whole body was tense with excitement.

"Please make this go away . . . unless you want it." He focused directly into her dark-blue eyes. "I *will* see how strong the wish is."

He shoved his lips into hers, hoping that she wouldn't say anything, and then slid his hands down her sides and slid his fingers through her belt loops.

His body was as flat up against hers as it could be.

Jenny breathed hard.

She wanted him too— very *badly*.

*Should we do this? He wouldn't be in pain anymore. I want to be the one he loses his virginity to. I'm . . . I'm ready, but . . . something still doesn't feel right. C'mon, conscience, **really**?*

He felt it. His eagerness quickly turned into anger.

"NO! Jenny! AGH!"

Demetri reared back and punched her truck.

CRUNCH!

"Demetri!" She put her hands on her hips despite her fear. "What the . . .? What the *freak*, dude?"

He locked onto her eyes, breathing hard. In one fluid motion, he shoved his right hand underneath the metal and then popped it back out with one hand.

It was as if it never happened.

"What? What do you want?" he tried not to yell.

Jenny turned away from him and felt the metal. She didn't feel anything abnormal. She couldn't believe it.

Jenny tried to push calmer emotions onto him, and he began breathing slower accordingly.

"Jen, you are *not* allowed to kiss me anymore. I *forbid* it."

She stepped back in aghast until she reached the truck.

Her face was as if she'd seen the dead rise.

He came up to her, close, still a little angry.

"If there *is* a next time, even if you take all the pain and desire away, I'm not stopping."

"Yes, master," she said automatically despite her horrified expression.

Despite everything, her heart reached out to his. It *wanted* to be conjoined with its mate.

He'd asked her to try not to start up another one of these *almost* situations.

Demetri looked through the shadows and into her dark-gray eyes. "Good girl. Now get in your truck, please."

She looked up at him meekly now. "Yes, master."

Her knees gave out when she tried to walk. Apparently, her body liked it when he was so in charge.

He caught her no problem and held her for a moment.

Jenny wanted to obey him, and she was pretty sure that it didn't have anything to do with being a genie.

She couldn't meet his eyes. "Thank you . . . *again*."

He hadn't taken his intent eyes off hers anyhow. He picked her to set her in the truck and gave her the seat belt to put on.

Jenny furrowed her brows. "I need a minute, please."

She was suddenly overwhelmed with a feeling of submission. All she could think of was 1st Corinthians 7, and that was good enough for her now.

But she *had* to obey what he said.

Demetri felt everything. Her feelings were more than clear. She wanted to give herself away, but his prayers were helping him block her desire.

He mentally prayed again, *Father, if there was ever a time that I needed the strength to fight a temptation off, I beg of you, please help me now.* He took a quiet breath in and fought off the scent of vanilla too. "Now . . . you have a *small* feeling of what it feels like for *me* when I can't have *you*. Start driving."

He shut the door for her and pounded over to his truck.

Jenny started up the engine again and began to pull away.

She sighed sadly. "Dear Father, please help me get back on track. These last couple days have been a huge and confusing test that I've been failing miserably at."

Demetri hopped into his truck and followed. His face was hard and serious. "Jenny Delemonte, you are going to be so fun to make love to."

* * *

At Jenny's house, Satan grinned. Knowing fully of the new developments in Demetri and Jenny's unique bond. He announced to Dalia that they had to leave.

"They're coming. We will watch from afar, and you can see how part of my masterpiece works out."

She grinned a half grin and gave him an expectant look.

They vanished and waited for things to play out.

* * *

Jenny pulled into her one-truck garage and hopped out to look at the damage in her garage light.

It looked completely normal.

"Wow . . . I can't believe it," she mumbled.

She walked outside and shut the garage door back.

Her motion lights on the front porch lit up the yard.

Demetri parked on her driveway and slid out too.

"Jenny, you're back!" A weaselly, little voice sprang out from next door.

Jenny rolled her eyes. "Mr. Mitts, isn't it past your bedtime?"

"By two hours and thirty-five minutes, yes, but I *had* to wait up for you, Jenny. I've been so worried! Woah"—he took a few steps backward in surprise—"are you wearing jeans? You look . . . wow!"

I should've known that Mitts would be waiting on me. She grimaced and scolded herself for not thinking to poof on a skirt before she came out into the open.

Mitts eyed Demetri. "What's *he* doing here?"

Demetri stepped forward with his back to Mr. Mitts and his body in front of Jenny's protectively.

He turned his head back slightly towards Mitts. "I'm here because Jenny wants to have sex with me."

Jenny's now humbled eyes burst open. *Were my emotions **that** strong? I don't want to anymore. I've had time to think!*

"WHAT!" Mr. Mitts nearly choked on air. "Jenny, don't do it! I-I-I'll call Mr. Conroy and tell him!"

Demetri smiled. "Go ahead. He already knows."

"What! No! I'm not letting you!"

Demetri let full cockiness lose. "Oh, but she's practically been *begging* me to." He turned to Mr. Mitts and grinned a "Take that" grin. Then he turned back to Jenny and whispered gently, "Ask me out loud to take you inside and tell me that you *want* me."

Her eyes burst open, but she obeyed. "Demetri, I want you to take me inside. I . . . *want* you now!" She stole a glance at Mr. Mitts and then Demetri's smug face.

Mitts was speechless for the first time in his nosey life.

Jenny had never seen Mr. Mitts's eyes so horrified.

Demetri began kissing her right in front of Mitts, pushed her backward into the house with his body, and locked the door behind them.

He pinned her to the front door. "C'mon, Jen, this won't work unless you kiss me back."

Jenny understood what he was doing now.

She looked up at him shyly. "I'm sorry, master. Believe me, I want to, but you forbade me to."

The last thirty minutes had been one of the first times he'd given her intentional orders, and she felt embarrassed having to follow such kinky commands. It was a good embarrassed though.

"Kiss me, Jen," he commanded. "Make a loud noise where *he* can hear it. We're going to get him to leave you alone if it's the last thing I do."

Demetri wanted her to feel comfortable enough to live in her own house without having to worry about the perv next door all the time.

Jenny obeyed.

Demetri banged on the front door.

Outside, Mr. Mitts ran up to the door and tried to open it. He heard a low sound that he knew instantly was Jenny's voice. It was followed by a bang.

"No! You're controlling her! She doesn't want *you*! Jenny! That's *my* Jenny! AGH!"

Mitts jolted his body up and down and threw a tantrum.

He wrinkled his face. "I *will* make you *pay*, Demetri." He stomped back inside his house and rushed to the window facing Jenny's.

Demetri brought Jenny to the living room. He opened the blinds so Mr. Mitts could see them.

The living room was dark, but Mr. Mitts saw their silhouettes because the kitchen light was on.

Demetri held Jenny up against the window and kissed her intently. He maneuvered down her neck to see if Mr. Mitts was watching.

Demetri couldn't believe his eyes. *He isn't even trying to watch inconspicuously. The little creep has his light on. I can even see the shocked expression on his face. Good.*

Mr. Mitts put his mitts on the window. "NO!"

Demetri moved back up to her mouth, lifted her away, and then shut the blinds. He took her upstairs.

Mr. Mitts couldn't see anything, so he quickly ran up his stairs too.

His tiny bathroom window faced her bedroom. He had to stand on the toilet lid to see.

Demetri commanded, "Make a bed appear."

She tried to clear her drunk mind enough to make one appear.

"Yes, master."

POOF!

* * *

Satan grinned from afar, and he thought to himself, *AH! She's fully submitted. He now has more control and more power! It's only a matter of time now. BWAHAHAHA!*

* * *

Demetri turned on her bedroom light after the bed appeared and then opened the blinds. Jenny was still wrapped around his waist. He kissed her neck again to see if Mr. Mitts was watching.

"No! You're violating her against her wishes! You keep your hands off my Jenny! Jenny!" His breath fogged up the little window; he frantically smeared it clean again.

Demetri took her to the bed.

Mr. Mitts screamed, "No! You're controlling her! You're brainwashing her!"

Demetri fell onto the bed with Jenny. He was on top.

Mr. Mitts could only see their knees.

Jenny laughed. "I see, you want him to *believe* that I'm taken so he will give up and move on, don't you?"

He smiled back down at her, "Yeah." His eyes shifted into solemnness. "You like it when I'm in charge, don't you?"

Her heart seemed to nod frantically.

Jenny pulled his face to hers.

Her mind drifted among dreamland, fantasyland, and reality. Her imagination went wild.

"Command me, Demetri."

His love-crazed eyes flashed with desire; he felt an emotion coming from her that he'd felt earlier at the trucks.

He realized he was finally able to control his mind.

Jenny had given him her bottle, making him her permanent master.

She'd accepted him as her master and now, she'd given him permission to command her.

Now he was in complete control.

Demetri didn't hurt. He felt alive and free.

Suddenly, dark-blue smoke seeped from her cuffs and swirled around him. It disappeared into his silver ring.

He felt the control overcome him and become a part of him.

Jenny gasped.

Demetri pulled back.

"What in the world?" they both said.

Mr. Mitts saw. "There's my proof! I *have* to save her!"

Jenny sat up quickly. "Oh no! What's happening?" She gasped again, "Mr. Mitts! He'll see!"

Demetri flung himself off the bed. He didn't see Mitts at the tiny window anymore.

He noticed a movement to the left, on the ground.

Mr. Mitts was running across the yard toward Jenny's house.

A frantic knock pounded the door.

"Crap. Jenny, he saw."

She scrambled to her feet, and they raced downstairs.

Jenny opened the front door. "Mr. Mitts, we're in the middle of something. Go away, please."

"JENNY! You're just confused right now. He's using some kind of evil power to make you want him." He grabbed Jenny's hand and tugged on her.

"Mr. Mitts! Please leave me alone! You've lost your mind!" She took her hand back.

Demetri stepped between them. "Mitts, stay away from Jenny!"

He ignored Demetri and tried stepping around him instead. Demetri nearly took up the whole doorway and wouldn't budge.

Mitts punched his stomach. "Ow! My hand! You broke it!"

"*You* punched *me*," Demetri scooted him away from the threshold.

"Harassment! I'm calling the cops! Oooh the pain! You're hurting Jenny too!"

Demetri crossed his arms. "I wish you would shut up for a minute!"

POOF!

Instantly, sound ceased from Mitts's lips, but his mouth kept moving. His eyes widened, and he stood there, petrified.

Demetri stared at him. "Mitts, you are *not* calling the cops again. Stop bothering them and mind your *own* damn business. I wish you never saw what you saw up there."

Nothing happened.

Mr. Mitts was still in the process of silently cussing Demetri out.

Jenny's raised her eyebrows. "Um . . . why is he still acting like he knows?"

Demetri tried something else. "I wish we were back at Conroy Renovations and none of this had happened yet."

Again, nothing happened.

Demetri gave Jenny an unsettled look.

She went up to Mitts again. "Mr. Mitts, I love Demetri. Please mind your own business and leave us alone!"

Mitts snatched Jenny's arm and began dragging her off again.

"ow!"

Demetri came forward, ready to punch him.

"No, Demetri. It's what he wants. He wants to be able to get you into trouble."

Jenny looked over at Mitts trying to gasp for his voice. She poofed him back into his house and shut her and Demetri inside hers.

She turned to him. "What are we going to do?"

Knock, pound, knock!

She sighed, exasperated. "Not again!"

Jenny opened the door a little.

Before either of them could react, Mr. Mitts scurried in quickly, gathered Jenny up with both hands, and began carrying her off as if she were a handful of delicious berries.

"Mr. Mitts, ow! Stop!"

Demetri pounded after the psychopath as he carried her away.

Her mind told him not to move.

It was against every atom of his body, but for some reason he obeyed.

Jenny vanished into smoke.

Mr. Mitts could speak again. "What did you do with her, you evil warlock! Imma . . . Imma hurt you!" He stuck up both fists and began strafing left and right.

"Mitts, shut up and get outta my way!"

Mitts didn't move.

Demetri picked him up and set him aside as if he were a feeble book stand. He ran to his truck and reached in to grab her bottle. He took the lid off and peeked inside.

"Jenny?"

Blue smoke swirled out, and Jenny appeared in the passenger seat. It was 12:00 a.m. Her decorative genie apparel adorned her.

"Jenny!" the weaselly voice exclaimed.

Demetri whirled around and realized Mr. Mitts had seen Jenny appear.

Mitts ran around to her side.

Jenny fumbled for the lock.

He screamed, "Open up, Jenny! I'll save you! He's turned you into some kind of sex slave! Just come with me!" Mitts scampered over to Demetri's side.

"Demetri, let's get out of here," Jenny begged him.

She vanished into the bottle, and Demetri shut the door and reached for the key.

SMASH!

Glass crushed beneath the sudden impact.

Jenny heard a muffled scream of pain.

Demetri's head rung.

Mitts opened the door, and Demetri fell out. He stepped on him and crawled inside to snatch the bottle. He scurried back out and then scampered into his house like the little rat he is.

Demetri managed to crawl a few feet over glass shards before the unforgiving blackness took over.

31

Slave

Demetri opened his eyes.

He saw a white light.

His nerves were numb.

Am I dead? he asked himself. He closed them again. *Just take me, Father.* He opened them again. "JENNY!"

He sprung up wide-eyed and looked around. It was all bright and blurry.

"Demetri . . . wait, hold on a second. You need to calm down," a vaguely familiar feminine voice told him.

"What? I, ow! Ow! I-I need Jen . . . Jen!"

He still couldn't make out who was talking to him.

I know that voice.

"Remember me, Demetri?"

"Yeah . . . yeah . . . Jen. I *need* Jen!" He held his head with both hands and squinted down at his lap.

"Jen? Are you on a nickname basis after only two days?" She laughed. "Tell me what happened. Where's Jenny?"

"She . . . she's been . . . TAKEN!" He remembered everything in an instant.

"What? What do you mean? Tell me what happened! Demetri, *tell* me!"

"Cali . . . stop yelling at me, please. It makes my head hurt worse."

"I'm sorry." She asked quieter, "Where is Jenny?"

"She's next door. Mr. Mitts took her."

"Mr. Mitts did this to you and took Jenny? Why?"

Cali couldn't believe Mr. Mitts had it in him to be so cruel. Weird yes. Cruel no.

"I need to get to Jenny."

"Demetri, you have a concussion. You need to stay here."

He stood slowly and stumbled toward the front door in a drunken state. He fell over a little and hit the wall. Cali was right beside him and helped him back upright.

She sighed. "I can see that no matter what I tell you to do, you'll be coming with me anyway, won't you?"

"Yes."

They'd made it to the door now.

"I feel awful . . . I need Jenny."

Cali opened the door for them.

Demetri struggled to keep upright as he half ran, half stumbled across the lawn. It was pitch black aside from Jenny's porch light.

"Why did he do this to you?"

Demetri wanted to be the one to ask questions this time. "How long have I been out?"

"I don't know. I've only had time to pick all the glass out of your cut and clean it. Don't worry, my dad was a nurse, he taught me how to properly clean a wound with glass in it."

"I'm weak." He suddenly felt pain, fear, and torture wash over him. "Jenny! I'm coming!"

"Hold on, you aren't able—"

"No! She needs me!"

They arrived at the door. Mitts had it locked, of course.

Demetri reared back and kicked the door.

The swift movement sent pain to his temples.

"Ow, my head!"

"Demetri, wait . . ." She thought that there might be a better way. "You've lost a lot of blood, and your head is bruised."

None of that mattered. He kicked it again and it broke through.

Cali gawked at his strength in this state.

"Mitts! You give me Jenny back, you fucking weasel!"

His head was in too much pain to try to think of a nicer way to ask. Um . . . make that command!

He wasn't in the kitchen or the living room, not in the bathroom either. Jenny screamed.

Great, he thought. *The bedroom, of course.*

He hurried up the stairs as best as he could. Cali supported him when he lost his balance.

"No offense, but you're a big guy," she grunted as she put his arm around her shoulders to help him up.

"None taken."

He wanted to sleep so badly, and he had the worst migraine headache to date, but he needed to get to Jenny.

The bedroom door was locked.

Demetri busted it down too. With a single kick this time.

He was running out of energy.

Cali just stood there for a moment, wondering if this was all real.

Demetri balanced himself. "Mitts!"

"Oh good, you've arrived," his weaselly voice called.

He had Jenny handcuffed to the headboard on his bed and had her bottle in his hand.

Demetri went for the bottle. Mr. Mitts quickly dodged him, and Demetri tackled only air to the ground.

Cali stepped in through the busted wood and took it all in. She saw Jenny cuffed to the bed in a harem outfit.

"Jenny! What . . . what did he *do* to you? Oh my gosh!"

Jenny had never been so glad to see Cali or Demetri for that matter.

"Cali!" Jenny called. "Help me!"

She rushed over to Jenny and pulled a bobby pin out of her hair and began to work on the lock.

"What are you wearing, Jenny? Did he make you put this on? Was he going to . . .? Mr. Mitts, you're a *creep*! I don't want to even *know* what you were going to try to do to Jenny! You're gonna go to jail for this!"

"Ha ha ha ha! The only one who's going somewhere is you. I wish that you—"

Demetri tackled him successfully this time and made an attempt for the bottle again. Mr. Mitts held it out of reach and then bashed the existing gash on Demetri's head with his knobby elbow.

"Ow!" Demetri called out.

Drops of blood began soaking into his blond curls

"Aht aht aht, Demetri." Mitts scurried from Demetri's loosened hold and fixed his eyes onto Cali. "I wish you would get lost!"

POOF!

Cali disappeared.

Jenny's hope vanished. "Cali! No!"

Demetri drowsily looked up at Mitts and stood again.

Anger filled his bones.

A little adrenaline kicked in. He felt a bit stronger being closer to Jenny.

"Jen, I wish *he* was the one handcuffed to the bed."

Nothing happened.

"You won't make her do things she doesn't want to anymore! *I* belong with Jenny! She's mine! I wish *you* were handcuffed against the *wall*."

POOF!

Instantly, Mitts's wish came true and Demetri had a perfect side view of the bed.

"No!" He tried with all his strength to break free.

Jenny's frightened heart stopped. It waited, petrified for what was next. First Cali was poofed off to who knows where and now Demetri was stuck too. There was no hope now.

Demetri's desperateness grew. "Jenny, just think about being somewhere else!"

Jenny looked at him helplessly. "I can't, Demetri! He took away my ability to wish! I *can't* stop him!"

Demetri felt so useless. He felt Jenny's pain. It tripled his own. It was a wonder that he didn't pass out again. His head spun and his lungs were short of breath. Sweat beads raced each other down his forehead. The pain was unlike anything he'd ever experienced before.

Mitts flashed Demetri a baneful grin. "I want you to see this, Demetri. This is what you did to me. Only Jenny didn't want *you*. She wants *me*!"

"I *don't* want you, Mitts! Keep away from me!" *Dear God, please help!* she prayed in her head. She bunched up her legs to her chest Mitts leered into Jenny's frightened eyes. "Jenny, I saved you from him. He only made you *think* that you wanted him." He came closer.

Jenny pressed her back against the wall as if she could fall through it and escape. "Stay away from me!"

He climbed onto the bed, bottle still in hand, crawled up to her and propped himself up onto his knees.

Her reflexes kicked him in the chest.

He lost his balance and fell backward but still kept himself on his bed.

"owww!" He held his chest. His face scrunched-up. "Bad, Jenny! You don't hurt your master! I wish that your legs can't move!"

POOF!

Jenny's legs became stiff with what felt like a thousand pounds of pressure. She couldn't budge them even a millimeter.

Her face was a mess of fear and tears. "I can't move!"

"Please Mitts No!" Demetri screamed.

Any last hope vanished completely.

Tears clouded her vision.

Mitts glanced back over at Demetri. "I want you to *feel* what I felt." Then he turned back to Jenny. "Jenny, look into my eyes and tell me that you *want* me. I've been waiting a long time for this . . ."

Demetri's eyes grew wide. "NO!

Against her will, she painfully looked into Mitts's eyes. She tried to fight through it with everything she had. It did no good. Her voice shook with disgust, "I . . . *want* you, Leonard."

"NO! MITTS! STOP!"

Demetri was frantic. He nearly busted a blood vessel trying to free himself from the cuffs again.

Mitts placed both his hands on either side of her. The bottle still trapped in his right hand.

Demetri uttered a prayer, "Father, please help us!"

He looked around for *anything*.

His every being fought a battle against exhaustion and severe pain. Sweat covered his pale face.

His brain; about to give up and succumb to the darkness of a concussion again.

His head; bruised blue and bleeding.

At least his blood was free to escape.

He had to think of something.

Demetri sunk his last ounce of energy into kicking the bed's wooden leg. "UNH!"

Mr. Mitts lost his balance and flung his hands out to steady himself. The bottle finally escaped his hands.

Mitts steadied himself and realized that he had dropped the bottle. He didn't have time to try to find it. Jenny was right in front of him. This was his chance; he'd wasted enough time! He was ready to hit Demetri where it would hurt most.

The heart.

"I'm so *close*!" He met Jenny's eyes. "You want me! I know you do!" He lunged forward to kiss her.

POOF!

Demetri and Jenny vanished.

Mitts hit his hard head on his hickory headboard and knocked himself out.

The extra devils left his head.

32

As The Wind Shifts

"Is *this* part of your plan too? They got away!" Dalia turned to Satan, crossed her arms, and shot him a mean look.

"Yes, Dalia. Normally, I *want* people to be impatient, but will you have some *patience?*" He grit his perfect teeth. *I'm getting tired of all her doubt in my abilities. I may drop her and go try my luck with Jenny again. She's willing to give up her pureness to Demetri now. Too bad Mr. Mitts failed, the imbecile! I put **ten** extra devils on his head you'd think that he would've been faster at getting into her pants! The pathetic little rat must've really not wanted to violate her. Why is there still so much **good** in this world? Ugh! The bond between Demetri and Jenny is quite impressive, it's beyond even **my** doing. I can't let them know that! I want to watch for a few days more, but how to distract Dalia? Hmmm. Oh! I know!* "Dalia." He turned to face her. "Why don't you go back to that little merchant guy for a while?"

"What? Are you *mad?*" she asked, her face, plastered with a horror-struck expression.

He turned to her with a manipulative grin. "I need things to play out for a little bit so that the plan can come together."

Her voice rose a few decibels, "You are wasting time! Let me just use my powers to trap her in there and then trade places with me!" She stamped her foot.

"It won't work, Dalia! We have to go about this carefully! Demetri won't let anything happen to her, and he *will* stop you! I've been doing things like this since the beginning of this earth. Trust me."

She stomped over, closer to him. "NO! I do *not* trust you! I only trust *myself*! I want to start doing things *my* way!"

He smiled and casually shook his head at her.

She instantly vanished.

I love seeing myself in people, but right now, there's only room for me. I need you to be gone.

*   *   *

Dalia appeared back in Mimir's shop without a burka. Luckily, it was only seven o'clock in the morning there, and Mimir hadn't opened his shop yet. He was currently stocking shelves and didn't hear her appear. He turned around to stack a different shelf, only to find her staring at him. He jumped back and his hands dropped all the coconuts he was holding.

His eyes lit up. "Dalia! You are back!"

He wanted to hug her, but he could tell by the expression on her face that that wasn't a good idea.

She crossed her arms. "Satan zapped me back here with you in this sorry excuse of a city! AGH!"

She stomped right past Mimir, went back into his bedroom, and locked the door.

Mimir sighed. His hands found all the coconuts and he put them in the sink to be rinsed off later. He headed for his room too.

I cannot believe I have been missing her, he thought to himself. He held his breath and knocked on the door. "Dalia, may I come in?"

She sat on his bed; her legs crisscrossed. "NO! GO AWAY!"

He rolled his eyes. "Please? What happened?"

Silence.

He gave up, knowing her stubbornness. His back slid down the door until he found the cool tiles; it might take a while.

"Please."

"Why do you care?"

She began to cry, but you couldn't tell from her voice.

"I care because you need someone to talk to, and I want to be that someone."

"WHY?"

"I am the only friend you have."

"We are not . . . *friends*!"

He sighed again. "Dalia, please stop yelling at me. Did I do anything wrong?"

She hesitated. "No."

"Then why are you yelling at me?"

"Because I am angry, and I do not have to tell you *anything*, Mimir!"

He shook his head in annoyance, stood back up, and unlocked the door with his spare key.

Dalia swiftly turned around and thrust her left hand in his direction.

He stopped, but nothing happened to him.

A sharp breath entered her mouth. "That con took away almost all my power!"

She still felt a little bit coursing through her veins, but she'd need to channel it for a long moment before she'd be able to use it.

"Dalia, the store is about to open. Do you want to cover the cash register for me?"

"No! I have bigger problems! Leave me!"

He walked up to her and gave her a stern face, "I will not. This is *my* house, and *you* are in it."

Dalia wasn't fazed by his sudden bravery; she crossed her arms like a stubborn teenager.

He bent down and got in her face. "Please, Dalia, help someone other than yourself for once."

"No!"

He glanced over her barely covered body and then back into her eyes.

A devious smile traced her lips. "You like what you see, huh?" she asked, hoping it would scare him off.

His face turned gentle. "Yes, I do."

Her eyes widened.

He leaned forward suddenly and kissed her.

Dalia reared her fist back to hit him, but it grew weak by the time she reached his head. Her hard-fisted hand turned into a soft caress for his face. She lifted her other hand to the other side of his head, and he wrapped an arm around her waist and scooted her back.

He didn't break their kiss.

Who knows how many thousands of moons had passed since she'd last kissed? She hadn't realized how lonely and broken she really was. Her head fogged up, her insides melted, and her body felt numb. She like putty in his hands.

He lifted her back even farther, and her head reached the pillow. He gently lowered his body down to hers and continued kissing her passionately.

People need love every day and Dalia hadn't had anyone to show her any. It was the first positive emotion she'd felt since she was young.

He came up for a moment to look at her. "Dalia?"

She never opened her eyes. She wanted him to keep kissing her. "Mmmm?"

"Will you work the register for me, please?"

Her breath was uneven. "I will do . . . anything you want, Mimir . . . but first, *please* keep kissing me."

He smiled. *Finally, she said **please**,* he thought and kissed her a little more forcefully.

33

Lost

Cali appeared on the damp ground in a dark forest. It was still nighttime, and the mist in the air thick. It tried to suffocate you when you drew in a breath. The moon shone through and lit a path through the brush. The trees were the tallest she had ever seen, and it was quiet. No sounds of mourning crickets whispering to each other, no frogs croaking their sad tales, no crows or ravens to sound their warnings of death, no wind to rustle the papery dead leaves and bury the cold hard ground.

She gasped for air and quickly stood to look around. The heavy mist stayed low.

"Hello? Is anyone here?"

The darkness began to close in on her.

She watched it for a moment and decided it was indeed moving toward her. She started toward the moonlit path, slowly at first, and then the darkness began chasing her.

"HELP!"

No one answered.

She ran a little faster and looked back. It still followed. She looked ahead and ran toward the light.

The only sound was her frightened footsteps trying to outrace each other. The frightened thumps echoed in her head.

Cali glanced behind her one more time.

That mistake caused her to trip.

She tumbled and rolled down an embankment.

Her hands latched onto a vine barely in time to keep her from plunging into a black pond of water.

Now stable, she breathed heavily and slowly sat up against the steep hill.

Her wary eyes focused into the still black water.

It drew her in and invited her to touch it.

She cautiously lowered her hand down to feel the black, murky surface.

Cali quickly retrieved her hand. "AH! Cold!"

It was the coldest water she'd ever felt. It was as still and cold as death itself.

She shook the water off and warmed her hand up with the bottom part of her shirt.

"Someone? *Anyone?* Where am I?"

Cali shrunk into herself trying to be as small as possible.

Her face buried itself in her knees.

Cold tears welled up around her eyes.

Suddenly, an eerie feeling alerted her neck hairs.

She lifted her head and threw her eyes over her shoulder.

It was the darkness again. It had caught up with her.

It crept over to where she was huddled and started to circle her.

Cali had nowhere to go. The frozen water of shadows wasn't an option.

The darkness kept circling like a serpent choking the life out of its victim.

She screamed, "NO! HELP ME, PLEASE! I'm not ready to die! Dear God, please help me!" She found herself on her knees and bowed over them.

Please! Help me!

The darkness prepared itself to consume her.

34

Guilt

Demetri and Jenny appeared back at his house, on the couch in the living room. He held Jenny in his arms as she cried.

"Jen, I got you. I got you. You're *safe* now. Shhh."

It took her a minute, but she finally looked up at him through sobs.

He felt her pain, suffering, stress, and fear on top of his own massive headache and terrible feelings of guilt and weakness.

"What happened, Demetri? How did he get me?" She held onto him tightly, but a new feeling of . . . distrust, maybe . . . came over him.

"Jen, I am *so* sorry." He closed his eyes and looked away. He couldn't bear to look at her. *This is all my fault.*

Jenny finally noticed dried blood on the side of his head and face, neck, and shirt.

She gasped, "What happened to you?"

He looked at her suddenly. He couldn't believe what she'd just asked.

"What happened to *me*? What about what happened to *you*?"

Jenny calmed her tears and her feminine caring side kicked in.

"Demetri, I already know everything that happened to me, but I don't know what happened to your head." She lifted a hand to move his head, so she could get a better look.

He didn't budge.

Her eyes filled with concern. "Let me see."

"No, Jen. It doesn't matter what happened to *me*. I promised both Mr. and Mrs. Conroy, I promised myself, and I promised *you*, that I wouldn't let anything happen to you, and I just broke that promise."

"Demetri, tell me what happened to your head, please."

"It *doesn't* matter. I should be able to keep you safe no matter *what* happens to me—ow!"

The rise in his voice had added too much pressure to his headache. He lifted his left hand to his temple.

Jenny gasped, "CALI!"

Demetri's head had hurt so much that he hadn't been able to think about Cali. His exhausted eyes widened as much as they could manage.

Jenny hopped up off his lap. "We've got to get Cali back here! I wish Cali was here with us!"

POOF!

"AHHHHHHH!"

A high-pitched scream echoed through Demetri's living room. Jenny and Demetri covered their ears and hunkered down. Cali had appeared right next to them on the floor. She was hunched over her knees, both hands trembled by her face.

Demetri tried to put his pain aside. Jenny's feelings of concern began to mask some of the pain.

"Hey, Cali, my walls are made of glass here."

He and Jenny bent down beside her.

Jenny hugged her, and Demetri placed his hand on her upper back.

Cali's eyes burst open. "J-Jenny? Demetri?"

Jenny came out of the hug and tried to comfort her by placing both hands on her shoulders. "We're *right* here. You're safe now."

"Where am I?" She looked around; a terrified expression was still fixed on her face.

"You're at my house. You're safe here," Demetri managed a warm smile.

Jenny searched Cali's large haunted eyes, "What happened to you?"

Her head tipped forward, and her tears fell to their death, "I . . . I don't know. I just appeared in this spooky black forest. The . . . the . . . darkness . . . it . . ." Tears streamed down and created a clear creek down her cheeks.

She couldn't finish. Her brain didn't want to accept that such a ridiculous thing had happened to her. It couldn't have been real, but her fear definitely was.

"Hey, don't worry, you can tell us later," Jenny hugged her again for good measure.

Demetri stood, "Hey Cali, stay here tonight, OK? Jenny can show you a room upstairs. Can *I* get you anything?"

"Um . . . OK . . . thanks." She looked up at him, "How did I get here? Did I pass out or something? Why are you still wearing a sex costume, Jenny?"

Jenny looked down at her genie outfit. The immodesty of it was the last thing on her mind; she hadn't been thinking of herself. The thoughts running through her mind now were: Demetri's head, Cali's safety, and thankfulness to God that they were out of Mr. Mitts's bedroom.

Demetri stepped forward a little, knowing Jenny didn't know how to respond. "Um, let's just get you a place to sleep, OK? It's almost one in the morning, and I think we're *all* exhausted."

Cali yawned, "OK, yeah, I'm so tired. Demetri, you need to have your head looked at."

He nodded once.

She lifted her hand to her throat, "Could I get some water, please?

"I'll get some for you. Jenny, go ahead and take her up to a room, please."

"Yes, mas—um . . . yeah, c'mon, Cali." Jenny guided her upstairs.

Demetri managed his way to the kitchen to get her some water.

Jenny took her to the room on the left across from Demetri's equipment room.

"Wow," Cali exclaimed when she stepped in.

Jenny gave a small smile and sat down on the edge of the bed with Cali.

"So, you and Demetri, huh?"

Jenny smiled at her shyly, "Yeah."

She yawned, "Wow, that's great, Jen."

"Cali, are you OK?"

"I-I think so. I'm OK now, but what I went through, Jenny, was it real? If it was, it was the scariest thing I've *ever* experienced."

"I'm not totally sure. I don't know what you went through. I'm just so sorry Cali!"

Jenny hugged her again and fought back tears.

Cali was happy to accept another hug. "It's not your fault Jenny."

If only you knew, Cali, Jenny thought.

Guilt knocked at her conscience's door. She felt like Cali's getting hurt was completely her fault.

"Do you want to talk about it?" she said instead, still clinging to Cali.

Cali sighed, "No. I just want to get some sleep. Jenny, what about you? What did he do to you? Oh my goodness, I completely forgot about that! I'm so sorry! Are *you* OK?"

"Yes, Cali, I . . . I'm OK *now*." Jenny looked to the side and furrowed her brows.

She still wasn't sure how Mitts was able to get ahold of her.

Cali's eyes turned to the bloodstain red bedspread. "Well, good. I'm *so* sorry I couldn't be more help . . . I can barely remember what even happened. I'm just glad you're OK."

Through bloodshot eyes, she noticed Jenny's neck. There were purplish-red spots in several places. Her eyes grew wide.

She gasped, "Please tell me Demetri gave you those hickeys and *not* that creep ball Mitts!"

Jenny quickly covered her neck with both hands. "Oh, um . . . what are you talking about?"

Her cheeks turned bright red.

Cali's eyes went wide with wonder. "Oh my goodness! It *was* Demetri! Jenny, it's only been *two* days, and he's kissed you *that* passionately? Oh my! Does Mr. Conroy know about this? Aren't they supposed to be making a business deal or something? Jenny!" She smiled teasingly, feeling a lot better. "Apparently, I have a lot to catch up on!"

Jenny couldn't meet her eyes. *More than you know*, she thought, "Um, heh. Yeah . . . I'll tell you about it tomorrow, OK? Hey, how did you know to come tonight? Did Demetri come get you or something? You walked in with him."

Her smile faded and she refrained from averting her eyes, "I just have wicked senses, Jenny."

Guilt tugged at Cali's conscience. She decided to break down and finally tell Jenny.

Jenny smiled and rolled her eyes.

Cali continued with a disturbed expression. "I, uh . . . actually just came back from a date with Stefan, and I came to your house to tell you about it. I know it was late, but I just had to tell you—"

KNOCK KNOCK KNOCK.

"Come in," Jenny called.

Demetri staggered in. "Here you go, Cali. Can I get you anything else?"

He'd brought up a tray and set it on the nightstand. The tray carried a glass of water, a pitcher for refills, and a few homemade snacks that had been stored in the fridge.

"Wow, Demetri! Thank you. That's more than perfect." She gave him a thankful smile.

"Good. I'm glad you're feeling better. If you need anything, Cali, I'm in the bedroom downstairs. *Please* ask, OK?"

He hoped that Cali wouldn't be too afraid to ask for something like Jenny had been.

She yawned again. "OK, thank you, I will."

"Well"—his eyes glanced at Jenny—"I'm going to take a shower real quick." He rubbed his neck. "Um, come tell me goodnight before you go to bed, Jen."

She gave him a smiling side glance. "OK." *Whew, I'm glad I didn't have to say master this time,* she thought.

Demetri still felt Jenny's wavering trust, and he knew exactly what she was thinking. He wanted to make sure he would have a chance to explain what had happened. A sigh escaped his mouth as he carefully made his way downstairs.

Cali poked Jenny and laughed. "Ooohhh!"

Jenny blushed and changed the subject. "Um, do you wanna tell me about Stefan tonight?"

She considered it once more and then changed her mind. "No, not tonight. I'm about to pass out. Are you staying in the other room or . . .?"

Jenny's eyes grew wide. "Cali! You know me better than that!"

Her conscience invited the guilt in.

Jenny had always been reserved, especially when it came to the opposite sex, but it'd been a whole other story with Demetri. She was hoping that some of her recent actions were just because she was a genie now.

Cali laughed. "Well, yeah, but it's been *a while* since you've had a *boyfriend*, and he is really, *really* nice."

"Yeah . . ." Jenny looked down again, feeling lonely all of the sudden. "I need to go see him. Do you want me to stay here until you fall asleep?"

She smiled with her lips together, "No. Go see him. He *really* likes you, Jenny. I can tell."

Jenny began to get up. "Are you sure you don't want me to stay, Cali?"

"Yes . . . go. It's OK," She gave Jenny one more hug.

Jenny gently broke from the hug after a moment and then switched the light off for her.

"Good night, Cali. Sleep in as late as you need to, OK?"

"OK," she yawned. "Good night, Jenny. Thanks."

"Good night, Cali." She smiled and shut the door.

Jenny tiptoed away quietly and then began sprinting down the stairs.

Despite her mixed feelings, she hadn't been able to touch Demetri in over twenty minutes based on the clock in Cali's room. She *needed* to be with him. Demetri was waiting for her at the bottom. She leaped into his arms from the third stair.

Despite Demetri's truly unbearable pain and exhaustion, he caught her and met her lips eagerly. He immediately felt better, and some of his pain melted away.

Jenny wrapped her arms around his neck and kissed him back with equal intensity.

He carried her to his bedroom and sat on his bed

"Ow." Demetri covered his head.

Jenny moved her hand quickly.

"Oh, sorry! I forgot."

He gave her a weak, tired smile. "It's all right. I barely feel the pain when you're in my arms."

She blushed. "Demetri, please tell me what happened to your head."

Her stubbornness came through loud and clear.

He sighed and turned his head away, the good side facing her. "Mitts hit me over the head with a . . . crowbar, I think. I barely saw it before it smashed my driver's side window."

Demetri met her eyes to accept judgment.

He felt like a failure.

Jenny's eyes had grown wider with every word. "Demetri! Oh my goodness, that could have killed you! Are you OK? We need to get you to the hospital!"

She reached to turn his head so she could see the blunt better. He let her this time. She kissed his forehead, not wanting to make his wound worse.

"Jen, I deserve this pain. Don't worry about me."

She took his face gently in both hands. "I want to *heal* you. You do *not* deserve this."

"Jenny, I do *not* want to use your power when it's convenient for me."

She began to tear up. "Demetri! You could have brain damage!"

"I'm just glad you're safe now. I'll be fine." He lifted his hand to move her hair behind her ear and tried to convince her worried eyes with his that it would be ok.

A pained look covered her face. "Demetri . . ." she said weakly.

"Jen, we have to deal with life's ups and downs as they come, and this is just an unfortunate down, and I'm going to deal with it like *anyone* else would have to." He kissed her forehead, "I'm *so* sorry I let you down."

"Don't be sorry. You got hit with a *crowbar*. I'm just glad you aren't *dead*! I probably can't bring back the dead, and I literally *cannot* live without you. I already forgave you, it wasn't even your *fault*, Demetri!"

He sighed. He felt like he could pass out any second now. He took her hands off his face and examined her wrists.

Above her genie cuffs, her skin was bruised where Mitts's wish cuffs had held her to the bed.

His blood began to simmer.

"He tried to rape you! He's going to jail for this!"

She sighed. "Let's just talk about it in the morning, please. I'm so tired I can barely keep my eyes open."

He really wanted to know right then what had happened to her, but his brain couldn't stay awake for very much longer either, and there wasn't anything they could do about it tonight anyway. Demetri searched Jenny's brain for the answers he so desperately needed to know, but her brain must have been trying to block the experience out.

Great, he thought. *She's been traumatized again. I can't believe I couldn't stop this from happening! Why didn't my wishes **work** back there?*

They were *all* exhausted and had each been through their own personal hell.

An aggravated breath rushed out; he mentally calmed himself back down. "Do you want to take a shower real quick?" He asked her.

"No . . . I normally would, but I'd fall asleep in there if I did. I'll take one in the morning."

"OK, good night, Jen . . . I . . . I love you."

He didn't feel worthy of her love, but he wanted her to know that he *did* love her.

She gave him a warm smile. "I love hearing you say that. I love you too."

Her body felt alive, but her brain was about to shut down.

He smiled at her. "Hey, I put your bottle back over there on my desk. Do you wanna sleep in it or . . . you can sleep with . . . *me* if you want?" He looked up at her, hopeful, "You've been through a lot tonight. You might sleep better in my arms."

That sounded so perfect, but she just . . . couldn't.

"I . . . I *can't*, Demetri."

He felt her disappointment and knew she really wanted to.

"I won't do anything, Jen, I promise."

She knew he would keep it but even so.

"Still . . . I just can't. I would rather try to wait. I'm sorry." She closed her eyes sadly.

"Jen, don't be sorry for respecting what your parents taught you. I understand. I just wanted to offer since we've all been through so much today."

"Thank you. I'll just sleep in my bottle."

"All right, see you in the . . . *later* morning."

She smiled. "Night, master."

Jenny squeezed down into her bottle.

"Good night, Jen . . ." He looked after her sadly, still upset with himself.

No matter how much Jenny tried to convince him that it wasn't his fault, he felt in his soul that it was.

Down in the bottle, Jenny crawled under the blanket.

This outfit isn't for sleeping.

She poofed on short shorts and a soft fitted shirt.

Her conscience tugged at her.

She remembered that she hadn't prayed yet.

A sigh escaped her lips. She was so exhausted, it felt like her body weighed a ton. Her body rolled itself over onto her stomach and managed to position itself onto her knees. Jenny prayed. As soon as she said "amen", she collapsed back down to her stomach and fell asleep.

Demetri turned his light off and practically fell into bed. He tried to fall asleep, but his anger kept his brain buzzing.

"AGH!"

He got back out of bed and got down on his knees and prayed too. A few minutes later, he crawled back in, calm now, and fell asleep a few moments later.

He was asleep for thirty minutes when he began dreaming about Mr. Mitts going to jail for what he tried to do.

A satisfied smile found its way across his sleeping face.

Down in the bottle, Jenny began screaming in her sleep.

She screamed.

And she screamed.

Demetri finally was able to achieve a deep sleep for once in his life and couldn't hear her tiny shrieks.

But he felt it.

His own dream of Mitts being in a jail cell was interrupted by the ache of Jenny's first scream.

His conscience tried to wake him up.

It created frightful blurry images. There was someone with an object, a *knife* maybe, coming toward him, and he couldn't move. All he could do was wait for his life to end. The blurred silhouette reared back with the object in hand and came down to stab his chest.

He woke up sweating, heart racing, breathing heavy. He gasped for air and looked around and realized it was just a dream.

Thank God, he thought.

Suddenly, he was overcome by tortured emotions. They ate away at his insides; he couldn't fight it off. He felt the same way Jenny felt in her dream.

"JENNY!" he called out.

He quickly staggered to her bottle.

"I hope this works. Aside from my wish to get us out of Mitt's house when I caught Jen's bottle, none of my other wishes have been working. I wish I was in there with you, Jen."

POOF!

Demetri instantly appeared inside the bottle with Jenny. She was in her bed curled up and crying in slumber. He lifted the blanket and crawled in with her.

"Jen, you're OK. I gotcha." He pulled her up against his body and held her tightly. "Jenny."

He kissed her head.

She wouldn't wake, but worried wails wilted into whispers of whimpering.

He kissed her cheek.

She subconsciously snuggled to him, safeguarded.

He kissed her lips.

Soon, she was silent and still. She wore a small smile in sound slumber.

Demetri stayed as long as he could before he knew he would fall asleep. But he was afraid that if he left, she would start screaming again.

"Agh. You're my weakness, woman, and you ironically make me stronger. I wish we were on my couch."

POOF!

They instantly teleported to his bedroom couch with her blanket still over them.

We slept here last night together. This should be fine . . . with . . .

He passed out.

35

Mitts's Punishment

Mr. Mitts woke up from deep slumber that night to a cold metal bench. His eyes shot open and he flung himself upright.

"Ow! My head," he complained in a tired, ragged voice.

He took in his new surroundings.

The walls were made of concrete and painted a dull gray color. The room was very small, and he suddenly felt claustrophobic. Steel bars blocked his only way out.

"NO!" He shot up off the bench and clung to the bars.

The bars wouldn't budge; he was trapped.

Mitts tried to remember how he got here. He held his head and crept back to the cold metal bench to sit. Memories fit themselves into place like puzzle pieces, but a few were missing.

He gasped, "Jenny! No! I didn't mean to! I—"

He realized there was no one around to convince, and he burrowed down into himself and pulled his knees to his chest.

"No . . . what was I thinking? What did I *do*?"

He began to wallow in his own tears when a faint whistle began echoing around him. He recognized the whistle and scooted closer to the bars.

The woman of the whistle walked past him and then came to an abrupt halt. Her eyes went wide with hope.

Oh my goodness. It finally happened! Mitts finally crossed the line! No more pointless runs to his house! No more reports to try to squeeze into the overstuffed "Mitts" file! Yes!

She backed up and slowly turned her head in anticipation.

"MITTS!"

He met her eyes sadly. "Hello . . . Officer Kelly."

She crossed her arms and stood firm. "All right, tell me, what finally got you canned?"

"I-I don't know exactly . . ."

He knew he deserved it, but he couldn't tell Officer Kelly that Jenny was a genie. He didn't want them going to investigate it.

Jenny must want me in here. I don't blame her. I deserve worse.

"Hmmm. Were you passed out or something?" She raised an eyebrow.

"Um . . . yes."

"OK, well, I have *got* to know what finally brought you in!" she said, fighting off her huge smile so Mitts wouldn't see. She skipped away with a content smile, "Don't go away! HA-HA!"

She wanted to do a little dance but refrained. A quick jig got the job done.

Mitts watched her walk away with melancholy eyes. He slumped back to the cold metal bench and leaned against the wall to try to sleep.

He couldn't.

He felt too guilty to justify sleep.

After thirty minutes, Officer Kelly finally came back. She no longer had a chipper demeanor about her. Her face was determined, bothered, and questioning. She looked at Mitts's lanky, pathetic body leaning against the wall.

"Mitts!"

He jumped and faced her at attention.

"I can't believe I'm saying this, but I have to . . . let . . . you go." She rolled her eyes. "No one knows why you're here or how you got yourself locked in a cell. Our cameras must've glitched because they don't tell us anything either. One moment the cell was empty, the next moment, poof you were here. It's the strangest thing I've ever seen."

"It's OK, Officer. I'd like to stay." He sat back down.

"What! You can't stay for no reason!" She crossed her arms.

He sighed. "Well, can I at least stay one night?"

She sighed now. "Fine. *Only* because it's nearly four in the morning. I'll drive you back to your house at eight sharp."

Mitts thought of the smashed front door; Officer Kelly would surely have questions. She was already suspicious and rightly so.

"No, Officer Kelly, I've caused you enough trouble. I see that now. I'm awfully sorry. If you can forgive me . . . I won't bother you guys anymore."

He at least wanted someone's forgiveness. He'd realized how screwed up his life was while he was trying to fall asleep in the cell. More than anything he didn't want to bother Jenny anymore. Nearly all his calls and false alarms had been focused around her.

Mitts turned his back to her. "I'd like to walk home. I need to clear my mind. It'll be good for me."

She was relieved that she wouldn't have to drive him. "OK, Mitts."

Shannon turned to leave, but her conscience tugged at her.

She sighed, knowing something was wrong. "Mitts?"

He leaned his head against the wall, his back still to her. "Yes, Officer?"

"It's been . . . I mean . . . don't feel bad. I forgive you."

She stared at him a moment longer and then walked away.

Officer Kelly assured him she would be back at eight to let him out.

Mitts gave a small side grin with troubled eyes. They were teared up again. *At least someone does. I wish Jenny knew how sorry I am.*

36

It's About Time!

The next morning, Jenny woke up in Demetri's arms. Her dark-rimmed eyes willed themselves open.

He still slept soundly.

She realized she was directly on top of him. She quickly put both arms on either side of him and lifted her chest off his. Her pelvis was on his stomach.

Demetri opened his eyes to see what was going on.

Jenny was staring at him, breasts in his face again.

His eyes grew wide too but for a different reason.

"Jen, don't move."

"Yes, master."

She couldn't move.

OK, I need to do this carefully. I don't want to freak her out, he thought.

He put his hands on her waist and lifted her as if she was a child and sat her beside him on the couch, locking eyes with her the whole time.

"I'll be right back, OK?" He quickly got up before she could see. "Oh, and you can move now." He went into the bathroom.

Jenny had more questions now than she did before. She let out a sigh and stared out the floor-to-ceiling windows. It was 12:30 p.m. and a beautiful Saturday morning, well, afternoon. She dragged herself off the couch and brought her blanket back into her bottle.

She felt like she could go back to sleep. *I need to take a shower,* she thought to herself. *Once again, I will be taking one in the **morning**. Err . . . afternoon.* She sighed. *I really don't like early showers.*

Jenny picked out another outfit and peeked out of her bottle to make sure Cali wasn't up yet and then came back out. She met Demetri halfway.

She was in her genie costume again.

"Good morning." He smiled and looked her over.

"Morning." She blushed and cut straight to the point. "Why did we sleep on the couch again? I'm ninety-nine percent sure that I fell asleep in my bottle."

He focused into her wondering eyes. "You had a nightmare last night, and your terrified emotions woke me up. So, I wished myself into your bottle and as soon as I wrapped my arms around you, you began to calm down."

She looked down. "Oh." She looked back up at him. "Thanks then . . . and for sleeping on the couch and not in my bed with me." She gave him a small embarrassed smile.

He matched her smile. "No problem."

Demetri wanted to kiss her so badly. His whole body wanted to pull her to him and hold her close again, but he refrained and found that it was a lot easier this time.

Good. I'm finally getting closer to my old restraint levels. I feel like a heel for everything I haven't been able to stop myself from doing with her. Even if she did want it, that isn't an excuse.

He looked down. He was glad she couldn't feel his feelings or read his mind.

Jenny tried to control her feelings as well. She was also getting a little better at it. She discovered last night that she could intentionally push her emotions onto Demetri to make him feel a certain way. She knew she had to be careful because she had also seen his temper, but she was sure that was mostly because of Derek.

Her eyes fell away sadly. "May I take a shower, master?"

Her cheeks didn't turn red.

Her heartbeat didn't speed up.

She felt like it was all her fault that he had gotten hurt. She was about to crumble into tears.

"Yes, Jen. I'm going to get started on breakfast."

He could feel a new jumble of emotions coming from her. This one was weird. Pain, longing, reflection maybe?

Then he recognized one for sure—guilt.

He shook his head, wondering why she felt guilty. Her pain made him hurt equally inside. Demetri gave her a harmless hug to cheer her up.

She smiled. He couldn't see it, but he felt it.

Good, he thought, and he smiled too. "All right, I'll be waiting for you. You can't take more than twenty minutes, all right? Cali is here, and we must start trying to learn to . . . *control* ourselves. One of us can't be the only one trying because that has failed in the last two days." His eyes were soft.

The more he tried to refrain from embracing her, the harder it became to actually convince himself not to.

"OK, I have to leave now." He fast walked out of his room and gently shut the door.

Jenny stared at his bedroom door. *Why did he practically **run** away?* She sighed and headed towards the bathroom. *I wish I could know how **he** felt for a minute.*

POOF!

A wave of emotions showered her. She knew them all immediately— pain, desire, refrain, guilt—and understood why he had to leave. She smiled and ran to the shower.

I have to hurry, or we might tear each other's clothes off in front of Cali!

There was just one emotion that she wasn't sure about. It bothered her a little and she wasn't sure if she really wanted to know the answer, so she didn't pry anymore into his mind.

I wonder why he feels regret . . .?

Jenny hoped it wasn't because he'd decided to help her figure all this out last Thursday. She was so afraid that it was indeed the answer that she'd nearly convinced herself that it was.

The shower masked her quiet tears.

Cali finally awoke. She felt great, surprisingly.

"Where am I? Oh yeah, I'm at Demetri's."

She crawled out of bed to stretch and took the tray back downstairs.

"Good morning, Demetri!"

He was finishing the eggs.

"Yes, thanks. Wow," she said, as she scanned everything he was preparing.

"I hope you like it. Just a few more minutes."

Demetri wore long dark jeans and a gray tank shirt that clung to his body.

Cali couldn't help but notice how ripped he was.

*Wow, no wonder Jenny likes him, **and** he cooks.*

"Cali!" Jenny hugged her from behind. "How are you feeling this morning?"

"I feel very rested, but I still don't feel good about everything that happened last night."

"Well, you will forget about all that bad stuff after you've had Demetri's cooking."

Jenny smiled big for Cali.

She hoped her eyes weren't red from crying. Cali would be able to tell instantly if something was wrong.

Demetri grabbed a hand towel from the bar and then turned to look at Jenny.

She was wearing a short white skirt today.

He dropped the hand towel and went wide-eyed.

The skirt came above her knees, probably a good six inches. Her blouse was a soft yellow with cupped sleeves and cut straight across her front, between her chest and collarbone.

*At least her **shirt** is covering because her **skirt** isn't. Please, God, be shorts underneath.*

"You've had his cooking already?" Cali raised an eyebrow.

Her cheeks turned rose. "Oh, um yeah . . . dinner. Mr. and Mrs. Conroy were here last night for the business dinner."

Jenny went around to the kitchen to help Demetri *and* to be close to him. She instantly felt a lot better.

If Demetri regrets helping me, then hopefully this outfit will change his mind. Or at least take his mind off it for a moment . . .

Jenny bent down to pick up the hand towel.

Demetri snapped out of it and looked away, even if she had bent down modestly by bending at the knees instead of the waist.

"Thanks," he mumbled and quickly returned his attention to the eggs.

Jenny's insides sank. His reaction wasn't exactly helping all her doubt right now.

Cali put both elbows on the counter and watched them work together. "Wow, so he knows you're dating? How did he take it?"

"He and Carrie both know. Carrie took it great, but Mr. Conroy . . . not quite *as* great. He's giving Demetri . . . a chance."

With that statement, Jenny remembered they were still officially dating. But for some reason, it didn't feel like they were anymore.

Jenny set the breakfast table, and Demetri finished cooking. Between the both of them, they didn't have to say a word to each other. Maybe the speechlessness was just because they both felt bad.

Cali raised her eyebrow again. "You guys work together like you've been doing it for years."

Demetri answered her, "Yeah. We have a . . . *connection* of sorts. I feel like I've known her for a long time." He smiled at Jenny.

Jenny blushed, and her insides warmed.

She couldn't stand knowing what his feelings were from earlier; she'd rather live in her perfect positive little naïve bubble.

*This is **killing** me! I don't know how he deals with my emotions all the time! I'm probably killing him inside right now too. I wish I could take back knowing how he felt earlier.*

POOF!

Jenny stood there, dazed for a moment.

All the hurt had vanished.

She noticed Cali and then Demetri. Jenny wrapped her arms around him abruptly. She couldn't help it.

"Woah! Jen! I have a hot pan in my hands!" His face turned red as he balanced it.

She blushed and unwillingly let go. "Oh . . . sorry."

Cali laughed and shook her head. "Jenny, what are you doing?"

She turned around to face Cali and changed the subject. "Time for answers! Cali, how did your date go with Stefan? Or if you wanna tell me later, that's OK too . . ."

Jenny thought maybe Cali wouldn't feel comfortable talking about it in front of Demetri.

Cali smiled, "Oh, no, I don't mind talking about it now."

"After you guys left the office Thursday, he asked me to go to eat with him. Then after I got off work, I met him at the restaurant." She stopped for a moment and studied the white countertop. "Jenny, he's . . ."

Cali just couldn't say it, so she decided to skip it.

"I just don't have that . . . *spark* with him. And I know the spark exists because *obviously* you two have it."

Cali glanced between them both and tilted her head with a knowing look.

Demetri and Jenny glanced at each other briefly. Jenny grabbed her right arm, and Demetri looked away and rubbed his neck.

Cali cocked her head a little more and continued. "Anyways, he's . . . I, um . . . I just thought I just needed to spend a little more time with him before I called it off. Just to be sure the spark wouldn't come later or something. So, I followed him to his place."

Jenny's eyes grew wide.

Cali continued. "We went inside and talked. Later, he pulled out some wine. Pretty soon, clothes were on the floor, and we were in the bedroom . . . well, you know how it goes. Well, I'm sure you don't *know, know* how it goes, but you *know* how it goes."

Jenny offered a small smile. She understood what Cali was trying to say.

"I fell asleep with him, and when I woke up, it was really late. I didn't want to stay the night though. I really wanted to see you and stay up late to talk about it like we always do when I have a date."

"Wow, Cali, you actually . . . did it with someone?" Jenny couldn't believe it. Cali wasn't the sleeping-around type.

"Um," Demetri interrupted. "I need to call John, all right? I don't need to hear this part. Breakfast is ready. If you guys want to go ahead and eat, I will join you in, um, about . . . *ten* minutes?" He wondered if that would be enough time for their "girl" talk.

"Ten minutes should be fine, Demetri. Thanks." Cali was thankful for his consideration.

Demetri gave Jenny a quick kiss on the cheek, which made her face scarlet, and then he went to his room to make the call.

Cali continued. "Yes, I did, and I was doing so *well* too, twenty-five years, ruined last night." She buried her face in her crossed arms.

Jenny rest her hand on her shoulder. "Hey, don't beat yourself up. You've been together for a little while. It wasn't like it was a one-night stand or anything."

"I mean, um . . . but I just wanted my first time to be with the *one*, ya know?"

She and Jenny moved to the breakfast table.

"You don't think he'll be the one?" Jenny sat next to her.

"No, I mean, he's . . . great. I just have . . . a feeling that he isn't the one for me."

Cali looked sad. Jenny didn't know if it was because she had lost her virginity or because she still hadn't found anyone she clicked with.

She sounds a lot like Lewis, but I don't think I should bring him up yet. "Hey. What happened, happened. You wouldn't have done it if he hadn't given you alcohol."

"True. I shouldn't have had some. It's all right, Jenny. I mainly just needed to tell someone. I *do* feel better telling you." She gave a small accepting smile.

Jenny felt a lot better too. "Is that *all* you wanted to talk about?"

"Well . . ."

Cali just *couldn't* tell Jenny yet, maybe not *ever*. Instead, she changed the subject.

"I do want to know what happened before I showed up last night."

Jenny looked down with furrowed eyebrows. "Mr. Mitts hit Demetri in the head with a crowbar, and then he dragged me away with him."

Cali's eyes burst open in horror. "Jenny! That's *awful*! He could have been *killed*!"

Jenny's eyes quickly found Cali's. "I know, that's what I told him!"

Cali tilted her head out of concern and put her hand on Jenny's arm. "What did Mitts do to you?"

"Well . . . let me go get Demetri real quick."

She went into Demetri's room and turned the corner.

"RAHHH!"

"AHHHHHHH!" Jenny jumped into the air.

"HA HA HA HA HA!" Demetri laughed.

"Demetri!" Jenny put her hands on her hips, and Cali came to the door's threshold.

"What happened?"

She looked at Demetri.

Cali screamed in terror too, "AHHH!" She clung to Jenny.

Demetri kept laughing. He took off his mask. "HA HA HA! I got BOTH of you!" He fell back on his bed still laughing.

Jenny raised one eyebrow at Cali. "Ready?"

"You bet!" Cali answered with a determined face.

They both grabbed a pillow and started hitting him with it.

"HEY! Jeez, I'm sorry." He shielded his face, still smiling.

Jenny and Cali laughed now.

"Stop! Please have *mercy* on me." He kept smiling and laughed a little more from Jenny's laughing.

Jenny stopped hitting him with the pillow.

Cali looked over at her. "Aw, c'mon, Jenny, you aren't going to give up *that* easily, are you?" She wacked him a few more times.

"Yes, I am." She gently touched Cali's arm. "I think we've gotten our payback now."

"Jenny, did you see that psychopathic, deranged clown mask he was wearing? That thing will give you nightmares!" She shot a more serious look over at Demetri.

Jenny went to pick the mask up off the ground. "Demetri, why did you have this thing on?" She held it away from her body with two pinched fingers.

Cali hid her eyes and turned away.

"I was trying to scare you. And it worked," he flashed her a triumphant smile, "and besides, Halloween is next month, I was going to see what you guys thought of it." He sat up in bed with a smug look. "I want to scare Lewis too. He is terrified of clowns!"

Jenny's eyes burst open, "I am *not* kissing you on Halloween if you wear this. It's absolutely repulsive." She gave it a disgusted look and tossed it at him.

"Aw, c'mon, it's not *that* bad."

He quickly put it on and started chasing them back into the main room.

They screamed and ran around the bar.

Demetri took it back off and laughed again, "All right, I won't wear it, but only if you go with me to find something you approve of."

Cali moved her eyes sideways and nudged Jenny. "You should wear your sexy genie outfit for Halloween, Jenny."

Jenny's face was painted clown-nose red, and Demetri rubbed his neck again.

Cali crossed her arms and continued, eyeing Demetri now. "You could role-play as her master and—"

Jenny covered Cali's mouth. "Cali!"

The color of Demetri's face matched Jenny's now.

"There!" Cali moved her hands to her hips. "That's my payback, Demetri. I also am *terrified* of clowns."

Demetri gave her a small smile. "Fair enough. I apologize, Cali. I only intended to scare Jenny if it makes you feel any better."

She smiled.

Demetri continued, "And to finish answering your question from earlier Jen, I just wanted to lighten things up a bit."

Jenny raised an eyebrow at him, "Lighten things up by darkening them with a demonic clown mask?" She crossed her arms.

His smile turned flat, "Sometimes light is found amongst the dark."

They stared at him for a moment and Cali broke the silence. "OK, let's eat. I'm hungry!"

Demetri pulled out a chair for both of them.

They both thanked him.

"Wow, Demetri, I've never had a guy pull out a chair for me." Cali looked up at him in surprise.

"Jenny never had a regular guy open the door for her either, until Thursday. What's the world coming to? Here, Jen, I also made you some hot chocolate."

"Aw . . . thanks." She gave him a shy smile. "But I really don't need it this morning. My throat isn't sore. Come to think of it . . . it wasn't sore yesterday either."

That's probably because I've been holding you for the last two nights, Demetri thought.

"I'll drink it anyways though. I can't turn down a cup of cocoa!"

"Would you like some as well, Cali?" he asked before he sat back down.

She gave him an appreciative smile. "Oh, no, that's *Jenny's* thing. I'm great with the orange juice right here."

"All right then. Let's give thanks and eat," Demetri said.

They did so, and then Cali took her first bite.

"OK," she said while still chewing, "*this* is the *best* breakfast I've ever had. I didn't know eggs could taste this good! What did you do to them?"

Demetri smiled. "I'm glad you like them, but sorry . . . I can't tell you what I did to them."

"Why not?" She took another bite.

Jenny rolled her eyes playfully at Cali. "Demetri is *big* into secret recipes."

"Ah."

Jenny turned to Demetri. "So . . . Cali came to my house late last night to talk about boys. What happened after that?"

Demetri responded, "I don't know. I woke up in your living room."

Cali answered them both, "When I pulled in, I saw that Jenny's truck had been smashed on the driver's side, and when I got out, I found Demetri on the ground."

"That's actually Demetri's truck."

"You guys have the same truck?" She gave them a look of disbelief.

"Yeah, except his is dark-blue."

"Hmmm, it was pitch-dark out. I thought it was yours. Anyways, I thought you were . . . *dead*, Demetri. I bent down to check your pulse. You were breathing. Then I kind of dragged you inside"—she gave him a tilted smile— "and then I was able to see the blood. Had I known you had been hit, I wouldn't have moved you."

They listened intently.

Cali continued, "I used some oils to bring you around a little faster than you would've on your own. You had me worried there for a while." She smiled at him. "But you pulled through remarkably fast actually, almost like . . . knowing that Jenny was in danger made you come around." She glanced at Jenny's now red face.

"Hmmm, well, I guess breakfast is the least I can do for you, Cali. You saved my life! If your date hadn't turned out as it did, then you wouldn't have come to Jenny's and kept me from bleeding out. Not to even mention what would've happened to Jenny."

Jenny smiled at them both.

Cali reflected for a moment. "Hmmm, well, I guess *something* good came out of it. I'm glad. That makes me OK with how everything happened. If it saved you and then enabled you to save Jenny, then . . . I have no regrets!" Cali sighed acceptingly.

Jenny grinned thoughtfully. "Things work out in a mysterious way like that sometimes, and you just have to look at the positive side to see it."

She was glad that Cali felt better.

Demetri turned his whole body to face Jenny. "All right, please tell us what happened to you now, Jen."

It had been eating away at his insides. He was tired of waiting for her to tell him.

"Um . . . well, I can't really *say* Demetri." Her eyes went wide, hoping he would get the message.

She had no choice but to tell him.

"But since you *asked*, I guess I will have to try my best to remember *everything* and tell you right *now* . . ."

"Wait!" He sighed. "You don't have to worry about it right *now*." He leaned his head to the side and rolled it back a little.

He *still* wouldn't be able to know.

"Jenny, just tell us what you remember," Cali requested.

"Um, it's just . . . *hard* right now." She looked into Cali's concerned eyes.

She hadn't wanted to tell even Cali, but Cali had never lied or kept anything back from her as far as she knew. Cali had just told her about the most intimate night she'd ever had. Jenny felt it was wrong to keep her secret from her best friend. So, she opened her mouth to tell her everything.

"Jenny . . .," Demetri said uneasily.

Jenny wondered how Demetri knew that she was going to confess.

Cali looked at them both eagerly.

"Demetri, I *have* to. Cali is my best friend. She will understand." She gave him a reassuring look and a little smile.

He breathed out a breath of air. "OK, Cali, brace yourself."

"Brace myself for what? Jenny, did Mitts get the chance to do something awful to you?"

She gave Cali an uneasy smile. "NO, no, but, um . . . there is actually something *else* that I need to tell you first . . ."

"Well, go ahead. You know you can tell me *anything*."

Saying that to Jenny pricked Cali's conscience.

She so badly wanted to tell Jenny what was really going on in her own life.

"First, I need you to promise you won't tell anyone."

"Jenny, I've *always* kept your secrets, and with especially everything that went down last night, I'm not saying a word about it. I promise I won't tell."

She met Demetri's eyes, almost for permission.

Jenny looked plainly into Cali's wondering eyes.

POOF!

37

This Isn't Real

*J*enny had made their breakfast disappear.

Cali jumped back and nearly tipped her chair over.

"What the *heck*?" She moved slowly. "OK? Did anyone just see breakfast disappear, or am I just sleep-deprived?"

Jenny furrowed her brows and informed her as plainly as she could, "Cali, *I* made it disappear. I am a . . . genie."

"What? Just . . . what?" She tilted her head and squinted her face a little. *I must still be asleep,* she thought.

Jenny rest her hand on Cali's arm.

She made breakfast reappear.

Cali raised her voice uneasily, "Um, OK, I'm dreaming! I'm *only* dreaming!"

A few deep breaths zipped their way into Cali's lungs.

Demetri just watched, on guard. He wasn't totally comfortable with this because it endangered Jenny.

Mr. Mitts already knew, and thankfully, his reputation wouldn't get him anywhere except the madhouse, but if he *and* Cali told, then an investigation might happen.

Jenny explained all about how she became a genie and the events that followed, but she left out the intimate parts. She even told her about their encounter with Satan's.

Cali listened with a fake smile. "OK. Now, I *know* I'm dreaming. I can't believe this dream is so real! That might explain Demetri's clown mask though too. I *hate* clowns. I wondered why I didn't have a bad dream last night. It's happening *now*."

Jenny stood. "Cali, this *isn't* a dream. You always tell me *everything*—"

Cali flinched.

"—so I'm not keeping this from you. Look."

POOF!

She conjured a folded extra set of clothes for Cali.

Cali's facial expression didn't change.

She truly had convinced herself that this was a dream.

Jenny sighed.

She knew it'd be hard to convince Cali. Cali was very science-minded.

Jenny handed the folded dress to her. "Why don't you go upstairs and take a shower? Put these clothes on and come back down. Maybe *then* you'll realize this isn't a dream."

Cali accepted the dress. "OK."

It was all she said; her face unchanged.

She backed up a little, never taking her eyes off Jenny, and finally turned around and walked back upstairs to take a shower.

Jenny looked back at Demetri and sighed. She let her head fall a little. "Did I do the right thing?"

He stood up and came to her.

She felt better when he touched her arm.

"Jen, you did the right thing if your conscience was fine with it. Cali is your best friend."

"Should we tell Lewis then too since he's *your* best friend? You guys have been best friends waaay longer."

The idea of him knowing too didn't affect her conscience in the least.

Demetri drew in a breath. "I guess we should, but I would prefer to not tell him until he has split with Mel."

Jenny smiled up at him. "OK. He's your best friend, so your rules."

Knock knock knock knock knock knock knock!

Demetri turned to face his front door with slightly annoyed eyes. "Jeez! Who the world?"

He let go of Jenny and briskly walked over. As he got closer, he heard muffled complaints going a thousand miles an hour. Demetri turned back to Jenny and rolled his eyes.

"Speak of the devil . . ." He opened the door and leaned on it casually. "Hi, Lewis."

"Man! Whatcha doin'?" Lewis said, face all scrunched-up in annoyance. "You changed your password on me? You tryin' to keep me out or some—" He noticed Jenny coming closer and stopped. "Ohhh, you didn't want no one comin' in here 'cause you *actually* busy this time. Ah, I see, I see, well, I'll just come back later a'ight?"

His feet backed away; a big smile covered his face as small laughs escaped his lips.

Demetri shook his head and looked down. "Lewis, get your butt in here. For the last time, we *aren't* doing anything."

Jenny smiled at him. "Yeah, c'mon in, Lewis."

"Well . . . if y'all are sure. OK!" He swiftly strut in with a big 'Lewis' smile, and Demetri shut the door behind them.

"What's up, man?" Demetri asked.

Lewis ignored the question. "Ah, y'all having breakfast?"

He noticed that there were three plates and got excited.

"Hey, you was expecting me? Great, man! It's about time! I can't believe it took you twenty-three years to be able to anticipate when I would show up." He sat and noticed the plate was riddled with crumbs. "Hey . . . someone ate all my food!" He crossed his arms.

Demetri rolled his eyes again and went to fetch Lewis a plate.

Jenny laughed. "Lewis, my best friend Cali is here. She'll be right down." Jenny thought excitedly, *Wow, they'll meet, and I won't even have to arrange it or anything! I really don't want Lewis to date someone like Mel. He deserves better.*

Demetri flashed Jenny a confused expression that she didn't notice and then handed Lewis his own plate.

"Thanks, bro. Hey, Jenny, Demetri *does* make better breakfast than me, by the way." He took a bite. "Mmmm, *so* good!"

* * *

Upstairs, Cali was in a zombified state. She let the water run over her head. *This water is real.*

Well . . . is it real?

Is my life real?

What is life?

Why am I here?

She snapped out it.

*Jenny is **not** a genie.*

*Jenny is **not** a genie.*

*That's ridiculous . . . right? Mr. Mitts isn't that type of man, weird, yes, dangerous, **no**. Demetri's clown mask, yuck. **Not** real. Jenny's story, heh, **not** real! OK, good, we are getting somewhere. This shower . . . is . . . **real**.*

She sighed.

Back at square 1.

She stepped out of the shower and dried off.

*Demetri's **house** is real . . . This **towel** is real . . . These **clothes** are real, even though she made them appear out of **nowhere**.*

Cali put them on and took a deep breath.

It was a beautiful olive-green dress with a V-neck collar and loose cupped sleeves. The waist had a slender black belt around it, and the dress loosely hugged her sides all the way down past her knees just a tad.

OMG. This dress is the one that I wanted so badly a couple of months ago but couldn't afford. She remembered that?

Scratch that.

*She poofed it out of thin **air** for me?*

Cali forgot about everything and looked in the mirror. She'd absolutely loved this dress in the store and loved it even more now that it was hers.

*Is it mine? I mean, this **is** just a dream, right? Well . . . I might as well enjoy the dream. I don't want this dress to disappear. Hmmm, I wish I had my brush and makeup.*

POOF!

Her brush and makeup appeared.

She stared at it for a moment before slowly poking the hairbrush; markings traced the handle in delicate cursive.

*This is my **real** brush. It has **my** initials on it . . . This is **my** actual makeup too. OK, well, I'll just . . . go along with it. Whatever.*

She gave herself another once over in the mirror and smiled slyly.

Let's just have some fun!

* * *

A couple of minutes before, Jenny had figured Cali was almost done, so she poofed her hair and makeup things over for her.

She crossed her fingers, *Hope it doesn't freak her out too much.*

Lewis talked between bites, "Yo best friend is here?"

Jenny returned to the conversation with a jittery feeling forming inside. "Yes. I can't *wait* for you to meet her."

Demetri held in a shudder from more girly feelings bouncing their way in. He successfully dissipated the feeling.

"Jeez, D., you got a house full of girls! You lucky, son." He shook his head and kept shoveling food.

"Lewis, it's not like that, and you *know* it."

Demetri stood behind Jenny and put his right hand around her right hip.

Lewis shook his head again. "Man, you guys act like you can't be apart for more than three minutes."

They both laughed kind of awkwardly.

Demetri raised an eyebrow at Lewis. "So, man, why you back so soon? Couldn't get enough of me? Or did you just want to see *Jenny* again?"

"Nah, man, I didn't even know that she would be here." He turned to Jenny. "You livin' with him now or something?"

Jenny's eyes went wide. "Uh, no, it's not like that. I actually . . ." She looked down.

Lewis hopped up to put his plate away, still listening.

Demetri followed Lewis with his eyes. "Um . . . a lot happened yesterday, Lewis, which also why Cali is here."

"Even though I'm still not sure how I got here," Cali said as she entered the main room.

Lewis turned around and began to say, "Hey, you must be Cali. Nice to meet you," but the second he saw her, he froze and went speechless.

"Cali"—Jenny smiled— "this is Demetri's best friend, Lewis."

Cali stood beside Jenny and gave Lewis a quick smile. She didn't even meet his eyes. "Nice to meet you, Lewis."

Cali was a receptionist and had to put on big formal smiles for everyone every day. In this "dream," she didn't feel like being caring, cordial Cali.

She turned back to Jenny and pointed to her dress with an ecstatic expression and began with the girl talk again.

Demetri walked over to Lewis and waved a hand in front of his face. With his right hand he made a walkie talkie noise by covering his own mouth. "Earth to Lewis, this is D1. Come in, Lewis. Over."

Lewis whacked his hand away. "*Very* funny," he said quietly.

He couldn't take his eyes off Cali.

"D.?"

Demetri put his arm around Lewis's shoulder. "Yes, Lewis?"

Lewis tilted his head toward Demetri's and whispered, "I-I don't know what to do, man."

Demetri whispered back with a teasing grin, "Well, actually saying words is an idea."

He smiled, glad he could finally tease Lewis about a girl for once. Lewis never brought girls over to his house, probably for that exact reason. He pulled Lewis into a headlock and rubbed his hair.

"Hey, man, watch it." He backed away from Demetri. "Not the hair!"

Lewis turned back around and ended up right in front of Cali.

He smiled and held his breath.

She stopped talking to Jenny and took a good look at him for the first time.

He extended his hand abruptly.

She raised an eyebrow and shook it, still not really meeting his eyes.

"Hi," he managed to say.

Jenny noticed how quiet Lewis had been. She noticed his dumbstruck hold on Cali too.

Good, she thought. *Maybe now he won't go on that date with Mel.* "Um, why don't we all sit down?"

Lewis turned to Jenny. He felt a little light-headed. "Good idea, Jenny." He headed for the couch.

Jenny sat Cali down beside Lewis and then went to sit by Demetri.

Everything was quiet for a minute.

Cali looked at everyone. "So, what happened to you yesterday, Jenny?"

Dream or not, she wanted to know what happened to her best friend.

"I really can't say." She looked at Lewis and then Demetri.

Demetri sighed and refrained from rolling his eyes. He was never going to learn what happened. He had been intentionally reading her mind all morning so he could find out, but Jenny was blocking it out, probably for very good reason.

"Lewis, if you tell anyone this, including Mel," Demetri said sternly, "I will kick your ass!" He looked at him with a stern look and put his right arm around Jenny.

Cali's eyes widened a little; Demetri meant business.

Lewis was surprised too. "Woah! Now I know my man is serious. He *never* cusses! All right, all right, man, I promise I will not tell, no matter what!"

Jenny tilted her head at them. "Lewis . . . I'm a genie."

Cali's intent eyes transformed into annoyed ones. "Oh *no*, not *this* again! C'mon, Jenny, can't we do something else in this dream besides talk about that? How about that other dress I liked that day too? You remember, the yellow one!" She smiled really big.

Lewis raised an eyebrow, "OK . . . obviously I *missed* somethin'? What's goin' on?" He scanned his skeptical eyes at everyone, even Cali.

They caught him up too.

Cali was bored.

Lewis squinted his eyes. "D.? You got hit in the head with a crowbar? Let me check you out." He got up to see for himself, whistled in amazement, and then sat back down beside Cali.

Lewis then turned to Jenny. "If that Mitts creep did anything to you, Jenny, don't worry, I'll take care of him for you."

Jenny smiled a weak smile and then continued. "Look, I can't tell you guys what happened until you believe that I'm a genie, or none of it will make any sense." She gave them each a serious look.

"I believe you guys, Jenny," Lewis stated.

"You *do*?" Cali shot Lewis a flabbergasted expression. "C'mon, Lewis, it is absolutely *ridiculous*."

"No, girl, I *know* Demetri, and he doesn't pull stuff like this. He's the most serious person I know. I don't know how, but Jenny is a genie." He laughed. "Man, D., no wonder you dumped Mel. This all makes *sense* actually."

"I didn't dump Mel because Jenny is a genie. I just ended an unhealthy relationship with her because I knew I could have a healthy one with Jen." He thought to himself, *Well . . . If we can overcome these extra temptations from the devil himself that is.*

Cali tilted her head at Jenny. "Wait, Mel as in the Mel who used to work at Mr. Conroy's?"

Jenny nodded.

Cali continued. "Wow, Demetri, yeah, it's *definitely* better that you ended that. She was an awful person to be around. Probably still is. People like her don't change easily."

Demetri furrowed his brows, which went unnoticed by anyone.

He still didn't believe Mel was a bad person.

"Cali," Jenny asked with hopeful eyes, "do you believe us?"

"Jenny, just go on with your story. We wanna know what happened already, dream or not."

Jenny wanted Cali to believe her first. "Cali, what can I do to make you believe?"

"I don't know." She flipped her wrists outward. "I mean, anything can happen in a dream, so I don't think you'll be able to do anything that'll convince me."

Jenny gave up. "Fine. But this *isn't* a dream. You'll see that as the day goes on."

Lewis studied Cali. With the new information, he was feeling more confident now. "So, you think you in a dream, baby doll?"

Cali's eyes grew wide; she glanced sideways in his direction. "Um . . . yes. This is a dream because this isn't *real*, Lewis."

Lewis couldn't help himself. Cali was the most beautiful girl he'd ever seen. Before she could react, he cupped the back of her head and pushed his lips into hers.

Cali's eyes burst, but since this was a "dream," she just let it happen.

She wrapped her arms around his neck and thought, *What the hell? Why fight it?*

Demetri and Jenny gawked at them in shock.

Demetri's expression changed first. *There's the Lewis I know,* he laughed in his head.

Jenny peeked over at Demetri with a hopeful smile.

"No, Jenny. Refrain . . . *please.*"

Demetri hated having to say that. He liked the disappointed look on Jenny's face even less.

Jenny's head fell a tad, "I just want one little kiss."

He grabbed her hand and kissed *it* instead.

That made her feel better.

She glanced up at him shyly, briefly before returning her eyes to the lovebirds in front of them.

Lewis and Cali were still kissing.

Demetri and Jenny glued their eyes to the floor and then the ceiling and waited a moment longer. Apparently, they had no plans to stop anytime soon.

Jenny pursed her lips awkwardly and pulled Demetri up and led him into his room.

"Jen, what's Cali going to do to Lewis when she finds out this isn't a dream?" He sat on his bed and waited for an answer.

"I don't know, but they *need* to be together." She peeked back out.

They were still going at it.

"What do you mean?" He got up and pulled her to him and sneaked one more look. "You don't think we should stop them?"

"No, Demetri!" she whispered. Jenny pulled him to the bed, sat down next to him. "I think they are perfect for each other. When I met Lewis, I thought of Cali. I just have a *feeling*." She smiled confidently.

Back in the living room, Cali had lost track of time and being.

Oh man, this is . . . the best dream ever.

Lewis had never felt so determined to keep kissing a girl.

Oh yeah, this one is the one for me. He leaned her against the armrest and hovered over her, lips still connected.

Cali's head spun. She felt butterflies in her stomach, and her heart beat uncontrollably. She detached her lips and held him away from her.

"What's wrong, baby doll? You finally realize this isn't a dream? True love's kiss is said to wake you up, so you know what that means, right?" He smiled down at her.

He had his "Lewis charm" back.

She stared back up into his dreamy blue eyes. "Yes, I know that."

Cali sat up and covered her face with both hands.

She began gently crying.

Lewis furrowed his brows. "Hey, girl, I'm sorry. Look . . ." He got off the couch, got on his knees, and brought her hands away from her face.

Her tears spilled over; she had a quiet cry.

"I didn't mean to hurt you. It's just you're the most beautiful woman I've ever seen. I *had* to kiss you. Please forgive me. I don't know if I could live with myself if you didn't, baby doll." He gazed deep into her eyes and meant every word.

She blinked a few times, trying to get the tears to stop.

He lifted his thumbs and wiped them away for her.

"It's not that, Lewis . . . It's just I've been looking for the *one*, and I've been waiting for a spark." She sniffed then continued, "I *finally* get one, and it's . . . in my *dreams*."

Lewis's heart pounded.

His eyes bulged excitedly.

"Cali, this ain't a dream. C'mon, girl, have some faith here. If you think that I'm the one for you . . . then will you please believe? For me?"

"Lewis"—she wiped away the last of her tears—"I would do *anything* for the one that I'm supposed to be with."

"OK, I'm not a dream. Have you ever seen me before?" He took her hands again.

"No."

"A'ight, your brain can't make up faces, let alone full bodies."

Cali believed that part.

"But—"

"Please just humor me in believing, OK?"

"OK, Lewis." She smiled at him and gently brought her hand up to touch his face. *He's so real feeling. Why am I being punished like this?*

"A'ight then. Stay here for me, OK? I'm gonna go get D. and Jenny, and she can tell us what happened to her now."

"OK, Lewis." She let her hand gently fall and watched him walk away.

"Hey, you two, I hope I ain't *really* interrupting something this time . . ." He knocked on Demetri's bedroom door.

Jenny opened it before he knocked three times.

"Oh, I ain't. Man, D., you have some serious self-control, brother. Being alone in your own room with a girl and all."

Demetri gave him a side grin of achievement.

Jenny bounded over to Cali. "Do you still think that this . . . What's wrong? Lewis! What happened?"

Lewis flashed them both a movie star smile. "Man, Jenny, she thinks I'm the one! Can you believe it? This is the *best* day of my life!"

He sprung up to slap a confused-looking Demetri a high-five and then sauntered back over to sit beside Cali.

"Cali?" Jenny sat on the other side and put her arm around her.

"Go on with your story, Jenny. I want to know what happened. I believe you, guys . . . I guess, but *only* for Lewis's sake."

Jenny furrowed her brows. It wasn't the answer she'd hoped for, but it was better than nothing. "OK," she decided.

She padded over to sit by Demetri, who was on the verge of ordering her to tell. He *needed* to know what Mitts did.

"So . . . I could tell my bottle was moving, but I didn't know that Mitts had it until I heard his rackety voice."

38

Christmas In A Bottle

"Hee hee hee, I got you, Jenny! You're all mine!"

Mitts scurried into his house and shut the door. He quickly locked all eleven locks and sat the bottle down on the counter.

He popped the cork off. "Come on out, Jenny! You're safe now!"

The devils rubbed their hands together evilly.

"Oh no!" Jenny hid underneath her blanket, like it would do any good. "I wish to be back with D—

Mr. Mitts eagerly rubbed the bottle.

Jenny automatically evaporated into smoke.

She wisped up and out and appeared next to Mitts.

He took a good look at her. "Jenny, you're . . . hot!" He moved his hand toward her leg, and she punched him in the face. "ow!" He held his nose and jumped around. "What did you do that for?"

"Stay back, Mitts! I don't like you like that."

"Yes you do, Jenny!" His eyes were wildfire, "Your feelings for Demetri aren't *real*!"

Jenny was afraid that *half* of that was true. She still wasn't one hundred percent sure that she and Demetri would even be together if she wasn't a genie. Sure, they both liked each other from the start, but after that, things were rocky until they tripped over the bottle.

Mr. Mitts started coming forward toward her.

She conjured herself a baseball bat in hand.

"I'm warning you, Mitts! I don't want to hurt you!"

"No, Jenny, there won't be any more of that. I wish you didn't have the power to grant yourself wishes while I have you." He smiled at her madly.

POOF!

The bat disappeared.

"What?" She looked at where it used to be in her hands.

He walked toward her. "Wow . . . that outfit doesn't cover much, does it? You're always so covered up; this is a . . . *pleasant* change."

"Mitts, stop, *please!*"

She covered her chest with her arms. She never showed her cleavage in public, let alone to creepy Mr. Mitts. She began backing up the stairs and reared her fist back again to punch him.

He took a step on the first stair. "I wish you wouldn't hurt me."

POOF!

She couldn't bring her hand forward. Her eyes were wide with hopelessness.

*He has taken away my ability to escape **and** defend myself.* She started to cry. "Please, Leonard, this isn't like you! Please!"

He stopped for one moment and shook his head to clear it.

"Jenny? What are you doing in my house? I mean, you are perfectly welcome . . ." He noticed her outfit. "Wow, is this a dream?" Drool formed in his mouth.

Jenny calmed a little.

The devils kicked in again with full force.

His eyes changed. "Jenny . . . agh . . . I . . . ahh . . . Jenny, I don't want to have to wish it! Come on now . . ."

"No, Mitts! NO!"

Jenny whirled around and ran upstairs into the first room she saw. She frantically locked the door and leaned against it with her back. She breathed hard, thinking for sure she'd be raped. She started to cry again.

"Jenny, Jenny, Jenny," Mitts sang. He grabbed the extra key above the doorframe and slowly slid it into the keyhole.

The metallic prodding of the key triggering the simple mechanism echoed in her brain.

Hope was dwindling quickly.

"No, Mitts, please don't do this! This isn't the Leonard Mitts that I know."

She dug her feet into the carpet and pushed against the door. She heard the key turn.

Click!

"Jenny, tell me you want me." He slowly turned the knob.

A tear hit the floor.

"I . . . want . . ." She breathed hard and tried to fight it with all her being . . . but couldn't. "You," she finished painfully.

Another tear soaked into the beige carpet.

Sweat beaded her forehead and her hands shook from fright.

He couldn't budge the door. "Then why don't you let me *in?*"

Jenny squeezed her eyes shut and prayed to God that she would make it out of this with her virginity. She had been ready earlier that night but *not* with Mitts. The experience had reminded her just how fragile her pureness was. On top of all her terrified feelings, she felt very unworthy for any miracle from him.

Please forgive me, Father. These temptations have been unlike anything I've ever been put through before. Please forgive me.

Mitts let out a low growl.

Jenny's voice was frantic, "I *don't want* you, Mitts! Stay *away* from me, please!"

He grinned. "I wish the door would open."

POOF!

The door burst open.

"Ahhh!" Jenny was flung forward but her hands thought fast and caught her weight. She quickly scrambled back around to face her predator but only to find him completely devil-crazed.

Mitts slowly came forward just enough to shut the door behind him.

"Stay back!" she yelled through tears.

His voice low and mocking, "Jenny"—he locked the door and began following her again— "it's me, Leonard, Lenny! You're *safe* now!"

"Am I, Lenny? Am I safe? I don't *feel* safe."

He dropped the key into his pocket.

She kept her eyes on him while trying to open a window. It was locked surprisingly, and she didn't have time to unlock it before he got too close. She jumped onto his bed and back off the other side. Her eyes scanned the room for anything to use to knock him out.

Not even so much as an alarm clock waited on his dresser or nightstands.

"Yes . . . Jenny . . . agh! You're *mine* now!" He lunged for her over his twin-sized bed.

She leaped away and started for the door.

Maybe she could break it down.

"I wish you wouldn't try to leave!" Mitts yelled quickly.

POOF!

An invisible barrier kept her from escaping.

Her hands prod and pounded against it.

"Please let me out! Don't do this!"

The devils in him loved toying with her.

He lunged for her again and chased her around the room a couple of laps.

Jenny's heart beat faster than it did during intimate moments with Demetri.

"Hold . . . *still*!" He lunged at her again.

Jenny had to stop, the red color in her face drained away. Along with it went all her hope.

He knocked her to the floor.

She couldn't move.

Tears rolled down her cheeks.

"Please don't . . ."

He gazed into her bloodshot eyes. "Stop crying, Jenny."

POOF!

Her tears ceased; forced to betray her.

"This is a *happy* thing. You and I *finally* can be together now!" Both his paws were placed on either side of her. He slowly bent down.

"Please don't, Leonard . . ." she whispered. Her face was turned away; eyes clenched shut.

He hesitated.

She opened one eye.

"I don't want to do it like this . . ."

Jenny held her breath.

He gave a small grin. "I wish you were trapped in my bed."

Jenny's eyes glazed over with disappointment.

POOF!

Her hands were cuffed to his headboard.

Trapped.

Her body didn't have much energy left but even her sweaty hands couldn't slip themselves out of the extra set of handcuffs.

Mr. Mitts heard a bang at the front door and distant muffled screaming.

"No! Your idiot *boyfriend* is trying to stop us!"

He realized that he didn't have the bottle. Mitts wished for it to appear in his hands.

POOF!

His wish was granted.

An idea came to him.

I can trap him too and make him watch us make love to each other.

Jenny screamed out, hoping to make her location known to whoever had just broken the front door down. She hoped it was Demetri, but at this point, she didn't care who it was or who else saw her in such a skimpy outfit.

Jenny just wanted out.

Mr. Mitts waited behind the way of his bedroom door.

A few moments later, Demetri busted the bedroom door down and nearly fell over from pain, blood loss, and exhaustion.

Jenny's extra exhaustion had been weighing down on him immensely.

He began to see colors.

The light in Jenny's eyes reignited with hope and gave Demetri the extra boost he needed to keep going.

39

"Tear In My Heart"

"Well, you know the rest . . ." She curled her knees up to her chest and rest her head on them sadly.

Demetri had contained himself to let Jenny finish. He had to let his anger out now.

He roared, "AGH!"

Everyone sat upright.

He leaped over the coffee table, swung himself over the couch, burst the living room door open, and ran as fast as he could out into his backyard field.

Lewis sighed. "He will be back in less than a minute."

"Are you sure?" Cali asked. "He isn't stopping."

"I'm sure, baby." He smiled at her.

Butterflies came alive in her stomach.

Jenny went to the window. "What's he doing, Lewis?"

"Uh, Jenny"—Lewis stood, walked over next to her, and rest his right hand on her right shoulder— "Demetri has . . . *temper* issues."

Jenny furrowed her brows in concern; she didn't want Demetri to be upset.

Lewis continued. "He joined track in high school, and continued it in college, to run off all his anger. He's really, really, really, *really*, angry right now. Probably the angriest I've eva seen him."

She searched Lewis's eyes. "How can you tell?"

He returned his wide eyes to Demetri. "Uh . . . 'cause he's back already." Lewis had never witnessed him running that fast before.

Jenny studied his behavior scientifically, wondering if it would be safe for her to go out there.

Demetri peered into the sky for a moment and then lowered his toned arms down and made fists. He slowly turned to meet Jenny's eyes for a brief minute.

She watched in awe at his displays of athleticism. A shy smile formed on her lips; she hoped it would calm him down a little.

Suddenly, a very confused Mr. Mitts appeared on his knees in front of Demetri.

Demetri gave Mitts a glare that could've given a deer a heart attack and drop dead. He reared his fist back, ready to bring it all down on him.

Jenny gasped. She ran out there as quickly as she could.

"No, Demetri, don't!"

He stopped.

His fist shook with anger impatiently.

Mr. Mitts screeched, shielded his face, and hunkered down.

Jenny shoved calm emotions into Demetri. It was difficult at first because she had to be calm herself to do it.

He stood there with his fist still in midair. "Jenny . . . *stop* trying to sway my mood."

She obeyed against her own will.

Lewis and Cali stood outside closer to the door. Lewis, out of instinct, positioned his body in front of Cali's just a touch. "D. I don't think I can let you do that to him."

Demetri ignored him.

Jenny pressed herself against Demetri in a hug and considered his wild savanna prairie, fire-lit eyes.

He couldn't help but regard Jenny's, which were gray.

The sun lit her irises, and the gray pigment glowed beautifully.

The tenseness in his body loosened.

A favorite memory reassembled itself.

This is just like the first time I'd seen her eyes light up in the sunlight. They'd been gray then too. Is this how she felt back then? I wonder why she was upset . . .

"Demetri . . ." Jenny shut her eyes and reached up to kiss his chest.

It felt like an eternity since she last kissed him. Her lips longed for his, but she was afraid that would make things worse. On top of that, she didn't like displaying public affection. Her intimate life wasn't anyone else's business.

He let out an annoyed breath. "Ugh! Why won't you let me punch him? He deserves to be taught a lesson!" He brought his arm down.

"Demetri, you didn't let me tell you all what I thought about it."

Demetri had been too frenzied to read her mind. He'd just been listening to her words and then his own thoughts had taken over.

His eyes flared. "What's there to know? He made you do things that you didn't want to do. He made you cry and scream, he nearly raped you, and you want to *protect* him? He belongs in jail!"

His anger had built again despite his momentary loss of thought from Jenny's melanin.

"Wait"—she made him meet her eyes— "he didn't even kiss me. Yes, he did the other things, but I don't think he wanted to." She turned to Mr. Mitts. "Lenny, you didn't want to do those things, did you?"

He slowly pulled his hands down to reveal his shameful face. "No, Jenny! I swear! I would never want to hurt you!" He started crying. "I'm so sorry! I don't know what came over me! That wasn't me."

Demetri glared down at his puny figure. "He can say whatever he wants now because he knows I'll pulverize him."

Jenny tried to get him to look her in the eyes again. "Demetri, the times that I called him by his name, it's like the *real* him was trying to get out or something. I believe this is Satan's doing. Lenny doesn't deserve to go to jail. I've lived next to him for a long time, and he's never tried anything like that before. He's certainly had plenty of opportunities, especially since I live alone."

Demetri sighed, not wanting to accept any of it.

He was reminded of Satan's promise that they would be separated and be sorry. He knew all too well how difficult it'd been to fight off the devil's temptations with Jenny. It actually made Mr. Mitts look pretty good if he fought it off that well, as long as that *was* the case.

He looked into Mitts's sorrowful eyes and decided to just go with Jenny on this one.

But his anger still needed an outlet.

If he couldn't punch Mitts in the face, then he *could* punch him in the heart.

He took Jenny into both arms, leaned her back a little, and kissed her passionately in front of everyone.

Jenny's whole body went weak, and yet she felt more alive than she had all day.

Demetri held her firmly against him. He controlled the situation and didn't even feel one ounce of temptation to *have* to keep going.

Good, I can control it. I finally don't feel like I have to tear her clothes off when I kiss her.

Mr. Mitts's eyes fell sadly.

All the hope of him and Jenny being together vanished from existence.

The punch to his heart was so forceful that it tore through.

Demetri slowly let her down and made sure she had her balance before letting go.

Jenny held onto him until she could think clearly. Her cheeks heated from the sudden realization that their kiss had been in front of everyone.

He glowered down at Mitts; his voice a warning. "Jenny is *mine*. You're lucky that she was here."

Lewis cleared his throat with authority.

Mitts began crying again. "I'm sorry, Demetri. I hit you with a crowbar . . . I-I've never done anything like that before. I don't even *own* a crowbar! I don't know what came over me. I'm sorry to both of you. Jenny . . . oh, Jenny." He brought his face to the ground.

Jenny bent down. "Lenny, please. This wasn't *all* you . . ."

He dared to meet her kind eyes.

"I forgive you, Lenny. Please don't cry." She gently lay her right hand on his back.

"I don't deserve forgiveness. Jenny, I'm so sorry!" He curled up in a ball.

Jenny stood and examined everyone.

Cali still didn't think this was real.

Lewis watched intently and silently, ready for whatever was next.

She took in Demetri, who had his tensed arms crossed. She tried to ignore his dreamy arms.

"I wish we *all* knew if Satan had anything to do with Lenny's actions yesterday."

POOF!

Everyone, including Mitts, was knocked back a little and went blind. There were a few unanimous *"woah's,"* as they threw their arms out to steady themselves.

Mr. Mitts, on his knees, nearly rolled back onto his bottom.

Previous events from yesterday consumed their sight. They saw Satan, in Jenny's house, telling Dalia that he would put extra devils on Mr. Mitts's head to show her what real power was like. The vision ended, and they could see again. They all either rubbed their eyes or shook their heads.

Lewis came forward a little, hands on hips. "Hey, Jenny, how about a little warning next time, huh?"

Cali flashed Jenny a nonchalant expression. "Cool, Jenny. A dream *inside* a dream."

It hadn't bothered her one bit.

Jenny shook her head plainly. She couldn't believe Cali *still* thought this was a dream.

Demetri stood in front of Jenny and then extended his right hand out to Mr. Mitts to help him up.

Mitts looked up at him meekly with a wet red face and weakly extended his hand to accept Demetri's.

Demetri helped him up and placed his hand on his shoulder. "Mitts, that was a lot of Satan's influence to fight. Jenny is right. The fact that you physically didn't do anything is no small matter. Thank you for fighting it."

He couldn't believe he was just thanking the man who *almost* did who knows what to his girlfriend, but he couldn't deny what he just saw, and Demetri wasn't past forgiveness no matter how bad his temper. He didn't want to have to stew about it for years to come. It was better to leave it behind in the past, so he could move forward on a positive note with Jenny.

Jenny gave Mitts a soft smile. "I forgive you. Please accept it. It wasn't all your fault."

"Jenny"—he hung his head— "thank you . . . Thank you *both*." He looked up slightly at Demetri. "I think it's best if Jenny doesn't stay at her place for a while or . . . even ever again . . . just in case. I *don't* want to be the one to hurt her. I've always tried to look after her, but I realize now that I've been too much. I apologize."

Demetri nodded.

Jenny smiled at Mitts's realization. *Hopefully he can finally have a normal life and make some friends.* "Bye, Lenny. I wish you the best," she said.

Mr. Mitts gave her a soft, farewell smile. He loved that she had finally called him Lenny; even Leonard was good.

Demetri thought about Mitts being in his own house again. He even threw in an extra thought about both doors that he destroyed being fixed and his hand being fixed as well. Although, it hadn't seemed to bother him since.

POOF!

He disappeared.

Mitts opened his clenched eyes. He was in his quiet little kitchen, at his sink. He turned around and notice his front door was fixed. He perked up a little and scampered upstairs to see if that one was fixed too; it was.

"Thank you, Demetri," he muttered to no one.

* * *

Satan watched unbeknownst to Mitts again.

Hmmm, he thought, *it would seem that Demetri is learning to control his temper a little better. AGH! That stupid girl is ruining him! In a "good" way! I cannot believe he did not even do anything to wimpy Mitts! They will pay for this!*

Enough was enough. He no longer cared about seeing his creation come into full glory. It was ruining everything!

All he wanted now was sweet revenge. And control of everyone's souls of course, but one thing at a time!

Or maybe I can get both at once.

He thought for a moment about what he could do next while Dalia wasn't holding him back.

Who can I mess with that would tear them apart?

He thought for another moment.

Ah! Bwahahahaha! How come I didn't think of that before?

Two people came to mind, and then he vanished.

Satan's work is never done.

40

She's Gone

Jenny flashed Demetri worried eyes. "You sent him back to his house, right? Not . . . jail or the middle of the woods?"

He gave her a satisfied half grin. "Don't worry about what I did, and trust me, OK?" He ran a finger along her jawline.

Her stomach flipped with that small touch. "Yes, master." Her cheeks turned pink saying it in front of Lewis and Cali.

They came over.

Demetri took a step away from Jenny. He could control his urges now, but he wasn't a fan displaying public affection toward anyone, even Jenny.

Cali spoke, "Jenny, this is a really weird and long dream. When am I going to wake up?"

"You *won't*, Cali." Jenny turned and pinched her.

She grabbed her arm where Jenny pinched. "Ow! Jeez! What was that for?"

"See? You *aren't* dreaming." Jenny crossed her arms.

"It will take more than a pinch to convince me." Cali crossed her arms too.

Jenny gave her a hopeless look and an idea came to her. She snapped her fingers. "I've got it! I know how to make you believe now!"

Cali got an idea too and returned Jenny's smirk. "Good luck, Jenny Ann." Her face turned smug face at the sight of Jenny's fiery red cheeks. She glanced at Demetri briefly and then back at Jenny. Cali gave her a "Take this" smile and continued. "Jenny Ann Dayton. Hmmm . . . that sounds pretty *good* actually. Don't you think so, Lewis?" She gently elbowed him.

Jenny stood, petrified; her heart thumped loudly in her chest.

Demetri's wide eyes matched Jenny's.

Lewis laughed. "Hey, that *does* sound pretty good. Good one, baby!" He held up his hand for a high-five, and she gave him one. *Definitely the girl for me. She even got D. with that one!*

She turned back to a still petrified Jenny and shrugged. "Hey, this is a dream, and you're 'apparently' getting ready to wake me up, so I wanna have some fun first. *That*"—she pointed at Jenny— "was for the pinch." She crossed her arms again.

Jenny sighed and grabbed her right arm, still embarrassed.

POOF!

Cali vanished.

Lewis threw his head back. Red and blue lights flashed in his brain. He glanced around, and then came forward quickly. "Hey! Bring her back! That was the woman of my dreams!"

"Relax, Lewis. She's in there on the couch."

He didn't waste a second and sped into the living room.

Jenny began to follow, but Demetri grabbed her right arm. She turned to him but couldn't meet his eyes. Her right arm still over her other spoke for her.

He tried to meet her eyes anyhow. "Jen, do *you* like the way it sounds?"

The only thing going through her mind was surprise that Cali had gone that far with her teasing.

She played dumb. "Um . . . like the way *what* sounds?"

Demetri let go of her arm and walked off toward the living room. "Never mind." He hid a smile. *That's what I thought.*

At that moment he decided to block out any more of her thoughts for now. He had learned how to keep them out and be able to just focus on his own. He wanted to let her have her rightful privacy.

If only I could learn to keep her emotions from clouding mine. That's hard to get used to.

Jenny followed him with her eyes.

She sighed. *Maybe he doesn't feel the same way. He's controlling himself better, maybe it's . . . disconnecting us a little? Driving a wedge?*

Jenny gave up and tried to control her own feelings. She didn't want

Demetri to know *everything* she felt, especially if she wanted it hidden. She forged the bubble in her mind again, hoping it actually worked.

Jenny followed after him.

He held the door open for her.

She didn't look at him but mumbled thanks.

Her feelings must've hid themselves pretty good because he didn't seem to notice any change in her mood.

Lewis turned to Jenny. "Jenny, what's *wrong* wif her? I can't get her to wake up!"

"Lewis, I'll wake her up in a minute, OK? She needs to be asleep right now. When she wakes up, she'll be able to accept everything from now on as reality." She turned to Demetri. "I'm going to need to use my power for this to work. Is . . . that OK, master?"

He nodded at her.

Jenny wanted him to say something.

She sighed inside and kept her emotions bottled up where they wouldn't be able to get out. Hopefully. Jenny placed her fingertips on her temples and thought carefully. She spoke out loud, so everyone would be on the same page. "Demetri's truck window is fixed."

POOF!

"My truck is here in the garage next to his."

POOF!

"Cali won't remember that Demetri and I are dating."

POOF!

"Demetri's head is healed as if the blunt never happened."

POOF!

"Jenny! I told you no. How were you even able to disobey me?" He thought back to what he had said and realized that he didn't actually *forbid* her to do it. *Crap,* he thought.

Lewis stood. "Wait, she has to do *everything* you say?" He turned his head to the side and squinted.

Demetri sighed. "Yes, Lewis. I'm her master."

"Shhh! *Both* of you! I'm trying to focus!"

They obeyed.

Demetri crossed his arms, feeling a lot better now that his headache was gone.

She continued. "Mr. Mitts's doors—"

"Wait!"

She flashed Demetri a 'what now' look.

"Jen, I already fixed those for him."

She was taken aback. "You did that for him?"

"Yes, I did. Don't act so surprised, please." He kept his arms crossed.

"Yes, master." She continued again. "Stefan will have memories of calling me to come get Cali after she got drunk."

POOF!

Lewis interrupted this time. "Wait, *what*? Some punk got *my* Cali drunk? Who this man, Jenny? Tell me! I need to know!" He hopped up to put his hands on her shoulders out of desperation.

Demetri stepped forward out of reaction.

"Lewis"—Jenny opened her eyes— "I'm *trying* to help you *both*. Please go sit by her in case she wakes up."

He sulked back over to Cali and sat beside her head. His hands gently caressed her beautiful pale face.

Jenny continued *again*. "They never had sex."

POOF!

Lewis flung up, steaming. "WHAT? He got her drunk *and* had sex with her!"

Jenny rolled her eyes while her lids were shut and ignored him. "He *only* called me to come and get her, so she'd make it home safely. We'll keep the part about him wanting to have another date with her Monday."

POOF!

Lewis tapped his foot with impatience and crossed his arms too.

"Cali's car is still there. Lewis will drive her to it after she wakes up. She will still think that me being a genie and everything else is a dream, for now."

POOF!

Jenny gasped and started to fall.

Demetri caught her.

Her heavy eyes fluttered open and shut.

He picked her in his arms and sat with her.

"Jen! Are you OK?" He brought his face close.

Her eyes closed, and a soft long breath escaped.

"Jen! Jenny!" He shook her gently.

He felt something radiate from her. Demetri didn't know what it was, but whatever it was, it scared him.

"Jen! Wake up now!"

Nothing happened.

He waited.

"Lewis! This is taking longer than it should!"

Lewis came over and held her hand. "C'mon, Jen-Jen, wake up! You freaking us out, girl!" He looked up at Demetri. "She's the only one who can wake Cali up. Man, if we don't fix this, *all* of us are screwed."

Demetri briefly flashed him a pained look.

All of a sudden, Jenny's silver cuffs began to glow blue.

"Woah, D.!" Lewis jumped back a little. "What's that?"

He noticed his ring; it started glowing too.

"Woah!"

"Man, D., what's going on?" Lewis studied the phenomenon warily.

"I-I . . . don't know, Lewis. This hasn't happened before. Jen . . . please wake up . . . for me."

His heart thumped loudly in concern.

He closed his eyes and rested his forehead on hers.

She began to feel lighter and lighter in his arms.

"What in the world!" Lewis exclaimed.

Demetri opened his eyes.

She was gone.

He felt her weight cease from existence.

"Lewis! Where did she go?" He jumped and looked around. "Jenny! Jenny! Come back!"

Demetri quickly scattered the books on his coffee table and frantically tossed accent pillows aside. "Jen!"

"Man, I don't think she's gonna be under that pillow." Lewis scanned the room.

Demetri stopped; he knew Lewis was right. *Where could she be?*

He bolted into his room and came back out with her bottle. He felt a little better as soon as he grabbed it.

He glanced at Lewis with determined eyes. "She's in here!"

Lewis shot him a look of insanity. "What? Man, how you know?"

"I can *feel* it, Lewis. Here, hold this, and *don't* drop it, OK?" He carefully placed it in Lewis's hands. "Jenny's life, and mine, are in your hands, Lewis."

"That's a lot of pressure, D." He was a little uneasy but held it firmly. "What you gonna do?"

Demetri locked his gaze on the bottle. "I wish to be inside with Jenny."

POOF!

Demetri appeared at Jenny's bedside.

She lay on her bed, unconscious.

He quickly crawled over to her.

"Jen!"

He turned her onto her back and lay his face on her chest to hear her heart.

It beat very slowly.

Demetri leaned down to kiss her. *Please, Jen, wake up. I love you,* he thought when their lips connected.

He held them there.

And held them there.

And held them there.

And finally, he felt emotions wash over him, and then he felt her kiss back.

Jenny wrapped her arms weakly around his neck.

Demetri slid a hand under her face and kissed her for a moment longer and then unwillingly parted his lips from hers.

He stared at her. "Jen?"

It took a lot of strength to open her eyes; she felt like she would pass out again.

He steadied her head.

"What . . . happened? Deme . . . tri?"

Her eyes closed again.

"Jenny, stay awake."

"Yes . . . master." She willed her eyes to be kept open.

They were bloodshot. Dark bags hung around them.

"Jenny, Cali is still asleep. You are the only one who can wake her. Lewis is going crazy up there."

Her heart felt sad.

Is that all he cares about? "OK. C-Cali. I wish to wake . . ."

Her eyes shut again.

Demetri felt a weight on his heart and pulled her up to a sitting position. He leaned her against his chest and scooted back against the wall of the bottle.

"Jen, just rest . . ."

He cradled her against him.

"I wish Lewis would safety set the bottle down on the coffee table and appear in here."

POOF!

Demetri felt a soft movement and a second later Lewis appeared at the foot of Jenny's bed.

"Man, something's controlling me! It ain't cool! What in the world? Where am I?"

"Lewis, we're inside Jen's bottle."

Lewis took his word for it.

He took in his surroundings and craned his neck to see up the tube in the ceiling. "Wow, man, I can hardly believe it. So, this is the alleged bottle, huh? I mean, I have to believe it one hundred percent now. Cool . . . OK, what's going on? Is Jenny OK?" He scooted over a little closer to them.

"I . . . I don't know, Lewis. She feels . . . exhausted."

"So, you feel what she feels too?" He squinted a little, trying to understand.

"Yeah, I feel everything she feels, and it's increasing. Her emotions can cloud mine. They can overtake mine completely. I don't think it will be long at all before she can control *me*. Ironic, huh?" He let out a breath of laughter.

He wanted to tell Lewis that he could read her mind too, but ultimately decided against it.

"Wow, dude, that's intense!" Lewis considered Jenny in wonder.

"I think all the wishing she did wore her out," Demetri said hopefully.

"Yeah . . . that could make sense. I mean, I'm no *genie* expert, but I could see it. Maybe this bottle is like a recharge or something?"

"Yeah . . . yeah!" Demetri lit up a little. "That's why she appeared in here. She didn't even have enough power to dissolve into smoke like normal."

Lewis furrowed his brow. "She *really* does that?"

"Yeah." Demetri brushed her jawline gently with his knuckles.

Lewis watched. "So, man, you really like her for her? Or do you like her because she's a genie?"

"Lewis, I know this sounds corny or whatever, but I knew that she was the one from the first moment I saw her."

His eyebrows shot up. "So, you gonna marry her then someday?"

"I-I don't know, Lewis. I want to, but she's still got feelings for an old boyfriend. I don't want to command her to choose between us. I want to let it be her decision."

He felt better being able to talk to Lewis about it.

Lewis gave Demetri a joking smile. "So, if you don't stay with her, does that mean I get my twenty dollars back?"

"Lewis! This is serious, dude!" Demetri shot him a look.

"Man, I'm just playin' with cha. But seriously, dude, you've got it made, bro. A woman who doesn't argue. She listens and respects what you want and *does* it, *and* she calls you master! That's the *dream*, man!"

"I know, Lewis, but I don't know if she obeys me because she wants to or because she *has* to. That isn't *love*, Lewis. I love her, but I'm not exactly sure if she really loves me or just *thinks* she does because I'm her master."

"You can't tell from her feelings?"

"No. Just because she feels something doesn't mean it's real . . . It's hard to explain. Girl feelings are more complicated. I just can't say for sure." Demetri studied her face.

"Man, you sound like you don't want her to be a genie."

He looked Lewis dead in his eyes. "I guess . . . I guess I don't."

"Man . . . that's some deep stuff. I don't even think I understand it all. Look, can't you like just set her free or something?"

"She wished to be free. It didn't work."

"But like, ain't you the one in charge and all? No matter what she wants, what you want is more . . . *powerful*, right?"

Demetri's brain worked overtime. "You may be onto something, Lewis."

"Wait, man, we need to wake Cali first, a'ight?"

"Don't worry, we will."

"Mmmmm," Jenny mumbled. She weakly managed to open one eye. A blurry figure was just a few inches away from her face.

"She's waking up now, Lewis."

Lewis started to say something, but Demetri teleported him up to the couch beside Cali again, full-sized.

"Yo, bro! Not cool! Give a man a *warning* first!" He crossed his arms for a moment and then rest his hand on Cali's face again.

Back down in the bottle, Demetri focused into Jenny's drowsy eyes.

"Jen, it's me. How do you feel?"

She opened her eyes a little more. They were still bloodshot and were completely gray-looking.

Maybe they're just gray?

"Demetri?" she asked halfheartedly.

41

My Master's Request

"I'm right here, baby." He stared into her tired gray eyes.

Despite her drowsiness, her *blue* eyes replaced her gray and burst open. She shot up in his arms. Pink slowly won the battle over the weak pale of her cheeks.

"You . . . you called me baby."

Demetri gave her a small grin. "Yeah, do you like it?" he asked softly. He rubbed his neck and hoped she did.

"Um, yeah, I do. It's just . . ." She looked down, embarrassed.

"What is it?" He waited patiently.

He felt certain old feelings returning.

"Um . . . it's just . . ."

"Oh, of course!" Demetri stood now.

She gently fell out of his lap and back to the bed.

"*He* used to call you baby, didn't he?"

Once again, she couldn't meet his eyes. She felt like she had betrayed him.

"I'm sorry, master."

Demetri didn't want to call her something that would remind her of another boyfriend.

"Derek. He isn't even *here*, I haven't even *met* him, and he's controlling what I *can* and *can't* call you!"

He paced.

Jenny kept her head down and grabbed her right arm.

"Demetri . . ."

Demetri bent down and put his fists against the bed on either side of her. He held his face close to hers.

"What?" He had a blank look on his face.

She slowly met his eyes. "I don't know . . ."

He sighed. "No matter what you say, I *know* you still like him. We can't date while you have feelings for someone else. I don't care how small the feelings are." He looked into her eyes and continued. "I don't know how you truly feel about me because of this genie-master stuff, but I *do* know your feelings for Derek are real." He looked down. "I'm not going to *make* you choose, but I am going to give you the freedom to be with who you want."

She gave him eyes that were full of pain, "Demetri . . ."

He didn't let her finish, and he couldn't look her in the eyes. "Jenny, I'm breaking this off with you."

His words hit her like a ton of bricks.

It hurt.

Her heart screamed no and reached for Demetri's as he backed away. It pounded and pounded, trying to break free and join his.

It didn't want to be broken.

The dust cleared.

"Demetri, no! You don't mean that!" Her eyes welled with water as she waited for a final confirmation.

"Yes, Jen . . . Jenny," he corrected himself, "I do." He crossed his arms and turned away from her.

She fell back a little, still exhausted. "We . . . we can't even *physically* be apart though." She tried to grasp onto anything to make him change his mind.

"Lewis and I have thought of something that I'm confident will work, but you need to wake Cali now." He turned his head slightly. "She . . . *needs* you."

And I guess you don't anymore . . . she thought sadly.

Demetri heard the thought more clearly than any other.

Demetri heard her sniff. *Aw, c'mon. Can't she see this is for the best?* He turned his head a little more out of concern.

She was sitting upright in the middle of her bed. Face buried in her knees, sobbing lightly.

He could see most of her bare legs.

Ugh! Pull yourself together, Demetri! he scolded himself.

When it fully sunk in that he was being completely serious, her emotions poured out uncontrollably.

She sobbed even more.

It hit Demetri all at once, but he was ready for it.

A tidal wave of feelings surrounded him and pushed him away from her. There were so many, and they were so mixed that he wasn't sure what any of them were.

He stood strong against them and the pain as she cried. He tried to combat her feelings.

"Jenny . . . pull yourself together, for Cali's sake." Demetri didn't know how much longer he could stand before he broke down too.

She quickly dried her eyes with her blanket and pulled herself together as best as she could.

Her eyes lifted to Demetri, who still had his back to her. "I'm . . . ready . . . master."

He sighed. "Don't tell anyone that we've broken up either, OK? Except for Derek. You don't even have to mention me to him, OK?"

"Demetri, I haven't seen Derek in almost two years." She stood.

"Well, I'm sure you have his number."

"I don't."

He sighed. "How do you *not*?"

"I did have it. Then Kurtis got me a new phone so that . . . people from school would stop bothering me."

Demetri turned back towards her a little but didn't risk meeting her eyes. He was sure he wouldn't be able to stop himself from scooping her up and changing his mind.

He furrowed his brows in concern. "Didn't you block them?"

"I did. But then they would use other people's phones and other profiles on social media. So, he just got me a new number and everything. I don't have any social media anymore."

Demetri listened.

"Anyways, I texted and called Derek's number. I had it memorized, of course, but he . . . never answered me back. So, I don't know what happened."

"Didn't you try his house?"

"Demetri, I never knew where he used to live, let alone where he lives now. That's a whole 'nother story in itself. He knows where I live, but as far I as I know, he's never attempted to come by and see me. He just disappeared after that . . . last time at my place."

"Do you wish that he'd answer if you were to call him?"

"I wish . . . I could hear his *voice* if I called him."

POOF!

Jenny gasped, "Demetri!"

Her heart raced.

He crossed his arms. "You're welcome."

"But—"

"Jenny, call him *after* Lewis and Cali leave."

She tried not to tear up again. "Yes, master." *If Derek answers, I don't know if I'll **like** his answer.*

Demetri sighed and positioned himself with his back facing her again. "Now are you ready to go wake Cali up?"

She wasn't tired anymore, but she felt worse than ever. "Yes, master." She looked down at her bed sadly and thought of Cali.

She poofed them up at Cali's side.

"woah! Man, D.! What did I tell you about giving me a *warning* first? C'mon, bro, you trying to give me a heart attack or something?" Lewis removed his hand from his heart and crossed his arms.

Demetri gave Lewis a hearty smile like nothing was wrong. "Sorry, bro."

"Jenny! You OK, girl?" He smiled at her in concern.

She kept her eyes glued on Cali. She tried to sound as chipper as she could manage. "Yeah, Lewis. Thanks!"

Lewis squinted a little.

Jenny smiled real big. "Um! I don't quite feel like myself yet. It took a lot out of me."

Lewis let out a breath of acceptance. "Well, I'm glad you're OK. You had us scared, girl!" He gave Jenny a quick hug.

She hugged him back tightly, hoping it wouldn't be the last time. "Let me get Cali up and going here."

Lewis smiled. "Great!"

She focused on Cali's peaceful face. "Lewis, this is going to be the 'first' time she sees you. You need to go over by the door and ring the bell in a couple of minutes like you're *just* arriving. Then go along with her stories, OK? And *don't* tell her I'm a genie. Or that Demetri and I are . . . dating." She closed her eyes briefly in sadness.

Lewis didn't notice thankfully. He sighed, "Yeah, I remember it all, OK."

He gave Cali one more kiss on the lips, hesitated, and then swiftly went to the door and shut himself out. Once outside he shook his head in disbelief. He talked to himself, "This is all so complicated. I finally find my woman and I have tuh wait around on all this mumbo-jumbo."

Back inside, Jenny smiled at Cali through heartbroken eyes. "Wake up, Cali," she whispered.

Cali opened her eyes and saw an unfamiliar ceiling. "Where am I?"

Jenny left her side and took a few feet back toward Demetri and looked down.

It had to be like everything was normal again, and Cali would instantly be able to tell from Jenny's face if something was wrong. She didn't have an excuse ready this time.

Demetri explained what "happened" to her. She slowly remembered exactly what Jenny wanted her to.

"Oh, man, my head. This is some hangover! I'm glad he called you instead of trying to take advantage of me or something."

She noticed that Jenny hadn't been looking at her. She was about to ask if Jenny was OK when the doorbell rang.

Lewis burst in. He didn't want to be away from Cali any longer, and he had to make sure she was OK. He briskly bounded over to them. "Hey, D., hey, Jenny, who's your friend here?"

He wanted to get right to the point.

Jenny rubbed her eyes with a pinching motion and sighed. *Smooth, Lewis,* she thought.

Cali gasped, "I-I . . . um."

Her cheeks turned red.

They waited in anticipation.

"Jenny! How did I get this dress on?"

Crap. I forgot about the dress. "Cali, I knew you liked it so much that I . . . went back to the store and got it for you. I thought it would be a nice thing to wake up in since you went through so much."

Cali ran her finger along the material in her lap. "Oh . . . Well, thank you."

Jenny gestured towards Lewis before she could ask anymore questions. "This is Lewis, Demetri's best friend." Jenny backed up again, so Cali wouldn't notice her red eyes. She could feel Cali becoming suspicious already.

Cali turned briefly to Lewis but kept her eyes on Jenny. "Hi, Lewis, nice to meet you."

She bounced off the couch and headed toward Jenny to talk about the dress and to see if everything was ok with her when Lewis took a step in her path and smiled.

Jenny sighed a breath of relief. *Whew! Thanks again, Lewis.*

"Hey, let me take you to your car, Cali. You can catch up with Jenny later."

"Um . . . I don't even know you, Lewis." She took a good look at him for the "first" time and gasped again. "I . . . I *do* know you! You . . . I just . . . *dreamed* about you." Her cheeks turned red.

All the emotions she felt toward him came rushing back too.

She returned her eyes to Jenny. "And you were a . . ." She laughed and brushed the thought away.

Demetri stepped forward. "Cali, he's my best friend. I called him over to take you to your car. He won't let anything happen to you, I promise. You can tell him about your dream on the way, OK? Then call Jenny later if you want."

She furrowed her brows, unsure. "OK. Um . . . Jenny?"

Jenny looked up briefly, closed her eyes, and ran at her with a hug. "Do what Demetri says, Cali. Call me later. Lewis is a *great* friend! I promise he won't let anything happen to you."

She tried to sound as happy as she could. She needed a hug from Cali badly right now. Her tear ducts felt like bursting over, and she wanted to talk about it.

"Ok, Jenny. I'll call you later." Cali turned her toward a smiling Lewis.

He gently took her hand, which Cali smiled at, and escorted her to the door.

"Bye!" Jenny called "happily."

"Bye, Jenny! Bye, Demetri!"

Demetri nodded. "Bye! See ya, Lewis."

Lewis was too enchanted to bid farewell.

As soon as the door shut, a little cry sound sang out from Jenny's direction.

Demetri sighed and began to turn towards her.

She couldn't hold it in any longer. She knew if she tried to run for her bottle, Demetri would stop her, and she didn't want to be stopped right now. She poofed herself there instead.

"Jenny!"

He knew where she was, and he knew he was right the closer he got to her bottle. He poofed himself down there with her and watched her helplessly.

Jenny heard him sigh. "How did you get in here? I wished that you wouldn't be able to." She was sitting in the middle of her pillows with her tear-stained face in her knees again.

He stayed in the spot he appeared in.

"What I want overpowers what you want, which is why . . . I'm going . . . to set you free." He looked down.

Jenny sniffed and lifted her head. "What? What are you talking about?"

"Jenny, as your master, I *should* be able to set you free."

She thought about the possibility of being free. Thoughts about what that would mean for her and Demetri raced against each other. She wouldn't be here with him anymore.

"No!"

He looked up at her in surprise. "Jen . . . don't make this harder than it has to be."

She started to get up. "I don't *want* to be free."

He sat on the edge of the foot of the bed. "Jenny, this isn't *normal*. You're the only genie in the *whole* world. It can't be like this! Genies shouldn't exist." He fought off her pain. "Can't you see how this is for the best?"

She crawled close to him. "No, I can't!"

He sighed. "I don't want to be able to order you around anymore. I want to know if we're supposed to be together, and I can't tell if this genie stuff gets in the way." He looked into her hopeless eyes.

"Demetri." She got up out of bed and came around to his front.

Demetri scooted back on the bed. He didn't want to get too close to her.

She leaped forward without warning and pressed her body against his. She kissed his lips and wrapped her arms around his neck.

His heart pounded and called to hers.

*NO! NO! No . . . no . . . mmmmm . . . yes . . . yes! AGH! Crap. You're **weak**, Demetri Dayton*, he thought. *This is a goodbye kiss, goodbye kiss, goodbye*

*kiss . . . OK . . . that's enough. No! I won't force her! I will **not** command her!*
She deserves a goodbye kiss if she wants one.

After another moment, he attempted to gently ease her off.

She forced *all* her desire and love onto him.

Demetri was overwhelmed with it; her desire was slowly taking control.

Feel me, Jenny commanded through thought.

Demetri heard the order loud and clear in his mind.

He couldn't fight it.

She moved both her knees on either side of his pelvis, her stomach pressed into his.

Oh dear God, please give me strength. He kissed her back hungrily, unable to fight her mental commands. He reached down and felt the back of her exposed calves.

Demetri slid his hands up her legs. He felt her lower thighs, and she willed him to keep going.

Oh man, your skirt really is too short, he thought.

He slid his hands up until he came to her hips under her skirt. His question from earlier was answered. *Nope. No shorts underneath.*

Tell me you want me, she thought again.

He mumbled it with his lips still attached to hers. His head felt clouded. He forgot what he was trying to accomplish.

Jenny ran her fingers through his hair and shoved her tongue into his mouth.

I'm going to give you what you want, Demetri. No more pain ever again.
Do you want me?

Demetri's eyes went wide. *Oh dear God, YES!*

She was willing for anything if it meant they could stay together.

Undress me.

By some miracle, he snapped out of it. He tried to push her off.

She wouldn't budge.

He came up for air. "Jenny, please . . ."

She sat back on her calves and furrowed her brows in complete despair. "I thought . . . I thought you loved me . . ." She gave him the saddest look he had ever seen.

His heart cracked open with the look she gave him.

"Oh, Jen . . . Jenny." Every word was like a cut through his heart, just enlarging the injury. "I *do* love you. Don't you understand? That's why I have to let you be normal."

"I don't want to be *normal*. I want to be here with you. I *want* you to be my master." Her eyes filled with tears again.

"I'm pretty sure that's just the genie in you talking. It isn't supposed to work like that. You need to *want* to be my *girlfriend* . . . if that's how you feel. *Not* my genie slave."

She lifted her fading blue eyes to his. "But you don't treat me like a slave."

Apparently, her blouse didn't cover as much as he originally thought.

He sighed. "I'd really like it if you'd get off of me now so I can think clearly."

She stared at him with betrayed gray eyes. "You . . . you don't mean that . . ."

"Yes . . . yes, I do. *Please*!" He leaned his head back and closed his eyes.

Jenny hesitated and then slowly got off. She sniffed.

"Please don't cry. You can go see if you're meant to be with Derek now."

She dug her eyes into his. "I don't *want* Derek in that way."

He felt it again. "Then what do I keep feeling every time you talk about him?"

"I don't know, Demetri!" She hid her face. "But he obviously doesn't want me either, so it doesn't matter anyway!"

He looked away, trying to stay calm. "Go call him now."

"Yes, mas . . . *OK*." She retrieved her cell phone from her dresser and dialed the same number she had a dozen times within the last couple of years before she'd given up.

Demetri turned his back to her and listened.

Her heart thumped repeatedly.

It rang once.

The thumping thumped around in her head loudly.

It rang twice.

The thumping ceased.

He isn't going to answer.

On the third ring, Demetri heard an unfamiliar voice say hello.

It was actually his voice.

Jenny gasped and then whispered, "D-Derek?"

"JENNY! *Baby*, is that you?"

Her heart began beating again.

"Oh, it's so great to hear your voice again!" Derek said.

Jenny tried to refrain from crying over the phone, "It is?"

Demetri felt anticipation.

"Yes! Jeez, I thought . . . I'd never be able to hear it again!"

"Why didn't you ever answer me then? I called you like a bazillion times!"

"Jenny, I never got a call. You texted me that you never wanted to see me again . . ."

Jenny's heart wrenched to the right.

"What? No, I didn't!"

"I've still got the message."

"Derek, I *promise* you that *I* didn't text it. I texted you a whole bunch of *other* stuff about wanting to see you."

"I didn't get anything else."

"That doesn't make any sense!"

"Jenny . . . I think . . . I think I know what happened now. AGH! How could I've been so stupid?"

"What? What happened?"

"I need to make sure first, but I'll find out and then tell you."

"Ok . . . so then . . . why didn't you come by if you wanted to see me?"

"Uh . . . that's complicated . . . but I *have* been coming by! I leave you flowers."

Jenny's eyes teared up. "Flowers? Those . . . those are from *you*?"

Demetri felt surprise and something else.

He was almost too afraid to try to figure it out.

"Yeah . . ." Derek said sheepishly.

"Why didn't you leave a note?"

"I thought you didn't want to see me. I didn't want to be annoying."

She felt a little happier. "You did all that for me?"

Demetri felt appreciation and love.

There *it is.* He closed his eyes sadly.

"Of course, I did, Jenny. I've always loved you, ever since middle school."

Jenny swallowed. "Do . . . do you still love me?"

Demetri waited.

Jenny waited.

"Yes, Jenny. I've thought about you *every* single day."

Demetri felt relief and wondering and love again. He couldn't take it anymore.

"Jenny, make a date with him," he whispered.

It was all he could manage.

Her eyes went wide. "Derek, I-I need to see you."

"Where are you? Are you at home?"

"I'm, I'm . . ."

"Tell him you're at home, Jen."

He couldn't help but call her Jen again. He felt her slipping away from him and this time, *he* needed something to hold on to. Her happy emotions were the only thing keeping him from breaking down completely.

They were the cause yet also the prevention.

Her feelings were so strong that his tears wouldn't spill over.

Demetri wasn't used to tears.

"I'm at home," Jenny answered.

"OK, I'll be there in fifteen minutes then. Is that OK?"

Demetri nodded.

"That's great, Derek. Thanks."

"Oh gosh, I can't wait to see you, Jenny."

"I can't . . . wait to see you either, Derek."

Demetri felt truth.

As soon as she clicked end, she collapsed onto the bed in a mess of tears again. She felt confused yet didn't need an explanation, excited yet guilt-ridden, hurt yet fueled by hope, rejected yet wanted.

Demetri felt equally as torn up inside. Someone might as well have taken a blender to the emotions she radiated.

I'll be glad when I can't feel her emotions anymore. "Jen . . ." He dried his eyes in secret and got up to face her.

She was face down crying into her folded arms.

He sighed and sat next to her. "Jen?"

She calmed down a little. "What?"

"Promise me that you won't let . . ."

Jenny sat up with her back to him now and finished for him. "I promise that I won't let him touch me anywhere sacred, OK? He never has." She kept her teary eyes on her gray comforter.

"Thank you."

She sniffed. "If it makes you feel better, he's never tried to touch me like that."

It did.

Demetri sighed. "Well, he has more self-control than I do. I've already violated you in so many ways."

"Demetri, you didn't do anything that I didn't want you to. And no, you haven't. You haven't touched my skin."

He let out a breath, clearly still aggravated with himself.

She turned to him with pleading eyes. "Demetri, this hasn't changed *anything* for me. I love you."

"Then why do I feel a flicker of guilt?"

She searched her own brain for the answer.

Derek had always loved her and been there for her. And apparently had never stopped loving her and would've always been there had something not interfered. He'd never overstepped boundaries. In all fairness, Jenny felt like she owed him one more chance, but she didn't want to admit that to Demetri.

Jenny apparently hesitated for too long.

"That's what I thought . . ." He looked into her torn eyes. "Jenny . . ."

She waited to hear what he wanted to say; surely it couldn't have made things any worse.

"I love you. And so, I set you free."

Author's Note

If you love someone, let them be free to make their own decisions. That's what God has done for us, after all.

TO BE CONTINUED

Thank you to my husband who had to put up with
me writing constantly for a month & who was a major
help to me both in inspiration and editing.

Thank you, reader, for taking the time to read my first
published book! I sincerely hope you enjoyed it!

Most importantly, I thank God for the work he's
done in my life. I would be lost without him.

My wish is that each person reading this series will learn a
valuable lesson to help them see the positive side of life.

If your hearts are open to it, I hope you can
seek help through God if you need it.

He's never failed me; sometimes it just takes time to see his work.
MORE EXCITEMENT TO COME!